T0149225

Other Books by Rue L. Cromwell

Cromwell, Rue L., Earl C. Butterfield, Frances M. Brayfield, and John J. Curry. 1977. *Acute Myocardial Infarction: Reaction and Recovery.* St. Louis: Mosby.

Wynne, Lyman C., Rue L. Cromwell, and Steven Matthysse, eds. 1978. *The Nature of Schizophrenia: New Approaches to Research and Treatment.* New York: John Wiley & Sons.

Cromwell, Rue L., and C. R. Snyder, eds. 1993. *Schizophrenia: Origins, Processes, Treatment, and Outcome.* New York: Oxford University Press.

Cromwell, Rue L. 2010. *Being Human: Human Being. Manifesto for a New Psychology.* Bloomington, IN: iUniverse.

Cromwell, Rue L. 2014. *A Time in China.* New York: Lulu.com.

You'll Like Linton

Linton

Rue L. Cromwell

YOU'LL LIKE LINTON

iUniverse books may be ordered through booksellers or by contacting:

iUniverse
1663 Liberty Drive
Bloomington, IN 47403
www.iuniverse.com
1-800-Authors (1-800-288-4677)

Because of the dynamic nature of the Internet, any web addresses or links contained in this book may have changed since publication and may no longer be valid. The views expressed in this work are solely those of the author and do not necessarily reflect the views of the publisher, and the publisher hereby disclaims any responsibility for them.

Any people depicted in stock imagery provided by Thinkstock are models, and such images are being used for illustrative purposes only. Certain stock imagery © Thinkstock.

ISBN: 978-1-4917-7102-0 (sc)
ISBN: 978-1-4917-7101-3 (hc)
ISBN: 978-1-4917-7100-6 (e)

Library of Congress Control Number: 2015910198

Print information available on the last page.

iUniverse rev. date: 07/31/2015

To Joe Dean

CONTENTS

PREFACE

It is the narrative record of a boy, the place where he grew up, and the people who lived there.

I had no intention of writing about my early years in Linton until my close friend Herbert E. Spohn urged me to. He was the son of a Jewish mother and a military hero father who was blinded while fighting for Kaiser Wilhelm in World War I. Herb had lost his entire cohort in World War II. The concentration camps, the Russian front, the Allied front, and the American bombing of his hometown, Berlin, into rubble—all of these had taken every classmate and friend of his youth. My stories made Linton a magical place—a Brigadoon—and they told him who I was.

Herb had lost such identity of youth. Serving as the seeing-eye dog for his blinded father, Herb was a proud Lutheran youth. When his father died, Herb, with his mother and brother, was relegated to the ghetto and substandard schools and became the target of spit and other harassment. Straightaway, his mother made secret plans to flee to Poland, where relatives accommodated their passage to America.

Herb arrived in suspendered lederhosen and with no English speech or comprehension. After high school and boot camp, he found himself back in Germany fighting his fatherland in the Battle of the Bulge. As Herb told me, one day in Frankfort, in his overseas cap and Eisenhower jacket, he caught a fleeting glimpse of his identity. He was an American GI.

Each person who reads this story has a place, time, ethnicity, race, or heritage that provides unequivocal identification. It is so embedded that he or she cannot envision what lifelong burden would come without such a base. So it was that Herb taught me that Linton was a magical place. He became the director of research for the Menninger Foundation in Topeka. He died on Pearl Harbor Day, December 7, 2013. An American flag covered his casket. This one is for you, Herb.

*　*　*

I grew up on the homestead farm of my great-grandfather Richard O. Taylor. He was the subject of my brother's narrative biography.[1] My great-grandfather was illegally sold into bondage in western Virginia shortly after the War of 1812. Living in a barn and sharing kitchen scraps with pigs, he ran away as the weather turned cold. Blindfolded on transfer and without orientation, he tracked the Ohio River and settled with a gristmill family in Flemingsburg, Kentucky. As an adult he and his own family removed by canal boat to Point Commerce, near Worthington, Indiana. He made his way to set up his homestead in Wright Township, Greene County, four miles north of Linton, Indiana. By fortune of being an early settler, his house, built on high ground in a forest, was a half mile from any public gravel road once they were later laid down. The house had no driveway or lane of approach. I grew up devoid of playmates or even peddlers and casual strangers until I entered school. I developed a world of

---

[1]　Harold D. Cromwell, _The Bound Boy_ (1995).

dreams that I kept as my own substitute playmates. From this private world sprang questions of who I was, what would come with tomorrow, and, beyond tomorrow, what eternity would bring.

This narrative biography consists of a series of vignettes. Rather than a chronology, it follows the treads of different stories, one after another. Some names have been changed to protect identities. I, for instance, have become Hanno Buchwald. Some characters may be composites of people I knew. Others may be imagined. Special acknowledgment is given to Jackie Kelly Aldridge, Lisa Temple, William Carlo Villacrusis, Neil Marvin Gerson, and Walter Katkovsky for comments about the manuscript.

Rue L. Cromwell
April 18, 2015

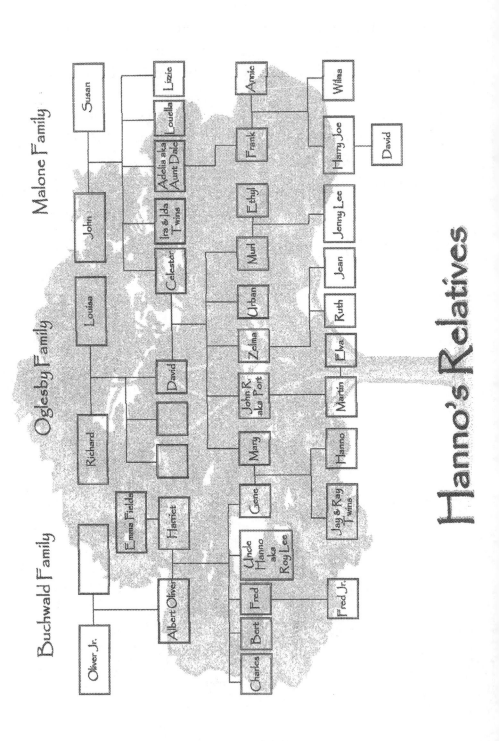

Hanno's Relatives

[1]

BLUE

People say you cannot remember stuff from before you were born. Hanno remembered something he did not know how to place. It seemed like it had happened before he was born, but he knew that he could not sell such a claim. There was a light-blue uniform field full of bubbles—not bubbles of gas that drifted to the top; these were more like globules suspended in the blue entity. There was no *me* as an observer separate from the blue. There was no beginning, no end, no time passing, and no space traversed, just blue with the slightly illuminated globules.

If Hanno had been asked to report his earliest memory, this would have been the first. But he could not call it similar to or different from some other memory. He could not say it was before or after. It was just blue and enduring.

[2]

HOMESTEAD

After Hanno grew up, he drove back to the old place once. He could see nothing but hundreds of acres of corn divided by the familiar network of gravel roads. He turned into a narrow lane where the mailbox had been. He drove over foot-high weeds with rows of corn swiping each side of the car. In two hundred yards, the lane quit. It had been used by trucks to haul out corn and fodder at harvesttime.

Hanno got out of the car and walked across the corn rows to where the old and new houses had been. He found a small patch of rubble at the top of the slope. Fescue grass mixed with the weeds. The well and the cistern had been filled in with rubble. A broken crock stuck out of the ground. Between two rocks was a clump of exotic flowers that had once been on Grandma Celester's rock garden. Hanno returned to the car and drove away.

In the soil among these cornstalks were a thousand stories. There was the story of a man, sold into bondage as a young lad, who had the courage to run from his illegal servitude. Later he had the courage to leave a bleak but secure setting in Kentucky to take his family by canal boat into a forested wilderness in Indiana. Life was to begin anew. There was the story of an ambitious daughter-in-law and her gentle but widely respected husband who built a two-story brick colonial house in an isolated location. There was the story of social and economic collapse as corporate coal interests dominated. The Oglesby homestead became only a memory, just like the Native American village that came before. Buried among these many cornstalks was the story of Hanno himself.

We go back to 1928. Although Hanno was born in the only hospital in Linton, Indiana, his recall of self began as a child who grew up on an isolated one-hundred-acre farm. Neither public gravel road nor private driveway led up to his house. How the roadless homestead came to be is one of the many stories across the bridge of time.

Hanno learned of thrice-told tales of his heritage. His maternal great-grandfather, Richard Oglesby, discovered this magical place. He was known as the bound boy. When not yet a teenager, he was sold into bondage by his father. It was 1814, and he was in what is now West Virginia. Once sold, he lived in a hayloft with pigs down below. He had first dibs over the pigs each day for the kitchen scraps. As the weather became cold, he ran away. This was not at all surprising. But having been blindfolded and tied down in the bed of a wagon when sold, he knew not which direction was home.

He found and followed the Ohio River for a good ways. It was a wandering escape. Fearing capture while on a packet boat, he turned south into the Kentucky hill country. Eventually, he found himself in Flemings County. A gristmill family adopted him, and he grew up helping run the mill.

As the wooden linkages of the mill became old and obsolete and after his adoptive parents died, Richard removed his wife and family by canal boat to Point Commerce near Worthington, Indiana. He then went across wooded land from the White River to his chosen area on high ground.

The year was 1854. Hanno's grandfather David was four when his family crossed over from Kentucky into Indiana.

As Richard and other old settlers moved in, their efforts were at odds with the welfare of the Native Americans. Rather than living from the richness of natural growth, the settlers were clearing land and fencing off fields and pastures.

This high ground that Richard discovered had once been an Indian village. On this ground in past centuries, happy times, hopes, and fears were experienced by the Plains Indians who prospered among the cool summer breezes while hunting, gathering, and planting.

Even in Hanno's time, with each spring plowing, he and his brothers found arrowheads and other stone artifacts. Like other old settlers, Oglesby cleared part of the virgin timber for farm fields and pastures. Part of the forest he left for firewood and wildlife. It was well populated with squirrel, muskrat, opossum, skunk, beaver, and raccoon.

As the European invaders established their colonies and moved west, the style of life of the Plains Indians was threatened by the sheer numbers of people staking land claims. Until then, it had been open, sacred, and free, but the arrow could not compete with the gun. A state was named. As a feeble honor, they named it Indiana, but, amid hundreds of sad tales, the Native Americans had to leave it behind.

The land seemed flat, and you could see for miles. Richard had staked it out in a prior visit. Both he and his wife, Louisa, were excited to face their new life full of unknowns.

For the settlers of the frontier, clearing land and stumps accorded the same respect as would be gained today from serving well in public office. Both contributed to the community's well-being. After centuries of seeking happiness, the sad exit of the Native Americans coexisted with the hope of the new settlers.

Clearing the land, however, was not the first order of business. One must dig at least one well. Without the well, water had to be hauled from a nearby stream to meet livestock and family needs. Hanno's great-grandfather, like many others, hired frontier well diggers to do this in advance of the family's arrival.

The second priority was to secure proper shelter for the livestock. Their protection was more urgent for family survival than building a house.

Richard Oglesby's house was among the last of his construction projects, and it is clear that his resources were running low. The house was partly of log and partly of rough clapboard. Barn latches were used on the doors.

The interior was never fully subdivided. However, it was large, strong in structure, and warm in winter.

After the Oglesbys settled in, Richard and Louisa were blessed by an influx of German immigrant farmers. They worked with each other to make a good life. They came to refer to the local community as their Gemütlichkeit. As Hanno grew up, all English sparrows were lovingly called spatzies.

The community, even without a formal organizing committee, often held ice cream socials and potluck dinners. One happy night before Thanksgiving, a potluck meal and a turkey raffle was held at Plum Branch School. Hanno was there. The families brought coal-oil farm lanterns and gasoline Coleman lanterns. Electricity was still a long time to come. People were pleased that Sam Risher had the winning ticket. He and his family were among those in hard times. Herman Bredeweg, who served as master of ceremonies, pulled a slip from the pot and read off Risher's name. The applause kept shy Sam from moving. Then Herman said, "I just talked to Sam Risher before we came inside, and he told me he did not buy a ticket. If he doesn't come up here in five seconds and get this turkey, I'm going to take it myself!"

With this, Sam Risher vaulted from his chair, knocking it down behind him, and he ran to the improvised stage. This brought laughter and more applause from the gathered families. Soon, Sam's wife let it be known that she indeed had not been told, and rightfully so. "I would have accused him of squandering. That ticket cost twenty-five cents, and I had already told him we couldn't afford that."

The Rishers would indeed not have had a Thanksgiving that year except for this bonanza. To contribute to the feast, some of the families wrapped up leftovers from the potluck in butcher paper to add to this unexpected holiday dinner.

From family to family, such warm feelings began to fade. As farms were sold off to the strip-mining company, some people were viewed as traitors. Some families quit speaking to others. The strippers and steam shovels breached the county gravel roads. This cut off their access to each other. Just as important, the blocked-off roads interfered with the time and length of mileage to get to town to do shopping and sell produce. Hanno recalled that some had to reduce the number of trips to town because of the increased amount of gasoline needed. Relations broke down within families as one brother decided to sell his farm and another brother was struggling to hang on.

An ordinance in early Indiana held that no child should walk more than one mile to a school. Thus these one-room schoolhouses were distributed every two miles, near the corner of a country square. Eventually, Plum Branch School (officially called No. 7) was gone. The road beside it and even the creek were gone too. Hanno's mother had gone there. It had burned down once. Hanno's brothers had gone there seven years earlier than Hanno.

As Hanno's great-grandfather Richard became a widower and grew old, his youngest son, David, stayed on the farm to care for him in his final years. During this time David courted and married Celester Malone, the eldest of the well-known and beautiful Malone girls of Linton. John Malone, Celester's father, had built one of the main commercial buildings along Main Street. In it he operated a highly successful haberdashery. (During Hanno's lifetime, the building was transformed into the Cozy Corner saloon.) Unfortunately John Malone died at age forty and left his widow Susan the responsibility for a household of daughters and sons. Susan lived another forty years. Every day for the rest of her life, she wore black to mourn her dead husband. The Malone daughters, Celester, Lizzie (Elizabeth), Ida, Adalia (Aunt Dale), and Louella, were the Linton equivalent of the Gabor sisters. Among Celester's sisters, Dale married a Letterman, great-grandfather of talk show host David Letterman. Ida married a Strietelmeier. Lizzie married a Davis, and Louella married a Fergas.

To raise seven children without scandal took a bit of doing. Susan Malone was an iron survivor. As a single parent with lifelong devotion to her dead husband, she took no prisoners. She ran her household with a metal fist inside a soft black kid glove.

Before the turn of the nineteenth century, after Richard had passed away, David and Celester began to build the *new house*. The year was 1901. Hanno's mother, Mary, was eight when her parents, Celester and David Oglesby, saw their construction completed. They moved from the old house into the new house.

Two decades later, Mary, the younger of David's two daughters, settled with her husband, Gene Buchwald, to care for David during his final years. It was 1934. Hanno Buchwald was a first-grader and six years old when Granddad David passed away.

Within five years of David's death, the homestead and the entire German farming community around it were in a state of collapse. World War I, the Great Depression, and the ominous advance of the coal-mining industry were all taking their toll.

The lyrics of a song said, "How ya' gonna keep 'em down on the farm after they've seen Paris." The words had truth. Some offspring were committed to leaving regardless of the prosperity or lack of it.

The coal-mining companies eventually discovered that a vast vein of coal lay beneath the entire community. The companies were lurking.

At the Oglesby homestead, Hanno sensed that another stress had come. When David Oglesby died, Mary Oglesby Buchwald was not the only heir. All of Mary's siblings were joint heirs. None of them had resources to buy off the entire property from the others. They decided to sell the homestead and split the money. It was Christmastime 1934, and the brothers graciously decided to let Mary and her family stay on until the twins graduated from high school at Midland in 1939. The siblings were grateful to Mary for the care of their father, to which they had not contributed. In turn, Mary, Hanno's mother, was forever appreciative for their kindness.

As a final expression of dignity and community spirit, the Oglesby siblings, including Hanno's mother, Mary, decided to sell the homestead to a neighboring farmer, Rex Kopfschein, rather than to a strip-mining company. This they did as a final statement of loyalty to the community of Gemütlichkeit. However, the collapse continued. Within a year, Rex Kopfschein sold the property to the strip-mining company at a significant profit. Within another year, he also sold his own farm to the strip-mining company.

While the homestead transaction was being negotiated, Kopfschein rented it to a tenant. On a cold night, the tenant allowed the stovepipe to become red hot. The soot in the flue and chimney caught fire, and the new house burned immediately to the ground. No neighbor, even Kopfschein, who sold the land to the strip-mining company, had known of the millions of dollars of coal that lay underneath.

The tract of one hundred acres—and much more—became completely stripped of coal. Today there is a stand of hundreds of acres of corn on the reclaimed soil—no buildings, no forests. Gone are the prosperous farming society, Plum Branch, the old house, and the new house. Gone.

[3]

HANNO'S WORLD

In his early days, Hanno Buchwald engaged as much with places and things as with persons. People were few in number. They were almost always family members and neighbors, all familiar and predictable. On the rare occasions of a trip to town, the strangers he encountered frightened him. Back at home, every tree and fence corner had its place.

The word *isolation* appears regularly in this story of Hanno and his family. Isolation was more than living far from town. It was more than not living on a public road or street. It was more than not having a nice long lane leading up to a farmhouse. Hanno lived where, to the outsider, there was no one clear means of approach. Was there a creek to cross, mud to mire the wheels, cows to slip through the gate, or a mean bull? When you got to the house, on which door did you knock? Did you yell from outside the screened porch?

One entrance was to drive among rows of fruit trees in the neighbor's orchard. Another was through the pastures with three latched gates. Another was a footpath through the woods, across a creek, and through a gulley. From the opposite direction of Plum Branch School, one could turn in from the county gravel road and go through two pastures with latched gates to the backside of the barnyard. With these confusing options, Hanno's family had few peddlers, salesmen, or casual family visitors to speak of.

Families who were intent upon visiting would sometimes be seen walking as a group across a pasture. They were afraid of miring the car in the mud. In such cases, Mary, Hanno's mother, would yell to one of the children, "Go kill a chicken!"

Yes, it was Hanno's world, but it was still dominated by one who lived and died before Hanno was born. Hanno's grandmother, Celester Malone Oglesby, had a vision and was determined to make it real. She envisioned having the best house in Wright Township. She chose as a husband a gentle and just man, David Oglesby. He was compliant and would give her free rein. Hanno took all these things for granted. The grandmother he never saw was a heritage and a destiny. The maple tree providing shade for the back porch was one small sample of her planning.

Hanno, when out of his crib, inhabited the kitchen. This linoleum surface was his first world. Later, it expanded to the dining room and the yard and then to the barnyard, the outer pastures, the fields, and the forest. Gradually neighbors came within his perimeter.

Hanno remembers the kitchen floor as his introduction to freedom. When his mother worked in the kitchen, she placed him on the floor. There he was free to crawl around on his own. He would crawl between and among the legs of the women as they worked. Hanno would watch as relatives and friends were greeted at the door and everyone talked and no one listened. Since he could not yet walk, he was carried around and rocked and kissed. If something was not to his liking, he would cry big. Big crying was his only means of control, and it was what he remembered most.

Soon, as he continued to play on the linoleum, Hanno's father would come home from the mines and sit beside him on the kitchen floor. One day, he brought a set of wooden blocks. Letters and numbers were embossed on each surface. His father showed him how to arrange the blocks into the ABCs. Hanno's grasp of this seemed to surprise his father. He did not know why. Later on in Hanno's life, he suspected that the alphabetic play might have been his parents' first sign that Hanno was comfortably alert.

The centerpiece of the kitchen was a large cookstove. Kindling was on hand to start it each morning. Since one cannot readily turn on and off a wood or coal stove, it was kept going throughout the day. A teakettle of water sang most of the time. At least two irons were always kept in back of the stovetop so to be ready to press clothing. The stovetop had round iron lids, and there was a special tool to lift a hot lid and get to the fire.

Across from the cookstove was a large worktable. The top was completely covered with a sheet of zinc. It served as the countertop to prepare food and wash dishes from dishpans. The zinc sheet allowed the table to be cleaned and scoured easily. On the end of the table, closest to the outside door, was a bucket of water. Hanging beside it was a dipper. This set of items was common to every house in the community, poor or starving. It was the source of drinking water for the family and for all guests. For families too poor to have a well, the soft water was collected from downspouts off the roof into a rain barrel. Concern about germs was never mentioned.

Since there was no plumbing, the kitchen was the storage place for water for other uses besides drinking. Cooking, bathing, washing up for a meal, mopping, weekly laundry, and watering plants and the pets all required an ample supply of water.

Later on, the family purchased a two-burner kerosene stove. This allowed them to avoid firing up the large wood stove for a short cooking chore. With the beautiful smell of the hickory kindling and coal, the stink of the little coal-oil stove was hard to get used to.

When Hanno's father, Gene Buchwald, came home each evening from his shift in the mines, he would place his cap with carbide lamp and his round aluminum lunch pail on the floor beside him. Hanno would sit on the other side. His father played with him and told him stories, a different story each evening. When in a very playful mood, his father talked and answered questions in rhyme. He rhymed the words that Hanno spoke to him. Each evening, Hanno could not wait for his arrival.

When Hanno grew older and could walk, he did not have to be watched in the kitchen. The dining room then became the center of his life. During the day, Hanno was always in his rocker. This was a small rocking chair that was a part of his grandparents' parlor furniture. Young Hanno could rock for an hour or more without stopping.

On snowy winter evenings, the family gathered around the welcoming Florence heater. On one side was the rocking chair. The dining table had been transformed with two coal oil lamps into a reading table for homework and for Gene's newspapers and magazines. Hanno sat at night and looked out the dark window into the reflection of the stove, chairs, and other objects in the room. They looked as if they were all sitting out in the yard. Yet he knew that in the yard there was nothing but snow. Two-dimensional reflections as he looked in the mirror in the morning made sense, but the reflection of furniture at different degrees of depth outside the window baffled him.

Hanno, for many years, lost track of why he was allowed to stay up after his older brothers went to bed. Later it became clear. As a preschooler, he had an intense fear that his parents would be killed or gone when he awoke. One repeated image was awaking in the morning to find his parents lying side by side on the wooden floor of their bedroom. Instead of looking like people with flesh and bones, they were like two mashed baked sweet potatoes. Although human-sized, they looked like they had been mashed with a fork. One could even see the fork lines. Melted butter fell into the grooves made by the fork. That, he felt, was the last he would ever see of his parents. Whatever the reason for the fears, Hanno was always eager to remain awake, simply not to miss anything bad going on.

The other memory Hanno had of his parents' bedroom was not so morbid. On the wall above the bed was a framed large portrait of his great-grandfather Richard

Oglesby. This picture was of a kind-faced man with a gray beard. Hanno was told later in life that the garb and hand position in the picture gave a clue that he was a member of the Masonic Lodge.

As Hanno grew still older, his fate was to have the same assigned chore as Oprah Winfrey did. While others were working in the fields and the kitchen, both Hanno and Oprah had to empty the chamber pots (a.k.a. slop jars) from each bedroom every morning. They would be rinsed and returned under the edge of the bed. That was an unattractive chore, but it had its good side. For the rest of the day, they had time to read. And read they did. Hanno would read while guarding the cows in the pasture. He would read in the quiet of the woods. There, he would find his mossy spot in the forty-some acres of uncleared virgin timber. His favorite place, however, was out behind the house on the grape arbor that his grandfather had built. He climbed up a gnarly vine about eight inches in diameter and found the place ten feet high near the top where the vines provided a comfortable seat. Shaded by a canopy of large grape leaves (good for nibbling), he read. As he read, he sampled the large, juicy Concord grapes. He dreamed.

As Hanno, later in adulthood, looked back on his tendency to daydream, he concluded that it made him more adept in creating new research ideas. There were always far more ideas than he could execute. Although he fell short in many scholarly skills, he felt superior to others in coming up with ideas. He often provided ideas to others for dissertations.

He was always dreaming. Early in college, people often told him they saw him smiling as he walked or ran across campus. Running and dreaming went together. Other people ran when they were late. Hanno seldom ran for that reason. He ran because he grew up with a long way to go to get anywhere. Then, sometimes, it was anxiety. Also, he just liked to run. He was good at it. In ROTC training camp, he won a gold medal for the three-hundred-yard shuttle race. He knew that as he ran around town and campus, others would assume he was late for something. He therefore did not have to provide an excuse. He continued to run and dream.

There were times when Hanno had to face reality rather than to dream. On such occasions, he did not always show his better side. Such was the case on the occasion of his paternal grandfather A. O. Buchwald's death. Hanno was still a preteen youngster. The family had a long trip to his funeral.

Young Hanno, living in the freedom of his rural isolation, had a great aversion to getting his hair cut. He saw no need for a clipping just for a funeral. His parents, siblings, uncles, and cousins pleaded with him to cooperate. To add to the conflict, Hanno was also resisting a tie for the clean white shirt. His mother took a roll of broad ribbon and cut off a piece to make a bow tie. When she finished, she took the scissors again and cut more off one end of the ribbon to balance the appearance. She then rushed away to get herself ready to go. Hanno decided that he could improve the balance of the bow tie. So he picked up the scissors and cut more off the other end. But he cut too much. This required going back to cut more off the original end.

One of Grandmother Celester's innovations in the new house betrayed Hanno's privacy. The wall between

17

the kitchen and the dining room was all cupboard space with doors on both sides. Between the upper and lower cupboard was an open space where dishes could be passed from one room to the other. Hanno's mom returned to the kitchen for water to wash her face. She glanced through the open space between the cabinets and saw pieces of ribbon and Hanno with the scissors in hand. The discovery led to punishment, a fast haircut with tears, the cutting of a new ribbon bow tie, a lecture, and a trip to the funeral with all the relatives unhappy with him.

Being a grandson of the deceased, Hanno sat on the front row in front of the casket. His only memory of the funeral service was looking at his dead grandfather's large nose with its single wart. It was the only thing he could see from the casket during the service.

Hanno knew that he had a remote historic relative on the Buchwald side of the family called Oliver Cromwell. Later in adulthood, Hanno learned that Oliver's nickname was "Nose Almighty."

On Hanno's farm, a survival existence did not mean starvation. Besides the fresh produce from the garden in summer, other great times of year were with hunting, fishing, and butchering. Baked squirrel was a delicacy. Squirrel gravy is a lifetime memory for anyone.

Rabbit stew was a staple food item. Although Hanno learned to shoot rabbits and squirrels, his older brothers were far more devoted and expert in hunting. Likewise, the twins did more fishing. The stripper pits were abundantly stocked with largemouth and smallmouth bass. Often when coming home from fishing, they would call ahead from the lane, "We caught the limit."

In a far pasture of the homestead was a pond. It contained the small but most flavorful of all local fish, the bluegill. Hanno used a cane pole with hook, cork, sinker, and earthworm bait. Minnows would also work if there were money for them. In the nearby grove Hanno would dig roots for sassafras tea if the fishing were not good.

Another treat for children came on butchering day. Pieces of pork skin and underbelly fat would be set aside for the lard press. The boiling-hot pieces of skin and fat were dumped into the heavy metal cylindrical vat. The lid closed, and the crank on top of the lid would be turned to force the contents to the bottom of the vat. At the bottom of the cylinder was a small spout. Out of it came boiling-hot liquid lard. Inside the vat was the pressed residue. It was a wheel of crisp hard cracklings. Once cooled, one could break off chunks to eat. It was shaped like a pizza pie or a wheel of cheese. It was so attractive in flavor yet unhealthy because of its residual fat content. Children were allowed only a small amount at a time, and the remainder was hidden or locked up. The cracklings were so good, one was willing to risk getting caught stealing them.

Hanno's father especially loved quail potpie. A mystery Hanno could never understand was why when his parents were in a prolonged quarrel, his mother would pay even closer attention to making the delicate quail potpie.

One farm chore that paid dividends was the making of butter. Hanno spent many hours moving the churn plunger up and down to produce the butter and buttermilk. He did not like to pump up and down on a churn handle for long periods, but he loved the result. After whole milk had reached the correct stage of souring, it was put into a tall crockery churn with a pole and plunger that went through a hole in the lid. As Hanno moved the pole up and down, the wooden plunger at the bottom of the pole would eventually accumulate butter. This left pure buttermilk in the churn. The butter captured by the plunger would be put into a wooden butter mold and pressed hard to remove the remaining drops of buttermilk. Inverting and tapping the butter mold removed a round pound mound of butter onto a sheet of wax paper. The butter mold had a flower design on the top.

The attractive part for Hanno was the buttermilk remaining in the churn. Unlike the thick homogenous buttermilk sold in the grocery, this buttermilk was a thin, smooth fluid of delicate flavor and with tiny flecks of fresh butter suspended throughout.

One of the big events occurring often in the summer was the making of homemade ice cream. The activity began at the icehouse down near the coal tipple, lumberyard, and railroad. The iceman would use a pick to split a huge block of ice and put a one-hundred-pound block into a gunnysack so they could get home with it. Each child had the rare opportunity to taste crushed ice then. Refrigerators and ice cube trays were yet unheard of.

Leaving the block of ice in the gunnysack, the next step was to crush the ice. This was done by hitting the sack hard and often with a baseball bat, mallet, the side of an ax, or any other club-like instrument. Invariably, one could taste the gunnysack along with the clear ice.

Next, a canister of ice-cream mix was placed in the freezer and the crank assembly was placed on the top. Crushed ice was poured into the freezer around the canister until it was one-third full of ice; then the rock salt was added generously to aid the freezing. When young, Hanno's first assignment was to watch the hole in the side of the freezer. If the melted salt water level reached the top of the canister, it invaded and ruined the ice cream. The hole on the side of the freezer allowed the salt water to escape. A small piece of ice easily blocked the hole and kept the salt water from escaping. Careful attention was required.

As the crank rotated the canister, the ice melted and the ice cream mix froze. The crank became harder and harder to turn. Finally it was declared "done."

The next question was who would lick the paddle? They removed the canister top. The paddle, fixed and unmoving as the canister spun around it, was lifted out and held vertically on a plate with ice cream sticking to it. Someone spooned off the paddle before the ice cream melted and fell off. Sometimes a child was chosen. Sometimes the privilege went to the person who cranked the hardest. Sometimes a visiting guest of honor was chosen. Sometimes it was Hanno's mom, who had prepared the mix.

Another special joy was when the big old tree in the east pasture had persimmons falling to the ground.

Another great taste experience was during apple-picking season. Hanno stood in Ferd's apple orchard barn in the heavily apple-perfumed air. He held his empty glass cider jug and watched fresh shiny apples dumped into a cider mill. The cider at the mill was a different experience from the one in the market where the cider had time to oxidize and was given preservatives. Another fine bubbly taste came when jugs of apple cider were left in the cool cellar and allowed to develop a quarter inch of foam at the neck of the jug. This was called hard cider.

Like almost every farm boy, Hanno learned how to kill a chicken. Spreading a bit of corn on the ground made the catching easier. When you caught a chicken, you grabbed it by the legs. Then you held the flapping wings with the other hand if you wished. You took the chicken to the bloody barnyard stump. You held the head down with your foot and continued to hold the legs as you raised the hatchet with the other hand. Hanno, uncoordinated as he was, learned to aim the hatchet onto the neck without missing it or hitting his foot. With the execution stroke, Hanno had to jump aside to avoid the spray of blood. The chicken's alternating leg reflexes would leave it jumping or tumbling in any direction. Hanno's father would grab his chickens by the head and spin the body in a circle with quick force. This was an option that Hanno did not like. If the neck was only broken but the head did not separate, there was trouble completing the task with a flailing injured chicken.

Later in life Hanno learned how differently children viewed chicken killing and butchering. With farm chickens, the practice of killing was familiar, but it was still not without emotion. A cardinal rule was that the chicken, turkey, or other animal to be slaughtered should never be a pet. They were difficult to kill. When on your plate fried, animals were difficult to swallow if they had been given a name.

In Hanno's world, like any farm boy's, his chores grew as he grew. After emptying the chamber pots, Hanno found his mother measuring whether he was ready to clean the thin glass globes of the coal-oil lamps without breaking them. On each Saturday morning one had to take the glass globes off the lamps and run wadded newspaper through them to remove the smoky film.

Then came the outdoor chores. An early priority was the safe opening and closing of the pasture gates when bringing the cows in for milking. Drivers of horse teams were at risk if they had to drop the reins, run to open the gate, return, drive through, and leave the reins again to close and secure the gate properly. Hanno, on his own, developed the skill of jumping off and completing this chore so that the driver could remain seated and in control.

Another broad area of responsibility Hanno picked up at an early age was managing the chickens. This involved checking twice a day on supplies. They needed a separate bowl for water. Unlike other livestock, they could not drink from the horse trough. Corn, both whole grain and crushed or mashed, was provided. A rail fence allowed the chickens access into the barnyard, while the cows could not get access to the chicken mash. Eggs had to be gathered from the nests at least once a day. A pan of crushed oyster shells or other calcium source had to be available for the hens to pick at; otherwise, their eggshells would become thin.

Hanno felt at times that the rooster was becoming too arrogant in dominating the hens. In such instances, Hanno would chase the rooster and try to catch him. The chasing tended to create a more humble attitude, and this pleased Hanno.

As Hanno became strong enough to carry the load, he assumed the unending task of carrying buckets of coal and water into the house. Even in these early years, Hanno was nicknamed "the absentminded professor."

The family would sometimes watch him from the window as he carried an empty coal bucket and set it under the pump spout before he realized that he should have gone to the coal shed.

Hanno watched as his father took to the milk stool. First, Hanno would spray the cow to ward off flies. Hanno was just at the right height to be slapped in the face by the cow's tail as it tried to rid itself of cow flies and horseflies. Then Hanno's dad would press his head against the cow's side as he sat. He held a sterilized aluminum pail firmly between his knees. (Otherwise, the cow could kick the pail over.) His two hands were placed confidently on the cow's *tits*. Hanno's dad was an excellent marksman. He would ask Hanno to open his mouth. When he did, his father would squirt a stream of warm milk into his mouth from the cow's tit. Very seldom did he miss. To relieve the cow's stress more quickly, the full udder was milked with diagonal sets of tits. In this farm setting, the cows were referred to as having *tits*, not *teats*. Hanno learned the word *teats* later on in life.

Hanno never got the hang of milking. As you squeeze the tit, you must squeeze your fingers, not as a group of four but in a motion of rotating downward. Otherwise, you would be squeezing milk up rather than down into the pail. Whenever Hanno tried, the cow would turn its head around to stare at him, as if he did not know what he was doing. Some cows were naturally cooperative. They were usually the best milk givers. An impatient cow would kick the pail over and walk away.

The family was living in the new house. By Hanno's reference points, they were both wealthy and poor. The early isolation affected Hanno one way or another for the rest of his life. It left its mark, both in dreams and fears. Hanno was left to his own devices for playing. Within miles, there was only one boy his age. This boy had a troubled father who forbade any of his children to visit neighbors. Hanno attached special importance to visitors, whether his brothers' friends, his parents' friends, relatives, neighbors, or salesmen.

An enjoyable place to explore was the old house, which was just a few feet behind the new house. The old house represented the previous generation. By the time Hanno was born in 1928, the old house had become a utility shed. One could still detect its history though. Richard Oglesby did not intend to live in this house as long as he did. Although the clapboards were from a sawmill, they were rough-hewn rather than smooth. The door latches and hinges in the interior were like those found on barn doors. Part of the building and the foundation was log. On one end of this cabin was an outside stone chimney. Inside was the large fireplace that at one time served for all cooking and heating needs. Within the fireplace was a well-constructed crane to swing cooking pots onto and off the hot coals. The fireplace had a fifteen-square-foot earthen hearth. This was necessary in order to protect the wooden cabin against sparks from the fire. The hearth, as Hanno knew it, was a black hard substance. It could not be swept clean. Hanno assumed that this hearth was a purchased fireproof substance. Actually, it was only the accumulation of wood smoke and candle smoke blackening the clay over decades.

Across from the fireplace, one quadrant of the floor space had been walled off as a private bedroom. During Hanno's time, of course, the house was not furnished as living quarters. Inside what had been the bedroom was now a corncrib. The remaining area was for tool and garden produce storage. Far from the fireplace was a large hogshead (pronounced hog-zit) with a lid. In this hogshead were stored potatoes, unshelled black walnuts, and rooted vegetables to be kept cool, dark, and dry. During the canal boat trip to Indiana, the hogshead became a center of attention at each mealtime.

Near the hogshead, bolted to the floor, was a cream separator. This newcomer was a hand-cranked centrifuge device that separated whole milk into cream and skim milk. Nearby was a churn. With vertical pumping it could produce buttermilk and butter.

Another source of exploration, not just for Hanno but also for the whole family, was the half acre set aside for special crops. Just outside the pasture gate and to the east was a small area for a special crop. During some years it would be planted with popcorn seed. In other years they planted lespedeza, alfalfa, potatoes, sweet potatoes, sugarcane, or watermelon. Hanno recalled spending days going from plant to plant to remove potato bugs. Most delightful were the sorghum-based popcorn balls and sticks of sugarcane.

On the rare occasions when a boyfriend visited Hanno the far west pasture was the favorite place for play. In winter, they could play tag and *it* along trodden paths in the snow. In the summer they could sail dried cow pies (cow manure). Only in Hanno's adulthood did the word *Frisbee* occur. Since kids were always barefoot in the summer, a great hazard and source of laughter was when someone stepped in a fresh, warm cow pie.

Hanno and his friends would often snack from little sour-tasting clumps of blooming sorrel grass. Hanno's mother would send him out with a dishpan to gather a mess of wild collard greens for supper. Different broad green leaves could be found in pastures and on the tops of certain vegetables. Like spinach, when boiled down with bits of cooked bacon, sugar, vinegar, and slices of hard-boiled egg, they made an excellent farm dish. Untold numbers of children were converted into liking a similar dish (spinach) by the Popeye cartoon strip. Popeye claimed unusual strength from eating it.

Hanno also enjoyed visiting the nearest neighbors. Just outside the southeast boundary of the farm lived an old couple, Sade and Corb Jones. They had a very small clapboard house. In their barn was an old Stanley Steamer automobile that had not been driven for years. A porch swing was suspended outside from a horizontal tree branch. They had a glassed-in porch with a couch that was called a glider. Suspended on the four corners, the glider could "rock" in any direction. None other existed like it in the community. On the side table of the glider lay a stereoscope. This device was mounted on a vertical post that served as the handle. You held it to your eyes and gazed into the shielded lenses as if looking through binoculars. A double picture was set in a frame at a given focal length. The double picture produced a single dramatic three-dimensional image. Many cards were available to view.

Sade and Corb had grandchildren who came to visit. The novelty of this company led Hanno more than once to stay there beyond his mealtime and get punished when he returned home.

Sometimes Hanno's family had a radio; sometimes they did not. The house had no electricity, gas, or modern plumbing. When they could afford a radio, it was a roman-arched tabletop model with wires to a car battery that sat on the floor under the table. An early country music singer was Bradley Kincaid. A popular song of that time was "The Big Rock Candy Mountain."

Sometimes, Hanno's family had a car; sometimes they did not. He was bundled up to drive to town in a girl's pink hand-me-down snowsuit. Hanno remembered the pink straps that went under his shoes. One strap had worn in two and flapped free. Dressed in this fashion Hanno had his first memory image of his hometown. On both the eastern and western city limits, there was an arched sign, high above the street. It was lit up at night and said, "YOU'LL LIKE LINTON."

[4]

WEEKLY ROUTINE

Hanno's memory of the farm was one of almost continuous work for the adults. Whether difficult or easy, there was no freedom of schedule. The men were bound to the milking and tending to the livestock down to the hour. The planting and harvesting had to be done within the limits provided by nature. For the women the duties tended to vary with each day of the week. There were no sick leaves, annual leaves, or long vacations. There were no extended weekends off.

Sunday featured a big dinner (always at noon), relaxation, and perhaps visitors. Sunday was seldom church day, except for Easter and Christmas. With a taxing shopping trip of nine miles round-trip the day before, time and resources did not allow regular Sunday church attendance. Yet, Hanno's mother was personally religious. One of the sorrows of her life was that her twin sons, Jay and Ray, went off to war without having been poured; that is, baptized in the First Baptist Church baptistery. Ray agreed to be baptized when he arrived home after World War II.

On Monday the fire was stoked up, this time for laundry. Large galvanized tubs had laundry brought to a boil. Into the boiling water went the OK lye soap. This was a medium-brown pound block of soap that looked like gjetost (Norwegian) cheese. Before using it, the round "OK" seal was pried from its spot. The clothes in the boiling-hot water were stirred with a broomstick. After this came the boiling-hot rinse water.

From the rinse water, the laundry, item by item, was hefted by stick or by hand into the rollers of the wringer. Someone cranked the wringer while someone else fished into the hot water and placed the item in the wringer. This team effort was hazardous since the person cranking could catch the other person's fingers in the wringer. This was a frequent occurrence, and Hanno's mother had a deformed joint on her little finger from such a childhood accident.

A common expletive issued by someone who had encountered misfortune in those days was: "I just got my balls caught in the wringer."

From the wringer the laundry fell into another tub. Then someone with apron pockets filled with clothespins hung the laundry on a wire clothesline in the backyard.

The wire clothesline was another hazard for young children when running at night in an unfamiliar yard. They were often shooting their Gene Autry pistols when a low wire would collide with their faces or necks.

Tuesday became ironing day. Almost all fabrics were ironed in those days. None were synthetic "wrinkle-free." None were preshrunk.

If in season, Wednesday was the day when they turned their attention to the canning and preserving of fruits and vegetables. They picked berries from the briar patches in the forest. To help ward off chiggers and poison ivy, Hanno and the other berry pickers had long sleeves, long pants, and then a salt bath at the end. The discomfort of collecting the berries and the salt bath seldom caused one to give up eating the fresh raspberries and blackberries.

Thursday and Friday were devoted to loose ends and cooking ahead for the weekend meals.

Saturday morning was the time everyone in the family had a bath. The soft cistern water was poured into a big, round galvanized laundry tub. Adults had to stand, but Hanno sat in the tub when his turn came. If the slick cistern water was in short supply, each person stood nude at a table before a small washbowl of hot well water. An alternative was to have one tubful of water used by more than one child. With a bar of soap and a washcloth (called face flannel in the United Kingdom), one proceeded from hands, face, neck, and ears to the feet.

As they took their baths, family members dumped all clothing into a laundry basket and donned clean clothes.

Then came the Saturday trip to town for shopping. Unless school was starting, the major focus of shopping was the Ax and Fry grocery. The family purchased items that could not be grown on the farm, like flour, Post's 40 percent bran flakes, rolled oats, salt, sugar, pork and beans, bananas, hot tamales in a can, salmon in a can (it was very cheap then but expensive later), sardines, saltine soda crackers, and peanut butter. Rather than grocery carts and checkout lines, each shopper held a list of items and waited in line for a fast-moving clerk. The clerk used a special pole to remove items from high shelves near the ceiling. He weighed and sacked various items. He would help the customer to the car with the many large brown paper sacks.

Once Hanno put his finger on the scales as the clerk was weighing. The astonished expression on his face pleased Hanno.

The merchants of Linton (called the Greater Linton Club) gave out drawing tickets for each twenty-five cents' worth of goods purchased in the stores. On appointed occasions, they held a drawing. A platform would be built along Main Street, and a big drum would be cranked. Some VIP would have the honor of drawing the winning tickets and announcing them to the crowd. On extra-special occasions, the platform would be kept in place for a band and street dance under the ornamental lampposts.

Even on a routine Saturday night, the downtown streets were festive. A confectioner's shop moved a popcorn machine out onto the sidewalk to sell heaping bags of buttered popcorn. Young couples, teenagers, and children would stroll up and down the crowded sidewalks, looking into shop windows, pausing to visit with friends, carrying their buttered popcorn with them. Ice-cream cones and cotton candy were also abundant.

The youngsters would be coming in and out of the Grand and Sher-Ritz movie theaters. There they had the weekend bonuses of serial episodes like *Hopalong Cassidy, The Cisco Kid, Drums of Fu Manchu,* and *The New Adventures of Charlie Chan.* Boys would argue the merits of Gene

Autry, Roy Rogers, and Tex Ritter in the debate over who was the best cowboy.

The northwest corner of Main and Vincennes was a panoply of activity and a counterpoint of human value. It differed from the carnival mood farther up Main Street. The central structure of this venue was the Cozy Corner Saloon. Unlike the ordinary squared-off brick corners of buildings, the Cozy Corner had the corner cut back into a diagonal main entrance of swinging double doors. Inside, at the far end, the signs "Gents" and "Ladies" were lit up above the two respective restroom doors. Between the doors was a small advertisement for the most recent beverage to come onto the market: 7-Up. Across the wall was a much longer sign for the leading beer of choice: Champagne Velvet. It was affectionately referred to as a "CV." Another popular beer was Sterling. Prohibition was over, and women sat with men at the booths but never at the bar. Interestingly, both the women, who would stop at one beer, and the alcohol-addicted men, who were exercising their last vestige of willpower, usually began with a short beer.

Later, during World War II, the often repeated joke was to order "airplane beer." The legend was that you drink one bottle and you P-38. (The P-38 was the famous Lockheed twin fuselage fighter-bomber of early World War II.)

Sometimes wives or children would come peeking into the side door, tired and wanting to go home, looking for their menfolk. Occasionally an impatient farmwoman would bolt in, sit down by her husband and his friends, and order a "dish of cream." Ice cream was not on the menu. In fact, there was no menu.

Outside the Cozy Corner, standing along the wall beneath the ornamental streetlamps, would be clusters of potbellied men, some with miner's caps, others with the straw hats they had worn all day on the farm. They would be enjoying conversation and a good cigar. Buster Brown would stroll along the curb, looking for cigar and cigarette butts in the gutter. Bert Sills, a prominent citizen with a peg leg, would also make his presence known. The potbellied men would be wearing suspenders and grasping them with each hand as they shared a warm story with someone they had not seen since last Saturday. Rarely, there appeared some young man in a jacket and tie. He would be carrying a flask.

Only a few feet away at the curbside—so close they could smell the beer breaths—was the Salvation Army Band. With a tambourine, bass drum, sliding trombone, and cornet, their songs included "Onward, Christian Soldiers," "The Old Rugged Cross," and "Rock of Ages." They were decked out in blue uniforms and garrison caps with red bands. The ladies would be in long garments of matching color with a stiff bonnet, also revealing a red band. One of the ladies went around collecting money in the tambourine. Sometimes a parent with two small children would stop and watch them play in wonderment. Otherwise, it was a Picasso-like scene where people in close proximity looked away into space as if all alone. Even when an offering was tossed onto the tambourine, there was no eye-to-eye contact. The potbellied cigar-smoker and the imbibing insider had an unspoken acceptance of the Salvation Army. They knew that their money would go for the needy.

Before the last piece of music, a lady would read a selection from the Scripture. Then they would pack their instruments and leave.

Hanno, as a preteenager, was overwhelmed by Saturdays after a week alone on the farm. Early on, he would accompany his parents to a drugstore soda fountain for a treat. He was afraid of the people at the tables around him. In a few years, when on his own, he would go to the Sher-Ritz and sit on the floor with other boys in front of the rows of seats. He knew not how to deal with the fast talk of the city kids and, on one occasion, yielded over a dime to a demanding kid. He had neither the language nor the fists to refuse and to defend himself, even with a smaller kid. His father had given him the dime for an ice cream cone and a Coke after the movie. After he returned to his father, he burst into tears. He could not be consoled. With severely injured pride, he could not accept his father offering him another dime. The dime could not replace his emotional loss. His feeling of defeat, remaining mute and defenseless, bothered him for years. Hanno mulled over the feelings of inadequacy and wondered if he would ever change.

A great day came in Linton when the ultramodern Cine' Theater was built. It had a genuine marquee with the name of the current movie in block letters. Inside was a spacious foyer and lobby. The floor was carpeted in red, and the seats were upholstered. On the ceiling was indirect florescent lighting that provided the magic glow of another world.

For the high-school kids and older, there was a Saturday midnight movie starting at eleven thirty.

Many people drove early to Linton to get a parking place. At the peak of the evening, every parking space would be filled. Cars would be driven slowly on Main and A Streets as people looked for an empty spot. Double parking was a common offense in those days. Older couples enjoyed getting their cars parked early, before the shopping, and then just sat there all evening long. They occupied most of the parking spaces. Television was yet to flourish, and radios often had too much static. Old people watched young people and children as the evening and their own lives faded slowly away.

[5]

JUMP

When Hanno was almost a year old, and as his parents confirmed, he achieved a feat that was talked about for years. He jumped off a train. The story goes this way.

Hanno's mother, his great-

Aunt Lizzie, his cousin Jean, and possibly another woman or two decided that it was time to take a holiday from the daily routine. They took a train a hundred miles north from Linton to visit Cousin Ruth in Indianapolis. Much planning was necessary. Hanno, still not walking or talking, was to travel with his mother. His father would take care of the twins. Hanno's first remembered image in this scenario was at the Linton train station. Hanno was in somebody's arms aboard the train. He could look down on his father, waving good-bye on the platform. Hanno realized for the first time that his father was not going. He began to cry—cry big. Hanno's father dropped his hand

and disappeared. He could see that Hanno did not want to leave him, so he hid.

Hanno can remember the women passing him around, happy to be getting away for a holiday, each trying to give him solace. He can remember very little of the passenger cars. The next memory was in Ruth's nicely furnished apartment. He was still crying, loudly. They debated about what was wrong. Hanno, of course, could not tell them that he simply wanted his daddy. They offered food, drink, and even candy; checked his diaper; and rocked him in their arms. They tried to get him to sleep in the crib they had acquired ahead of time. Nothing would quiet him.

Plans had been made to go out for the evening and leave Hanno *sleeping* in the crib. They finally made the decision, difficult or welcome, just to leave him there crying.

Once they left, all was quiet. Beside the crib were some maroon velvet draperies. Hanno realized that there was no one to cry to. So, he stopped. He slept a bit. Later, when the ladies returned from their outing, he began crying again. One might say that he spoiled their trip.

Hanno does not remember boarding the train to return home. What he does remember was what happened when the train arrived in Linton. As people were disembarking from the passenger car, Hanno's mother asked the conductor to hold him as she got her luggage. The conductor stood with Hanno at the top of the steps down to the platform. Hanno spotted his father alone and smiling at the foot of the steps on the platform. His legs were bent under him in a position to spring. The moment he saw his smiling father, he sprang.

Hanno did not see the flabbergasted face of the conductor, as his mother reported. What Hanno did see was the flabbergasted face of his father. He did not know why. Hanno sailed through the air, and his father caught him down on the platform.

His father, still recovering from his fright, confided a few minutes later that he had no confidence that he would be able to catch Hanno. All Hanno could remember was joy. He remained in his father's arms the rest of the way home.

[6]

FIRST SOLO VISIT

When Hanno was one year old, not yet able to talk, he ran away from home. He went over a half-mile path to the Erlichs' farm. He was aware of all the smiles, mirth, and warm greetings as he arrived. One of the Erlich boys was sent to Hanno's home just as his alarmed parents came out to look for him. Hanno's parents found him perched atop a high chair, eating cottage cheese. Only later did Hanno realize that the smiles and special courtesies were because he was stark naked during his visit.

[7]

ROOSEVELT TOILET

The one outbuilding not mentioned in the previous description of the homestead was the two-holer outdoor toilet. This building and its furnishing, more than anything else, defined the social and economic status of the family. From an academic distance, people are divided roughly into upper, middle, and lower classes. For those who are proximal to such casting, the levels of vertical discrimination are both more numerous and more exact. Better than anything else, Hanno discovered that he could determine the social standing of a family by visiting their toilet and rating it.

Level 9 was one in which, instead of toilet paper, a random assortment of corncobs had been pitched into a pile on an unwept floor. The cobs were rough, sometimes having single grains of corn and pieces of shuck remaining.

On level 8, cobs would be more neatly placed in a box, parallel cob to cob, and the floor otherwise was kept swept and clean.

On level 7, a selection was made from only white, rather than red, corncobs.

The corncobs of level 6 were not only white but they had been prerubbed against each other so as to make the texture of the cob soft to the touch. Such accommodation seemed to be chosen most often by old maidens or old widows living together in pairs, once endowed with money but no longer. Pride had outlasted their fall.

On level 5, there were no cobs. Instead, there was the current issue of the Sears Roebuck catalog, from which one tore individual leaves for toilet paper. This level was so close to that of the Buchwalds that Hanno's mother would speak disparagingly of this class. They seemed to lack forethought. From year to year, the members of this level would need to make a Sears order and the page that displayed the item had already been torn off and used. They would have to go to their neighbor's house in order to seek assistance in making the Sears order.

On level 4, the family reserved past issues of the Sears catalog for use in the toilet.

The next level, at 3, was the one where Hanno's family resided. This involved having in the toilet a previous year's issue of the Sears Roebuck catalog. In addition, a roll of store-bought toilet paper was kept in the house and was put out in the toilet on days when company was visiting. In addition, a bucket of quicklime and a ladle was kept on the floor of the toilet at all times. This allowed the customer to ladle a cupful of lime down a hole of the toilet either before or after it was used. This was done for both sanitation and odor.

The next level, level 2, was referred to in common language as the standard Roosevelt toilet. This name derived from the fact that the first generation of these toilets was constructed by workers in the WPA (Work Projects Administration) of F. D. Roosevelt's New Deal administration during the Depression. Each toilet was constructed atop a below-ground reinforced concrete septic tank. Only one seat was inside the toilet, and it had a wooden lid, seat, and metal hinge. It was placed at a diagonal within the toilet in order to provide more foot room. Chemicals were put in the concrete septic tank, which greatly reduced, or at least changed, the odor. The septic tank could be easily emptied by a special truck with a suction motor, large hose, and storage tank. Both the truck and the person who used it for the toilet cleaning were referred to as "honey dippers."

The Roosevelt toilet was a major advance in sanitation and public health. Toilets of the earlier era and lower class levels required the contents to be removed by shovel and wheelbarrow. It was wheeled away for burial or disposal. The name Roosevelt is burned into the memory of the country folk throughout the land where these toilets were being built.

Unfortunately Hanno's father was unable to get a job with the WPA, which provided numerous jobs in roads and parks, as well as toilet constructions. Likewise, he was unable to get a grant of clearance to have a Roosevelt toilet built on the homestead property. The reason was one of local political patronage. Preference to be given jobs or to have a Roosevelt constructed for them went to

Democrats. Gene Buchwald was well known to be an avid Republican. He used the words *radical Republican,* which might have been an oxymoron. Such discrimination was not sanctioned in Washington, but it was often practiced "here and there."

Level 1 in the hierarchy went to those families who had access to city water and sewerage lines or who could afford to have wells and septic tanks installed on their property. This allowed indoor plumbing and traditional urban bathrooms.

The memorable experiences with the homestead two-holer came when Hanno had to bundle up in a heavy coat and overshoes. He would trudge in the crunchy snow in below-zero weather past the old house. He would push a snowdrift away from the wooden toilet door. He would sit on an iron-cold wooded hole. He was told it would make him a better person. This baffled him. It still does. Like the stars and the idea of eternity, he could not understand the concept.

Hanno's dad learned a compromise. Before leaving the warm house and before putting on his heavy coat, he would unbuckle his belt, trousers, and suspenders. Then he would wrap up in his warm coat and head into the snow. He had complete faith that his pants would not drop to his overshoes. This took more courage than Hanno could muster.

As for retiring to one's bedroom, the outhouse would be replaced by a slop jar on which one could sit.

A very rare item—Hanno's family had only one available in the entire house—was a commode. This was a square piece of mahogany furniture of stool height. Its appearance was similar on all four sides and the top. It was so neatly designed that one could not detect that the top was hinged. If given this knowledge, one could then not tell on which side the hinge was located. If one lifted the correct edge on the wooden top, the object would open up into a slop jar, fitted inside, and the hinged top could be used as a backrest during one's transaction.

There were occasions when a guest did not know the word *commode* when introduced to it and certainly did not know which side of the wooden top to lift. When Hanno was in high school, he had occasion for his girlfriend (from the city) to be an overnight guest in the spare bedroom. Hanno's mother made reference to the commode but did not provide a users' guide. After pulling up the wrong side in an encounter after midnight, she then spent hours in distress. At last, as daylight broke, she found her way to the forgiving outhouse.

[8]

DAD

If one is shaped by kin and community, both for positive identity and for contrast, it is appropriate that Hanno give an accounting of those he felt were important to him, both in direct contact and in events of heritage that preceded him.

Hanno's father, Gene Buchwald (born 1888), was the fifth of six sons born to Harriet and Albert O. Buchwald of Cory, Clay County, Indiana. Before Gene, there were Charlie, Bert, Dale, and Fred. Gene was born two years after Fred. Gene's heels were hardly out of the womb when Harriet was pregnant with the baby later to be called Uncle Hanno. This is the baby for whom young Hanno was named.

While Harriet was pregnant with her last child and was still nursing Gene, she pursued her favorite pastime of reading German and French novels. During this reading, she was taken with a boy character called Hanno Buddenbrook.

"That shall be the name of my child," she declared. "Or, if it is a girl, I shall call her Hannah."

It was indeed a boy, and he became Hanno.

Within three weeks, however, Harriet passed away from birth complications. The infants Gene and Uncle Hanno found themselves in a motherless household. Their four older brothers were unforgiving for their arrivals and for the attention they commanded. They were cruel to Gene and Hanno. They fought with outsiders and with each other. Their father, Albert, was in grief, out of control of himself, and unable to control his sons.

Harriet's unexpected death was a turning point for Albert and for all the boys. Albert and Harriet had an ideal Indiana family life. He was a Hoosier schoolmaster, and they owned a promising farm. He was an inspired teacher in a one-room country schoolhouse. The frontier society of Indiana held in high esteem a teacher who could advance the book knowledge of its children. Also in high regard were the farmers who could clear the fields of rocks and stumps to reach a productive crop growth. Albert met both of these symbols of status. Also, his own father, Oliver Junior, had been a member of the Indiana legislature from Worthington and a distinguished citizen.

Harriet was a natural-born manager. She was successful as a mother, housewife, and overseer of farm activity. She was raising boys, which contributed to the economic promise of a farm family. Her interest in books made her attractive to the other farm wives, who often wanted tutorial help for their offspring. She minded the family budget in the absence of her husband, who was getting greater and greater esteem from his brilliant teaching and willingness to serve the community. Albert enjoyed his good life. Above all, Harriet was the love of his life.

Harriet's death left Albert in a state of prolonged grief, and his boys, all of them, suffered from both the loss of their mother and the diminished attention from their father. Albert delegated more and more of the farm responsibilities to them. Among themselves, they fought for a pecking order of authority. They offered no leniency to each other.

When Gene was thirteen years old and the boys had the burden of the farm, the pupils of Perry Township raised money and presented Albert with a gold-headed cane. At the same time, Albert had a home life and farm that was reeling out of control. His grief over the loss of his life's love was compounded by his duties as a single parent. The community increased its demands on his time, and the farm duties, which Harriet was no longer available to supervise and nurture, were neglected. The more work he delegated to the older boys, the greater their discontent.

Uncle Hanno was not greatly affected by his mother's death as such. After all, he was only a few weeks old when she died. He did not remember her. His grief came not from the loss of her but from the abuse by the older boys.

With Gene, later to become the young Hanno's dad, it was a different story. He was old enough to become bonded with his loving and nursing mother. Her death was like a physical blow. He quit growing, and he developed stomach problems. It became apparent that he could not endure the abuse of his siblings and the inevitable failings by his father. Finally, as Gene became the physical runt among the strapping brothers, his father had to make arrangements to place him with Harriet's mother. His maternal grandmother, Emma Fields, took Gene over in loving memory of her daughter Harriet.

Living with his grandmother, Gene finally began to prosper. He gained some weight, but he remained with stomach problems and a passive, dependent nature for the rest of his life.

The central theme of Gene's young life was loss. He lost his own mother at the peak of his natural attachment to her. Then he lost his sense of dignity when he was unable to cope with his brothers. People said he was not tough enough.

Gene became sensitized to the humiliation of living under the care of his grandmother while his brothers continued to work the farm. He had a private feeling of worthlessness. At the hint of criticism of his toughness, he would fight or curse people so that they would not see him as weak. He developed a lifelong need to seize some immediate feeling of status, pleasure, and self-worth. He learned not to trust time. Any endeavor that required a delay for some greater and more stable reward turned him off. To extend a bet when others faltered showed his courage, and this was more important to him than a later reward. He expected failure. Failure was painful. By consequence, much of his behavior was impulsive or for the gain of immediate status and appearances. Even his positive achievements failed to remove his self-doubts.

From the beginning, Gene was the smallest boy in his class. He was living in the village of Cory, Indiana, with his grandmother, and he helped out in the apple orchards come picking time. In spite of his size, he gained some respect in school because of his intelligence. By consequence, he got two double promotions during grammar school. He skipped the fourth and sixth grades. These achievements enhanced the tragedy of his personal chaos. Even in the first three grades, he was always ready for a good fight if teased about his height. After two double promotions, however, his size as an eighth-grader became freakish to the others. Not only was he smaller but also his emotional interests did not match those of his fellow eighth-graders. They had become teenagers in their thinking. The teasing was incessant, and the little runt was sure to retaliate.

One day during recess, Gene sneaked up quietly behind a boy who had teased him earlier. With a very fast and strong move, Gene gave the boy a swift kick in the buttocks, timed so that the bell would ring and class would come to order before the boy could fully retaliate. Gene then discovered that the school principal was right behind him holding the bell as he kicked. Gene was not about to yield to the principal's punishment, so he ran out the door and across the schoolyard. The principal dropped the bell and came in pursuit. Gene was headed to the lot next door where a new school building was under construction. Bricks were piled high, and Gene thought he could find a place to hide. The principal, however, was right on his heels. The kids were rushing out of the school building to witness the unique event.

Gene grabbed a load of bricks and began throwing them at the principal. Now it was the principal who turned and ran from Gene. Like a dog sensing his dominance, Gene ran after the principal, throwing the bricks as he ran. By then, almost the entire school was out to watch the eighth-grade runt chase their principal and stone him.

Since the pupils of the school had witnessed his retreat, the principal did not assume the mantle of love and forgiveness. Before the close of day, Gene had been expelled from school. As it turned out, this became the last day of Gene's excellent academic career.

Some former teachers who remained impressed with Gene's intelligence urged him to bypass high school and enter normal school. A normal school was the term used then to refer to what later became a state teachers college. Such changes were possible, but Gene lacked the motivation to follow this guidance. Somehow he knew that he could not be the runt on his own without a supportive and nurturing person being with him. So, he continued to live with his grandmother and work odd jobs.

Again, even while people bragged of Gene's courage, he quietly viewed himself as a loser. Few things in life gave him any other view—except one. Gene could run. Soon his name was known throughout Clay County. Although Gene was small in stature, his body matured into the shape of Michelangelo's statue of David. His legs could rotate like the flywheel of a combustion engine. Some claimed they could not even see his legs as he ran.

Foot races, while popular in rural Indiana, were always informal. Usually they had no timing. In Gene's case, someone went to a local retired schoolteacher who owned the only stopwatch in town. With it, a group of young men measured out a level pasture for one hundred yards. One young man brought his pistol with real bullets. The local high school was not accredited, and they had no track team. Gene was not actually a student anyway. In this small town, no one knew what to do or where to go to get Gene's time officially recorded. He and his competitors would take off their heavy work shoes and socks. They would roll up their pant legs, take off their shirts, and run barefooted. In this kind of setting, Gene was clocked more than once at 9.5 seconds for his one-hundred-yard dash. But they indeed did not know that the world record at that time was 9.6 seconds. They did know that it was safe to bet on him. He had many races. Nothing ever came of it. Years later, at age fifty, Gene could outrun his three sons.

It was during the running competitions that Gene learned that his brothers were planning a trip to find work out west. This immediately sounded attractive, and he wanted to join them. Gene could sense that his fear of being abandoned was wearing off for whatever reason. He wanted to prove himself.

The pressures within the Buchwald household could not last. The older boys were fed up with the endless work with little reward. Perhaps they were also tired of fighting each other. The older ones were surprised when Gene and Uncle Hanno both sensed the spirit of adventure and wanted to join them. The boys had heard about gigantic wheat fields in the state of Washington that needed farm labor. It was a chance for freedom and fortune. Albert, despondent and alone, saw his dreams of a prosperous farm go to rubble. Without hesitation, he gave the older ones his blessing. He knew they would have gone anyway. Gene was already gone from the farm. There was little his father could say. Although he felt that Hanno and Gene were too immature, he finally relented. If nothing else, he wanted Hanno around for company. But he gave that up.

The boys' sojourn out west was at first a colossal success and then a colossal failure. They were all tough farm boys, even Gene and Hanno. So they got good jobs as hired hands. They did their work. The pay was good.

Cutting free for the first time, however, they squandered their money as they made it. It was a summer of drinking, gambling, and, for the older ones, chasing the girls. As the harvest season came to an end, they had no money. They all sought assistance from their father to get money to travel back home after one harvest season—all, that is, but Hanno.

Having remained the scapegoat of the older ones, Hanno had taken a job on a different farm in order to distance himself from his older brothers. He was lucky to have received some mentoring and advice from the farm owners.

To the day they died, Uncle Hanno's brothers were in hot dispute about whether Hanno was actually contacted when they made the retreat back home. Either it was a cruel abandonment of their little brother, a miscommunication in who would contact him, or Hanno elected to make his life out west on his own.

Thus Albert could not rejoice over the return of his boys. He still missed his wife. He missed his farm. Now, with Hanno gone, he could not be consoled. He struck out to find Hanno and bring him back. But Hanno had moved on to other work. The farmwork was over until the next season. No one knew where Hanno was.

With the onset of World War I, Albert knew that Hanno was of age for the draft. So he made inquiries of the War Department to trace Hanno. They were to no avail. (Years later, it was learned that Hanno had changed his name to Roy Lee.)

Later, when Albert died, heartbroken, he willed his gold-headed cane to his son Hanno in the hope that he might return.

Getting back home to Cory, Indiana, from the west, Gene was left to feel that the trip had been yet one more failure on his record. This circumstance led to a new adventure: joining the US Navy. It has never been clear if Gene chose this on his own or if his father persuaded him. Again, in the Navy, Gene was a social failure.

As expected, Gene was smaller than the other recruits. He was assigned to a hospital in Washington, DC, as a medical orderly. During his tour of duty, he had a chance to see the famous oversized bathtub of President Taft.

In the mix of Navy and other military personnel in the nation's capital, it did not take long for people to realize that Gene was a country bumpkin. Indeed, Gene was aware of it. The complex diagonals, circles, and grid pattern of the streets confused him. One night in a driving storm of sleet, Gene circled the Capitol building two times before getting his bearings.

On another occasion he wandered into an upscale barbershop. He did not know how to deal with a situation he could not afford. He could not admit he could not afford their services. Upon entry, an attendant helped him off with his coat. Another attendant put it on a hanger and began brushing it with a whiskbroom. In the barber chair, Gene was given a set of choices he did not understand. As his hair was clipped, another attendant began to manicure his nails. Gene began to worry about what he would be charged. He was seeking a fifty-cent haircut. He had only

$2.15 with him. When he was finished, he grabbed his coat, threw his entire $2.15 to the cashier, and ran out the door without speaking to anyone.

Various experiences left Gene as a scapegoat in his barracks because of his lack of knowledge of city ways. Gene appealed to his father to help get him out of the Navy. However, his stress level and his stomach problems got the better of him. He was given a medical discharge with a 10 percent service-connected disability.

It was not long after arriving home from the Navy when Gene's grandmother, Emma Fields, died. She had rescued him from his father's farm and nurtured him. She had treated his stomach with gentle foods. Now he felt the void from her quiet passing. Just as significant in Gene's life history, Emma had left him an inheritance.

The inheritance came at a time when Gene was least able to think of the meaning of life and long-term goals. Too much pain and humiliation had passed under the bridge. He had to grab pleasure while it was available. Otherwise, it would be gone.

Gene had seen a lot of the recent fashions on the streets and in the windows while he was in Washington, DC. His first step was to outfit himself in what might best be described as *Great Gatsby* outfits. Gene chose a derby hat, colored dress shirts, a light-colored suit, and tan leather sporty shoes. Gene was very conscious of wondering what it would feel like to be the best-dressed guy in town.

Gene's next step was to buy a horse. This was a time when all successful young men had a horse. He wondered what it would be like to have the best horse in town with that horse pulling the best buggy. Gene purchased a horse that had won ribbons in horse shows. He bought a buggy that matched his outstanding horse.

As Gene was regaling himself with a new image, the young ladies were not far from his mind. In spite of that, it came as almost a surprise that ladies whose eye he could not hope to catch before were happy to be seen with him and to spend time wining, dining, and partying. It was easy to gather a small group of close friends who could spend time in party. And it was always Gene who picked up the tab. He became popular. It was easy to start believing they were attracted to him, not his money.

Gene became more and more attracted to one girl, Lola Risher, who was most happy to be in his company. It is safe to say that his resources began to reach bottom as he bought gifts and entertained her. He fell in love and wanted to marry her. To his shock, she turned him down. He was suddenly out of money and out of a girlfriend. Throughout all of this, the importance of having a good stable job did not occur to him.

Depleted in cash and broken in spirits from a failed romance, Gene decided to move to Linton, Indiana, and look for work. His brother Fred was a fireman there.

Soon after Gene arrived in Linton, Fred transferred to the police department and was shortly murdered. On February 9, 1915, a burglar had broken into Harley Miller's tavern after midnight. Fred, on routine night merchant rounds, spotted the partially open door. Untrained in police techniques, he opened the door wide and stood in the doorway. He looked into the darkness within the barroom.

With the backlighting from the street, Fred was well in view. The burglar shot into Fred's silhouette with a pistol.

The burglar was identified while trying to get away. He was Frank Toricello. Within less than a week, he was traced to a hotel in Indianapolis. A group of policemen surrounded the room, opened it with the house key, and found Toricello shaving with half of his face fully lathered. The policemen grabbed his wrists so that he was immobilized, prevented from using his razor or the gun from the bedside table. Booked in the police station and put in a jail cell, he remained with lather on one side of his face. He was found guilty and sentenced to life in the penitentiary at Michigan City, Indiana.

While losing the emotional support he expected from his brother Fred, Gene received some unexpected reflected fame. He became visible in the community as the brother of one who had given up his life in public service.

Gene knocked around at various part-time jobs. One of these jobs was to deliver flowers from the shop of Lizzie Malone Davis. Lizzie was profoundly deaf, and she successfully managed a large business by depending heavily upon young hired help.

This job presented two opportunities. First, it was the opportunity to meet Mary Oglesby. Second, it was the opportunity to drive Linton's first car.

Lizzie had ordered a Model T Ford for $400. It was ordered from a Sears Roebuck catalog and came to her house in a kit. She paid her nephew Murl Oglesby a hundred dollars to assemble it. This task took a full day. Although Gene admitted his stress while teaching himself to drive, it was nothing compared to the stress endured by the car. Fortunately, the gears survived their stripping.

Mary Oglesby had come to town to live with her grandmother, Susan Malone, and attend high school.

Things did not work out well. Then when Mary's sister Zelma left her job with Aunt Lizzie, Mary lost no time in taking it. Mary became very skilled in how Aunt Lizzie read people's lips. She was soon able to carry on a conversation with Aunt Lizzie without speaking but with lip movement only. She could deliver gossip or privileged information without other people present understanding.

As fellow employees under Aunt Lizzie, it did not take long for Gene and Mary to begin dating. Their romance flourished. One day, Mary approached Gene in great distress. She had not had her menstrual period. She was certain she was pregnant.

The response that Gene made to Mary and how he made it portended the nature of their relationship for years to come.

First, he was disposed to do the right thing. He would protect Mary from the social disgrace of having a child out of wedlock. He could still hear his late grandmother Emma's words ringing in his ears. Such a decision also validated his desire to show himself a "real man." This recent romance in Cory as a playboy also illustrated his search for a macho image as he defined it.

Second, he could not stand failure and humiliation, and he could not stand for another person to experience the same. He put pride in himself as a loyal good buddy. Even his Sunday school experiences while living with his grandmother taught him the notion of God and Jesus as one of personal caring. The deity was seen as one who would walk with you. Prayer to Gene was an individual walk in the garden to talk things over, one with One.

Third, he was keenly aware that Mary had features that he could not find in himself. He knew that he was a person of impulsive decisions, one to escape immediate problems but then to regret it. He saw Mary as a life manager, seeking to control when things were not right and even when they were. Thus she could provide something he lacked in his makeup.

Was he in love? After the recent rejection when he fell deeply in love, he was no longer sure what love meant. All he knew was that, under these circumstances, he felt deeply committed to Mary and needed her.

Under these circumstances, Mary, in the days that followed, experienced the relationship as one where she was completely protected and loved. Mary had grown up in the shadow of Zelma, who had been looked on by both men and women as one of the outstanding beauties in the county. Everyone, even Mary herself, was drawn to Zelma. For Mary it was a new and wonderful feeling to have someone interested.

Immediately after the rushed marriage, Mary announced the pregnancy had been a false alarm. It was seven years before they had children. For the rest of his life, Gene did not know whether he had been tricked into marriage or if Mary was truly distressed by a late period. For Gene it made no difference. The topic was never raised until their son Hanno queried the story of their marriage during the final year of Gene's life. It was a raucous, continually quarreling marriage of fifty-four years by a couple who could not be torn apart.

Such is the story of how Hanno's two parents met and married. With all the fighting, almost daily, neither of them ever spoke seriously of divorce. They wished only to vent their frustration and hate and to destroy each other.

The nature of their fighting had a consistent pattern over the years. Mary would lambast him with bad labels like "a failure," "a drunk," "a bad husband," "unreliable," and the like. She was capable in anger of throwing a pot at him. Gene expressed his anger in a different way. Never once did he say a bad word about her character. Never once did he resort to any hitting or physical violence. Instead, there were impulsive expressions of anger such as, "God damn you," "To hell with you," and "Go ahead and cry. I don't care. The more you cry, the less you will piss."

He would bend over with a stomach pain as he received the epithets that she hurled. He was quite capable of just walking down the lane, leaving the house, and returning in a day or three.

Back to their early days of marriage, Gene, to expand his income, worked as a chauffeur for Welch and Cornett Funeral Home. Mostly, he drove to Indianapolis to pick up bodies from the train station and bring them back to Linton for burial in Fairview Cemetery. Sometimes, however, he was called upon to drive the hearse or a family car from the funeral service to the cemetery.

Leaving these part-time jobs behind, both Gene and Mary took jobs in a defense plant, Delco Remy, in Anderson, Indiana. Gene was an inspector on an assembly line. He referred to this job as the most advanced he ever had.

Two years after their marriage in 1914, Gene was drafted into the Army for World War I. Gene was shocked at being drafted since he was married and had been medically discharged from the Navy. He had assumed that he was exempt and would not have to go to war.

Once the draft orders were cut, Gene was assigned for training at Camp Taylor near Louisville, Kentucky. Gene's reaction to the Army was positive. From his experience in the Navy, he was more familiar with military procedures than the other men being drafted. He often claimed the Army "made a man out of you." Gene had humorous stories about recruits from the mountains of Kentucky, who could not read and had never experienced indoor plumbing. They lacked knowledge of which bathroom fixtures were intended for which purposes. He no longer played the country bumpkin role as he had in the Navy. Pictures were taken of him and his comrades in their campaign (Smokey the Bear) hats. Notable were the comic poses of Gene with his platoon as they stood unsmiling at strict attention. Gene, also with a straight, unsmiling face, would have his body tilted at forty-five degrees and held from behind by the soldiers in the front row. Another picture had a stern-looking sergeant with a bulldog face seated while Gene stood beside him with a serious face but with one leg cast across the sergeant's lap. Gene loved to play the clown. For him, the playfulness went hand in hand with the poker and drinking. Gene was the mischievous fun-maker of the troops.

Plans were being made to ship his unit into combat in France when, to the delight of the world, Armistice Day was declared. Gene was discharged shortly afterward.

Gene and Mary returned to Linton after the war. Mary had been very lonely and not accustomed to the larger city ways in Anderson. Also, no relatives were available.

During the years immediately following Armistice Day, a confluence of events led to a major change in the lives of this young couple. With Mary working in her aunt's flower shop and Gene taking up part-time jobs, they were making only a hand-to-mouth existence. Also, Gene created problems in the marriage because of his occasional benders. Not only were savings getting expended, but also Gene would often borrow money for gambling and drinking. In addition, Mary's mother, Celester, died. This left Mary's father, the aging David Oglesby, son of the Bound Boy, with an increasing burden in farming and caring for the homestead. Then also, Zelma, Mary's older sister with two baby daughters, Jean and Ruth, had contracted a fast spreading cancer (melanoma) on her leg. She was not expected to live. This meant that in addition to Mary's duties with Aunt Lizzie, she needed to provide medical and personal care for Zelma. Her two little daughters needed care and eventual custody. Finally, after seven years of marriage, Mary had become pregnant. As it turned out, she made up for lost time by having identical twin boys. With all this to deal with, Mary's father became the center of attention by losing his memory (that is, developing Alzheimer's disease).

This situation resolved itself through a series of both beneficial and forced events. First, Mary became unable to work and provide income because of her caretaking responsibilities with her sister Zelma, the daughters, and her father. Second, two revelations became apparent in the personal characters of Mary and Gene. Mary could not adjust to the continual cacophony and demands of crying babies, either her own or her sister's. She became increasingly anxious and unable to cope. She had clearly become inadequate to the task. Gene, on the other hand, while childlike in his immaturity and desire for immediate gratification, turned out to love the father role and to love children. He had joy in playing with and caring for them. He picked up some of the responsibility where Mary was failing. They owned no house but greatly needed one for the child care.

The one beneficial event was that Zelma was a very careful and successful businesswoman. With her boardinghouse, she had accumulated a modest savings. She left it for the care of her two daughters. Mary and Gene became the heirs apparent for custody of Ruth and Jean. Since their number-one necessity in child rearing them was adequate housing, they drew from Zelma's fund as the down payment for a mortgage on a small house. It remained arguable whether this was a legitimate way to spend the money intended for the daughters. For immediate practical purposes, there was no question.

Since Gene was heavily involved in the rearing, a series of vignettes should be presented to show the kind of humor, jokes, and stunts he loved to perform as his children were growing up. Young Hanno witnessed some of these and cherished others as a part of family history.

At one of the concerts at the twins' high-school the school's best singer was introduced for an a capella rendition of "Jack of Diamonds." After the teacher's elaborate introduction, the boy stood alone under the spotlight. The auditorium lights were darkened. The boy, well trained for his craft, stood solemnly looking upward, waiting for the audience to become silent. Suddenly, from out of the darkness came Gene's shout: "Someone should first play 'God Save the King.'"

Once Gene had an opportunity to visit the Grand Ole Opry in the Ryman Auditorium in Nashville. While a rousing country music song was being played over the air and the house was packed, Gene jumped out of his seat into the aisle and began clogging. His children dragged him back to his seat.

An evening party was being held for the birthday of a lady who was a French miner's daughter. Along with homemade ice cream and cookies, someone had brought in a car-battery-operated radio. Amid the static, a hillbilly song was found. Gene immediately asked people to move so he could roll back the carpet. Then he asked one of the unsuspecting wives to dance with him. Gene's sons were mortified, but to their surprise, the wife who danced enjoyed it thoroughly and others joined in. Mary did not dance.

Such happy evenings Hanno often associated with the trip home late at night. Tired and happy, the family walked across pastures and planted ground in the moonlight, discussing various humorous and interesting events that had occurred. The moon helped guide the way. There were acres and acres of lightning bugs popping on and off across the fields. On a nearby fence post, a whippoorwill was speaking its name. High on a tree off in the forest, a little screech owl screamed as if he were watching the world come to an end.

The next major event in the early marriage years was of no little importance. The lieutenant governor of Indiana, the honorable E. L. Hardesty, asked for a private audience with Mary and Gene. Hardesty had roomed in the boardinghouse run by Zelma. He shared with them that he had been in a prolonged and deep love affair with Zelma. On her deathbed, Zelma had asked him to take care of raising her children. Learning of the difficult circumstances of Mary and Gene and realizing that the problems would be great for them to raise all four children, he proposed that he and his wife legally adopt Ruth and Jean, assume custody of the fund, and place them at the disposal of his personal resources when that fund was spent. Since Mary was already overwhelmed with the burden of childrearing and Gene, while enjoying it, had to give up work time on occasion, the transaction was carried out through the court and a cordial relationship remained between the two families to the end of their respective lives. Even though in later years, Mary became a "heavy house cleaner" (woodwork, windows, heavy furniture) and Gene became a janitor and a night watchman, the lieutenant governor and his family never failed to invite Mary and Gene to their annual Christmas reception in their home. Along with prominent VIPs of banking, business, and politics, Mary and Gene Buchwald were served up the Honorable Hardesty's favorite hot Christmas drink, Tom and Jerry.

Another unexpected bonanza that came with the birth of the twins was the amount of attention the community paid to Jay and Ray. They were indeed very good-looking and almost impossible to distinguish. More than one couple literally wanted to buy them (i.e., pay thousands of dollars for the privilege to adopt them). These offers were declined without conflict or regret. Both Gene and Mary claimed there was nothing in the world that would induce them to give up the twins. Meanwhile, the twins were showered with many gifts of nice clothing, toys, and playground equipment.

As if the problems in childrearing, custody, income, living quarters, drinking and gambling were not enough, it was now confirmed that Mary's father David's

Alzheimer's disease was advancing. He was becoming incapable of managing the farm alone. At this point a number of problems were solved by the young family moving from Linton back to the homestead, four and a half miles north.

And so it was to be. A final coda was added to the plan by Gene. He took on his first full-time job since he moved to Linton. He became employed as a coal miner. Before and after his shift in the mines he took on the farmwork. David was freed up to stay with the twins.

Unfortunately, in the mines, Gene got hit on the shoulder by a slate fall. He was disabled for several months. During the chiropractic treatment, Gene could still manage the farm chores. All of this meant that his distress did not prevent him from slipping off the farm to visit a saloon.

Once transferred to the farm, Gene and Mary already knew very well that their lives would be governed by a routine that must be repeated every day, every season, and every year. For Gene, this routine represented a toggling back and forth between minding the farm and escaping it. Some of the escapes to pleasure were benign, and some led progressively to his downfall and dysfunction late in life.

Gene genuinely loved the activity of being a father. As the twins, born in 1921, were growing up, he became involved with the school, which was providing poor reading instruction. He visited school authorities and did his own tutoring. Later, when the twins were in high school, he felt the coach was being unfair when choosing his own relatives over the twins to be on the basketball team. He had no money to buy a basketball or a basketball goal, but he protested. He delighted in board games, playing cards, singing with them, and teaching them to use a gun safely and to hunt. Squirrel, quail, and rabbit potpies became favorite dishes after these hunts. At an early age, he bought them .410-gauge shotguns. He got fishing tackle so that they could use a rod and reel. He taught them to collect flint arrowheads and other Native American artifacts as the plow turned them up on the planted fields. He taught them to collect specimens of butterflies and moths. He taught them to trap and to tan hides of ground animals from the virgin forest. They strove to exceed their father in their knowledge of names of birds, names of trees, and even names of weeds. They wandered for hours through the fields and woods, never following a trail or path. They would seek out the hedgerows and the hollow logs where their interesting friends would be residing.

Seven years after the twins' birth, when Hanno was born, the path was different. First came the storytelling and the alphabetic blocks on the kitchen floor, and then came the rhyme.

They discovered that Hanno was not well coordinated, could not throw a ball straight, and could not aim a gun well. Yet Gene discovered that Hanno did well in recognizing words. Also he could use numbers. Besides alphabetic blocks, Gene bought Big Little Books for Hanno. These were about five by five inches on the face and about two inches thick. One book contained the story of Frank Buck, who went into the jungle to capture wild animals and pythons for the zoo. Another book was about Shirley Temple, whom he had seen in a movie. Hanno told his family that her date of birth was within a year of his own. He announced to them that he was going to marry her. While his mother and brothers laughed at the idea as incredulous, Gene taught Hanno to live on dreams. Most notable was his dream for a pony. Gene granted that request and discussed with Hanno what color he wanted, where they were going to have its stall, and what name to give it. Hanno's brothers and mother would tell Hanno that there would never ever be a pony, that there would never be enough money for a pony. Jay and Ray would say, "There is not even money for a basketball or baseball or football. There will never be a pony." They were right. Hanno did not agree. He believed. His dreams of a pony were so vivid he, as an adult, feels grateful that his father let him own the idea of a pony.

Years later, when he learned of it, Gene enjoyed reminding Hanno that he was born on the same day as Mickey Mouse. The first Mickey Mouse cartoon, "Steamboat Willie," was released on Hanno's birth date, November 17, 1928.

There was one thing about his father Hanno did not like, but he never had the courage to say so. Gene, having had so many failures in his own life, could not tolerate seeing a child have this experience. So he would always let Hanno win at cards. If Hanno's luck was running well, Gene would not cheat. But if Hanno's luck or skill were not good, his father would cheat by making silly mistakes in order to allow Hanno to win. Hanno much preferred that his father would allow failures to happen and then analyze them in order to improve his skill.

With Hanno especially, his father enjoyed answering with rhyme. If Hanno asked if he must catch a chicken for Sunday dinner, he might say, "You can catch the chickens if you run like the dickens. If you throw down some corn, the rooster might blow his horn."

With Hanno's father's ever instant rhyme, Hanno would get caught up in the game. He would try to give his father a question to which he could not rhyme. Hanno always lost.

"Dad, what do you think we'll have for supper?"

"I'd like some peas, if you please. I'll have my milk. It makes my stomach feel like silk."

"But, Dad, how about an orange?"

"An orange is a citrus. I'll pass it up. I know it is fit for us as juice in a cup."

On occasion, Hanno addressed his dad as Foozy. Foozy was a character in the comic strip *Alley Oop* in the funny papers. Foozy talked in rhyme, like Hanno's father did.

After Hanno was grown a bit, his mother used him as a two-way hedge in order to keep Gene from drinking and not coming home. His mother sent Hanno along with Gene to ensure more sobriety and a more certain return. This is what happened on the day Gene went to vote. Political candidates were always browsing around the polls with a good supply of whisky. Every vote was worth a good swig.

On November 8, 1932, a few days before Hanno was to become four years old, he and his father were trodding the path from the orchard into the forest ravine. They were heading toward Fairview Road to pick up a ride to go vote. Hanno, holding his father's left hand, was taking care on a path made for people going single file. Gene looked down at Hanno and, for his own amusement, asked him if he was going to vote for Hoover or Roosevelt.

"Hoover," Hanno replied. Hoover was a name Hanno had heard before. He had never heard the name Roosevelt.

By the time they had reached the road, Hanno had changed his mind. He told his father that he would rather vote for Roosevelt.

"How did you make this choice? Why did you change your mind?"

"I knew the name Hoover, and I thought it was a smooth, pretty name. Then I thought more about Roosevelt and said the name to myself over and over. I decided that Roosevelt was prettier. I will vote for Roosevelt. He has the prettier name."

On other occasions the hedge was in reverse. Gene wanted to run away and get a drink. He knew that his wife disapproved. However, he also knew that there would be less turmoil if he took Hanno with him. He always gave a fake excuse, such as the need for cigarettes, gasoline, or Bromo Seltzer.

On May 6, 1939, when Hanno was ten and a half, Gene called him out to the cornfield and they walked to the east pasture gate. They got in the car and headed for town. They drove directly to Harley's Tavern. Gene ordered a Coke for Hanno and a short beer for himself.

Hanno soon learned that this was not a routine day. It was the day of the Kentucky Derby. A radio was hooked up behind the bar. John, the tall bartender, was drying glasses and putting them on the back bar. He chatted with Hanno's dad and offered to buy his pool ticket for the Kentucky Derby. Dad refused. John then offered to buy half the pool ticket and split the winnings, if any. Dad refused.

Two weeks before, Gene had purchased a pool ticket for a dollar and had drawn the favorite of the day: Johnstown, Son of Jamestown. Since Jamestown had been a winner, people today expected no less of the colt.

Soon the race was on. Johnstown was positioned in the fifth gate. Within the first quarter mile, he swerved to the inside lane. With a mile yet to run, he took the lead. On the backstretch, a nudge sparked him ahead by six lengths. He won the race with speed to spare. The contents of the pool were turned over to Hanno's father. His father immediately called for a round of beer for everyone in the room.

Harley's Tavern was on Main Street at that time. It was there that Hanno got his first sensory overload of a pissoire. This was a trough urinal that could accommodate three men side by side. It was in a room with no door.

Other activities that stood in the way of focus upon the farm were Gene's general sense of fellowship and loyalty to friends. This loyalty, of course, broke down when Gene followed his addictive impulses toward gambling and drinking. On such occasions, he would borrow money from friends when he had no means to pay them back.

An illustration of Gene's commitment to friendships is the story of when a posse of sworn deputies with shotguns raided the homestead in the middle of the night. Gene's drinking and gambling buddy Cyrus Jones, one of the sons of Sade and Corb Jones, played loose with money. He was frequently charged with cashing bad checks.

Cy considered Gene his best friend. One day, Gene was approached by a car mechanic who had cashed in a check that was made out to Cy by Gene Buchwald. The check indicated that Gene had paid Cy a sum of one hundred dollars for farm help. The check had bounced, and the mechanic wanted his money. Gene looked at the bounced check and recognized that indeed his name had been forged as the signee. In fact, Gene had not hired any work from Cy, had no knowledge of the check being prepared, and had never owned a checking account. One might think that this would be a dirty trick to pull on one's closest friend, but Cy actually knew that Gene had no bank account and would suffer no loss.

A warrant was made out for Cy's arrest, and he left his residence and went on the run. Cy thought of hiding out with his parents on the adjacent farm, but he knew they would be looking for him there. He figured that the least likely place they would look for him was at the home of the person whose name he had forged. He had a long talk with Gene along the barnyard fence. Hanno found it unusual that he was asked to stay away. Finally Cy left and returned shortly with a suitcase and extra clothing. Hanno and the rest of the family were told that Cy would be spending the night.

Around two o'clock in the morning Hanno was awakened by the noises of a dozen men roaming through each of the rooms of his house. They found Cy in an upstairs bedroom, and he surrendered without resistance.

Hanno's father held no resentment toward Cy or toward the mission of the posse. However, he was extremely angry with them for intruding upon the twins' bedroom. When they arrived, Gene made a plea to them not to wake the twins. Hanno was already awake and curious about what was going on. As usual, he assumed that any company was good company. The posse ignored Gene's request and entered the twins' bedroom after locating Cy. They had awakened and were in a sleepy, confused state. In reply to Gene, the leader of the posse threatened to arrest Gene for harboring a criminal. Nothing could be proved, so life returned to the routine. Gene reaffirmed his loyalty by taking his family to visit Cy in jail.

On another occasion, Bill Staggs, another of Gene's sporting friends, was severely ill with kidney failure. Someone conjured the idea that fresh food and fresh air might ward off his demise. He moved in with the Buchwald family, but with modern dialysis treatment being unknown, he finally returned to Linton to his grandmother's house to die.

This incident might have gone forgotten except for the memory of young Hanno that Staggs would lie helplessly on a day bed and look at pictures of ladies' hose in the Sears Roebuck catalog. Hanno asked him if he was looking for a gift to order for a lady friend. He answered, "No," and said no more. Only years later did Hanno realize that Staggs was only admiring the feminine beauty of the legs of the models. The hosiery was irrelevant.

As Gene progressed in age and addiction, it was increasingly apparent that a disconnect had occurred between his hostile views of institutions and his loyal views of friends. Specifically, Gene expressed intense hatred toward the United Nations and the Catholic Church. Yet his closest individual friends were Catholic or of a foreign ethnic origin.

"How can you be so negative against the Catholic Church, and at the same time, Bill Staggs, your closest friend, is Catholic?"

"But he is different. All the rest of Catholics are like what I say."

Then if he acquired a new friend and discovered him to be Catholic, the same cycle was repeated. He could not detect the logical flaw in his thinking. He always relegated unknown persons to the negative stereotype but not the known members.

Entering into any constructive argument would cause his speech to become louder and more emotional. Certain truths became self-evident. The anger expressed had very little to do with the nature of the institution, even as he defined it. Logical intervention failed to persuade him. A solution was achieved when Hanno would pick up a guitar and sing a song like "My Bonnie Lies over the Ocean." His father would immediately join in. To Gene, music was magnetic. In a minute or two, all disagreements with Hanno were converted into love and harmony—for Hanno and for the whole world.

When Gene's brothers' families came to visit, Gene would be anxious in advance for fear old, unresolved arguments would break out. So, Hanno's father prepared himself in advance of the relatives' visits. He would have a folding card table, a deck of cards, and beer handy. The moment they got in the door, even before they had their hats and coats off, Hanno's father would suggest that they play cards, in particular, euchre. Invariably, all would agree. Soon the Buchwald boys were shouting with pride over a chance trick they had won, or almost won, from their own strategies. Following suit was a must. Renegging was a loss of face. "To play it alone" was the joy of the day. Hanno, as he watched, was impressed that the players could not only monitor the status of their own cards, but they could keep an account by inference of what another player was holding in his hand. This was done on the basis of which initial cards were played, what was discarded, and what was revealed inadvertently on the bottom of the deck. They each kept an eagle eye on the dealer. Hanno could not understand why the game was still fun when so much energy and memory went into it. Each of the brothers could remember very well what hands other players held a game or two previously. They were in the middle of proving that they had the intelligence of a college-educated person, and this was the only way of coming close to that.

Shortly after the onset of war with the Japanese attack on Pearl Harbor, Gene got a job in Terre Haute as a mounted security guard. With this job, Gene came home on weekends. This respite, which Mary and Gene had from each other, created a noticeable lull in their quarreling. Civility in the household increased. The death of Jay at Pearl Harbor added a new dimension to their marriage. Along with the prolonged period of grief over the loss of Jay, both Gene and Mary developed networks of friends and support that helped them get along when they were indeed together. True to the spirit of the entire nation, Gene was forbidden from mentioning the item being manufactured at the Terre Haute defense plant, even to his family. Hanno heard a rumor once that the plant made bombsights.

As Hanno was living through his teenage years during the war, the use of the car and his dad's permission were matters of grave importance to him. Gene and his family had a 1940 Studebaker. Gasoline was being rationed, and tires could not be purchased. Eventually, every tire on family cars was recapped with the hope that the heated-on rubber would last out the war. Every time Hanno got the car, he was told to stay in town, that the tires would not last a trip out of town.

On one occasion Hanno and Bill Marshall had a Boy Scout banquet they were invited to attend in Washington, Indiana. They made it to the banquet without mishap. On the way back, on the outskirts near the Phil Harris Golf Course, a tire went flat. It was past midnight. As one boy got the tire out of the trunk, the other one got the lug wrench to take off the flat tire. The lugs would not budge. After this came a number of problem-solving moves that made matters worse.

"Try the wrench in the other direction."

"Hey, let's try the wrench on a wheel on the other side of the car, and see which direction is right."

"Okay. Let's try it together."

Finally: "Let's roll down the window so that we can hang on to the side of the car, and we will both stand on the lug wrench and force it to go."

After about two hours of working, they gave up and walked into town. Hanno walked on to his house on Black Creek Road. He woke up his dad and explained the problem. Gene guessed at the answer. The lugs on the right side of the Studebaker went in the opposite direction from the left side. The boys had forced the lugs the wrong way so hard that they froze them into place. Gene told Hanno to go to bed, and Hanno slept well into the next day. When he awoke, his dad had taken care of the matter. After trying it himself, he had the car towed in to a mechanic. The mechanic, with some difficulty, used a blowtorch to get the lugs off. The mechanic reassured Gene that such things had happened before with the Studebaker.

The night's frustration was nothing to compare with the amount of teasing Hanno and Bill endured because they could not get the lugs off the car.

The greatest problem with the car came on senior prom night near the end of the war. On this occasion, Gene made Hanno promise that he would not leave town with the car because the tires were so bad. Hanno made a false promise. During Hanno's time at Linton Stockton High School, planning to take a drive out of town was as important as attending the prom itself. Horace Meurer and Hanno decided to double-date, and the plan was to go to Vincennes. It was thirty-seven miles away from Linton, which would be described as "not that far."

The major story from this night was that they had four flat tires during their trip. On the way down to Vincennes, Horace and Hanno changed one tire on the road. As they arrived at the café in Vincennes, a second tire was going flat. They were fortunate to have a service station open nearby. So they had both of these tires repaired as they had a small snack in the restaurant. Heading back to Linton, they again had a flat tire on the road. Horace and Hanno changed the tire with the spare. Then as they arrived in Linton, they had the fourth. It was a tiring, dirty, grease-filled night as they arrived back in Linton. It was much later than the expected hour for the dates to be home from the prom.

Hanno's date was a Catholic girl named Rose Fernando. During that era, Linton was well reputed for its ethnic, racial, and religious prejudice. In consequence, Hanno's relatives and neighbors had raised their eyebrows. With the war near its end attitudes were quickly changing all over the world. Within less than a decade a Catholic boy from Sullivan was happily married into Hanno's family.

No time was wasted in getting their dates to their respective homes in this early morning hour. It was the only time Hanno ever had to pay careful attention not to stain his date's white formal gown from the various grease spots on his suit, shirt, and tie as he kissed her good night. Rose's house lights were on as they arrived, and Hanno dared not ever ask if she got scolded for her late arrival.

Getting home at two in the morning, Hanno found his mother in no happy mood. In spite of the grease stains, she accused Hanno of having his first experience ever at sexual intercourse. Hanno's dad, however, moderated the conversation by arguing that Hanno should get to bed. Again Hanno slept late the next day. Before he awoke, his dad had found the tire tool where Horace had pitched it on the floor of the backseat of the car. He used this as evidence to attempt to allay Hanno's mother's accusations.

These were times when Hanno, without giving credit, found his father to be the most supportive person in his life. In spite of the fact that Hanno disobeyed his father's orders, his father gave him nothing but support rather than anger. Although significant time and effort was required of Gene to have the car towed, to get the lugs loosened with a blowtorch, to repair some tires himself, and all the untold things, he overlooked Hanno's transgressions and was his friend. Hanno knew deeply that, were he right or wrong, his father would always be on his side. Hanno did not foresee his father's collapse.

[9]

TALK

E arlier on, before entering school, as it so happened, Hanno enunciated curse words. In the family's remote venue, the baby's new words stood out. Even his grandfather, who used only "T'care, t'care" and "Dag nabbit," as his sole expletives, found Hanno's precocious vocabulary enjoyable. When relatives or close neighbors visited, Hanno displayed his lexicon. He brought laughter as he swore at them like a drunken sailor. Through ordinary rules of learning, Hanno expanded his gift until his cursing became fluid poetry.

Then one day came the event Hanno had never anticipated. His dad and mom had talked it over ahead of time, for sure. Although his mom was usually the source of discipline, she assumed a passive, quiet role.

It was in the kitchen that Gene Buchwald addressed his son: "We want you to quit using swear words. It is a bad habit. Please stop it."

"No," said Hanno. "I like them."

"But we want you to stop."

"To hell with you."

At that point, his father took him by the shoulders and shook him. Hanno became angry and yelled, "Keep your fuckin' hands off of me!"

Hanno's father grabbed him again and gave him a slap on the bottom. "Stop it!" his father exclaimed.

"Go to hell!"

Hanno's father pulled Hanno over his knee and slapped his behind.

"Stop that, you son of a bitch," said Hanno. "That hurt."

The father slapped Hanno's behind two more times.

"Get your fuckin' hands off of me, you bastard!"

The father restrained Hanno's escape and paddled him several times.

Hanno began to cry but also became louder. "Quit that, you lily-livered son of a bitch. I'll cuss if I want to."

Hanno's father paddled his son several times again. Hanno screamed with pain. With his crying and screaming, his expletives were shorter in order to allow him to catch his breath.

"Shit on you!" Hanno blurted but kept crying.

Hanno's father, still persistent but now angry, paddled Hanno harder.

Hanno screamed, "*Shit!*"

His father did not let up but continued his manual punishment with great alacrity.

Hanno was now crying too loud and too much for curse words or, in fact, to say any words fully. Even as he struggled to catch his breath, he emitted a *ha-va-va* sound with the quivering intake of air. Hanno felt his world turn upside down. He was no longer the cocky boy who could entertain people with his talk. He did not know what he was. His body shook. He was unable to predict his own destiny. He could not even recount what had happened. For a while, he became totally mute. He continued to shake and to whimper in an uncontrollable way.

Hanno's mother handed a glass of milk to his father. "Here," his father said. "Do you want to drink some milk?"

Hanno was unable to speak, unable to drink the milk, and unable to shake his head no. He was unable to look at anyone or anything. Hanno did not resist as he was laid into bed. He whimpered and made sucking noises, still trying to catch his breath. Finally Hanno went to sleep.

Like an animal brought to heel and obey, Hanno was broken. Forever after, he lacked the full zest of spirit with words that he had had before. There was a measure of loss of confidence. If he had to face the outside world restraining his swearing, of which he had been so proud, what else would change? What else would become unacceptable as he grew up and left home?

[10]

MOM

Mary Oglesby was born in May 1893. She was the fourth of the five children of David and Celester Malone Oglesby. Mary's eldest brother was Porter Oglesby, the only one in the family with red hair. Then came Zelma, followed by Urban and, soon after, Mary. Following Mary came Murl, the little brother to whom she felt close. All the children were born in the old house, but during Mary's early years, work was heavily afoot in building the new house.

Mary told Hanno she could remember little of living in the old house, although she lived in it until she was seven. She remembered the earthen fireplace hearth and crane for hanging pots for cooking. She remembered the home-molded candles and the exciting new coal-oil lamps. Life was primitive.

Then, when Mary and her family transferred into the elegantly designed two-story brick colonial-style mansion, their style of life was beyond all other homes in the community. Mary moved into a bedroom she shared with her older sister Zelma.

Mary had mostly unhappy memories of home life during her earlier years. One was the harsh physical discipline of her mother. Many times, she referred to being "knocked across the room" if she did something wrong. She also referred to this as "coming from the school of hard knocks." Mary grew up in the spanking culture. "Spare the rod and spoil the child" was her mother's motto. As an adult, Mary continued in the spanking tradition, but she always insisted that her ways were more moderate.

Mary's father, David, on the other hand, was a mild, loving soul. He was gentle with the children, friendly and fair with the neighbors, and adored by relatives as the family role model. The neighbors elected him as justice of the peace since he was good at settling fence and other disputes. He enjoyed marrying people and was even known to marry young couples as they stood in their buggies outside the Oglesby home.

Unfortunately for Mary, David's main focus of attention went to her brother Urban, just older than she. Urban was unusually bright and appeared to have the greatest promise of all the children. Early in life, he developed epileptic seizures. At that time, however, seizures were a mysterious and feared infirmity. The best guess regarding Urban's ailment was that he banged his head when falling off the roof when the new house was under construction. Superstitions were rampant about seizures. The state of Indiana built a home for epileptics in Greenfield. While

Urban was yet a boy, he was placed there. He remained there until he died, except for returning home each Christmas. Urban's father devoted all possible attention to him before he left. He was greatly in despair when Urban had to part with the family.

What this meant was that Mary did not get the generous share of paternal love she would have desired. Urban captured her father's time and attention. Celester had a one-and-done creative streak, but she was not strongly maternal. She was already burdened with three when Mary came along. Zelma was put to very hard work in cooking and housekeeping. Mary was the young, clumsy annoyance getting into trouble or failing to do things right. Getting her little finger caught in the wringer during laundry left her with a lifelong impairment. A family photograph taken when Mary was eleven showed her as if she were prepared to explain that it was not her fault.

The other major childhood memory for Mary was the universal view of older sister Zelma as the beauty of the family. The view was so widely and openly held that Mary had no idea of offering competition. Instead, it was settled fact. Mary was not looked upon as ugly or homely; she was just seen as plain.

Zelma, however, turned people's heads along the street with her full, curvy figure; graceful walk; plump, smooth cheeks; thick hair; and blue eyes. Mary was both proud and envious of Zelma. She wished that she could be viewed for one shining moment as being so pretty.

Mary feared her mother's discipline, but she was blind to her mother's unique gift of creativity. Being so isolated, she could see nothing outstanding. Actually Celester was a spectacular and engaging person, albeit raising children was not her favorite sport. Hours of work went into the finer points of the house design, and her husband, David, let her have her way. She had her unique rock garden full of flowers most of the year. She had her pet raccoons. She had her creative washstand made from a boxcar axle and wheel.

She was well known among family and friends for her "crazy board." Celester collected family memorabilia and cemented them onto a board of landscape proportion. It hung on the parlor wall. Each item told a family story. Among the hundred or so items was a piece of melted glass from the first Plum Branch School, which burned down before she had children. David's father, the bound boy, had helped build it. There were political campaign buttons, such as from William Jennings Bryan's campaign. Centered on the board was the porcelain face of a doll. It had bright eyes that would close. It was referred to as a boy's doll and was owned by Porter, her first child. (No one ever asked or explained why Zelma and Mary had only cloth Raggedy Ann–type dolls, whose eyes and mouths were sewed on with yarn.) There was a glass tube that had been used to treat (unsuccessfully) her sister Lizzie's deafness. A tiny medicine bottle came from when Murl had a high fever. Corked inside the bottle was a sprig of hair from a favorite deceased aunt. Also present was a small gold coin. Embedded in the board was the wishbone of a fowl from a memorable Thanksgiving feast. Various glass miniature pictures were also present.

Hanno and the twins grew up assuming that every family had a crazy board. It was a prized item to be handed down to later generations.

Mary inherited her mother's lifelong search for attention. Mary said that at a wedding, she wanted to be the bride. At a funeral, she wanted to be the corpse.

In spite of the splendid house, the one hundred acres of homestead did not have the soil for prosperous farming. No one knew that millions of dollars of coal lay just beneath.

The family investment in the house precluded long travel vacations that other families enjoyed. Yet the mansion was very effective to accommodate the relatives and friends visiting from afar. There was never any new land acquisition, and no upgrade into motorized farm equipment occurred. Except for Porter's "boy doll," there were no toys of significance. Yet, throughout her childhood and adulthood, she retained a strong sense of family pride. To go on the dole (referred to then as relief and now as welfare) was absolutely forbidden. The children and the family learned to go without, rather than to accept charity.

As with all the children who grew up on this isolated homestead, the coming of age for school was a big event. It meant having more contact with friends. Mary was an average to good student, but she liked girlfriends and girl talk. She would often get into trouble for whispering in class and for writing and passing notes.

A major chore for Mary at home was to help take care of her little brother, Murl. Little existed in Mary's world that gave her a sense of adequacy and confidence. She seemed never to be able to please her mother. As true of all younger kids, she could not do things as well as her older siblings. She was not as pretty as her sister. The only thing left was Murl. Only with Murl did she have a sense of accomplishment. The span of age gave her a head start. Being female enhanced her early growth and height beyond that of Murl. Most of all, she learned that she could play the role of teacher with Murl and tell him some of the things she learned in school. Fortunately, when Murl reached first grade, he was a better student because of Mary's attention.

Mary had other occasions to look upon others as superior. When she reached the seventh grade, Viola James, a close friend, was in the eighth grade. When Mary reached the eighth grade, Vi had completed summer normal training and was hired as the Plum Branch schoolteacher. She had lost Vi as a friend but gained her as a teacher. Losing a friend, Mary felt, was far more important than gaining a teacher.

Since no high school existed in the homestead vicinity, it had been anticipated for years that leaving home would be necessary if an Oglesby child was to attend. With Zelma, this entailed taking a live-in job with her Aunt Lizzie in the flower shop and greenhouse. Since Zelma occupied this position, Celester made arrangements for Mary to move in as a housekeeper with her own mother, Susan Malone.

Even though Zelma's transition from the cocoon-like homestead to Aunt Lizzie's flower shop in the city was a comfortable one, Zelma nevertheless had written bitter letters back home to complain of her loneliness.

Moving in with Grandma Susan, Mary had it even worse. It was out of the frying pan and into the fire. The whole year was a disaster and failure in Mary's life. Without Celester realizing it, Susan had grown old. She no longer had the flexibility and patience to raise a young high-school girl like Mary. Susan had already raised eight children and had become set in her ways as an elderly widow. No assistance by Mary around the house met with Grandma's approval. Much of Mary's conduct, as a newly emancipated young woman, met with disapproval. Her tendency to hit Mary during a dispute was even more likely than with Mary's own mother.

Maybe things in the living situation could have been tolerated if school had gone well. It did not go well. In high school, each subject was in a separate room, and she knew no one. At Plum Branch, everyone was in the small room, and she knew all of them. After she had found her way to all of her high-school classes, it became a bit easier. Before that, Mary was devastated with fright.

Then came the fatal blow. Mary had a learning disability. She could not take lecture notes. In grade school the assignments were either in the book or written on the blackboard. In high school they were always given orally, and Mary could never get them down. Even worse, the material to be learned was usually given by lecture. There was no other place to review it. When the teacher gave information by oral presentation, she was helpless to copy it down.

Mary concluded that these problems represented a disability, and she declared herself incapable of proceeding on in high school. Looking back, one may ask how much her fright and profound feeling of inadequacy contributed to it.

Suddenly, at the right time and the right place, something happened that Mary could call good. Zelma was quitting her job with Aunt Lizzie. She had become engaged and was planning to marry.

When Mary took Zelma's job with Aunt Lizzie, she began what was perhaps the most free and happy period of her life. She hit it off well with Aunt Lizzie. Aunt Lizzie, profoundly deaf, found it easy to read Mary's lips. In fact, Mary contributed to the communication by being the only person who ever learned successfully to move her own lips without speaking or whispering yet be understood. Mary would raise two fingers to the side of her mouth to signal her intent and then convey to Aunt Lizzie confidential flower-shop transactions or, more likely, juicy gossip about other women in the community. Occasionally there was a naughty story or joke they did not want the nearby children to hear. Mary loved to talk on Lizzie's newly acquired telephone. She was part of the first group in Linton to have telephones installed. She enjoyed friendships with close girlfriends and relatives. Many Kodak box-camera pictures were taken of the girls swimming at Muir's Lake. Also, they took pictures in comic poses—dressed in men's garb while smoking pipes. Mary had inherited her father's early gray hair; she had white hair at age twenty-six, like so many other descendants.

Back then, the Eastman Kodak Company sold box cameras for only a dollar and then made their profit selling film. This film was usually developed by local photographers, which helped boost the sales.

Mary, for the first time in her life, was getting a feeling of confidence and control. She was not anticipating criticism at every turn. Even more exhilarating in Mary's young life, her fear that she would never attract a boyfriend or get married was beginning to wane. Aunt Lizzie had hired this young man, Gene Buchwald, part-time for flower delivery and odd jobs. His brother had just recently been murdered while on the Linton police force. He was from Clay County and seemed to come from a good family. Mary and Gene had considerable contact working in the same setting. Mary enjoyed his entertaining her by showing off. A romance began to blossom before deaf Aunt Lizzie knew what was going on.

Lizzie had a great zest for life. She loved going fishing and camping in an old straw hat. She loved Sunday rides on an airplane at the city park. Besides the telephone, she also wanted to be the first in town to get a Model T Ford.

The first of a series of tragic events began as Murl completed the car assembly for Aunt Lizzie. Murl had become very talented in mechanical work and was starting a business of assembling new Model T's in one day for a hundred dollars. Shortly after assembling Aunt Lizzie's machine, Murl got his arm caught in a threshing machine as he was stuffing cornstalks into it. He was only sixteen. For years, the story was told that Murl was so talented with machinery that he reached in with the other hand and reversed the machinery to retrieve his mangled hand. It saved his life, but he lost his left hand and arm up to the elbow. Murl continued in his work as a mechanic despite this handicap.

Among all of the family, Lizzie was the most robust in dealing with adversity. People sometimes said that she compensated for her profound hearing loss. Her adopted teenage daughter, Elizabeth, emotionally disturbed since birth, died during this period. Lizzie's husband had a major heart attack and died. He had owned Linton's major bakery and delivery center in the alley behind the Grand Opera House (later the Grand Theater). One had to know Aunt Lizzie very well in order to detect the deep grief she felt from these personal tragedies. On the surface Lizzie was always vigorous and moving on.

Life did not go well for Mary's sister Zelma. She quickly had two beautiful little girls, Ruth and Jean. Her husband, already with a reputation as a rounder, could not keep a job. He abandoned her and the two children and was not heard from thereafter. With her husband unemployed, Zelma began running a boardinghouse. Like Aunt Lizzie, she was a successful businesswoman. Immediately, however, she developed cancer, a melanoma on her leg. It was a fast-moving affliction, and she soon became an invalid. Care of the children fell upon Mary's shoulders, and at the same time, total care of Zelma fell to Mary as well.

Zelma's prolonged illness with the suffering of intense pain gave Mary a fear of cancer for the rest of her life. She developed various superstitions about what might have caused it. One hunch was that she bruised her leg often on the front of the hot cooking stove on the homestead. Before Zelma passed away, it was already becoming apparent that Mary would be the heir to take custody of Zelma's two baby girls.

As all of these tragic events were happening in town, out on the homestead, things were not going well either. Celester died suddenly just after Zelma did. Since Mary had become tied up with full-time bedside care for Zelma, she had no choice but to leave Ruth and Jean, still only five and seven years old, to stay with their grandparents. While Celester was on her deathbed, Ruth and Jean grew up under the care of tender, loving Grandfather Oglesby. They had the fondest memories of him for the rest of their lives.

Mary's deathbed care of her sister Zelma had compromised her job with Aunt Lizzie. She was becoming unable to complete all of her duties. All of her lifetime insecurities were aroused again. She would have prolonged anxiety attacks throughout the day and spells of hysterical collapse during periods of acute pressure. She feared a loss of relationship with Gene. A great redeeming influence, however, was Gene's quieting demeanor. He did not get bogged down—in fact, he reassured her in the face of stressful demands. Finally, unlike Mary, Gene enjoyed caring for and playing with Ruth and Jean.

Once Zelma's tragic death finally occurred, the problems shifted. Zelma had accumulated a significant savings for the benefit of her two children. Mary's thought was immediately to buy a house and move Ruth and Jean into town from the homestead. It was during this time that Gene and Mary had their hasty marriage. This followed on immediately with the mortgaging of a small shotgun house. (A shotgun house is one in which you can look in the front door and out the back. It was like looking through the open barrel of a shotgun.)

Mary had to drop her work with Aunt Lizzie in order to meet the child-care responsibilities. They brought Zelma's girls back from the homestead to the little house in town.

Mary was overwhelmed with the caretaking, but this did not last long. Mr. Hardesty, the Indiana lieutenant governor, asked for a private meeting with them. In this meeting, he confided having a deep love affair with Zelma. On her deathbed, she had asked him to take care of her children. Knowing of Mary and Gene's difficult circumstances, he offered to take legal custody of the children. After their fund was expended, he pledged to continue raising them with his own resources. Well after Zelma's death, Mary was entranced with Hardesty. She realized how envious she was of her late sister. Hardesty, however, was unresponsive to her mild flirtation. All he wanted was a formal, cordial friendship with Mary and Gene and to acquire custody of little Ruth and Jean. Indeed, Ruth and Jean in their new Hardesty family led well-educated, prosperous, and glamorous lives. With all the jet-setting, travels about the world, however, they did not give up their love of Linton and of their own blood and kin. They were especially warm and loving to their Aunt Mary in future years.

Yet Gene could see that Mary was more rather than less stressed with this move away from the homestead. So, since Gene had friends in Anderson, Indiana, and speculated that Mary might get a new start in that environment, he suggested they leave Linton. Mary got a good factory job winding armatures with copper wire on a Delco Remy assembly line. For Mary, it was worse than before. She was separated for the first time from all her friends, from Aunt Lizzie, and from the homestead. She was more lonesome than ever before. Gene had a job as an inspector. He found it to be the best job he would ever have in his life.

The next big surprise occurred when America entered World War I and Gene was drafted. No one expected it. Gene was both married and had a medical discharge from the Navy. With the Navy and the Army under different cabinet administrations, however, the Army gave no heed to Navy records. Mary remained in Anderson lonely and miserable throughout the war. Fortunately, however, the war was over just before Gene was to be shipped overseas.

Getting out of the Army, Gene decided with Mary that they should return to Linton. For a period, Gene did temporary work for Aunt Lizzie and also for the Welch and Cornett Funeral Home. Mary put in work for Aunt Lizzie during her regular maid's vacation and weekends off. Finally, after seven years of marriage, Mary became pregnant. This catapulted her back into her emotional insecurities. Gene played a split role of being a caretaker of his pregnant wife and a boy playing hooky to drink and gamble. Finally came the shocker. Mary's pregnancy was to be a set of identical twins, Jay and Ray. They were so identical in appearance and so good-looking that they brought special attention in the small community of Linton. In fact, they were showered with gifts of expensive clothing and offers came to adopt or "buy" them.

As all of this was happening, Mary's father, now a widower on the family homestead in Wright Township, was showing increasing signs that he would soon be unable to care for himself or the farm. The inevitable pattern of aging and the warning signs of Alzheimer's disease led the young couple to sell the small house and move in with Granddad. The twins would therefore be raised in the isolated farm setting.

Mary's father, David Oglesby, was still alert enough to help take care of the twins, play with them, and bounce them on his knee. He was also energetic enough to do light farmwork. Mary's husband got a job in the coal mines to help support the family.

When the twins began school, they had a reading problem, which was always blamed upon the teacher. Gene said the teacher was letting the children "read the pictures" rather than the words. Not all learning was in the single schoolroom of Plum Branch. The twins, even in the primary school years, could range far into the forests, fields, and stripper hills. They were each other's companions. Each moth, birdcall, or terrapin was something to behold. Together they turned a venue of isolation into a crowded menagerie of nature's wonders. They dreamed of the day when they could own a rod and reel, a .410-gauge shotgun, and a pair of hip boots for checking the trotlines.

Home at night beside the fire burning inside the polished chrome and blackened Florence heater, they would sit on a rocker or on Granddad's lap. They would listen to stories of his own father, who was sold into bondage and escaped to follow the broad Ohio River into the mountains of northern Kentucky. It was a world of sawmills and catfish that they never expected to see firsthand. So from Granddad's stories, each built his own beautiful and exciting image of personal adventure.

Mary told Hanno of his own arrival. Just as she had told him about the years before, after another seven years, there came another pregnancy. Mary and Gene had been married fourteen years and had seven-year-old twins. Mary was thirty-five, and Gene was forty. Hanno could not have been a planned event, no matter the occasional debate. It was 1928, and, for Indiana, the Depression was already under way. Up until Mary's time, all births were conducted at home with a midwife. With Mary's chronic anxiety and episodes of panic, her births were planned in the Freeman Greene County Hospital in Linton. Perhaps it was better that way. The baby was large. It was a forceps delivery. Nothing went easily. After three days in the hospital, little Hanno was brought home to meet Jay and

Ray. Jay and Ray were accustomed to competing with each other for their mother's attention. They had not anticipated that Mom time would now be cut more than 50 percent, given the needs of a helpless infant. For seven-year-old twins, sometimes pampered and admired for their identity, it was not an occasion to celebrate.

Hanno came out of the blue into this family. He kept many memories from his infant days, although he could not fit them together along a time line. The most remembered fragments from his infancy were of crying. All events, it seemed, either began with crying or led to crying. The second set of images was of being carried—almost always by women. Since crying was the major memory, the carrying often entailed being rocked, soothed, fed, and urged to stop crying. Only rarely during this period did he recall being held by his father.

Another group of memories was about the lady who picked him up often kissing him on the face. Hanno did not like to be held by everyone, and he did not like to be kissed by anyone. Only years later did he associate being kissed with affection. At this early age, the kissing was associated with having his face washed by a floppy, sloppy washcloth. He resisted both. Hanno was too young to apply much reason or query.

Almost all of the next set of memories was about the kitchen. With the hot cooking stove, the floor was always warm and inviting on a cold day. The floor was linoleum and easy to crawl on. Mary liked to add a bit of status whenever possible, so she referred to it as their "Congoleum" floor. Only later in life did Hanno learn that this was a commercial name for the floor material.

Years later, when electricity came to the countryside, Hanno could see that calling a refrigerator a "Frigidaire" or even a "Kelvinator" had more appeal to her. For Hanno the name made no difference.

Sometimes the isolation was broken for Mary as some cooperative activity or favor came up with the nearby neighbors. This could involve such things as canning vegetables, getting fresh items from the truck patch to market, quilting, or letting someone use her telephone. It was the only telephone in the farm community. Neighbors, like Sade or Corb Jones, Maybell or Jack Erlich, or the widow Mattie Kramer walked in and out of the kitchen where Hanno played and Mary worked. This always broke the monotony, and Hanno was especially attracted to Jack Erlich, who was nice to him and gave him some attention. While learning how to talk, Hanno shortened many words. Jack Erlich came to be called Jac-Kelly.

As time passed, the trips by Jack became more frequent. Charmed by him, Hanno would always follow him into another room if they left the kitchen. Hanno was accustomed to his older brothers not wanting to be followed. Hanno always persisted, and likewise, he persisted with Jac-Kelly and his mother. Sometimes she would produce a toy that required him going out into the yard to play. Toys were rare, however. Then there were the occasions when Mary would give Hanno an empty water pail or coal bucket and tell him she needed him to go to the pump or the coal shed right away. While it was frustrating to give up time and attention from Jack, Hanno obeyed.

Sometimes when Hanno returned, his mother and Jack would no longer be in the kitchen. Hanno was too young to see any significance in it, but sometimes he would find his mother upstairs dressed only in her underwear. Hanno would ask what she was doing, and a frequent answer was, "Oh, I was just showing Jack a new dress I bought, but he is gone now."

Hanno accepted her word and did not try to look for him. Hanno had not an inkling of what romance, an affair, or an impropriety was. The same was true when Jack was leaving one day. They came downstairs, and neither noticed Hanno beside the stove behind the kindling box in the corner. They embraced each other and kissed on the mouth. Then Jack departed.

One evening the family was gathered as usual about the Florence stove with chilly weather outside. The twins were sitting together below the stovepipe that entered the wall. Hanno was in his favorite rocking chair. Mary was on a chair in front of the stove with a basket and was darning socks. Gene was on a chair at the dining table reading the newspaper. The twins were chattering away about an older girl in their school whom they saw kissing her baby brother.

"Here is how Mom and Jac-Kelly kiss each other." Hanno spoke up. "On the lips." Hanno held up the back of his fist and kissed it.

Jay and Ray broke out in loud laughter.

"You nut!" said Jay. "People don't kiss each other on the lips. That's silly. They kiss on the cheeks."

"And why would Mom be kissing Jack anyway? He isn't a baby!" said Ray.

Mary immediately produced an alert smile. As Jay and Ray finished their laughing comments, Mary said in jest to Hanno, "How could you come up with a silly joke like that? You have never told a joke before."

"That was not a joke. That was just stupid, as usual." Jay got in the last word.

During all the laughter and talk, Gene, at the table behind Hanno, did not look up. He turned the page of the newspaper and kept reading.

Hanno sat in his rocking chair, surprised and perplexed. It was clear that the rest of the family had not seen what he had seen. It was also clear that his mother did not want it seen or known when she called Hanno's comment a joke. She not only knew she was being untruthful, but she also knew that Hanno knew. Hanno was accustomed to his brothers putting him down and laughing to belittle him, but in this instance, they were not informed. Hanno's mother, informed of her own conduct, was willing to misrepresent it even when she knew that Hanno was aware of her falsehood. Hanno, meanwhile, although a witness, was unable to see what significance, if any, was attached to the conduct of his mother and Jac-Kelly. Now he knew that, whatever the meaning, it was something his mother wanted quiet. Hanno knew that he would end up with punishment if he persisted to argue. He made his own decision not to talk about it again.

Mary and Gene did not ever express affection in front of their children. Hanno had no idea that this kissing on the mouth indicated affection. He did not even know what affection was or if affection was wrong. If not wrong, why should it be kept a secret? *Secret* was a word he knew. He did not know why his mother never discussed this with him, as she did other things. Quite the opposite, she chose to try to conceal it with a falsehood. Whatever it was, he knew it must be something important for her to do that.

This was the second time in Hanno's life when, in thinking about a matter, he realized that he was on his own. The other instance was when Hanno watched his older brothers get home from school, race immediately to their mother, and compete with each other in search of sympathy for all the bad things that had happened during the day.

"Richard hit me at recess."

"Sarah looked at my art book and did not tell me."

"Joan took my notepad and turned it in to the teacher."

"The teacher was mean to me because I did not finish my arithmetic."

Their mother, usually repairing clothes, also seemed disturbed and overwhelmed with this onslaught. Hanno, as he listened to his brothers and without saying so, vowed that he would never come home and bother his mother with such things. He could see his mother's anxiety and helplessness. He could see that such things should be dealt with on the spot rather than later at home. He made a private commitment to himself not to convey to his mother what had happened at school and certainly not what required resolution.

Regarding his mother and Jack Erlich, there was no one he could go to for discussion or direction. Not only did he make a decision on his own, untethered to advice, direction, support, or disagreement of another, but he also decided it was something not to be discussed with others. His case would not be presented to anyone for approval. No one knew that Hanno had chosen this guiding tenet, known only to him. Like the isolated homestead on which he lived, Hanno would have a part of himself isolated from others. In a major way Hanno, who was still learning to talk, was his own person. He was developing rules in a private world he did not share with others. To some extent, it involved pride. Mostly, it was just scary and lonely.

As the weeks and months went on, Hanno's attraction to Jac-Kelly dwindled to nothing—not because he disliked him but instead because of confusion about the events that he still did not understand. Also, as his speech improved. Hanno learned to refer to him as Jack or Jack Erlich.

As the relatives and neighbors saw it, Hanno was growing like a weed. This meant taking on more chores. Hanno became able to take on the responsibility of not only bringing in buckets of coal and water but also "guarding the cows."

Guarding the cows was a distasteful, boring chore for Hanno. His mother would try to encourage some enthusiasm by telling him that this made him a cowboy. It entailed going out into the pasture, finding, if possible, a shade tree to sit under, and then watching a herd of cows and calves, usually between seven and ten. The stated reason was that the fences had not been fully mended yet and the cows might break through and get into the green crops not yet ready to be harvested. If this happened, the greenery would make the cows sick. It was a reasonable story that Hanno accepted. He never felt he was duped or was being told a lie. At the same time, there was the blatant disregard for the fact that these assignments were always on days when Hanno could spot Jack Erlich in his work hat and bib overalls walking across the orchard path toward the house. On more than one occasion, in his own boredom and frustration, Hanno would make a mad dash toward the house. As expected, he would find his mother only partly clothed and explaining that she was trying on dresses. He would ask, "Where is Jack?"

"He has gone home a long while ago." He always accepted this response from his mother without question. It never occurred to him that he was being lied to and that Jack was hiding very nearby.

To allay Hanno's complaints, Mary would often give him a very attractive sack of lunch, a Thermos or glass jar of Kool-Aid, and one or two books.

Then one day, the inevitable happened. Timed at the right minute after Jack left his house, his chubby wife Maybell made a jog across the half-mile orchard path to the Oglesby homestead. No one in the neighborhood kept doors locked or knocked on doors. When a person arrived to visit, he or she would open the door a few inches and yell, "Anybody home?" This time, Maybell did not yell. She quietly opened the screen door and crept up the stairs. She quickly realized her worst suspicions. Only the noise of her fast steps and the door openings made her departure known. Seeing what she had come to see, she turned about without a word and marched home.

Maybell must have had her strategy planned in advance. As Jack arrived home, she, in a storm, immediately insisted upon a separation and that the two no longer remain under the same roof. Second, she asked for a divorce. Third, in the coming days, she struck out along the gravel roads, visiting all of the neighbors who had a friendly or working acquaintance with her or with Mary. Since she knew that Mary was from a highly respected family and held close friendships with many women with the aid of her daily telephone conversations, Maybell made the astute decision that she should strike first in informing the community that Mary had stolen her husband. Her recitation was well practiced by the time her list of visits was over. The text was that Mary Oglesby Buchwald was trying to steal her husband, that she and her husband were having a love affair, that it had been going on for some time, and that she finally visited the house unexpectedly and caught them in the act. In consequence, she kicked him out of the house and he lived in the tack room of a pig barn on the far end of their farm. Divorce papers, she said, were pending. Although all farmwomen liked to talk, Maybell was not one who was endless in her visitation. Having made her recitation, she would arise and walk on to the next house.

Maybell and Jack had two boys of high school age. When the incident happened, they clammed up. Not a word was ever spoken by them about the incident. No one ever knew whether this silence was their own decision or whether they had received orders from one or another parent.

Jack indeed moved into the pig barn. It was down in the valley among the trees, far off the road. It was across the road from Corb and Sade's place and looked like a ramshackle unpainted vacant property. Actually it had a very solid structure. Years earlier, with prosperity at its peak, the community held Halloween parties there. People came in masquerade. Bonfires were built for wiener and marshmallow roasts. A large coffeepot and a beer keg were always present. Musical instruments and lots of candles and lanterns provided light for dancing, inside or out, depending upon the weather. Ghosts would appear from the haymow. Hanno had been fascinated with the satin-lined musical instrument cases. Almost everyone was familiar with this place during the happier days.

Jack set out immediately with carpentry tools to build a solid partition in the barn. On one side, he constructed a kitchen, a combined bedroom-living room, and storage space for himself. On the other side, he upgraded the deteriorating parts to make a working barn for five or six pigs. One had to go outside to get from the residence to the pig side. Jack winterized the walls and ceiling. He kept the premises scrubbed clean.

Jack had few visitors. Except for trips to town for shopping, he kept to himself. His two children were seen visiting him once in a while. Hanno visited once to deliver a package from a neighbor. He saw the layout and the remodeling, but Jack was not at home. After a few short years, Jack was found dead in his small quarters.

Hanno's mother's reaction to Maybell's tactics was also immediate. She had a long talk with Gene, telling him that she had been in a big fight with Maybell. The fight, she said, went back to the early days when they were pupils at Plum Branch. She warned that the fight would last for some time and that she needed all the sympathy and support he could give her. She also explained that Maybell was at war with her own husband. She was accusing him of being unfaithful to her and said that they were separating. She explained to Gene that Maybell was spreading lies about her. Maybell, she said, had found some kind of evidence that Jack was stepping out on her and she decided for some reason that Mary was the sweetheart in the situation. She explained that she got all this information from Annie Letterman on the telephone.

Never was this saga discussed with the twins or with Hanno. However, neither was it concealed. The twins and Hanno were not forbidden to listen to their mother talking about the matter on the telephone or to friends on the street or elsewhere.

Mary knew that her reputation was at stake. Although she did not have a list of people and she did not travel door to door as did Maybell, she nevertheless waged a counter-campaign for the next two years. Since Hanno was still not old enough to be left alone in the homestead or in town, he was very often by her side as she interrupted a conversation to present her case. The monologue was made to both men and women but usually, of course, to women. The typical scene would go like this.

Some lady on the street on a shopping day would engage in conversation with Mary. Mary would interrupt their topic to ask, "Have you heard about what Maybell Erlich has been saying about me?"

"No." The answer would always be no. Hanno wondered how many times this "no" was to avoid admitting they knew the recent gossip.

"Well, it is terrible. She has been spreading the lies everywhere that I am having an affair with her husband. She says that I am wicked, that I am trying to take her husband away from her. I don't know who would want her husband in the first place, but she is even claiming that she has caught us together in the act of being unfaithful. Can you imagine that? I don't know what to do about it. She won't talk to me. I think that there would be no reasoning with her if she did talk. I'm so angry I won't talk to her. Maybell has certainly had a falling out with Jack. I have no idea how long that has been going on. I cannot imagine what woman would want to become his sweetheart. There may be someone else he has his eye on, but it certainly is not me. I have never seen him flirt with another woman, and like I said, I cannot imagine anyone being attracted to him. Yet, here I am, the victim. I am the one she has picked as breaking up her marriage. She is an evil woman. It is so nonsensical. It is unbelievable. What do you do in a situation like this?"

Time and again, Hanno, beside his mother, would listen to this script with little variation from one time to another. What Hanno had difficulty understanding was why she was not telling the truth to the other person. Even more upsetting to Hanno was that she knew that he knew that she was not telling the truth.

Once Hanno's mother finished such conversations, she would move on without a word to Hanno, who had heard it all. She would neither confirm her lie or deny it or ask Hanno what his feelings were about it. As this matter became public, Hanno was also aware of the impulse toward loyalty. It would be proper that he should shield his mother, that he should be protective of the family name. Yet, to do so, he would be shielding her right to tell lies. Hanno did not find Maybell an attractive person, but he knew that she was telling the truth.

It is likely that no one came directly to Mary with this accusation. She was so assertive in introducing it that she never gave the other person a chance. In addition, Hanno noticed that his mother was changing her lifestyle. She became socially active to put herself deliberately in the public eye. While she had previously attended church on an irregular basis, she now attended regularly and, while there, would place herself into special groups. These were groups where gossip about her might come up if she were not present. She likewise sought out occasions of other school and neighborhood meetings to be present. She would regularly query her telephone friends to see if they had heard of anyone speaking ill or questionably about her character. If so, she would seek that person out and confront him or her with the script.

As Hanno continued to grow and learn what *love affair, sex, faithfulness, loyalty,* and other words meant, he tried to see his mother in ways more broadly than the Maybell-and-Jack-Erlich saga. Within the saga, she let her son watch her lie to others, yet she expected him to tell the truth in other matters. She was ready to punish him if he did not. If Hanno lied about something to protect his own interest, like stealing food from the pantry or tapping into the Concord wine jugs in the cellar, then he took the usual physical punishment that was handed out also to other children in the community.

As for his mother, however, he tried to build a picture beyond lying. Zelma had existed as this spectacular older sister who had overshadowed her. She was bound to be left with a craving to have just a bit of the attention and affection Zelma had received. Zelma was battling the loneliness of leaving the homestead and her loving father when she married unwisely. So also Mary was aware that she, in flight from her mother Celester's discipline, got even worse treatment from her grandmother Susan. Perhaps the failures in high school also helped prod her toward a marriage unwisely and impatiently. Mary had been aware of her husband Gene's drinking and gambling habits even before they were married. She was aware of his flamboyant behavior that attracted other women. She was aware that her husband could betray her. But she also knew that Gene was not of the character that would pursue a long-term affair. He was more committed to the joys of the here and now. At most, he was capable of only a one-night affair. Mary knew that she was not happy with this half cup of a marriage. She was often resentful of the gambling losses that left family needs unmet. It was reasonable, as Hanno thought about it when he was older, that his mother would want to retaliate or meet personal needs in an affair. Hanno often saw his mother melt when she was given the slightest compliment from another man. Yes, she needed this affection badly.

Yet Hanno could not escape the fact that he was watching his mother live out a double life, appearing one way in certain situations and another way in others. She knew she was doing this. He knew she was. And she knew he knew.

Hanno grew into a different relationship with his mother than did the twins. The twins competed with each other for her attention and affection. They would quickly do her bidding in order to preserve this source of maternal affection. In this sense, she had a power and control over them that she did not have over Hanno. As in any mother-son relationship, Mary expressed and sought affection from Hanno. Sometimes Hanno saw her as too hungry, and he was not willing to provide it. He often resisted her maternal advances. He kept his privacy and distance. Mary seemed to have a thrill in washing her sons' private parts. Early on, Hanno insisted that he wash himself.

Hanno's resistance to his mother's affection did not deter her from making extraordinary sacrifices for him. She wanted him to make something of himself. When

Hanno was in high school and especially when he was in college, she would work long and hard hours in menial labor when it was clear he needed money. His father was never considered a reliable source.

Mary never learned how to spend lavishly on herself. When having an upscale restaurant dinner with her lady friends, she would look at the menu prices and then order a vegetable plate.

Hanno appreciated these extraordinary efforts and said so in generous ways. Yet Hanno felt compelled to keep a reserve. This distance existed but became irrelevant with the tragedy of war. With the Japanese attack on Pearl Harbor, Jay was immediately missing in action and Ray remained in the South Pacific without leave for the duration of the war. The prolonged grief experienced by Mary changed the entire family.

Mary spent her life reaching for that magical status of being significant. If she reached it, it was in the planning of her own funeral, which is described later.

[11]

BODY 101

Hanno's awareness of sexual differences went back to his earliest memories. While his mother and other ladies were still carrying him around, and certainly before he could talk, he was aware of and attracted to the female shape. In his earliest memory, he wanted to be a girl. He felt cheated in that girls' figures were more curved and attractive, and he was stuck with being a boy.

Then there was a transition. Here the memory is blank. Hanno cannot remember whether he was still being carried, whether he was crawling or walking, or whether he was talking. His attraction to the female figure remained the same, but he preferred admiring that figure from the perspective of a boy. For want of a better word, he developed the view that the female figure could best be enjoyed not by having the figure but by being a *consumer*. This was the role of the boy and the man.

Clearly, Hanno had developed his foci of attraction with the woman's form. Among the various body features, the hips were first. The breasts were next, but they were a close second. Then came the legs and the total contour.

Faces of women did not play a role in this ranking. It was as if faces were on a different dimension. Hanno was in the first grade before he could say that one girl's face was prettier than another's. Even then, the attractiveness of faces, the hair configuration, and the likelihood of a smile in a male or female were all mixed together. As Hanno grew up, these rankings did not change.

*   *   *

Hanno's parents gained some amusement out of the names they taught Hanno and his brothers for body parts. Even before he could talk, they referred to Hanno's penis as his *doodlewhacker*. It was called nothing else but doodlewhacker. Growing up on the isolated homestead, he never received any alternative to call it anything else. Before being tucked into bed at night, Hanno's father would say, "Have you remembered to drain your doodlewhacker?"

When Hanno was in the sixth grade, he and his family moved off the homestead. They lived on Black Creek Road, and Hanno attended Black Creek elementary school. Unlike Plum Branch, this was a two-room schoolhouse. The first four grades were in one room, and the second four in the other. Hanno had an argument during recess about naming. A boy, Dale Evanston, argued that the correct name for the boy's organ was *penis*. Hanno asserted that the proper term was *doodlewhacker*. *Penis*, Hanno explained, was a foul or slang word that one should not use in good company. *Doodlewhacker,* in contrast, was the proper scientific designation for the male organ. Hanno was the more persuasive, and he won the argument.

All of this raises the question of how young ones learn the nature of evidence. What was the effective observation that made Hanno right?

By the time Hanno reached high-school, life experiences had shown him to be wrong about both doodlewhacker and penis. Hanno had picked up the other slang terms for penis, such as *dick, peter, prick,* and *pecker,* but he was really surprised when he learned that doodlewhacker was not even a part of common parlance.

*　　*　　*

When one does not have sex education in the schools or from the parents, one may well ask, "Where does a child learn it?"

One may learn a little bit from having a sibling of the opposite sex. One may learn a little from having a baby in the family whose diapers must be changed. Hanno had neither of these.

The remaining alternative was "dirty" or "sexy" jokes. And this was not an easy way to learn. From the stories and terms used in dirty jokes, one must do considerable triangulation in order to fit one joke after another to the place and nature of body parts in real life. Hanno was left with the perplexing question, "How can it possibly all work together?"

*　　*　　*

Hanno and his buddy Dale were slowly walking along the lonely gravel road. On one side was the forest, with squirrel nests high in the branches. On the other side was a cornfield with a couple of unwelcome crows. Dale was carrying a hiking stick. Hanno had thrown his away. Both were barefooted, and their bib overalls were rolled up to their knees. It was August, and by this time, the gravel no longer hurt their once-tender feet. They had not worn shoes since school was out, and, frankly, they did not welcome putting them back on for the opening of school.

"I would like to jack up Grace Bedwell," Dale said. "She's really looking good. I wonder if you can do it standing up."

"I don't know."

"The problem with all these dirty jokes, none of them tell you how you can get it in."

"That's right."

"Someone told me that there are three holes. Right together. One to pee from. One where babies come from. Then there is the asshole."

"Yeh, I think that's right."

"Then, how can you be sure you are getting it in the right hole?"

"I don't know."

"I don't want to look dumb in front of a girl and do it wrong."

"You won't be in front of her. You'll be on top of her."

"Wise guy."

Hanno and Dale were heading down to the bridge. The Plum Branch Creek ran underneath. Ordinarily, it would be about four to six inches deep. But east of the bridge, there was a drop-off. The water was three feet deep in one spot. There was no room to dive in, just a hole. There was no room to swim. Neither boy knew how to swim. But you could take off your clothes and get completely under, even put your head underwater. There was no place else you could do that. There were no snakes, hardly ever, only tadpoles. The only problem was that if a car came by over the bridge, the people inside could see you naked in the water. They would honk and yell and laugh. The sons of bitches.

"I hear that Brad Evars and his older brother are screwing their little sister all the time."

"How can they do that without getting caught?" Dale said.

"They wait until their parents have gone to town. Then they go down to the big barn behind their house and lock all the barn doors but one and crawl up into the loft. She resisted at first, but with the two of them, they held her down. Then they promised to give her their candy and darn near anything else they got. Oh yeah. They told her that if she told, they would tell all over school what she was doing, so everybody would know."

"I don't believe that."

"I don't know. That's what I was told. Not by her brothers. I wonder if her bright-red hair and pigtails would make her more easy to go along with it."

"By the way, Dale, your own sister is really starting to look good. Up there in the seventh grade, girls always get taller. Your sister doesn't have the tits that some have. I've got the hots for her. I think she likes me. She pushed me in the swing a few times. Do you think she would do it?"

"Go to hell." Pause. "You stay away from her."

"Hey, there is this other seventh-grader. Shorter than your sister. But when I stood next to her at school, she smelled like a number-two lead pencil."

"Which end?"

Hanno looked puzzled. "More the eraser end, I guess?"

"No, I mean which end of her?"

"You go to hell also."

They saw the bridge and began to run. They jumped down over the drainage ditch alongside the road. They began taking off their clothes, trying to see who would be first to get into the hole.

*　　*　　*

Hanno's Uncle Murl, his wife, Ethyl, and their daughter Jenny Lee were among those who often made the trek four and a half miles north of Linton to spend a day visiting.

Jenny Lee was a year older than Hanno, but no less than a boy, she was an exciting playmate during their preschool and early elementary years. On this visit, Uncle Murl did not come. Not yet a policeman, he was busy in his auto garage.

Hanno's mother and Ethyl were very close. Both were verbose, eager to talk and share. The moment the door opened and the two families faced each other, Hanno's mother and Ethyl would start talking simultaneously on different topics. Neither would relent to listen to the other. They were happy to see each other and to unload more than to listen. To Hanno, as a preschooler, this made no sense. Talking, he felt, was secondary to listening and understanding. So, one day, Hanno yelled, "Stop!"

Both women stopped talking immediately and looked at Hanno. Finding that he was in no distress, they continued talking.

A patch of pebbles lay by the house. They had been rinsed by decades of rain and were muted blue in the bright sun. They had been laid down for some reason by Hanno's grandmother Celester long before he was born.

On this day, Hanno and Jenny Lee sat on the pebbles. It was a day that brought the greatest turmoil of Hanno's childhood.

Jenny Lee loved to play with Hanno and, in particular, to climb Hanno's grape arbor. Hanno had a wagon but otherwise no balls or toys to play with. So, after climbing a while, they sat down on the patch of blue pebbles.

"Do you want to see my bottom?" she asked.

"Sure," Hanno said, not knowing exactly what she was referring to.

"You are not supposed to tell about this. Do you promise?"

"Sure," Hanno said.

She arose, took off her panties from under her short dress, and sat down again on the pebbles, facing him. With her legs apart, she showed Hanno the vertical slit in her smooth skin. There was not much to see. Hanno said nothing.

"Now," she said, "you've got to show me yours."

Hanno saw no reason to object. He unbuttoned the fly to pull off his short pants. He pulled forward his penis and his scrotum. She looked at them for a moment. She took hold of them, feeling and looking underneath.

"I knew that boys were different from girls. I learned that from kids at school. This is the first time I have had a good look." Still holding his scrotum, she said, "What is this called?"

"My bag."

"Mine is more handy than yours. I can keep stuff in mine. I call it my pocketbook. I can keep pebbles in it. Once I kept a penny in it before I spent it on candy. Do you want to see?"

"Yes," Hanno said but with some hesitation.

She picked up a pebble and inserted it into her vagina. Hanno watched with intense interest.

"Do you want to put one in?"

"Okay," Hanno said. He picked up a small pebble and pushed it into her vagina. He sat for a moment in wonderment without talking.

"That's a very handy thing," Hanno finally said.

"Yes, and boys don't have it. I'm glad I'm a girl and I've got one. It is something special."

At that moment, Hanno felt envious of her. He wished that he were a girl and had a vagina. You could do all kinds of things with it.

Trying to regain some sense of esteem, Hanno then pointed out to her that his bag served as a pocketbook too. "But it won't open. I have two balls in it, but they will not come out."

"Let me see." She took Hanno's scrotum in both her small hands and felt for Hanno's testicles. She did not press hard or hurt him. "Your bag has a line of bumps that go on back between your legs."

"Yeah. I don't know what they are for."

"That is really nice. It is too bad you cannot open your bag and get to them. I like mine better."

"I do too."

Hanno recalled very well that he was indeed envious of the female body shape back when he was being carried.

Jenny Lee then said, "I can put my finger into my bottom. Let me show you."

Jenny Lee inserted her forefinger into her vagina and then took it out.

"Would you like to put your finger in there? I will let you."

"No. I don't think so."

Why Hanno said no he would never completely understand. Maybe it was like venturing too far into the unknown. Forever after, he regretted declining this invitation.

Suddenly, from the open screened window just above came a loud scream. It was Ethyl, Jenny Lee's mother.

"*Jenny Lee*! Come here at once!"

As Aunt Ethyl left the window, she continued to scream. Hanno took off running. Jenny Lee took off in another direction. He headed north to the chicken house. He hid in behind the bars on which the chickens roosted. It was a long way to the woods, and he would be in plain view all the way. This was the quickest way to get out of sight. He had not considered that it was also one of the easiest places to be found.

Jenny went in the direction of the old house, but she went right by the door where her mother exited and grabbed her. She was dragged inside the house. Since all the windows were open in the heat of summer, what happened next could easily be heard.

Hanno did not know what with, but he could hear clearly from the chicken house that Jenny Lee was receiving a beating. It was a beating such as he had never heard before—and has not heard or seen since. From the sound, Hanno knew that Ethyl was not beating her daughter by hand. It must have been a hairbrush, hand mirror, a book, a piece of stove wood, or such. She beat her daughter and still screamed at her. After the first beat or two, Jenny Lee began screaming also. But the beating went on and on. Ethyl ran out of words but kept screaming. Jenny Lee kept screaming. Finally Jenny Lee could no longer scream. She succumbed to a series of long moans and wails of a softer, quieter defeated nature. They were intermixed with her gasping to get her breath. Still, Ethyl continued. When would it ever stop? Finally, it did stop.

Hanno's brothers arrived home to find Jenny Lee in a state of collapse and Aunt Ethyl in a distraught demeanor with tussled hair. Hanno could hear sounds of Ethyl loading Jenny Lee into the car and leaving immediately.

The twins, around thirteen years old, were highly curious as to what had happened. They received a full explanation of all details of the day after Ethyl and Jenny Lee drove away.

"But where is Hanno?" they asked.

"Hanno ran away somewhere. I don't know where he is, but let him be. He'll be back."

Hanno heard pots and dishes, and he knew that supper was being prepared. Although he had never had a beating such as given to Jenny Lee, he was fully expecting that his mother would be coming to the chicken house with a large whip. He anticipated a beating equivalent to what Jenny Lee had received. No one came. Hanno's dad came in from the fields at the end of the day. Hanno's brothers were eager to share the news of the day with him. He did not leave the house and come for Hanno either.

Finally, Hanno heard everybody eating. He wanted to leave the coop and go home, but the feeling of terror and anticipation that it was now his turn kept him from budging. He was not hungry, but the smell of the chicken droppings beneath the roost and all around was becoming unbearable. Time passed. Hanno knew that supper was over. It was getting dark. Finally, he could wait no longer.

When Hanno went into the house, he was met with a profound artificial quiet. His brothers, who would have been the first to torment and tease him, were away in their room. He was expecting to get at least a lecture from his father, and it was either postponed or not to come. He was expecting his mother to have the switch ready and for her to whip him and give him a lecture never to do that again. Instead, she asked Hanno if he wanted something for supper. She had a plate set aside and a glass of milk. The event of the afternoon was not mentioned—ever. Yet Hanno knew—he thought he knew—that he was to receive punishment. Jenny Lee had been beaten so hard it was impossible to reason otherwise. Hanno could find no explanation for the unequal treatment. Yet, as Hanno waited and waited, nothing happened.

Hanging in his thoughts now was the unfairness if Jenny Lee were to get so battered while he did not. His most sensible deduction was that the error of examining body parts was so grievous that some special time was being reserved and then he would really get it—worse than Jenny Lee. He did not dare to bring up the topic, and he could not understand why his mother and father said nothing.

Hanno was so traumatized by Jenny Lee's beating that he was even feeling guilty toward her for not taking his share.

Why was she getting all the punishment and he was getting none? Was it because she was a girl and Hanno was a boy? Was it because his folks reacted against this extraordinary beating by doing the opposite? Was it because his parents were more tolerant of childhood exploration? Was it both or all? Did they have a double standard that put the responsibility on the girl? Was it that Jenny was a year older?

As that day began, Jenny Lee, Hanno's first cousin, had been his most exciting and favorite playmate. As the day ended, he settled on one of the possible explanations of what had happened.

Jenny Lee and Hanno had done something terribly wrong, the exact nature of which Hanno, and perhaps Jenny Lee also, did not fully understand. Jenny Lee was apprehended and punished beyond belief for her part. And at any moment, also, Hanno would be the recipient and realize his worst fears. It was only a matter of waiting and bearing the terror of anticipation.

The problem with such a formulation was that it would be a burden forever unless there was the fulfilling punishment.

If only there could have been five minutes of talking with Hanno openly about the event, a lifetime of anxious apprehension would have been avoided. Hanno is still waiting.

With Hanno's brothers, the situation was quite different. In their view, there was this young lad born into a once happy family and his arrival ruined it all. This became an opportunity to even the score. They knew that they could arouse Hanno's misery each time the incident was mentioned.

During those years, there was a folk spiritual, "Hand Me Down My Walking Cane." The lyrics went like this:

Oh, hand me down my walking cane.
Hand me down my walking cane.
Oh hand me down my walking cane.
Goin' to heaven on the midnight train
For all my sins are taken away.

Since Jay and Ray had been confined to their bedrooms during Hanno's return, they had ample time to compose the following words:

Oh, I wouldn't do what some people do
Oh, I wouldn't do what some people do.
Oh, I wouldn't do what some people do,
    just like Jenny Lee and you.
Now people will know the things you do.

Hanno's brothers were excellent singers, both solo and duet. They sang in the school choir and in musical comedies in high school. They sang around the house daily. Little did Hanno realize on this morning in 1933 that he would be serenaded with this song until his brothers entered the military in 1940.

At first, they sang the song to Hanno in front of their parents. The parents were amused by their creativity. Soon, their parents sensed that Hanno's misery with each rendition was not going to subside. They forbade the twins from singing it. Their sense of joy and power over Hanno's torment was too much to give up. So they persisted whenever Hanno's parents were absent.

Hanno, with wits at end, finally reported these transgressions to his mother. Busy with housework, she told Hanno to go out into the woods and find a good switch. She would whip both of them, she said. Hanno promptly began the search in the forest. Wandering far, he found a switch that the six-year-old could see would match the torment he had received. It was a branch about six inches in diameter and about eighteen feet long with all the subbranching and twigs. Lightning had torn it from a tree trunk. Hanno could not carry it, but he dragged it back to the house. He showed his mother. He was hoping that she would ask him to go find his brothers and bring them in. Instead, she was overcome with laughter. She shared her mirth with Hanno's father, the nearby neighbors, and people on the phone that Hanno did not know. In the end, the tree branch was put on the woodpile, and Jay and Ray only got a good talking to.

A couple of years later, Hanno and the twins were sitting in the shade of the maple. They were playing with the collie dog. When the dog began paying more attention to Hanno than to them, Jay began singing the song. Hanno was carrying a pocketknife. Actually the knife belonged to Ray. Hanno was not considered old enough to carry a knife.

Hanno opened the pocketknife and hurled it at Jay. With Hanno's poor throwing arm, the knife veered toward Ray and penetrated more than an inch into his leg. All knew that Ray was this time innocent and not the target.

Their mother was in the kitchen, just outside of hearing range. Hanno expected the worst for his deed.

To Hanno's surprise, the twins did not call to her. They said nothing to Hanno. They headed directly to the pump in the barnyard. They washed the wound but could not control the bleeding. They had no recourse but to seek their mother's help. They knew that she would demand an explanation. Hanno was still sitting in the yard with the dog. The twins trumped up a story about the knife. Their story did not hold water. She knew that something had to have provoked Hanno to use the knife. She knew well of their daily torment with the song, and it did not take her long to extract a valid confession.

Once again Hanno escaped the jaws of severe punishment. His brothers were lectured about their behavior and told they got what they deserved. Hanno felt Jay failed to get what he deserved and Ray got what he did not deserve. Hanno was forbidden to have a knife in his possession anymore.

Later in the evening, with Jay's first opportunity to be alone with Hanno, he promised Hanno that they would get back at him and that he would suffer more than Ray did with the knife wound. The twins were fifteen, and Hanno was eight. Hanno saw them as big and powerful. Hanno saw no reason not to take these threats seriously.

The day after the knife incident when Jay was away from home, Ray came to Hanno in the yard. Hanno expected the same taunting and threats, but Ray sat down and played with Hanno for a few minutes. Then he quietly left.

Ray showed a kindness that Hanno had never experienced when the twins were together. For the first time ever, Hanno became aware of differences in their characters. Jay was the more dominant, assertive, and vindictive. Ray, without Jay present, was the more gregarious, warm, and friendly. He was more likely to invest time visiting over the fence with neighbors. Yet, when they were together, they followed Jay's dictum. To avoid being caught singing their taunting song to Hanno, they would hum it often beneath their breath.

The fateful visit of Ethyl and Jenny Lee to the homestead on that beautiful sunny day was the last time anyone saw or had contact with them. As Ethyl sought a divorce, Mary followed her oft-used rule and gave up a relationship with a very close friend in favor of her blood kindred. She acknowledged to many that she saw great faults in Murl that caused a breakdown in the marriage. Yet she never communicated again with Ethyl.

Murl, the one-armed mechanic, finally had to give up his garage business, and after years as a constable, he became a member of the Linton police force. He became the expert stolen-car detective because of his outstanding memory for license plate numbers. In those days without air-conditioning, the policemen sat on the sidewalk during the day in a row of chairs in front of city hall. The major traffic route to and from Linton was before them. Murl's reputation for spotting stolen cars was spoken of and tracked in terms of the number of stolen cars he identified each week.

He kept a picture of Jenny Lee upon his dresser. He wrote her once a month but received no reply. He received only a Christmas card once a year, each one of which he treasured. He was never sure the letters got to her. When Hanno asked about her, Murl would speak in a choked, low, tender voice, barely a whisper. A tear would come to his eye. Yet he knew nothing of her life.

Hanno met Jenny Lee and her husband years later at a wedding in Michigan.

*   *   *

"Have you ever jacked off?" asked Billie.

Hanno looked at him, a bit astonished, and, at first, said nothing.

After school, Billie White had asked to walk home with Hanno along Black Creek Road. Hanno's family had moved closer to town, just a mile north of the city limits. Hanno was now in the sixth grade at Black Creek School. Billie was in the fourth, therefore in the lower room. Thus Hanno did not know Billie well. What he did know was that Billie was a somewhat restless and talkative kid who made straight A's, the top kid in his class. If not for his top grades, his hyperactivity would have put him into more trouble.

Finally, Hanno said, "Yes. Almost every guy does it. Everyone that I know of. I knew a Boy Scout in town that claimed he had never jacked off. I don't know if he were telling the truth or not."

"I jacked off last week—for the first time, really. I've been playing around with my dong a lot but not real jacking off."

"I should tell you. This is something that most guys do not talk about. Their own experience, I mean. They talk and joke about it in general. You shouldn't be talking like this to everyone."

"You're older. And I want to talk."

"Okay." Hanno was somewhat curious.

"Last week at the end of jacking off, there was a kind of a burning feeling, like you wanted to pee. It felt good."

"You *came*. That is your *come*."

"Is that what come is?"

"Well, once you get older and get hair around your doodlewhacker, you get something wet coming out."

"Like pee?"

"No. It's kind of like, well, library paste."

"I've never seen that. You say it comes when you get that burning feeling?"

"That's right. And what you are talking about is called *orgasm*. You are having an orgasm."

"Orgastum?"

"*Orgasm*. If you want to talk more, why don't we go inside our barn where no one will hear us?"

Hanno's family had just one acre of land, but it used to be an old farmhouse and there was an old, small unpainted barn. It was used now as a garage and a toolshed. The barn had a clean, empty loft of two-by-twelve lumber flooring.

Up in the loft Billie said, "Let's jack off together so I can see how you do it."

They sat on the floor, cattycornered from each other, and unbuttoned their flies. (Zippers were starting to be used, but not for their pants yet.)

"By the way, there is an official word for this, other than *jackoff*."

"Yeah, I know. My sister told me. Is it *menstrubation*?"

"No, no. You got it wrong. It is masturbation."

"Masturbation."

"And what we are doing now, two of us together, is sometimes called mutual masturbation. It's when two or more guys do it together."

"Gosh!"

"And one other thing. That come that we were talking about? You've heard of having sex with a girl?"

"Sure!"

"Well, when the guy puts his dick inside her and when he comes, that come stuff is what makes her pregnant and they have a baby."

"No, that's not right. That cannot be right. I'm sure of that. I know about sex with a girl from jokes, you know, but that's not what causes babies. I'm 100 percent sure of that. My folks would never, never do that. And they had us as babies, and I'm positive they would not do that."

"Then where do you think babies come from?"

"Well, I don't know. Maybe from kissing. Or maybe they just come along naturally when two people get married."

Hanno considered entering into persuasive debate with Billie. But then Billie had such an unshakable view about his parents. Hanno decided he would leave his view alone.

Hanno shifted the topic. "One of the funniest stories I ever heard about mutual masturbation was, well, ah, the Bloomington High School football team, once in the locker room before a game, they decided to have a jacking off contest to see who would come the fastest. So, one of them got a stopwatch and when he said, 'Go!' they all started. Well, the guy who won made it in thirteen seconds. But when the coach walked in the door, almost all the players were still going. That really stopped the contest. The whole team was caught."

"I can't believe that! Where did you get a story like that?"

"It's true. A guy named Jim Hazleton told me when he came home from the Navy. It was some time ago, and

Hazleton was on the team. He took part in the masturbation contest himself. He has a bent, broken nose to prove it."

"He got a broken nose ... ah ... in a jacking off contest?"

"No, no. He got the broken nose on the football field, you crazy."

"Well, what did the coach do about it?"

"That's why it's so funny. He couldn't do anything. It was just before a game with another school. He couldn't kick them all off the team. There would be no team left. Can you imagine a coach contacting the referees and the coach of the other team and telling them that he was cancelling the game because his team was masturbating? And can you imagine him contacting almost each and every parent to tell them their son has been kicked off the football team for masturbating and then cancelling the rest of the season?"

"But what did he do"

"There was nothing he could do. They just suited up and played the game, and after a locker room talk, nothing was said about it ever again."

"That's really something."

"Yes, that's something. I'm sure you will not hear of such a thing very often. But the thing that always bothered me was, why be first at coming? I thought that the whole idea of sex is to enjoy it all as long as you can."

"I can see that. Last week, I watched Sullivan play us. During the game, I was wondering if some of those guys even knew how to jack off."

"You can bet on it."

The two heard Hanno's mother calling.

"Gosh," said Billie. "I got to get going. It's late. It was swell talking to ya."

[12]

BODY 102

During World War II, various means were used to sell government bonds. At first they were Defense Stamps and Bonds. Then they were called War Bonds. Some local bond drives were activated by having a "war show." Like a Barnum and Bailey circus or a Bill Cody Wild West Show, this was an extravaganza. On Oliphant Field, the Linton Stockton High School football field, an active Army outfit would divide up into two camps and attack each other. With the help of well-placed fireworks and blank bullets and shells from weapons, the loaded bleachers would experience M1 rifles, Browning automatic rifles (BARs), mortars, and light artillery pieces. Soldiers would charge, get wounded and be carried on stretchers, fall dead, take prisoners, and such. At the end, many children stayed around to watch the soldiers gather their equipment, clear the debris, and retire to their bunks and sleeping bags in the high-school gymnasium.

While many soldiers were asking where the "babes" were, one burly soldier with a tender, gentle voice was clearly attracted to the boys who had gathered. This soldier, known only as Bob, approached Hanno and Richard. He asked if they could show him around town. From the beginning it was apparent that Bob was mentally abnormal and intellectually subnormal. Yet there was something attractive about his gentle, vulnerable attitude. He was nice. He bought them ice-cream cones. He was so barren of defensive posture or macho arrogance that he sparked a sense of wanting to protect him. When it came time to go home, he wanted to walk Hanno and Richard home. Hanno was staying with his aunt Lizzie. On the way Bob showed Hanno and Richard a grip on their thumbs with Bob's huge hands. The grip could cause pain in two ways. He could press down and hyperextend the joint so as to cause pain. Also, if one tried to get his thumb free, he would inflict pain on himself.

When they reached their residence, the soldier wanted a kiss good-bye—on the lips. Richard was comfortable kissing him without resistance. Hanno refused. Bob insisted and increasingly applied pain to Hanno's thumb. Attempts to free his thumb produced so much pain that Hanno finally yielded. Once he was kissed on the mouth, the soldier released the thumb and had no further requests.

About two years later, the war show was repeated. Hanno and Richard had talked often about the strange burly soldier. Their curiosity and attraction exceeded the brief moment of pain he imposed. They went looking for him and found him in his quarters in the gym. Fellow soldiers stared at Hanno and Richard. They did not intervene. Again, he wanted a kiss good night. Again, Richard yielded and Hanno refused. Again, Hanno got the painful thumb treatment. Again, his gentleness returned once he received his good-night kiss.

*   *   *

Hanno was not unlike most high-school boys, who became increasingly interested in girls. During his freshman and sophomore years, while in a convocation in the auditorium, he would gain eye contact with and flirt with those he felt were the very best-looking girls in the school. He was pleased that they flirted back, even when seated with their regular boyfriends. These girls would be the sources of daydreams when alone and wet dreams when asleep. However, he did not have the confidence to pursue them.

*   *   *

Hanno dreamed of having a date years in advance, and he finally had his first date during his sophomore year at Linton Stockton High School. Hanno, correct or not, felt many obstacles competed against a person like him when seeking a girlfriend. If you had asked him, he would have said that the first asset to competing for and keeping a girl was having a car at your complete disposal. The second was being a town person. He felt that country kids, both male and female, were not part of the "in" group. The third was having money. Hanno did not match up on any of these. If someone else had been asked, he or she would have said that it was only a matter of Hanno's self-confidence.

Girls intimidated Hanno. When around them, he spoke few words. For this reason, communication was not always clear. Hanno had ample occasion to encounter Becky Ann. They not only had classes together, but they also attended the First Baptist Church together. To their embarrassment, their friends caught them holding hands under a shared hymnal. The Sunday night meetings of the Baptist Youth Fellowship (BYF) led to a habitual late movie afterward at the Ciné Theater. Then there was the period when Cecil Jesse joined the church as pastor. He and the Sunday school / math teacher Bonna Baughman packed their cars with kids and had many wild car rides to other towns for a Coke and snack, with lots of singing and backseat cuddling on the road.

Becky Ann was a perfect fit for Hanno, and all their friends knew it. Hanno, meanwhile, was in love with the town girl all the boys with cars and money were chasing. Hanno knew he could not compete. Becky Ann had eyes for two of the varsity basketball players, but she felt she could not compete. Hanno's first romance was by default.

The one incident to stand out in memory for all time, however, was the basketball game. Becky Ann and Hanno made it a habit to go to all the home basketball games of the Linton Miners. The Linton team was good, and the basketball gymnasium was packed. After a very close game against Terre Haute Garfield with Clyde Lovellette, Linton played Bicknell, a small school that was not so athletically strong. During the game, a member of the Bicknell team got a severe kick in the testicles while scuffling for a loose basketball. The impact was so great that the boy yelled loudly and rolled to the floor, grabbing his crotch with both hands. He continued to groan and roll over. The ball players had great empathy and held back. The bleachers were filled with hundreds of people without an empty seat. Both the Linton and opposing sides went dead silent. The referees were leaning over the boy.

Suddenly, in the quiet, as if from a midnight lake, Becky Ann yelled out, "I think he's faking. I've been hit there many times, and it never hurt me like that."

The hundreds of fans on both sides burst into laughter and turned to look at Becky Ann and her companion. Hanno Buchwald instantly wanted to be somewhere other than Linton, Indiana.

It was a milestone embarrassment for Becky Ann, but the crowd also scrutinized Hanno. It appeared to the other boys he had not kept pace in the classic tutorial game of touch, and all of his and Becky Ann's friends now knew it. They had imagined scenarios of more adventurous sexual encounters, and now they knew better.

Hanno, during this time, thought of himself only in terms of his Linton niche, but he was participating in a transition of life that comes for all boys and girls throughout humankind. When you think about girls, you also dream about them. When you dream about them, you also have wet dreams. You wake up in the morning to find a little puddle of come has been ejected from the penis onto the bedsheets and pajamas. What can you do to keep your mom from discovering this? Hanno learned that there was not much you could do.

*   *   *

Another event that represented a milestone in Hanno's life trajectory was when he first creamed his jeans. This would occur while thinking of a sexual scene or even without any provocation. Hanno had his first experience of it with passionate kissing. The preferred term for such cuddling and kissing was *smooching*. With such embraces and a kiss, Hanno suddenly found his underwear filling up with come. The event was exotic beyond all experience, but it left an aftermath of concern. Still being fully clothed, boys like Hanno were concerned that a wet spot would come through and show on the front of their trousers. Also, Hanno found it a bit uncomfortable to have soaked undershorts and to have to wait until he got home to clean up. These concerns did not discourage Hanno from the wonderful experience of smooching. As he and Becky Ann became more and more comfortable embracing each other, holding body parts, and kissing, the exotic experience could become mutual. Fully clothed, Becky Ann's body could be pressed tightly against his genital area—sometimes in the backseat of a car, sometimes while dancing—and Becky Ann and he alike could feel a sudden onset of throbbing as his penis was emptying out its fluid into his undershorts. Simultaneously, when all in love was right, Becky Ann would grasp a piece of Hanno's sleeve, her head would drop back with lips slightly apart, as if in slight pain, and a soft cry would emerge from her lips. Finally, she also was spent.

Following this unstoppable action by their bodies, they were back to awareness of each other as if placed together alone in a tent beside a mountain lake miles from other people. They had only themselves and their attachment to each other to touch their awareness. They were in a world of their own.

* * *

A well-known but undiscussed event during Hanno's high-school years was the classroom crisis with an uncontrollable hard-on.

The best example from Hanno's time happened in history class one day. For Tommy Kelly, the conditions were right for the perfect storm. The seats and desks were the old traditional type in which one sat on a flip-down seat and the backrest served as the front of the desk for the person behind you. As you sat down, you slid in behind and under a desktop with shelf space underneath for supplies. Your legs extended so that your feet were below the flip-down seat of the person in front of you. For a tall person, it was tight quarters.

Another feature was that Mr. Gabbard, the history teacher, allowed seating by personal choice. This presented the opportunity for girls to seek seats close to Tommy Kelly, the outstanding and good-looking varsity basketball player. Each girl was looking for eye contact, a flirt, or at least a friendly smile.

The next feature was tight undershorts. Jockey shorts and other briefs were designed to keep the genitalia in a pouch under close surveillance, therefore preventing testicle damage or the penis from protruding freely down one trouser leg or the other. If a sexual thought or a natural hormonal surge occurred, the penis elongated. The stimulated end of the penis met its obstacle. This magnified the stimulation, and erection proceeded all the faster. With the tight undershorts, there was no room for the penis to elongate and expand. The physical restraint created even greater stimulation and greater erection. The tight underwear resulted in an elongated penis that was being bent at right angles. The bending brought uncommon pain.

This was what happened one day to Tommy Kelly as class was being called to order. Tommy began to have a great hard-on—and, with it, even greater pain.

If admiring girls had not been sitting beside, behind, and in front of him, he could easily have grabbed his crotch and freed his penis from its cul-de-sac in two seconds. However, to do this, he would appear to be fondling his crotch, and he was too shy to attempt it.

With Tommy's intense pain, beads of sweat were visible on his forehead. Hanno and some of his buddies were pointing and drawing attention to Tommy. They winked at each other. They had been there. The girls were puzzled about what was going on, and they became more attentive. Tommy scooted his legs forward as far as they would go. It did not help. Then he scooted back so that his back and buttocks were tight against the back of his seat. It did not help. He put one leg forward and the other one back. It did not help. He reversed and wiggled around in his seat. It did not help. He tried to divert attention by focusing upon his history book.

The teacher, Mr. Gabbard, sensed an atmosphere in the class that indicated misconduct was taking place. He scanned the class carefully, but he could not find what the problem was. The only thing different was that Tommy Kelly was intently studying his history book, and Mr. Gabbard had not handed out the assignment yet.

Fifteen minutes after Mr. Gabbard began teaching, Tommy's problems were history.

*   *   *

In high-school dating, Becky Ann was expected to be back home by eleven o'clock. This allowed Hanno to play a double role in the vital balance of seeking and exposing affection. Among the students, there were the *smoochers* and the *buttercuppers*. For each activity, a car was required, and, almost always, it was borrowed from the old man. After a movie, dancing at the Teen Canteen, or some similar entertainment, the smoochers drove out into the countryside and found a place to park and smooch without disturbance.

The idea was to be far enough away from the residential area so as to attract no local attention. But also there was the necessity to find a place where you could see cars coming. The buttercuppers, also called bushwhackers, had the sole purpose of discovering and exposing the smoochers. They would shine lights on the car and try to rattle or tease the smooching couple.

"I caught you! I caught you."

So, after Hanno took Becky Ann home and kissed her good night, he would drive back downtown to Main Street around the Ciné Theater to join the gang of buttercuppers. These were typically guys of high-school age who had not yet started dating but were so heterosexually oriented they saw great sport in catching a couple by surprise. Some kept records of the number they caught per week.

It was great fun. The high points were in catching the difficult-to-catch. Sammy Doolittle and his girlfriend had been going out to park and smooch for ages, and nobody had found where they parked. Hanno was a part of the group who cracked the riddle. A few miles outside of Linton on a country road was an arched bridge over a rail track. If one pulled up to the crest of the arch, stopped, and turned off the lights, one could see for miles in all directions. If one detected a car, one started the motor and left long before the other car's arrival.

On one quiet late night with just a bit of moonlight, Hanno and his buttercupping group left to check out the hunch that Sammy and his girl were using this spot. At least two miles away, they turned off their headlights and rolled down all the windows. Everyone watched the shoulder and ditch so as not to drive off the road. In the dark, they found the T-intersection with its road going off to the left only. They turned on this road and continued to drive very slowly. Within a half mile, they came to the bridge. They could see the silhouette of Sammy's car atop the bridge. They drove up to the top of the bridge, turned at an angle toward Sammy's car bumper, and turned on the bright lights. Up popped two red, embarrassed faces. The secret was over.

Having been a regular buttercupper, Hanno had many friends who knew very well that he and Becky Ann had not been discovered. Of course, Hanno declined to tell them his secret spot. It was a long time before Hanno and Becky Ann were caught, but finally, they were—and in grand style.

Hanno had many relatives in the funeral business, and he had become familiar with the entire Fairview Cemetery.

In the southeast corner of the cemetery, where the roads were somewhat irregular, a small side road often went unnoticed. Becky Ann did not object to the graves, so it became the location for hot smooching for many months. Finally, however, one moonlit night, their secret came to an end. Suddenly, not one but two cars accosted them. They blocked Hanno's exit from the area. The cars were filled with Hanno's close buttercupping friends. Having ensured that Hanno and Becky Ann could not leave, they got out of the car and chatted and laughed with them for a while. Hanno's game was over.

*   *   *

A word about the Teen City Canteen is well deserved. It was a gathering spot for teenagers regardless of whether they went out smooching or buttercupping later. It featured a great dance floor, a jukebox, booths along the sides, a pool table, and a Ping-Pong table in back. A patio out front would be filled with people in good weather. A snack counter inside was run by a lady who served as chaperone, but you never knew that, even if you asked her.

As a total high-school crowd, the young people were proud of it and guarded its reputation. Smoking, drinking, and vicarious sexual activity were not allowed, even in the parking lot. Street drugs, as we know them today, were not in use. It was where most Linton kids learned to dance slowly and to jitterbug. Hanno had many arguments with his uncle Murl about the place. The Linton police strongly suspected that it was a den of sexual inequity, and they wanted to close it down. They could not believe that such a place could be run without police supervision.

One can only say that during those years, the integrity of the place was protected by all. Students reported any misconduct, and students corrected it. Such an idea could not be successful if the students did not have such a sense of ownership.

Smooching was an advanced art of expressing affection that did not require condoms or birth-control pills. Hanno had a job working in the Rexall drugstore. Some girls and women would seek out the soda fountain girls to order Kotex or other sanitary napkins, but a great many high-school girls would deliberately seek Hanno to order Tampax or Kotex—deliberately, that is, to expose his shyness.

*　*　*

One day during the war, Hanno was in the public library studying a Boy Scout merit badge manual. He had to test a Scout on the merit badge topic of rocks and minerals, and he was not well informed.

Hanno was seated on a low bench beside the row of merit badge manuals. Margaret Cooper had left the library on a short errand. Around the corner from Hanno in the next room, two ladies were talking. They were unaware that anyone was in the library. One was a member of the First Christian Church, and the other was a member of United Brethren. Both were known for the active work they did for their church and the community. One was a leader in the local chapter of Mothers of World War II.

Both of the women had sons killed at a very early age. One lady had her son killed in combat in the early days of the war in Europe. Hanno knew her best because his own family had a son killed. Their discussion led Hanno to stop his reading and listen carefully.

One of the women made the comment that the greatest heartache of her son's death was that he might not have lived long enough to make love to a girl. To her it seemed that anyone who had lived to the adult age deserved the joy of making love. Her son may have missed that joy.

The other woman immediately agreed. She shared the same heartache. Her son had died in an auto accident shortly before he was to graduate from high school. During their talk, she told the story of an evening when she waited up for him. Taking the family car, he had gone out on a date. There was a time set for him to be back home with the car, and he had violated it. He was an hour late. When he arrived home, he had a bit of sweat on his brow. She scolded him as would be appropriate, and he went to bed without discussing the evening. She confessed that she hoped and prayed that this minor perspiration of the brow meant that he had had sexual intercourse with the girl he was out with.

The other woman then discussed her fragile hopes. Her son had dated little until his senior year in high school. In the most significant date, the evening was interrupted when the son backed the car into a ditch and required towing to get back onto the road. There were two other dates. She wondered if there had been sufficient time on either of those dates to make love. Then when he was in boot camp and shortly thereafter in combat, he did not write about having any dates. She was left hoping that some secret intrigue might have happened somewhere so that her son could have enjoyed the wonderful experience of loving.

Hanno listened to their full conversation with both interest and perplexity. Here were two women, both religious and with prominent reputations in the community. If they had found evidence that their sons had engaged in any sexual activity, they would certainly have been punished. Moreover, the mothers would have made every effort to cover up the behavior had it occurred. Neither of them spoke from the perspective of the girls being dated. They spoke only of what they wished for their deceased sons. Hanno was overwhelmed with the contradictions that occurred in the boundaries of being human.

Hanno once described this reversal to a colleague in Australia. Immediately she responded, "Sometimes it is better to grow up in a country founded by criminals rather than Puritans."

[13]

PLUM BRANCH

Of all places academic, whether undergraduate,
postgraduate, or postdoctoral, those three years in
a one-room schoolhouse in southern Indiana beat
them all.

—Author, 2012

Hanno spent his first three school years at Plum Branch,
Wright Township District 7, in Greene County. Plum
Branch was a one-room redbrick schoolhouse. As fate
would have it, Hanno's years there were the last in which
the school existed. The venue and model for grammar
school learning faded away into the generations struggling
for a more civilized and informed society. Like Brigadoon,
who knows? Perhaps one day Plum Branch will return.
Read closely.

Plum Branch School got its name from being on the southern slope of the creek with the same name. The creek originated in the virgin forest on Hanno's family homestead. There had been a grove of wild plum trees well before the time of the Native American village that once occupied the high ground of the Oglesby estate.

Hanno's mother had attended Plum Branch. It burned down, and the Oglesby menfolk had a part in rebuilding it.

With the Indiana schoolhouses came the Indiana schoolteachers, earlier called the Hoosier schoolmasters. They were an unusual lot. Held in high esteem for their education, they made very little money. Schoolmasters were looked up to, but you would not want your daughter marrying one. Beware of the young man who can afford neither a car nor a cow.

Take a look at the kind of community in which Plum Branch was placed. The school itself had no electricity, running water, or telephone. On the road to and from school, Hanno and his friends spent idle moments throwing gravel at the glass insulators on the newly placed telephone poles. Once in a while, when lucky, one of the rocks would hit. It would crack the glass and cause a humming sound. The boys imagined that they were interrupting someone's conversation on the party line.

Grown-ups had a moral code often no more esteemed. A party line would be assigned to three to five families. To place a call, you rang up central. (Central is now called the operator.) If the person's line you were calling was not busy, central put you through. The code 315R2 meant that you rang the 315 line two times. If you needed to make a call and someone was already speaking on the line, then you were supposed to observe privacy, hang up, and wait. This was where the eavesdroppers-gossipers were separated from the regular folk. The gossipers would hold a hand tightly over the mouthpiece and keep the receiver to their ear. As soon as the conversation was over, the gossiper would call a fellow gossiper and report all the information.

Hanno's mother and Annie Letterman became established as the two town leaders in the craft of gossip. They were so proficient that when other women wanted an update on gossip, they would not listen on the party line but would simply call Annie or Hanno's mom for a synthesis.

Moral codes find their own levels. The gossipers were not always evil. Sometimes, by this clandestine means, they would pick up an outstanding recipe and pass it on. Because of the hazard of spoilage during canning season, sometimes sterilizing procedures would be passed on by gossipers who overheard. Once a man broke his arm when his tractor overturned, and a gossiper's spouse showed up immediately to drive him to the doctor. Once in haste, a number was called incorrectly to ask about canning corn. "Do you scrape the cob?" were the first words said. "Yes," came the answer, along with a few tips. After hanging up, both parties realized that they had no idea whom they had been talking to. If Hanno's friend broke an insulator, the community looked first for some redeeming value in him. Plum Branch sat as a cocoon amid this complexity.

The barefoot days of summer of 1934 were coming to an end. Hanno's brothers were preparing to enter the eighth grade, and Hanno was excited about his first entry into school. At the beginning of each school year, parents were provided a list of school supplies necessary for the year. For the first-graders, this list included the currently used reader *Trips to Take*, two number-two lead pencils (yellow with an eraser on one end), a cube of art gum, a box of crayons, a package of colored construction paper, a pair of small scissors with rounded rather than pointed tips, an inkwell (that fit into a hole on top of the desk), a bottle of Skrip ink, a pen holder and two metal quill pens that fit into the holder, a bottle of mucilage, a bottle of library paste, a blotter (a thick absorbent paper about the size of a postcard), and a folding aluminum cup with lid.

Each day the teacher would refill a five-gallon tank of water. The tank had a small faucet at the bottom. Each pupil was taught to pull the concentric rings of his or her cup upward until the upper edge of each tier fit tightly with the ring just above. There were few water spills. Almost all the spills, it seemed, came from dipping the metal quill tip pen into the inkwell. If one pressed the pen too hard on the paper, all the ink came off onto the paper. First-graders made frequent use of the blotters.

Lunch buckets were not on the supply list. Not everyone could afford one. Those without buckets brought a sack lunch and often envied the others. Almost all of the lunch buckets were black and rectangular, with a high rounded lid that could store a thermos bottle.

The beginning of school always brought a new pair of shoes. Since everyone was growing, there was no hope that the shoes taken off in the spring would still fit. They were either discarded or, more likely, handed down.

Then, as always, clothing had its fashion. The standard dress for boys was bib overalls, and no one felt honored by them. The increasing desire, as one advanced toward puberty, was to have a pair of trousers with a belt. This meant that you were old enough to have hips so that your pants would not slide down. No one wanted suspenders.

Most despised of all were knickers. Hanno had two pair, handed down from his older brothers. These were not undergarments as in Britain but instead were pants that buttoned or buckled just below the knee and required calf-length stockings.

Every boy dreamed of having a Lindy cap. Seven years before Hanno attended first grade, Lindberg had flown solo across the Atlantic. The aviator's cap that he made popular had no brim. To allow Lindberg's radio earphones over it, the cap fit tightly over the skull and had flaps that snapped together under the chin. Although fashionable, it was a snug fit and kept the ears warm. In warm weather, the flaps were fastened over the head. Hanno's mother found a suitable hand-me-down.

The alternative to the Lindy cap was the toboggan. Nowadays it is called a ski cap or knitted cap, but then the only word was *toboggan*. Few knew the word *ski*. Just as today, it could be folded above the ears, pulled down over the ears, or stuffed in a pocket.

The number-one envy of every boy was a pair of high tops. This was leather footwear that cross-laced and tied just below the knee. Hanno's dream of having a pair was never met. (If you had high tops, you still had to get regular shoes for church, funerals, and weddings.) For fantasy, the high tops fit the role of explorer, aviator, or even cowboy with stirrups and spurs. At Plum Branch, they were especially valuable when trudging through thicket and underbrush.

Hanno's first day at school was an event to remember. Heavy rains had come, and the half-mile lane out to the east gravel road was very muddy. Hanno's dad did not want to see him get his new shoes and pants muddy on the very first day. So, his father hitched a horse to a single tree and pulled Hanno on a farm sled over the deeply rutted muddy lane. Hanno's dad walked beside the sled in overshoes. The sled was a homemade box fifteen inches high—with no bench. Hanno sat on the floor. Just a few inches of sled runners separated the floor from the mud. To keep Hanno from feeling babied, his dad agreed to let him walk the final quarter mile on the gravel road.

As Hanno walked by the Fiscus and Bedwell houses on the left and the Old Billy Powell cornfield on the right, he could see the schoolhouse in a small clearing with the deep forest behind it. This was to be a major physical venue in Hanno's life for the next three years. Hanno stepped off the gravel road onto the inclining shale driveway. Shale had been brought in from a local mine. It was cheaper than gravel but could combat the mud with its austerity. Farther along the school boundary beside the road was the girls' toilet. Along the adjacent boundary beside the corn and soybean field was the boys' toilet. In between, behind the schoolhouse, were two basketball goals. Beneath each goal was only dirt. On a dry day it was smooth; on a rainy day it was muddy and slippery. Midway between the two goalposts was a faint patch of grass. The entire playground area was relatively small.

At the back of the cleared playground were paths leading into the dense forest. Some of these paths led to Plum Branch Creek at the bottom of the hill. The creek ran under the gravel road through a large metal corrugated aqueduct with concrete poured over it. With no sidewalls or rails, a car out of control could drop off into the water.

The water was usually ankle deep and slow moving, except for one popular deep spot. It would rise to almost knee high after heavy rains or a snowmelt. Hanno already knew from his brothers that it was a great place at recess to take off one's shoes and wade barefoot. One could then approach the afternoon with relaxed pleasure. The only trouble was finding where you had put your shoes.

Plum Branch Creek always had lots of minnows, and during summers, local men would often take nets and seine for them. They were dropped into a minnow bucket as bait to fish for the big ones elsewhere. Hanno was excited to watch the tadpoles develop. They would begin black and very tiny, grow in size quickly, and, after a few days, begin to grow tiny front and hind legs. Finally, they would lose their tails and come to look like young frogs, which they were. The tadpoles were numerous and easy to catch. A more matured young frog was more difficult. It hopped fast, and you had to grab it with your hand. During summers, when the frogs were loud at night, adults or high-school kids would come gigging. They would catch enough frogs for a frog leg feast. If one did not make much noise wading in the water, a frog under a flashlight would not move. They were easy to gig and put into a gunnysack.

Once in a great while, student explorers would encounter a snake. This brought a lot of attention, and sometimes the snake was destroyed. Hanno's Uncle Murl Oglesby, a one-armed policeman in Linton, loved to seine for minnows, but he was deathly afraid of snakes. If he saw a snake, he would run, curse, and go on to another creek to seine for minnows.

As Hanno continued to dream before entering the school door, he imagined going on to the forbidden stripper hills and holes. If one followed the creek, it would eventually empty into one of the many stripper holes. During this period in the early 1900s, strip mining was already under way. A steam shovel would be moved in and dig a long strip of soil out of the ground. How deep the dig was depended upon how deep the coal vein was. The "strip" would be at least fifty feet wide, if not wider, to allow the steam shovel room to swing around and drop coal into the beds of trucks. These trucks would be lined up to haul the coal product away.

If the coal strike was large, and it usually was, then the steam shovel would dig another strip exactly parallel, so that the unwanted clay and shale from the second dig would be dumped in the huge original furrow. Just as on a plowed field, as furrow after furrow was overturned, the end result was rows and rows of stripper ridges. Then one long, deep stripper pit would remain unfilled. It would fill up with water from fifteen to forty feet deep. These pits were stocked with bass and bluegill. Occasionally muskrat and beaver also occupied the habitat.

During this era, the mining companies left the acreage of stripper hills as they were, and the Conservation Club planted evergreen trees on the hills. Later, the mining companies were required to flatten the hills for farming.

Just as important as fishing, the stripper pits became the site of all the local swimming. There were no swimming pools. With no supervision, there were occasional drownings. Shakamak State Park, where Hanno learned to swim, was more than ten miles away. It had supervised swimming and locker rooms for girls.

Everyone in the stripper pits swam in the nude. Girls were never seen either swimming or fishing. Sometimes, as sport during summer, some adults would bring their lady friends to show off the nude swimming. This caused all the young boys to huddle in the water until the onlookers got bored and left.

The Plum Branch pupils were told not to go into the hills, but the temptation was too great. Groups of kids would take their lunch and explore. They would follow the winding creek to where it emptied into the stripper pit. They could wander along the edge of the deep stripper pits, looking far down for the larger fish. They would climb the clay hills and organize clod fights from the molded clay. There was a strict rule against putting a rock into the molded clod ball.

For Hanno's new school experience, the stripper hills became the last and farthest level of the Plum Branch curriculum.

Hanno took one last look down the hill toward the creek and then entered the school building. The first thing that struck him was the smell. As one walked in the door, one was met with the aroma of the newly oiled wooden floor, the crayon smell, the new books, the newly varnished teacher's desk and chalk trays, and even the soapy smell of the newly scrubbed fellow pupils.

Inside the school, after the bell, came the next part of the education. Students were assigned their seats, and they put their books and supplies away in the storage space beneath their desktops. In the universal fashion, the front of each desk was the backrest of the student in front. With as many as eight grades during any given year, the desks were in eight vertical columns facing the front of the room. Each column of desks corresponded with a specific class level. Across the front and along the side walls, the blackboard was made from large slabs of pure slate. In the middle, above the blackboard, was a map case. Also, high on the walls on each side of the map case were the framed pictures of George Washington and Abraham Lincoln. George Washington, with his teeth pressed together, looked as if he would spare no quarter, especially while he had this annoying headache. Abraham Lincoln always looked as if he would give a pupil the benefit of the doubt if he or she were accused of whispering in class.

The most notable thing about the room was the absence of the teacher's desk in front. Okie Astrup was the teacher. Placing his desk in the back of the room was not an idle decision. If he were in front of the room, you knew when he was watching you. If he was behind you, you were in constant uncertainty. Sometimes you thoughtlessly took a chance to whisper or throw a paper wad—and lost.

Recitation was the centerpiece of the class activity. On the first day the students had a practice drill of the procedure. On a strict schedule, the classes would be called in turn to recite. They would rise from their desks and stand with their toes along the line. The line was painted on the floor in front of the teacher's desk. Here they might be asked to report their assigned homework, answer questions, or read from their textbooks. If it was time for arithmetic problems, the class would retire to the blackboard.

The teacher's desk was slightly elevated on a platform. This allowed Astrup to scan occasionally over the reciting class onto the backs of the heads of the other children. They were expected to be silent and upright in their seats. The recitation was interrupted any time there was whispering, a pupil playing with the red curls of a girl seated in front of him, or other misconduct among the seated pupils. This included the passing of notes or the shooting of paper wads with rubber bands.

After the allotted recitation, the pupils were given homework and excused to their seats. Another class would then be called to "toe the line."

Each day in school brought a new experience. The leaves of the trees turned yellow, gold, and brown. Halloween came, and students cut out pumpkins, black cats, and witches. Christmas came, and Hanno learned the little piece he was to say before the assembly of parents. Each day, when they returned from noon recess, the pupils in the lower grades went to the blackboard nearest to their seats. There they would write the numbers in proper order as far as they could go. The upper left corner of the blackboard began with 1. Without words to explain it, Hanno could soon see the structure of three- and four-digit numbers of the decimal system. Each column had ten digits.

Another experience from first grade was singing. On a side blackboard, Mr. Astrup put the lyrics to "Nobody's Darling but Mine."

Come sit by my side, little darling,
And place your cool hand on my brow.
And promise me that you will never
Be nobody's darling but mine.

The five kids in Hanno's first grade were not expected to read these lyrics, but they were expected to sing along.

From that early experience, Hanno knew how to spell the word *darling*. *Darling* was not a first-grade word, so it became a landmark in his education. It was a good word.

The joy and advantage of the one-room schoolhouse was that the faster your class recited and sat down, the sooner you could sit and listen to the fascinating things being taught at the other class levels. Although one was supposed to be tending to one's own homework, Hanno did not do so unless he was being watched. It was easy to pretend you were reading a book when you were actually listening. Some kids without foresight or planning would not have their books out, and the teacher would detect such and ask why. Since the teacher had to attend closely to the grade level reciting in front of him, this monitoring of the other classes seldom caught anyone.

Okie Astrup was a teacher who could make history come especially alive. Whether it was Washington and his troops crossing the Delaware, the Gettysburg Address, or Lincoln's anguish in the telegraph office as Sherman's Army was out of communication, you felt you were there. With the winter of suffering at Valley Forge, the entire schoolroom was transported to the scene. Each pupil braved the freezing waters and the deep snow. The students could not wait until the next day's episode. The homework was done later.

The joy of the one-room schoolhouse was not limited to listening to the classes ahead of you. You could also review what you missed in a previous year. Learning how to use the tenses in a sentence or how to carry over in subtraction could become clearer if you listened to it a second or third time. Among the many choices, you could also attend to what was taught at one's own grade level.

Punishment at Plum Branch was both strict and consistent. It occurred on three levels: a stern reminder, the nose in a ring, and the whipping. Stern reminders were very rare. In most cases a transgression took place with full knowledge and understanding of the rules. If the misconduct was more deliberate, then the second level, nose in the ring, was called for. As many as three, four, or five might be undergoing it at the same time.

With any such transgression, the teacher asked Hanno (or another urchin) to arise and come to the blackboard. When facing the blackboard, which was always dusty with chalk, Hanno was asked to get as high on his tiptoes as possible and then touch the blackboard with his nose. One's nose always had enough oil on it to leave a mark. Then the teacher asked Hanno to step back. The teacher would then take a piece of chalk and draw a circle about three inches in diameter around the nose mark. Hanno then had to regain the position on tiptoes, place his nose on the blackboard within the circle, and remain there until the teacher excused him to go sit down.

Hanno had his share of occasions to participate in this ritual. He might turn around and look at Newt in the seat behind him or look at the material on Newt's desk. He might whisper. He might even try his marksmanship with a paper wad. Unlike some of the other students, the punishment for Hanno seemed a kind of transaction. Hanno continued to be the top of his class, if not the whole school. The teacher was always cordial as he administered the ritual. Hanno was always cordial in his participation. Hanno finally came to feel that the exercise on his nose made it grow.

One day, a shy, small, blonde first-grade girl was caught whispering and was required for the first time to have her nose in the ring. Mr. Astrup was involved in a recitation and overlooked her briefly. A student in class noted her distress and pointed to the teacher and then to her. As the teacher looked, there was a broad stream of tears that ran from the circle on the blackboard down to the chalk tray. She had been crying in complete silence. The teacher asked her to return to her seat. He did not give the consummatory lecture warning. She continued to have tears at her seat. Never again was she asked to approach the blackboard and put her nose in a ring.

The whippings were for more severe transgressions, such as lying, stealing, or hurting someone with intent in a fight on the playground. Throughout elementary school during this era, teachers had different practices. Some had wooden paddles hanging in view on hooks. Some had razor straps hanging there. Some used their belts. Women teachers usually used rulers or sent children to the principal. At Plum Branch, in keeping with its natural setting, a switch was broken off from a limb in the forest and trimmed down to be suitable for the job. At Plum Branch the whippings were done in the entranceway outside the room. Other pupils saw nothing, but they could hear it well. Sometimes twigs or a piece of the whip broke off and flew through the open door. No other pupil ever seemed to know exactly what the crime was. More than one of Hanno's friends said that they would far prefer whippings over lectures by their fathers when they got home. Hanno's conduct at Plum Branch did not merit any whippings. In spite of all the discussion, a whipping occurred only two or three times a year.

Hanno made a strategic mistake in the middle of the first grade when he found that the encyclopedias were in a nearby bookcase. He set a goal to start with *A* and proceed, page by page, through to *Z*. Each time he finished reciting, he would go immediately to the bookcase. The teacher, however, became annoyed that Hanno was not returning first to his homework just assigned. He forbade Hanno to go to the bookcase until he completed his homework. This humiliated Hanno, so he dropped the project altogether. Here was an instance where Hanno, in his own private world, made a decision about what was right and what was wrong. He had an unspoken disagreement with his teacher. In retrospect, Hanno realized that he also erred. He should have persisted with the encyclopedia project at a different time.

Hanno committed another transgression that was never detected. After Hanno was able to master the word *darling* in the first grade, he became especially proficient in spelling in the second and third grade. On each Friday afternoon, the teacher conducted a spelling bee for all grade levels of the school. Hanno tended to excel in this spelldown. In more than one Friday, he and two eighth-grade girls were the only ones left standing before Hanno finally missed his word. One day Hanno decided that he would miss a word in order to break the spell (pun intended). The teacher called off *beautiful* on the weekly written test. Hanno put down "beuatiful." As the test ended, the teacher graded the spelling cards. Holding his marking pencil in hand, he said, "All correct, as usual." Hanno's heart sank as he watched the teacher start to enter the grade. Then he said, "Oh, wait!" He paused. "No," he said. "One is wrong." All in the room heard. The teacher looked disappointed as he entered Hanno's score. Hanno felt relaxed. He now belonged.

At home, another event occurred during the Plum Branch years. In the first grade, following the Christmas program for the parents, Hanno went home for the holidays with his bag of candy. It was December 21, 1934.

On December 24, Hanno awoke and came out into the dining room. To his surprise, the cot on which Granddad slept near the warm Florence heater was all neatly made up. The pillow was placed carefully below the top sheet and blanket. That amount of care to bed making early in the morning was odd. On some days, the cot would go all day without being made up.

"Where's Granddad?" Hanno asked.

Hanno's parents feared that Hanno, being close to Granddad, would collapse in tears. Emotion was something the parents believed was bad for young children. The made-up cot cornered his parents, so they had to disclose.

"Grandpa passed away last night. The hearse from the funeral home has already come. They took him to the funeral home."

Both of Hanno's parents were uneasy. However, the outpouring of tears did not occur. Instead, he was curious about the details.

"How could the funeral car get all the way to the house through the snow and mud?"

"It didn't," said Dad. "I took him by the horse and sled over to the mailbox. We called and arranged to meet the hearse there."

So, as it turned out, barely more than three months after Hanno's landmark sled ride to the first day of school,

Granddad had his farewell ride away from the homestead he and his wife had put their hearts and lives into.

As usual, Hanno's parents left him alone to go about their work, and as usual, Hanno dreamed. He was too young to imagine the future, too young to miss his old partner, too young to be driven to tears from his loss. He understood only about the present. Hanno was starting to build his own private world, of which other people were not a part. In so doing, he sat by the Florence heater and did something that he would continue to do for the rest of his life when someone died. He would dream back of the good memories and say good-bye to the one who had passed on.

The dreams had a pleasant allure. Hanno dreamed of teasing Grandpa David, and he would say, "Take care. T'care." Both he and his Grandpa liked to rake leaves, and there was only one rake. They would sometimes fight over it. He was stronger and he won. Grandpa would put Hanno across his boney knee and jostle him up and down as he sang (How it hurt!):

Old Dan Tucker was a fine old man.
He washed his face in a frying pan.
He combed his hair with a wagon wheel,
And died with a toothache in his heel.

As the family worked in the fields, Hanno's job was to keep an eye on him. He had developed a bad memory. If he wandered off by himself, no one would know the direction. The forest? The gravel roads? The pastures or stripper hills?

As a preschooler Hanno discovered his job was important but a challenge. Grandpa would often arise from his chair and say, "It is time for me to go home." Hanno quickly learned that the old man would not accept his account of the facts. Hanno could not just say, "You *are* home."

Hanno quickly learned that he was too small and not strong enough to restrain him. And it was up to Hanno. There was no one to call for help. But Hanno found the solution. He would allow Grandpa to leave the house and walk down the lane. He would then run to catch up.

"Grandpa," he would say. "Where are you going?"

"I'm going home."

"Can I go with you?"

"That's fine."

After a few steps, Hanno would then say, "Grandpa, you made a wrong turn. There is your house, back there."

"Oh? Yes, yes. I see. So I did."

Grandpa would then return to the house, take off his jacket, and sit back down in his chair as if nothing happened. If queried at end of day, Grandpa would say that he was taking care of Hanno. And maybe he was.

As Hanno returned from his dreams a touch of sadness remained. Granddad's body traversed in the bottom of the sled. It was only eight inches above the sled runners that plowed the mud and snow. It seemed that Granddad deserved better than that.

Granddad's life had been a heroic one. The homestead was where his daddy, the bound boy, had raised him. It was where he stayed on and cared for the old man to the end. It was where he brought Celester to marry and raise a family. It was where they, as a couple, struggled to build the two-story mansion. It was where he had brought in granddaughters Ruth and Jean when their mother died.

Hanno did not realize until years later that he played a silent role in his grandfather's death. When he entered the first grade, a significant balance of energy took place on the homestead. Hanno's caretaking work was replaced at school by the panorama of new experiences. Even when he returned home, the school-related activity took up his attention. Without giving it much thought, he overheard his parents saying what a burden the caretaking of Granddad had become with Hanno gone. For Granddad, the departure of Hanno during the day was a major loss. He lost his only true companion. There was no occasional grandparenting duty, no story to tell, and no song to sing. He was no longer of any use.

That Christmas of 1934 was a sad but memorable one. Hanno could see the sadness in the grown-ups. Granddad passed away on December 24. Hanno's parents had to be on hand for the days of receiving visitors to the casket. Hanno spent the holiday hours on the carpeted floor of Harry Welch's office in the funeral home.

Because of the expense of the funeral and the expenses of living and eating in town, Hanno's parents were truly broke. Hanno's brothers each got a pocketknife and two large oranges for Christmas. Hanno was given two large oranges and a cardboard toy cat that mechanically wagged its tail as it rolled across the floor. Harry Welch (who had saved his own cast-iron train from childhood) surprised Hanno by buying him a tin train, spring-operated, that ran on a circular track. Harry got down on the floor in his office and helped Hanno assemble the track.

As well as the soft gentle facade he felt required of an undertaker, Harry Welch also had mischievous tricks. Often with babies and children, he would fold a handkerchief into his hand to resemble a rabbit with long ears. The impromptu puppet would then perform several antics. For adult entertainment, he had a factory sample of a casket six inches long. The casket had a secret opening in the bottom. When unobserved, Harry would powder his thumb and slip it through the hole in the bottom of the miniature casket. He would then tell an onlooker that he wanted to show an example of his embalming. In the casket, he said, was a thumb that had been severed from a man killed in an accident. He would then open the lid of the casket, and the powdered thumb would be resting on a pink satin pillow. He would say, "I embalmed this thumb separately and put it in this little casket. Don't you think that is a good job of embalming? Looks natural and alive, doesn't it? Touch it to see how soft it is." If he could persuade the onlooker to touch the thumb, Harry would do a quick thumbs-up. Even adults would startle and jump.

As best Hanno can recall, he remained in Harry's office during the funeral service itself, but he was brought out immediately afterward for the final viewing of the body. During this final viewing, Hanno's uncle Porter Oglesby began to cry. Hanno's father jumped immediately to Hanno and tried to drag him away so that he would not witness this emotion. His father was too late, and Hanno saw Uncle Port crying from the loss of his daddy. Hanno immediately began to cry.

After the burial service at Fairview Cemetery, Hanno's family finally returned to the homestead. When Hanno arrived home, he went immediately to his school material and opened his first-grade reader, *Trips to Take*. He read to himself the first lesson he had received back in September:

I am Jack.
I am a boy.
I have a dog.
His name is Tan.
I have a pony.
His name is Dan.

I am Jill …

As Hanno read these words, he became eager to go back to Plum Branch. He had said his good-bye privately to a very lovable grandfather, and he was ready to move on.

[14]

GRACE

The incident happened when Hanno was in the first grade at Plum Branch. It raised the hair on the back of his neck. For seventy-two years, Hanno told no one. You will soon know why. It was 1935, and the country was in the Great Depression. The pupils of Plum Branch did not fully realize this. All of them were poor. All of them felt uncommonly rich. They went barefoot all summer, and they learned about the Depression from their parents fearing they would have no shoes to start school in September.

It was early spring, still snowy, and Hanno was enjoying the Plum Branch experience. Okie Astrup, he felt, was one of the greatest teachers. Hanno would sit quietly and listen to the upper classes recite. He came to feel that what the higher grades studied was far more interesting than the exercises given the first-graders.

Hanno's class of five first-graders had just been called to recite. They took their homework and textbooks to the back of the room and put their toes on the line.

Near Hanno's seat was an erect coal stove. A small fire was burning inside. Its belly became red-hot on cold winter days. Even though it had a partial shield around it, Hanno was left burning on one side of his body and freezing on the other.

Absolute silence was expected throughout the rest of the room when a class recited. The students knew from experience that Mr. Astrup could scan the room while conducting a recital. As first-graders, Hanno's class members were not exactly clear that teachers did not get paid well. No one within miles could afford a tractor, but almost every family had at least one horse. Almost all families had a half-dozen cows. They provided dairy and beef products for the table or to sell. But Okie had none of these. He did not make enough money from teaching to get a farm started. No cow was available to provide milk for the baby. Instead, when summer vacation time came, he took on jobs with neighbors, putting up hay, picking fruit, and doing other projects.

Okie's house was the first one north of the school. You went down the hill, crossed the bridge over Plum Branch Creek, and ascended the next hill. All was forest on either side of the road. Hanno's mother once made a cloth doll for the Astrup baby. When Hanno and his mother brought it to the baby, it did not occur to Hanno that no cow, horse, or pig was around. It was said that teachers did not get their rewards in this world. They must surely get them in the next.

On this day, shortly after the noon hour, as Hanno had finished toeing the line, a surprise visitor appeared in the doorway. Mr. Astrup was stunned to see his wife and baby. Acting very distraught, his wife was shouting, pleading, and yelling. She raved that Mr. Astrup was not paying attention to the support of his family, that there was a shortage of money for food, rent, and the baby's needs. She said he did not provide any hope for a better house, better income, or better future. Mr. Astrup's response was to remove himself to the opposite side of the room from her. With the baby in her arms, she approached him at times with apparent intent to hit him. He would immediately move and remain opposite her. With all the student seats in the middle of the classroom, the teacher, his wife, and the baby rotated around the perimeter. He was pale and speechless.

With Mr. Astrup remaining silent, his wife continued for almost an hour. Finally, she grew weary and exited the room. Mr. Astrup, without making any comment, resumed his usual teaching duties. But now he was sober and subdued.

As usual, recess came and everybody was immediately out on the playground. It was not too difficult for Garry Powell and George Lawson to carry out their plan. They got together with every single group playing on the schoolyard.

Garry and George were eighth-graders. Hanno knew them, but until that day, he had been more concerned with his own age group. So it came as a surprise when they interrupted Hanno and his mates. They talked of what had happened in class. They told all the students not to tell their parents, neighbors, siblings, or anyone ever about what had happened. They asked them to go about school and home as if this incident had never happened. Hanno and his playmates stood quietly and listened. Garry and George looked them intently in the eyes. Hanno had never seen them so serious. They did not want to see their teacher humiliated in the community, and they felt confident that the money problem would get solved. Hanno and his playmates promised.

Certainly, if Garry Powell and George Lawson had not made the rounds to visit all the pupils during recess, this happening would have been the first topic to spring from the lips of the young ones the instant they arrived home. Instead, if anyone asked, it was just a routine day.

Now, after all those years, all the principal players in the drama are dead but Hanno. Okie Astrup, like his father, the school bus driver, lived to be over one hundred. During his prime years, Okie became legendary for one-room schoolhouse education. The Great Depression is in the past, but the public attitude and policy toward schoolteachers can still be found. The real legacy was the group of students, what they had learned, and what they later sang. He was deserving of the title of Hoosier schoolmaster.

As Hanno tells of this day, his thoughts focus with respect and gratitude for the two eighth-grade Plum Branch boys. There was nothing special about them, Hanno thought. Isn't that right?

[15]

NAME

Hanno was not free of the tendency to want to conform. He did not like to stand out as different from others. As mentioned before, when he became aware that other kids were looking on him as different because he was a good speller, he deliberately misspelled a word on his weekly spelling test to rid himself of the stigma.

It is not surprising then that Hanno became preoccupied with his name. By the time he was well into the first grade, he had determined that no one he knew had the name Hanno—none, that is, except his Uncle Hanno, for whom he was named. At least around Linton, the name was an oddity. The longer he thought about it and the more comments that strangers made, the more he wanted to change from Hanno to another name.

Arming himself to face resistance or refusal from his parents, he approached them. He informed them that he was unhappy with his name and wanted to change it.

To Hanno's utter surprise, both of his parents were accommodating. It was as if they had already anticipated the possibility.

"You decide what name you want, and we will go to the court and have it changed."

So came the second surprise. Not only were they willing to have his name changed, but also they granted him total responsibility for choosing a new name. Thus it was that Hanno was left alone to choose a new name. Somehow, the satisfaction Hanno anticipated in having a new name was at least partly from winning over the resistance. Since this resistance did not exist, the joy of having a name change diminished. Another factor was in the choosing. One by one, as Hanno examined new names, he did not like them.

The name that came close was Paul. For several days, he thought about naming himself Paul. Finally, in a close call, he decided he would prefer Hanno to Paul. There seemed to be more pride in the name Hanno.

Neither Hanno nor his parents realized it, but Hanno's Uncle Hanno, for whom he was named, actually did change his name. He had chosen the name Roy. This did not keep Uncle Hanno from being pleased to learn there had been somebody named after him as Hanno.

It took about a month, but finally, Hanno was ready. He went to his parents and announced to them that he could not think of a better name. Hanno, it was going to be.

In years to come, Hanno's major memory about this period was that, while he often disagreed with his parents' decisions, especially in child-rearing, this was one instance when they made a superior decision. To be in charge of one's destiny and to be without counter advice allowed Hanno to be more stably committed to his identity.

[16]

PONDERING

When one is placed in the middle of a scene where there is little to look at and nothing is changing, one's balance of awareness leans away from attending to external events. Instead, one is driven toward dreaming and thinking. One deals with material already collected and how it is collected. When Hanno was assigned to guarding cows, this was what happened.

The reason for guarding cows was controversial. Whether the cows needed to be guarded—whether fragile fencing might allow them to get into green crops—could be argued. Whether the green crops would sicken them was more certain. That Hanno's mother used this task to get Hanno away and to provide privacy for her own affair was the viable explanation.

Regardless of the origin of his task, Hanno reported significant subjective events from his gazing. In the remote southeast corner of the homestead was a pasture with one lone shade tree in the middle. Hanno would sit on the ground and lean back on the trunk of this tree. Occasionally, he would count the cows in order to ensure that none had strayed. While doing this, he noticed something he called "delayed counting." To do delayed counting, he would choose a given target, such as the head of a cow amidst the herd. He would passively gaze at that spot for four or five seconds. Then, before moving his eyes away, he would close them in order to capture the image he was observing. He would turn his head away from the cattle but keep his eyes closed. If he had held his focus steady, he could now, with eyes closed, still see the image of the cows. At this point, he could count the cows as they stood in the image. If he chose, he could count other objects in the scene as well. The image lasted at least four or five seconds.

Hanno would then usually open his eyes, look back at the herd, and count them to check the accuracy of his delayed counting. Hanno could usually count up to twelve to fourteen objects before the image faded.

Years later, when Hanno was in college, he learned that these enduring sensations were called *eidetic images*. Unfortunately, by this later time, Hanno had lost his eidetic skill. Did Hanno become a good speller because of his skill in eidetic imagery? He does not know.

The other two experiences were more frightening to Hanno. They involved words. The words were *eternity* and *infinity*.

Eternity, as presented to Hanno, was defined as endless time. Hanno did not feel he had a full grasp of endless time. All things came to an end, he felt. Nothing lasted forever. There was even the love song, "Till the End of Time." Yet, if one were to identify a marker in the ongoing stream of events that was the end, then there *had* to be something beyond the marker. Hanno's thinking led to two ideas: (a) any marker to designate an end point in time would always imply that something would occur beyond that marker, but (b) with distant markers, a point in time would come when the outer limits of the time span cannot be defined. That is, we could count and measure things and thereby grasp an understanding. Beyond the imagined "last marker," we would be unable to count, measure, observe, or apply traditional mathematics. We would be out of control. Hanno found himself unable to confirm or disconfirm that eternity itself must come to an end. The idea was upsetting.

Infinity, as it was presented to Hanno, referred to endless space (or distance). Hanno had learned if the stars and planets of other systems were toward the outer edge of the universe, then other heavenly bodies not visible were likely beyond. However, the idea of infinity represented a different challenge. As usual, Hanno began his thinking with what was proximal. Proximal objects had limits designated by length, width, and height. By definition, if all three were designated, then the object was finite. To become infinite, at least one of the measures must be violated in an amount that exceeded measurability. If one looked off into infinite space, then one had a natural presumption that, sooner or later, all things must come to an end.

Yet, if you got to the end, there must be distance beyond that. If the distance beyond that was some designated outer limit, then that was not infinity. If, however, the outer limit was not identifiable, then finite space had been breached. However, at the same time, the criterion for infinity had been met, the outer domain defied measurement. The role of mathematics, counting, or other observation was precluded. If there was no math, counting, measurement, or other observation, then there was no apprehension. Either infinity was, by definition, beyond apprehension or fraudulent. With such uncertainty, Hanno could not abide. As with the notion of eternity, he returned to the house trembling.

Hanno had worked himself into a panic. At his young age, he was thinking of eternity and infinity as absolute concrete features of reality, separate and independent from any human being. As Hanno viewed the contradictions in the terms *eternity* and *infinity*, it seemed as if no concept anywhere could be firmly trusted. He felt the earth had been torn apart. He could not share this with the twins, for they would ridicule him. He could not share it with his parents, for they had come to accept absolutes without question. He was alone and frightened.

He realized, as an educated adult, that all constructs were merely frail human attempts to develop a code for communication, that all words, including *eternity* and *infinity*, were only arbitrary tools that lasted as long as they allowed human beings to anticipate the events unfolding before them.

History has shown that a newborn must start from a bleak beginning to create concepts and counting. Certain ones of these methods become broadly applied and highly useful. Once we can carry these out without awareness of our actions, we confer on them the status of being absolute, even though we were the imperfect creatures that created them. But then, when we discover that these taken-for-granted notions are flawed and unable to solve certain problems, then we undergo a revolution in what we call absolute truth. But Hanno did not know this earlier on, when he was frightened by these ideas.

Then concepts are not absolute in meaning. They lack any certitude beyond the limits of the person who invented or used them. Hanno came to realize that human beings create a reality from the sum of these observations and ideas, but then, once created, it is not to be viewed as absolute and transcendent beyond human beings. Instead, human beings, as imperfect creators of constructs, transcend reality and its respective constituents.

[17]

STORM

There is no way to describe it. It seemed that nothing different was going on. Yet there was. Hanno, like other young children, had this sudden impulse to run, run fast. Then came the nosebleed. Not every child was prone to nosebleeds with a drop in barometric pressure, but Hanno was. True, he knew of no such phrase as *barometric pressure* and would not know until years later. Yet something was happening.

Hanno's mother would get him a large bleached cloth to hold to his nose and catch the blood. She would have him hold his head back so the blood inside his nose would clot more quickly. Hanno's mother kept these ripped up cloths in a clean bushel basket. He did not know why until he was fifteen and worked in the Rexall drugstore when he saw the richer ladies of the city come in to buy Kotex or sometimes Tampax. He had known of no such items. Still later in life, he connected these to the basket of bleached cloths.

The drop in barometric pressure and the coming storm did not seem to energize the adults. You could only see it in the children and the farm animals. It was when Hanno's father saw the cows "bulling" each other that he knew it was time to make haste. *Bulling* means that the Jersey milk cows will climb onto each other's backs as if trying to copulate. Hanno's dad would call to Hanno's brothers, "There's going to be a goose drownder. Get the horses into the barn."

Sometimes during these few minutes before the downpour, a pair of light-blue river birds would fly by. It was a strange new sight because they did not inhabit the area. The drop in barometric pressure seemed to throw them off course. When this happened, it instilled panic in Hanno's father. He was not ordinarily superstitious, but an event such as this got to him.

The father's job with an oncoming storm was to avoid danger. The horses would stampede with lightning and thunder. They could possibly injure themselves. As the first step, they had to be in the barn with the door-latched top and bottom. No one should be caught standing under a tree to avoid the rain. No one should be near any metal equipment, such as a pump or iron cable. One of the neighbors had been killed on a tractor. Another hit a high wire with his corn planter.

So, one by one, the Buchwald family would gather inside the house. The gathering place was the screened porch, where all would watch the oncoming storm. All were safe from the pump, downspouts, and cables from the lightning rods. Some sat on the concrete steps leading into the inner house. Chairs were brought out for others. During nosebleed time, a bucket of fresh, cool water was brought from the barnyard well, and Hanno's mother made Kool-Aid. If the storm was in cool late fall, Hanno's mother and father might have some Sanka or Postum.

They would settle in and watch the oncoming spectacle. With the new house being on high ground, they could see the storm coming from miles away. There were distant bursts of lightning and then, after many seconds, the soft rumble of thunder. As the black clouds gathered, they could see sheets of rain falling in rhythm on farm fields a mile away. All of the family would speculate about whether the storm would continue in their direction. The adults' views depended upon whether the crops needed it. The young people wanted it too, simply for the excitement.

The lightning began to come closer, the thunder louder. Soon they would see a single burst of lightning, followed in a split second by a large, startling blast of thunder. Then they knew they were in the path of violence. They would discuss whether the house, one of the farm buildings, or a barnyard tree might be hit.

With the large storms it was almost certain that one or two trees in the forest would be hit and have split trunk or main branches. Once such a tree was found, and if it could not survive, it was usually put on the list of work items to be sawed down and chopped up for firewood. However, if it were the disappearing black walnut, it would be preserved for furniture making in high-school wood shop.

With the lightning and thunder hovering overhead, a strange few seconds of quiet occurred until that first heavy drop of rain banged onto the tin roof of the pantry adjacent to the screened porch, then another and another.

The atmosphere, even inside the screened porch, became more intense, cool, and quiet.

As the storm picked up, increasing from the patter of drops into a steady and then heavy downpour, the question turned to whether hail would follow the onset of the rain. If hail came, the tin roof above the pantry would bang loudly. The family would see hail stones bouncing off the shale and the grass outside the porch. For Hanno, who had never seen a refrigerator with an ice cube, this was the most exciting of all.

Once the rain became continuous, the pent-up energy was turned into song. Hanno's mom would step into the kitchen for the pitcher of Kool-Aid or (non) iced tea. Hanno's brothers led the singing, although his father and sometimes everyone joined in. Hanno's brothers were especially good at harmonizing with such songs as "Red River Valley," "Wreck of the 97," and "Casey Jones." On one such occasion, a classmate Billy Headley was there with his guitar in order to practice for a high-school musical concert.

Hanno cannot recall a time when any of the family returned to their regular work after a storm. Usually it was dark before the rain completely stopped. Hanno's mother would go up to the second floor after the deluge to see if any neighbors' homes had been hit. If still daylight, she would look for the plume of smoke. If dark, she would look for the glow in the sky. The next morning, if there were newly plowed ground, Jay and Ray would put on overshoes and wander through the wet sod of the field. If any flint arrowheads or tomahawk heads showed up from the plowing, the heavy rain would have washed a surface until it was detectable. Hanno, fully recovered from his nosebleed, would observe and remember.

[18]

TWINS

The story of Hanno's two brothers may be found not only in this chapter but also in other chapters concerning the war, the family, and Hanno.

The twins were born in November 1921, and Hanno was born in November 1928. Thus the twins had seven years to garner the full attention of their parents. For this group of siblings two peak periods of conflict occurred. The first was when Hanno came home from the hospital. The second was when the twins entered high school and Hanno was in the second and third grades.

The first peak is common to all families, as older siblings must share parental attention with a new and helpless infant. The second peak arose from the fact that entry into high school brought a new crop of friends who came visiting the Buchwald house to see Jay and Ray. Devoid of playmates at the isolated homestead Hanno was also attracted to these newcomers. The attraction was so strong that he felt that he would never have friends his own age so attractive. The attraction was reciprocated and these friends enjoyed spending time with Hanno as well as Jay and Ray. Since Jay and Ray were also deprived of social contact, the anger and competition toward Hanno intensified.

In the peak of this negative reaction, Jay told Hanno that he and Ray were going to take a butcher knife from the kitchen and cut Hanno up into small pieces. Then they would scatter these pieces widely through the countryside. In this way, no one would ever find him. Finally, people would come to forget that Hanno ever existed. With this threat came the usual rider that if Hanno reported to his parents the execution would come sooner.

Unfortunately Hanno was of an age where he took such a threat seriously. He believed. For the first time in Hanno's life, he developed a persistent anxiety. Rather than being focused upon the conflict with his brothers, he came in general to expect that something bad was going to happen to him. His orientation toward seeing the positive satisfactions in life—just having fun—was replaced with an effort to keep ahead of some threat, injury, or death that was going to overtake him. He became fearful that he was mentally ill, although he did not know exactly what that meant. As time passed, the details of these events faded from memory. Only the nervousness remained. Then with writing and talking, the details returned to match the emotional pain. Even now, Hanno has the fear that there may not be a gravestone or marker to identify his remains. He wants it to be known that "there once was a time when a boy named Hanno Buchwald walked the earth."

When the twins were together, they acted in unison to oppose Hanno. When apart, Jay remained unchanged. Ray, however, relaxed his resistance to Hanno. He would sometimes act warmly, play with him, and talk to him. Ray's general personality was to be more sociable and conversational with everyone. He treated Hanno the same.

After Hanno became an adult, he realized that his parents treated him and the twins differently. The twins were treated as sportsmen, skilled craftsmen, and artists, whereas Hanno was treated as more fragile in health. This was probably because of the frequent nosebleeds, nervousness, and his dangerously avid bookworm habit. His mother, superstitious as she was, suspected that to read a lot, like Uncle Urban, could cause poor eyesight and epilepsy.

The twins were given fishing rods and reels, .410-gauge shotguns, fly rods, and steel traps for trapping ground animals. They prepared and dried the animal hides for tanning.

Hanno expected that he would be given the same presents when he came of the same age, but it did not happen. Hanno was given a bamboo fishing pole, fishing line, a sinker, a cork, hooks of different sizes, and lots of books. Hanno caught bluegills in the pasture pond on the homestead. With an available shotgun from the house, he shot an occasional rabbit or squirrel in the near woods or in the garden. He did not participate in the long hunting and fishing trips with relatives and family friends. Early on, Hanno's father had invited the twins to come along.

The gifts bestowed upon Hanno at each appropriate age were mostly books. Like the gifts for the twins, the books were chosen and given by his father. This difference may have occurred because his father discovered that he was nimble with alphabetic blocks and numbers. First came the Big Little Books about Shirley Temple, Frank Buck (jungle explorer), Tarzan, and others. Later came youth novels, such as *Dick Prescott's Second Year at West Point* and *The Young Engineers.*

Unfortunately Hanno, with this pressure, did curb his reading. He continued the habit somewhat with a flashlight under the covers. Once he went to school, however, his reading could no longer be controlled.

As for other playthings, neither the twins nor Hanno ever owned a basketball (almost unheard of in the Hoosier state), a baseball, softball, or bat. The family was too poor to have committed themselves to these luxuries. Whenever money was available, Hanno's mother was mindful that if there was not enough for presents for all three, no one got anything. Finally in high school, with the twins already in military service, Hanno used his newspaper route and yard-mowing money to buy a softball. How wonderful it smelled! Then a family whose son had perished gave him a baseball glove, a football, and a Boy Scout bugle. It came to be that Hanno's athletic ability was limited to running. The twins, unable to practice basketball at home, participated on the junior varsity team in a limited capacity.

As the twins graduated from Midland High School in the 1930s, the Depression was highly evident. During the summer before their senior year in high school, Jay was hired for farm labor at one dollar a day. But this was only temporary. The twins considered the Civilian Conservation Corps (the CCC). Their father had been rejected from the WPA for being on the wrong side of local politics. The twins' high-school graduation approached, and there was no local work. One day they seized upon the idea of joining the Navy. The outcome was that Jay entered the Navy right away. Ray remained home for a while and then joined the Army.

A significant event in the life of Hanno came on the day his brother Jay left home to go to the Great Lakes Naval Training Station in Evanston, Illinois. Jay was eighteen, and Hanno was eleven. When the hour came for Jay to catch the bus for Terre Haute, he went throughout the house and basement to say good-bye to each family member. Hanno was in his room working on homework. He could hear the parting words as Jay said his proud good-byes. He then stepped out of the front door and headed down the driveway. Hanno, realizing he had been passed over, arose and stepped out on the front porch. Jay, hearing the screen door close, turned and looked back. Hanno said nothing. Jay raised his arm slightly to Hanno and pointed his thumb down toward the ground. Not only did he decline to say good-bye, but also he refused to wave properly to Hanno. Jay turned away and continued walking. Hanno, saying nothing, returned inside.

Hanno had years of training from Okie Astrup at Plum Branch School about how noble it is to serve and, if necessary, to die for one's country. Hanno felt a pride in his older brother going off to serve his country. As World War II loomed, Hanno easily set aside the hurt feelings arising from Jay's unresolved sibling conflict. It was a time in history when it was all about the war and the demands on the home front.

[19]

AUNT LIZZIE

As Hanno grew up on the farm, he assumed that every family had a person like Aunt Lizzie. Some families do. They are the lucky ones. In the early days, Hanno took Aunt Lizzie for granted. What he did not take for granted was Aunt Lizzie's house. For a farm boy, it was a look into paradise. It taught Hanno how town folks lived.

Standing out most in memory was the lightbulb. It was amazing how one could screw a lightbulb into place, then turn the black switch, and the room was filled with light. What remained mysterious for many years was how electricity was consumed. To Hanno, the switch was the determining factor for electricity consumption. If the bulb was unscrewed, leaving the light off, Hanno assumed that the electricity would still be flowing unused until the switch was also turned off. Hanno would be annoyed at his father for unscrewing a bulb from a double socket but not turning off the switch. Years later, Hanno understood that a closed loop (circuit) of electric wire had to go from a lamp or appliance to the source generating the electricity and then another wire back to the lamp or appliance. Also, it was not clear until later that the breaking of that loop, whether by switch or otherwise, would stop all electric flow. Initially, to Hanno, any switch left closed (or on) was wasting electricity into the air.

Another fascination was with the flush toilet. It had been perfected in the 1880s by two British gentlemen, Thomas Crapper and Richard Humpherson. Hanno discovered that a small lever would release a tank of water into the toilet bowl to remove the waste and that it would refill to the proper level without running over. More than once Hanno turned the lever just to watch the action.

Yet another item of attraction was the spinning wheel. This one was not fully assembled to deal with yarn, but it had a small crank handle that allowed the large wooden wheel to be turned at high speed. Putting a pencil against the spokes of the big wheel produced a satisfying noise.

Another item of curiosity was the steam radiator. Turning the knob at the bottom right made the radiator become hot and eventually warm the room. More interesting, however, was the variety of sounds. At first there was a jolting sound throughout the house as the radiator was kicking in. Later, there was the pleasing purring and humming sounds as the radiator was happily doing its work.

In examining these objects, Hanno would sometimes cut or scratch himself. When he did so, Mercurochrome, or iodine later, would be applied to the wound. The red stain from the medicine helped Hanno feel much better.

Another feature in Aunt Lizzie's house was the Atwater Kent radio. It was a black metal cabinet with dials. Atop it was a round metal-framed speaker of fourteen inches in diameter. Aunt Lizzie had bought it back in the 1920s in hope that it would penetrate her deafness. She was never able to hear it. The signal was so strong, however, that it gathered many relatives during the world heavyweight prize fights of the 1930s. Hanno well remembers listening to the Joe Louis versus Max Scheming fights and the James Braddock championship. The static and other electronic interference were always there.

The central focus of interest for Hanno was the piano. Here Hanno profited greatly from the fact that Aunt Lizzie was profoundly deaf. (Back then the proper phrase was *stone deaf*.) This allowed Hanno to play uninterruptedly for hours. Such noise, and noise it was, was not entirely welcome to others. Also living in the house, and dependent upon Aunt Lizzie, were two of her sisters, also widows. There was Aunt Dale Letterman (great-grandmother of David Letterman) and Aunt Ida Strietelmeier. While both were disabled, they had the misfortune of being able to hear. It did not take long for one or the other to go to Aunt Lizzie and ask her to have Hanno stop banging on the piano. They knew Aunt Lizzie could not hear the noise. Thus, she hardly ever tended to take them seriously. Hanno was often allowed to continue. From this free exposure, Hanno learned to play "Chopsticks" and the Indiana University alma mater. Hanno was not a natural musician.

Aunt Lizzie, the youngest of the dazzling Malone girls, was the most aggressive and outgoing of the group. She was widowed and lost an adopted child long before Hanno was born. In spite of being deaf, or maybe because of it, she established a business as a florist. She was among the first group in Linton to have a telephone. Her first phone number was 6, then 66, and then on to larger numbers. She was the first in Linton to purchase a car. As mentioned elsewhere, this was a Model T Ford, purchased in a kit for $400 from the Sears Roebuck mail-order catalog. Hanno's father, just recently hired for delivery, was the first to be asked to learn to drive it. The sturdy car survived the stripping of gears.

Aunt Lizzie also eventually learned to drive. Being deaf before the rules of traffic and safety were adopted, Aunt Lizzie drove as if herding a cow along the road. If she was on the left side or the middle of the road and a car or bus came over the hill to face her, she considered it an act of mutual participation as to which was the passing side.

Aunt Lizzie was more adventurous than just having a phone and a car. She liked to fish, to hunt, and to camp. A Kodak picture revealed Aunt Lizzie sound asleep with both feet protruding from a tent. She loved flying in an airplane. It was a time when on Sunday afternoons, a pilot might land in the open field next to Haseman's Grove and take people for a half hour plane ride for a fee. She also loved to plan and take trips.

Aunt Lizzie's home and florist shop was on First and E Street Northeast. The backyard had a large L-shaped greenhouse with its own heating system. The porch was enclosed and converted into a flower shop. The flower shop had the large icebox for both cut flowers and food. It had floral displays for sale. The shop had bulletin boards for her sales notices and numerous articles of humor and general interest. Her favorite personality was Will Rogers. She kept articles and sayings by him on the wall of the flower shop. Most daring among the wall hangings was a framed picture of a cartoon figure in a tuxedo leaning drunk against a lamppost. The caption read:

A friend is not a fellow
Who is taken in by sham.
A friend is one who knows your faults
And doesn't give a damn.

During the 1930s and 1940s, this was a very daring poem for a lady to display. A Linton lady, even in business, was not expected to use the word *damn*.

As typical of Linton, most of Aunt Lizzie's flower business was for funerals. This did not stop her from posting a sign outside her house: "Send me flowers while I can smell them." Another read, "Say it with flowers."

Famous also among the memories from Aunt Lizzie's home was the milk and ice delivery. Each delivery was made with a single horse-drawn wagon. The milkman kept his horse in a slow pace without stopping. He would run to the houses with the milk in glass bottles with cream gathered at the top. He would grab the empty bottles and trot back to the moving milk wagon and get the milk for the next house. The milk was left outside the door.

The ice wagon required more time. In each house was a square sign with 25, 50, 75, and 100 at each base. This sign was placed in the window in the position so that the erect number indicated the number of pounds of ice needed. Usually Aunt Lizzie needed a hundred pounds.

The iceman used an ice pick to make clean straight cuts in the block of ice. He used tongs handily to carry the ice.

Aunt Lizzie kept among the cut flowers in her icebox a large ceramic pitcher of iced tea. No one's iced tea was like Aunt Lizzie's. It picked up the aroma of roses and other flowers in her icebox.

Aunt Lizzie was always blunt and outspoken. If she gave a wedding gift and the bride did not acknowledge it promptly, she would claim the late thank-you card was suspected to be a birth announcement. Once when discussing a former female acquaintance with Hanno's mother, she asked, "Does she still stink like she used to?"

Without sign language by hand, Aunt Lizzie used only lip-reading. She was highly skilled. Hanno's mother developed a skill, when talking to Aunt Lizzie, to move her lips without saying words or making noise. Aunt Lizzie could understand with no problem. As mentioned previously, this lip moving was usually done to discuss some scandalous or wayward behavior of a woman in the county. Hanno many times tried to move his lips without speech, but Aunt Lizzie could never understand him.

Aunt Lizzie took no prisoners when it came to telling stories. Once when she thought Hanno was out of reach, she told his mother a story about Lieutenant Governor Hardesty. Hardesty grew up in Linton, owned property, and had adopted two of Hanno's cousins. Yet he was a political figure, the object of many rumors, and loved to display his masculine demeanor. Once on Main Street in front of the People's Trust Company, he was chatting on the sidewalk with some of his constituents. Out of the bank came the elegant Mrs. Hamilton, fitted out with veiled hat and kid gloves. She spotted Lieutenant Hardesty, threw her head in the air, and marched by him without speaking. Her shunning was apparent to all present. After a moment of silence, Hardesty said, "I made love to her last night, and this morning, I do not get even a simple hello."

Aunt Lizzie loved surprise parties. During Hanno's seventeen years living in Linton, Aunt Lizzie must have had at least fourteen of them. Should she see people laughing, she would never attribute the laughing to herself. Instead, it was a show of happiness for her presence. This was illustrated once dramatically when all the relatives and friends were gathered in her front room with the lights off, waiting for her and Hanno's mother to return from shopping. People sat, stood, and huddled in wait. Finally, the outside door to the flower shop came open. In hushed silence, all were prepared to sing "Happy birthday to you." As the shop door closed, Martin Oglesby, a young prankster, released a long, loud fart. Immediately, he yelled, "My father Port did that!" This event brought an uproar of laughter as Aunt Lizzie opened the door to the living room and turned the lights on. In the turmoil, the "Happy Birthday" song was forgotten. Aunt Lizzie attributed all the laughter to the joy people felt in her presence. And she said so. And no one disputed it. She did not learn about Martin's expulsive prank.

Hanno was sometimes the butt of Aunt Lizzie's humor and quick wit. It was not often that all the great-aunts had sufficient health for an outing together. However, on one occasion, Aunt Lizzie arranged a picnic at Spring Mill State Park for Aunt Dale, Aunt Ida, Hanno's mother, Hanno, and herself. In many ways this was an exciting experience for Hanno. It was his first introduction to olives. They were stuffed with pimento. He ate the stuffing separately to examine each flavor. He had the rare experience of bologna on white store-bought bread. Store-bought white bread were a delicacy that he would often eat by itself. Homemade bread was onerous.

One event, however, became the center of attention for the elderly ladies. Hanno discovered a hole in the ground, a few inches in diameter, that emitted cool air from a natural underground cave system. On a moderately hot day Hanno went to his mother and his great-aunts to share the discovery.

"It really feels good having the cool air go up your pant leg," Hanno exclaimed.

Hanno's mother immediately translated his comment to Aunt Lizzie. The old ladies in their seventies with ankle-length dresses took special note of Hanno's phrasing. They laughed and laughed. To Hanno's embarrassment, this quotation was the highlight of the day.

Only once did little Hanno elicit humor from Aunt Lizzie. He drew a dilapidated house with a broken roof and missing doors. Below it, he placed the caption "The Poor House." He showed it to Aunt Lizzie and got a modest chuckle. In those days, the county charity hospital that took in people too poor to feed and care for themselves was referred to as "the poorhouse." Youngsters were told that if they did not make something of themselves, they would wind up in the poorhouse.

Aunt Lizzie was a joyous, giving person. This was an era without Social Security or welfare, at least for farmers. Lizzie's two sisters had been left destitute with the deaths of Joe Letterman and Jake Strietelmeier. Aunt Lizzie took them in as their respective husbands died. Lizzie's oldest sister, Celester, living almost five miles north of Linton, brought to Lizzie her own two daughters, first Zelma and then Hanno's mother, Mary, to provide exposure to town, school, work, and future husbands. Her home provided a gateway in and out of life.

Aunt Lizzie was vigorous in building her business and spent her money freely both on the business and on her own adventurous spirit. People, without asking or investigating, assumed that Lizzie was independently wealthy. The thought of being a beneficiary in Aunt Lizzie's will was of no little interest. Aunt Lizzie attracted a broad perimeter of relatives. Her house each weekend became the automatic gathering place for relatives, invited or not, who visited her at least once a week and "adored" her.

This popularity and affection was a major goal and source of satisfaction in Aunt Lizzie's life. She always had a gift from her greenhouse to give them to take home.

Hanno knew Aunt Dale the best. Her major failing with age was her eyesight. Hanno was fascinated by her snap-shut spectacle case and her magnifying glasses. She was also very religious in that she would continue to try to read the Bible with her magnifying glasses. She also had a little Motorola radio from which she sought religious music. With aging, however, her perception and judgment was not all that good. One day, she summoned Hanno to come listen to some wonderful religious music. Hanno discovered that the music was "Deep in the Heart of Texas." Long after she was gone, Hanno discovered that Dale was a nickname and that her real name was Adelia. Aunt Dale always made him think of the O. W. Holmes poem with the lines, "If I should live to be the last leaf upon the tree in the spring, let them smile as I do now at the old forsaken bough where I cling."

Aunt Ida was harder for Hanno to get to know. Most of the time, she was in a grumpy mood—and for good reason. Unlike the other two Malone sisters, Ida was always in considerable pain from her legs and back. She had a crutch to move about, but movement was rare for her. It brought still more pain.

Lizzie herself had a strict personal discipline. She would take regular baths at a reserved hour. She took vigorous callisthenic exercises and maintained a very narrow waist for her entire life (with the help of a corset). She went to the library and brought home at least ten books each week and would not touch these books until bedtime. She would then read late into the night until she fell asleep.

Aunt Lizzie had one mental quirk. It was kept secret by those who knew of it. During her regular baths while undressed at the bathtub, Aunt Lizzie would become convinced that boys were climbing upon her garage roof and looking into the bathroom window. The belief was clearly irrational. No boys were typically in the vicinity. Even if they were and if they climbed on the garage roof, the angle of vision was such that it was impossible to see anything but a portion of the ceiling inside the bathroom window. Aunt Lizzie would call out with emotion to her assistant, who managed the flower shop and telephone. If Hanno's mother were present, Aunt Lizzie would yell also to her. The call was always to chase the boys off the garage roof. History had proven that there were never any boys there, so Aunt Lizzie's persistent calling was always ignored. To Hanno, who was eventually given explanation, it seemed unkind.

Time passed, and a surprising thing happened. Everyone assumed that Aunt Lizzie had a great fortune since she had taken in her sisters and had invested heavily in an attractive flower shop, greenhouse, and delivery business. She always had money to take trips and to bring others along. She was endlessly accommodating to guests. Suddenly Aunt Lizzie sold her house and business, moved into a modest one-bedroom apartment, and had only a limited amount to spend for her essentials. The large cadre of relatives who had visited her and adored her every week failed to appear or to communicate. Aunt Lizzie was heartbroken and angry. She had kept the lifelong view that she was of high value and loved in her own right. She felt her money had no bearing upon their affection for her. Now with limited means, she learned differently.

Hanno's mother, with all her shortcomings, had family loyalty as her highest virtue. She did not forget that Aunt Lizzie had cared for her dying sister Zelma, for her aunts Dale and Ida during their widowhood, and for herself early in life. She had enhanced the lives of everyone around her. So, as Aunt Lizzie became frail, disabled, and poor, Hanno's mother became Aunt Lizzie's final caretaker. Aunt Lizzie was assertive all her life, and she was not one to die passively. She declared to Hanno's mother that she had put into her will that she was to be placed in the casket on her stomach. In this way, she said, her relatives could give her one last kick. Hanno's mother was appalled. What Aunt Lizzie was doing would embarrass the family.

Aunt Lizzie would become frustrated that she was bedfast in her final days. In a rage, she would throw her bedpan across the room. Hanno's mother abided by Aunt

Lizzie's rage but learned always to dodge. When Lizzie passed away, Hanno's mother went to great lengths to make sure the will was not opened until she was already in the casket and buried. The funeral was a large one, as would be expected for one of Linton's prominent citizens. Finally, when the will was opened, the item directing that she be buried on her stomach was missing. Aunt Lizzie had played her last joke. In the will, Aunt Lizzie left the proceeds of her estate to the First Baptist Church. It came to the total of forty-eight dollars plus some items of furniture. Despite her early hearing loss, Aunt Lizzie quickly became the center and inspiration o the entire family circle. She had lived a heroic life.

[20]

ELVA AND MARTIN

A unt Lizzie led a spectacular life, and everyone knew and talked of it. Some people lead lives where their deeds are rarely mentioned, either by themselves or by others. In the generation following Hanno's great-aunt Lizzie, a couple assumed a central role for identity and welfare in Hanno's family. They came together, they loved, they gave, and then they were gone. Their mark was so ever-present that one assumed that they would live forever, that there would always be a Martin and Elva.

Martin was Hanno's first cousin, the son of Port. Hanno's first memory of Martin and Elva was as a toddler at the family homestead. When they were courting, they would often make the four-mile trek to the family farm. When such guests came, it was the custom to open up the parlor. Everyone could use the grandparents' furniture of fine wood and black leather. Hanno had never seen a young unmarried couple in love. He had never seen a couple sit so close together and cuddle. So, Hanno got his baby stool and placed it in the parlor opposite them to sit down and watch. He watched every romantic gesture. They were so wrapped in each other that they were unaware Hanno was there.

When Martin was a boy, he became an excellent taxidermist. After he and Elva married, he became a mortician and funeral director. Martin was not lured to dead things and never held his profession as the mark of his identity. Instead, he shared a lifelong passion for fishing with Harry Welch, a local funeral director, and Harry became Martin's role model. More than that, however, Martin probably felt he belonged to a niche. His father Port was the custodian of the town's Fairview Cemetery and was the major gravedigger. (Martin hated mowing the graveyard grass for his father.) Aunt Lizzie, as a florist, had funerals as a major source of business. Both Hanno's parents helped out in the flower business and in the funeral home.

Whenever Martin and Elva were described, it always seemed an exaggeration. The hours of their lives that were devoted to others challenged belief. Wherever family needs might occur, either Martin or Elva was there. If a person became an invalid or went to a nursing home, either Martin or Elva visited every day and answered his or her needs. If an acute mishap occurred, either Martin or Elva was there to help.

When Martin's mother was in a nursing home with Alzheimer's disease, Martin visited her every day until she died. Hanno's own mother, developing Alzheimer's and struggling to stay out of a nursing home, let Elva take over her finances. (Elva having had many years of work in the bank. Elva was furious once with Hanno's mother. She approved some traveling shyster company to put on a new roof when the existing roof was only a year old.

When Hanno's mother went to the Rest Haven nursing home with Alzheimer's disease, either Martin or Elva visited her every day thereafter. They did the same for the younger daughter attacked by multiple sclerosis. At the beginning of this nursing home stay, Elva and her daughter Sharon took charge of the estate sale of the contents of Hanno's mother's house.

The population of Linton did not move much during this era. Each year on Memorial Day the entire town would gather at the cemetery with baskets of flowers. The Salvation Army and the Boy Scouts were in uniform. The American Legion would march in, blow taps, and fire three volleys of shots for the honored dead of World War I. Then a town VIP would offer an emotional patriotic speech to honor these veterans. Relatives would drive in from other states. Many flowers were sought so that the neighbors' graves from generations past could be decorated as well as one's own relatives'. Hanno grew up in a society where death was not shunned or feared. It was a significant part of community life.

Memorial Day was well named. It indeed was a day of memories, emotion, and satisfaction. Dear friends would often see each other not having met since last Memorial Day.

The Boy Scouts did their good deeds by helping people find graves. They pumped water for the flowers. Once on Memorial Day Hanno's Scout friend Jerry Rupert saw a tall, slim, awkward man coming down the road to the cemetery. His jacket was too small. His tie was not at all tied properly. His clothes were out of place and did not match. Jerry offered to help and was able to find the tombstone the man was seeking. It was the grave of a baby girl. The man removed his hat, dropped to one knee, put his single flower upon the grave, gazed down, and soon shed a tear. He looked away from Jerry in embarrassment. He got up and left the cemetery without speaking to anyone. He had completed the task he came to do.

From Martin's position in the funeral home, he was an important part of the infrastructure that made Memorial Day a big event each year.

Martin, during the same period, recruited Hanno to be an usher to help take up the collection on Sunday morning at the First Baptist Church.

When Hanno was in college at Indiana University, he usually hitchhiked home from Bloomington. When he arrived in town, he would go immediately to the funeral home. Hanno would first walk through the viewing rooms to see if anyone had died that he knew. Then he would go to the back office area to visit with Martin for an hour or so.

Later when Martin had entered the nursing home and Elva was home alone with her TV, telephone, and pacemaker, Hanno would often call her. He knew it would be several hours before Elva's daughter got off work to come to check on her. After a satisfying hour of conversation, getting caught up on the Linton news, Hanno once was concerned that he was wearing Elva out with the conversation. Hanno told her this and said he should get off the phone. She protested. She disclaimed any tiredness and said that during the day, she was unable to get out of the house because of her health. Moreover, her friends that she might potentially visit were dead or else confined to their own houses and unable to visit her. So, with that, Elva and Hanno continued to talk on the telephone for two more hours. And from then on, whenever they talked, it was usually about that long.

Hanno always thought of Martin as an unlikely funeral director because of his humor and raucous laughter. But then Hanno discovered that Martin's demeanor was highly effective in putting people at ease. People came to the funeral home in grief or trying to figure out how to look to be in grief. Hanno could see how people relaxed with Martin's greeting.

Martin did not talk freely of his funeral work. When Hanno urged him to, Martin would not mention names. Once, with Hanno's urging, Martin told of an accident in a heavy rain after midnight in Wright Township. Martin got a call to come with an ambulance. On a gravel road, a car had slipped over a bridge railing into a swollen creek. They waded through the mud and water to the car lying on its side. They pulled out one dead young man. They took him by stretcher to the ambulance. Coming up onto the shoreline of the creek, Martin spotted two shoes in the loose mud turned up by the car. Martin and his helper pulled on the shoes until they retrieved a complete body buried in the mud. They then returned to Linton with the two bodies. As per usual protocol, they called the coroner to come to the funeral home to examine the bodies and make out death certificates. As they were having coffee and waiting for the coroner, one of the bodies coughed. The young man who had been completely submerged in mud was alive and survived.

Only once did Hanno see Martin slip from his demeanor. Many years after leaving Linton, Hanno had come home from Nashville, where he was still teaching at Peabody College and Vanderbilt University School of Medicine. He made his usual first stop at the funeral home to see Martin. In the viewing room inside the front door was a little casket with a year-old child whom Martin had just laid out. She was a beautiful little girl with golden curls who suddenly got pneumonia and died. Instead of her hands being together or crossed on her chest, they were arranged in an irregular position with one arm curved above her head as if she were only sleeping. The other arm was slightly away from her side at a relaxed angle. The natural beauty of the little girl moved Hanno. Hanno then found Martin sitting in an empty viewing room nearby. He explained to Hanno the circumstances of the little girl's death. They sat down and talked. It was their usual talk of Linton news. Suddenly Martin grabbed Hanno's arm. "Come!" he said, and he hurried Hanno to the woodworking shop in the rear of the building. Hanno was puzzled about what was going on. Martin then explained to him that he heard the front door latch. He was sure it was the little girl's young parents coming to view their daughter for the first time. With a choked voice Hanno had never heard, Martin said he did not have the heart to greet them. He could not conjure the control to talk to them. On that day Hanno felt blessed when seeing a hidden side of Martin's character.

[21]

On My Honor ...

H anno's brothers graduated from Midland High School, Wright Township, in 1939. Since 1934, when their granddad passed away, it had been planned to sell the homestead as soon as they graduated. The proceeds of the sale went to Hanno's mother and her brothers. Concurrent with the sale, other farms were being sold, one after another, to the strip-mining company. As pastures, buildings, small forests, gravel roads, and Plum Branch School were being destroyed, the Buchwalds were leaving a way of life to be gone forever.

In its place, however, doors of opportunity were opened for Hanno while others were closed. Just one mile north of the Linton city limits, the Buchwalds bought a square wooden house of four rooms and a full basement. It was on one acre of land, which allowed for an ample garden. A dilapidated unpainted barn served as a garage. The horses and all but one cow were sold, and a pasture area was rented from a neighbor for the cow. This cow served to remind the Buchwalds they were farm folk.

The house had electricity—barely. One single bulb was suspended from the ceiling in each room. There were no wall switches or outlets. In one room, a Y-shape double plug was screwed into the socket dropping from the ceiling. The lightbulb on one side could illuminate the room, and the other side had a plugged-in electric cord dangling down to the toaster on the table.

Deep in the Depression, no jobs were available for Jay and Ray as they graduated. They were both busy enlisting in military service. Jay was accepted into the Navy. Ray was repeatedly rejected from the Navy and finally resigned himself to join the Army. The moment Ray joined the Army, the Navy recruiter told him he had decided to prevent brothers, especially twins, from going into service together. He felt war was imminent, and as it happened, war indeed came. With it, the government soon formally ruled against recruiting siblings into the same unit.

These events left Hanno essentially as an only child, living within walking distance of grade school, high school, and town. His isolation was over. He walked to first-aid classes, music classes, and to the park where badminton equipment could be checked out. The stripper holes were available for unsupervised swimming, fishing, and camping. Hanno could visit the library freely and have his own library card. The only obstacle was that his mother felt excessive reading led to epilepsy. During the summer, a bus was hired to take Linton children to Shakamak State Park, eleven miles away, for free swimming lessons.

Hanno, like every boy and young man at the time, learned the advertised hair items. He quickly learned that witch hazel and brilliantine were out of style. Coming into style were Vitalis and, even better, Wild Root Cream Oil. An appealing commercial by a male quartet was on the radio. It went like this:

You better get Wild Root Cream Oil, Charlie.
Start using it today.
You'll find that you will have a tough time, Charlie,
Keeping all those girls away.

Radio introduced combined commercials: "Ipana for the smile of beauty; Sal Hepatica for the smile of health." Roadside signs featured the renowned poet:

Don't stick your elbow
Out too far.
It might go home
In another car.
　　　　—Burma Shave

The radio was flooded during the day with soap opera, such as *Oxydol's Own Ma Perkins*, but detergent was beginning to outmarket soap chips. For boys after school, there were programs like *Don Winslow of the Navy*, sponsored by Fleers Double Bubble Gum, *Jack Armstrong, the All-American Boy*, sponsored by Wheaties (the Breakfast of Champions), and *Henry Aldridge* ("Coming, Mother!").

Other favorites on the radio, especially for Hanno's great-aunt Dale Letterman, were fifteen-minute religious programs. They often had a male quartet sing an opening theme song. One of these featured a bass:

Give the world a smile each day
Helping someone on life's way.
From the paths of sin, bring the sinners in
To the Master's fold to stay …

Another was:
On the Jericho Road,
There's room for just two.
No more and no less.
Just Jesus and you …

Like all the other boys, Hanno began early and secretly shaving his face, although there was actually no whisker to shave.

For the learning of proper values for living, Hanno had the family's chosen First Baptist Church. Closer to town, Hanno was now expected to attend every Sunday. During this period, however, the Council Scout Executive was visiting Linton in order to stimulate interest in new Scout troops. As it turned out, the Scouting had the greater impact on Hanno's moral and spiritual imagination.

Harold V. Boltz, Scout Executive for the White River Council, based in Bloomington, had been at odds with leaders in Linton because he declined to use the Linton Scout Camp as part of the summer camp season for the surrounding eight counties. Boltz decided to ignore the town leaders and Troop 57, the oldest troop in town, and begin making trips to Linton to contact churches and organizations that might be interested in starting a troop.

He enjoyed checking in at the Roosevelt Hotel and eating in their dining room with his frugal expense budget. Eventually, he had six organizations that had recruited a Scoutmaster and six to twelve youngsters.

And so it came to pass that on December 1, 1941, a ceremony was held in the auditorium of Linton Stockton High School to install six new troops.

Hanno's Uncle Murl had informed Hanno that the Linton Conservation Club was sponsoring a troop and was looking for kids. It was the answer to Hanno's dream. Leon Moody, a young postman and newlywed, had agreed to be the Scoutmaster, and Robert Blevins, just out of high school, had agreed to be assistant Scoutmaster. They had their meetings in a vacant storefront building on Vincennes Street near the old Ford dealership. Hanno found an ideal fit in this troop. When he left Plum Branch, he entered Midland School. The fourth- and fifth-grade classes each had their own room. His social development was behind others his age. He often spent his playground time with kids in lower grades. Now in the troop, Hanno was thirteen and almost all others in the troop were twelve. With them he was a leader. With his own peers he was only a skinny kid without athletic skill. He had read, even studied, the Boy Scout manual. He not only knew the requirements for Tenderfoot rank but also could help the other Scouts learn the knot-tying and other requirements. Immediately, Hanno was made a patrol leader. As Hanno was helping the other Scouts on Tenderfoot requirements, he was also beginning on his own second-class requirements. He did the mile-long Scout pace as Leon, his Scoutmaster, timed him. He built a fire and cooked a piece of bacon on a stick.

His Scoutmaster passed him but declined to eat Hanno's campfire cooking. He cooked his own and ate it.

Six days after the instillation of troops came December 7, 1941, "a day to live in infamy," when the Japanese attacked Pearl Harbor. On that long Sunday Hanno executed his duties as a paperboy with the *Linton Daily Citizen* and *Indianapolis News*. Although Hanno did not know it, it was a day that would change his life and the lives of many others.

About two weeks after the troop inauguration, Leon and Bob came to Hanno at the end of the troop meeting and told him that this would be their last meeting. Both were draft eligible, and both had decided to enlist rather than wait to be drafted. They had tried to get their own replacements for the troop with the Conservation Club but had failed. Hanno remembered well the words that changed his life.

"Take care of the troop until we get back. We'll see you after the war."

The weeks and months that followed were clearly the most emotionally tormented of Hanno's life. A number of demands came upon Hanno that he was not prepared to meet.

One of the stresses came from Hanno's feeling guilty over being given authority that he felt he had not earned. Immediately, new boys coming into the troop required someone to pass them on Tenderfoot requirements, which Hanno had only recently passed himself. Some charter members of the troop were eager to move on into requirements of second-class and first-class rank. They wanted to be tested and meet requirements that Hanno had not even reached himself. For example, some of the troop wanted to pass requirements for the merit badge, Rocks and Minerals. In normal times, there would be an expert from the mines available who would test the boy on the requirements. Now, however, no such expert existed; moreover, it was an unfamiliar area to Hanno. Soon, Hanno found himself on a daily trek to that place where only Margaret Cooper's voice spoke up loudly—the Andrew Carnegie Public Library. There Hanno read and read again the merit badge books that told what to ask and what to test. It still did not keep him from feeling like a phony. No one provided an answer for what else to do. No one was there to forbid him from doing it. He signed the advancements in rank and the merit badge applications, and the Bloomington Scout headquarters did not object. Time marched on. Troop 50 was the only one of the newly established troops that survived. All the others dissolved from lack of adult leaders.

It was not long until the anxiety about assuming a new role as boss became hollow. Hanno's profound inexperience and incompetence began to catch up with him. His years of isolation, not learning to work and play and fight with those his age, became a liability.

As soon as Hanno took over the troop, the annual selling of Christmas trees was already under way in downtown Linton. Then came appeals from the government for collection of critical scrap needed for the war effort. Huge amounts of paper were needed for molded products, such as gas masks. The call was so urgent that the national Scout headquarters created an Eisenhower Medal for every Scout who collected at least two thousand pounds of paper. Every Scout in Hanno's troop earned one. Other drives were carried out for scrap metal, aluminum, and tree planting on the stripper hills.

A typical troop meeting agenda involved the opening ceremony, roll call, announcements (e.g., paper drive, weekend hiking trip, special events), review of advancement and who needed time scheduled, demonstrations, a competitive game (e. g., Simon Says), and the closing ceremony.

The typical church basement where they met was furnished with wooden folding chairs, one or two long dining tables, a piano, a piano stool or bench on rollers, and a kitchen equipped with dishes, pots, and pans. As kids of Scouting age gathered and waited for a meeting to start, their natural activity level drew them toward noisemakers and anything with wheels or rollers. In a church basement, the best noisemaker was the piano. None of the boys ever had piano lessons. The pounding on the keys would wane only slightly after the meeting started. The boys would want to see how many of them could sit on a single piano stool. In case the ivory was loose on a key, some boy was compelled to try to remove it. If the ivory were completely missing on a key, some boy would check out the other keys by prying on them. Even more attention getting were the furniture items with rollers, such as piano stools and swivel chairs. The boys would put the stools on their chests, run as fast as possible on the concrete floor, dive forward, and glide as far as they could with chests on stools. In only a brief time, the furniture, even folding chairs, began to break as the legs gave way to such abuse.

The greatest attention-getter of all was a fight between two of the boys. Any boy in the troop would immediately leave what he was doing or the troop meeting itself in order to watch a fight—even those loyal to Hanno and committed to the troop's success.

Hanno's attempt to secure discipline made him doubly aware of his inadequacy. What he did was either overkill or underkill. Hanno's first impulse was to ask troop members to quit their unwanted activity. Ordering them to stop and directing them to another activity did not work. When Hanno yelled or screamed, he knew he was no longer in control. Hanno's next strategy was to declare group punishment for repeated misdeeds. This entailed the paddling machine. The paddling machine was a form of punishment wherein the whole troop lined up in single column behind one of the patrol leaders. Each boy had his legs apart. The victim got on his hands and knees in front of the column. As fast as he wished, he would crawl through the tunnel between the legs. As he did so, each boy in the column would swat the victim on the buttocks as he passed. This was an easy punishment to apply. The swats on the buttocks depended upon how fast the boy could crawl under the spread legs and how hard the participants swatted. It was the one single decision that the boys in the troop relished. At least some shared the frustration from the disruptive antics. All of them seemed to enjoy rendering up punishment to another when there was no risk to self.

Hanno's leadership problems came down upon him in short order. The first was that three of the Scouts, feeling abused and bruised, quit the troop.

The second occurred when the church elders of the First Methodist Church learned of the damage done to church property. Immediately, they gave Hanno notice not to come back. This was a blow that immobilized him. However, since he was volunteering at the time to clean ashes from the stoker coal furnace in the basement of his own First Baptist Church, he asked permission to meet in this familiar setting. Not a month went by, and the elder in charge of his maintenance work asked Hanno to have the troop leave and not return. With this state of affairs, some Scout in the troop got permission for the troop to meet in the United Brethren Church, but the details of this agreement are lost to Hanno's memory.

This cascade of events led to the worst period of Hanno's life. Possibly, Hanno thought, this would not have happened with another boy who had not grown up in isolation. Another boy would be savvy to defensive skills, excuses, and the blaming of others. It was not that Hanno chose to avoid excuses and blame. The options simply were not there. Very simply, he had made a promise to his Scoutmaster, and he was not keeping it. At least, with the troop conduct, there was no assurance of keeping it. The promise was made in the setting of a country newly at war, a highly patriotic population determined to keep the war effort going and not forget the combat troops overseas. This obligation of every citizen was magnified by the attention paid to Hanno's own family. With a brother missing in action at Pearl Harbor and his twin serving in the same combat zone, his family was preparing to have a pennant placed in their front window with one blue and one gold star. Hanno felt his failure all the larger when viewed in comparison to his brothers and family. Jay was Greene County's first combat casualty. Even this was not the beginning of feelings of personal patriotism. In the one-room schoolhouse, Plum Branch, in Wright

Township, Hanno lived through the heroic exploits of the men at Valley Forge and of so many who gave their lives so that America could be free and could prosper. Hanno saw his failure and inadequacy within the light of all that had gone before. And, yes, despite severe conflicts with his siblings, he was proud of their service to country and the resolve they had instilled in the Buchwald family. By any standard he could conceive, he had let the troop, his departed Scoutmasters, his country, his church, his family, his brothers, and himself down.

To Hanno, only he was responsible and only he had failed. He was forever outside of the proud long line of Americans who held up the torch when their time came. He held his emotions until his parents were away from the house. He then sat motionless in his grandfather's rocking chair and cried. He did not want to live. He could not conceive of a time in the future when things could be any better. He tried to hide from the world. He wanted to be dead. He could not make himself do his homework or his chores. He could not attend class or take action in any other way. Crying did not cleanse his disposition. He had no desire to eat. Exhausted, he would fall asleep, but he would wake up in the middle of the night, obsessed with his failures. There was no one to talk to, no one he wanted to talk to. His parents were rightfully preoccupied day and night with the fate of the twins. Jay was possibly dead, and Ray was in a vulnerable area of Hawaii, where defenses were broken and occupation could come at any time.

Days passed, and no one noticed Hanno in his darkest hours. At night his thoughts could not be taken away from each upcoming troop meeting. He wanted to hide and not turn up. He could not let himself do that. He considered quitting the troop. As he contemplated this, he thought about which Scout would take over. Troop 50 had patrol leaders, but they had not been active in organizing. Even so, one of these three patrol leaders was the only possibility.

As Hanno continued to obsess about this, he imagined three new troops with the three patrol leaders, Drexel Pope, Bill Marshall, and Jerry Rupert, each having his own troop. Even as he imagined it, he knew it would not work, as they were only twelve.

How this idea emerged into a new leadership structure, Hanno never figured out. Until then Hanno began a troop meeting with the spoken command, "Troop 50, fall in!" Hanno knew well that this would draw the attention of only a few. Now Hanno planned to dump most of his own responsibility by yelling, "Patrol Leaders! Fall in, the Troop!" Then Drexel, Bill, and Jerry would be hustling each to be first to get their patrol to stand at the line on the floor. Then, as part of Hanno's new structure, each patrol lined up at attention and their leader called the roll. The patrol leader then reported the roll call to Hanno. The first patrol to complete these steps was recognized by having the troop flag placed by their position for the rest of the meeting.

On the very first night, it was already apparent that this new procedure of assembly was working. A part of Hanno's naïveté was removed. Initially he felt guilty for shirking his own responsibility. To the contrary, the patrol leaders enjoyed their new duties and began to grow in leadership skills as the Scouts in their own patrols began depending upon them. Hanno had not previously realized the delegation of authority led to better troop functioning at every level.

[22]

CAMP CURRIE

As the troop began to get a greater sense of purpose, it was time to start planning for summer camp.

The idea of a week at summer camp was exciting to this Boy Scout troop. Most of them had never been separated from their parents for a week. It was a time when the troop members had to be engaged in mowing yards and finding other jobs to earn the precious eight dollars for the registration fee plus a bit of spending money. It was a time when Hanno was reminded that his family was not the only poor family. Not one Scout had his camp expenses bestowed fully by parents. With some, this expense was out of the question. For some families, a sturdy pair of hiking shoes, extra underwear, and wool socks were a cost they could not afford.

In the end, only eight out of the twenty-four made the trip. Of those, half had full Boy Scout uniforms. Others usually had a Scout shirt only. One new Scout had no official Scout garb or equipment. None of the group owned a sleeping bag. All brought blankets from off their beds. However, good times were coming. The war economy was picking up, and the Depression was still there but winding down. The Scouts of Troop 50, a small band of brothers indeed, were off to Camp Currie.

This camp was having its final year. It was soon to become a small part of the Crane Naval Ammunition Depot. This depot was a heavily guarded field of mound-like sodded structures with grass covering three sides and the top. The platform and doors on the concrete face allowed munitions to be stored within and taken away.

Both the new Crane and dilapidated Camp Currie were nestled in the fringe of foothills that had been pushed up eons ago by a glacier during the ice age. The area was not attractive for fancy living or quality farming. The irregular thicket was, however, suitable for a Scout camp or wildlife preserve.

The magic of summer Scout camp, or of any summer camp, is not to be found in its physical facilities. It is usually in being free from parents and teachers, having exposure to a cadre of staff and fellow campers who would yield exciting new friendships, and the chance to learn new things about oneself. Despite its limitations, the week at Camp Currie in 1942 presented its unique magic. It rained every day but one.

The tents were from surplus World War I Army stock and had a single center pole, a square base, no flooring, and room for eight cots.

One could see why this facility was only a rank better than the Scout facility in Linton. The dining lodge was more sanitary and accommodated larger groups.

The terrain and the prior use of Camp Currie had worn the grass and ground cover bare in many places, so the place earned the reputation of Camp Mud. That said it all.

The lake (better called a large pond) had an improvised but adequate swimming area with the nonswimmers, beginners, and advanced swimmers in separate areas. A small boat dock accommodated two rowboats and a canoe.

Troop 50, being the new kids on the block, did not draw the choice unit site during this crowded week. Tents had been erected off in woods at right angles to the path between the dining hall and the other camp units.

During the first night in camp there was a heavy downpour. Experience varied from camper to camper depending upon the terrain under his cot. Hanno's troop did not know it, but the older campsites had only clay and mud under the cots. Since Troop 50 was in an undeveloped site, the water passing from high to low ground beneath the cots had weeds, grass, leaves, clay, and mud in mixture. One cot had a mound under it, where one camper had put his socks and shoes, the only dry ones in the morning. Another cot had uneven ground under it, and rivulets formed to float registration and merit badge papers a few feet down the slope. The rivulets left a miniature demonstration of land erosion. One kid yelped with terror as he put on a shoe. A small chipmunk had chosen the nastiest shoe in which to spend a dry night. The animal dashed away, likewise in terror. Two scouts had brought clothesline, and the lines were tied to trees and filled with wet clothing.

There were no footlockers, so one's belongings, merit badge papers, and other perishables had to be stacked atop the bed at one's feet. Mattresses were called tics. They were long white cloth bags filled with straw and smelled when wet. The beds were steel metal frames with steel folding legs. Within the frames was a network of small springs and wires that provided some elasticity if sitting or lying on the bed.

One day Hanno's campers heard a loud howl from another camp unit. A nature guide visiting the unit speculated that the yell came from someone practicing for the upcoming Order of the Arrow ceremony. Later they learned that a boy had sat down naked on the cot springs and his testicles had dropped between the springs. When he arose, the springs came together and arrested his testicles. Fortunately the wedging did not create permanent injury.

All the routine things that are familiar to a veteran camper, Hanno and his buddies were experiencing for the first time. A bugle directed the main activities. "Reveille" was sounded to arise in the morning. "Assembly" sounded the request to stand in formation. "To the Colors" was for the flag-raising ceremony. "Mess Call" sounded for the call to eat. "Retreat" and then "To the Colors" were for the flag-lowering ceremony. "Tattoo" was for retiring to quarters. "Taps" meant lights out and bedtime.

One center of attention was the canteen. As always, the soft drinks and candy bars were available but rationed. Within minutes after arrival at camp, kids were walking around with brightly colored strands of lanyard material, braiding their lanyards and other objects. Veteran campers were teaching new campers. Other construction kits were available in the canteen. Popular among these were leather moccasin kits, but most campers had to wait another year and save up their money for these.

The dining hall was the camp's only permanent structure. It was a unique experience for the new campers. A Scout was appointed each meal to say grace before eating. Scouts with the shortest graces found themselves to be the most admired among the half-starved campers. This brevity reached its peak when a staff member, who had returned from the Merchant Marines with an injury, offered, "Bless this food. For Christ's sake. Amen."

Near the end of each meal a camp staff member walked among the tables holding a tabletop flag. When he found the neatest table, he placed the flag on the table. It remained until the next meal. Competition for this flag often became intense, and campers were expected to keep their plates and glasses lined up in a row across the table. Individual cereal boxes at breakfast had to be cut open and folded in a uniform way.

Another highlight of the dining hall was the singing at the end of the meal. One song, popular at the time in all summer camps, was "Billy the Goat" or "Didn't He Ramble." It went like this:

We speak of Billie the William goat
A beast of great renown.
He had a habit of rambling in
To every place in town.

Didn't he ramble? He rambled.
He rambled all around.
In and out of town.
Didn't he ramble? He rambled.
He rambled till the butcher cut him down.

Various verses were composed to fit the occasion.

Tuesday was the only night of the week without rain. The campers were tired from the day's activity, accustomed by then to the camp surrounding, and ready to go to sleep shortly after taps was blown. However, at two in the morning there was a great commotion. A young Tenderfoot Scout in another tent near Hanno was screaming and crying. Others in the tent, awaked, asked what was wrong.

"It is a bear! I am sure of it. I heard him. Just outside the tent."

"You were dreaming," someone said. "Go back to sleep."

"No. No. I was not dreaming. I was awake. I am sure of it."

The commotion was so loud that the kids in adjacent tents could hear. Bears were unknown in these parts, but other wild animals were indeed there. It made sense to be prepared.

"Everybody get your shoes on. Pants too over pajamas if you like. Someone get to the woodpile and hand out two sticks of firewood for each Scout. Bears will run away if you bang two sticks of wood together or bang on a mess kit pan or something. Everyone who has a flashlight, get it out. Warn the other tents if they are not awake."

Almost everyone in the entire camp unit was awake. A very few were being shaken and were asking what was going on. If not a frightening experience, it was highly exciting.

When the entire camp unit was out of bed and armed with their clubs and flashlights, a plan was laid out to cover the entire perimeter of the campsite. All were to be quiet and listen for the bear. All was quiet. Finally the boys began whispering, "He's gone, I guess."

Some grumpy kid still not fully awake said, "Let's get back to bed!"

After discussion, all agreed. Most of the Scouts felt it was a false alarm and that there had been no bear. The young Tenderfoot loudly protested, "Yes! I heard him. I heard him."

All the campers and camp leaders finally got back into bed. No one had heard anything that remotely sounded like a bear.

All became quiet, and the campers, one by one, were falling asleep.

In the tent between Hanno and the Tenderfoot boy, a Scoutmaster, Mr. Edwards, was prone to allergies. The vegetation of the deep forest was kicking up an attack. He had to rise from his cot and clear his postnasal drip. In a triad of sounds, he snorted inward through his nose, had a long cough to bring up mucous from his throat and lungs, and then spit under the rolled up wall of the tent: "Snaaark-haawk-tooey!"

"*It's him! It's him!*" screamed the Tenderfoot. "*There he is again! The bear! The bear! He's back. I hear him!*"

"That ain't no bear, Scotty. That's Mr. Edwards clearing his throat. Quiet down, and everyone get back to sleep."

The final scream had aroused everyone. After some mumbling and grumbling, sleep was exactly what they did.

On Wednesday, the White River Council Scout Executive, Harold V. Boltz, visited the camp. Very shortly after he arrived and observed the activities, he lost his temper. He was upset because no program was taking place. Hanno did not understand what Boltz was talking about. Hanno had never experienced a summer camp with a program. To him everyone was busy building kits from the canteen, playing cards in their tent during the rain, and drying out their gear.

In fact, what was intended for the week was a number of nature hikes, each based upon some merit badge item: bird identification and birdsong hikes, rocks and minerals hikes, friendly (edible) and unfriendly (poisonous) weeds and ivies, life-saving lessons, swimming form and safety, rowing, canoeing, rifle marksmanship, the use of a compass, and other skills to find one's direction. With so much rain early in the week, these sessions, one by one, had been cancelled. After two or more cancellations, a decision was made to cancel the entire topic because not enough time remained in the week to complete all merit badge requirements. Boltz did not like this decision.

Boltz was not a person to seek a private audience to criticize someone. He would blast away at the staff members, individually and as a group, for all to see and hear. When he found out that no instructional programs were taking place, he became the *unhappy camper.* And he decided that others would be the same.

Harold V. Boltz was a robust man well over six feet in height. Even in his Scout shorts, he cast a dominating physical presence. He went at everything in life with full throttle. When criticizing the camp staff and camp director, he took no prisoners. When leading a song, he was the loudest and most energetic. When saying a prayer of grace before a meal, his voice was the most reverend. When he was complimenting someone on an action, well, you knew that you had been complimented. When he chaired a meeting, you knew he was in control. When Boltz came to Camp Currie, the camp director took on the role of Boltz's personal assistant. Yet Boltz did not arouse fear or hate. Hanno felt this was true because he showed a sincere interest and support in one-on-one relations with people. The sound of Boltz's last name gave an idea of his personality. Hanno was soon to have his surprise encounter with the "big one."

[23]

INTO THE ARROW

Before camp, Hanno had never heard of the Order of the Arrow (OA). On Thursday, a representative from the OA visited Hanno's troop campsite. He described the OA as a national Scout camping honorary fraternity. He explained that neither OA members nor individuals taken into membership determined who entered the organization. OA members were chosen by fellow campers who had lived and camped with the candidate. It was a vote by peers to elevate someone from their own ranks. This person should have all the attributes of a good camper who gave unselfish and friendly service to others. Since people who get in have no voice or vote over who gets in, a minimum of lobbying and politics are involved.

All the camping units were now casting their ballots to raise some individual from their own ranks. It was a blind ballot. Representatives are passed out blank paper slips and collected the vote. Hanno had been so busy that he knew not of his fellow Scouts' regard for him. He chose the name of one of his patrol leaders and turned the ballot in.

At the evening meal an OA member demonstrated how to wear a blanket for the calling out ceremony. Stripped to the waist, one draped the blanket over one shoulder, allowing one arm and shoulder bare. After the meal, as twilight neared, an OA member appeared in the camp unit. He was dressed only in a breechclout, moccasins, and a headband that had one turkey feather. In addition to his summer tan, he had donned some ceremonial face paint. He asked that each Scout put on his blanket and form a single column. He then announced that under penalty they were to maintain silence from then until they returned from the ceremony. They were to watch carefully and to listen. Hanno's troop filed away and soon merged into a longer line of over seventy blanketed campers. For the new ones especially, there was a sense of wonder at the total quiet of the moving throng.

They proceeded along a trail in the forest until they came to the long grassy slope overlooking the lake. As they approached, they could hear the beating of a single tom-tom. In the center of the grassy area was a tall pyramid of wood, prepared for a bonfire. The long single file of campers formed a circle around a wood stack. By that time, night was beginning to fall. Small groups of OA members, dressed also in breechclout and moccasins, were dancing toe-heel with alternate bowing and reaching for the sky. Yet all was quiet except the drum.

Then from out of the forest came a more elaborately clad person dressed in Indian garb. He approached the firewood, raised his arms in the air, and spoke.

"To the wood of the forest, from which comes light and warmth."

With this, some noticed that a flame burst forth in the top of a tall oak tree at the edge of the clearing. Then a flaming arrow, mounted on a guy wire, slid quickly down the wire for forty yards into the middle of the pile of firewood. Already soaked with kerosene, the logs of the firewood suddenly became ablaze. It illuminated and warmed the faces of the campers.

The costumed warrior then went to each of the four directions of the compass within the circle. He raised his arms each time and saluted the four directions.

"To the north, which brings the cold. To the east from which come the sun and life. To the south, which brings the warmth and growth of plants. To the west from which comes the harvest and the color of falling leaves."

Then out of the forest came a column of four more, also dressed in elaborate Native American garb. At the front of the line was the chief of the OA lodge, donning a formal Indian feather headdress with a trail of feathers falling down his back. Following were costumed figures dressed as a medicine man, spiritual man, and huntsman with bow and arrow following the chief. Other costumed OA members were running back and forth around the outside of the circle. The chief and his party proceeded silently around the inside of the circle. The outside warriors identified elected candidates and quietly stood behind them. Suddenly the chief stopped his procession and turned to stand in front of a blanketed candidate. The chief slapped him three times on the shoulder and then, unexpectedly if possible, gave him a push backward out of the circle. The warrior standing behind him would catch him in case he fell toward the earth. He then attended to straightening his blanket and demeanor. The chief advised the candidate to take a position at the end of his party and follow.

Hanno was one of the seven called out that evening. When all candidates were chosen, the chief led his entourage into the forest where a small secluded meeting area had been set up, either with a small campfire or Coleman lanterns were used for light. The chief told Hanno and his fellow candidates that they had been removed from their circle never completely to return. For the rest of their lives they were being asked to commit themselves to a higher purpose of brotherhood, service, and joy to others. The candidate was to submit himself to the needs of his fellow man without expectancy or purpose for any reward or recognition. They were then told that if they wanted to decline this obligation, they must do so now. They could be escorted back to their camping unit with grace and dignity. No one chose to decline.

From a script, read or memorized, the chief of the lodge and three other members described the spiritual meaning of this quest for extraordinary lifetime service to others. Candidates were then advised of the initiation to earn final acceptance into the band of the Order of the Arrow. They were to spend the night in the forest with a partner but without speaking to him or anyone. They were to subsist from then until the end of daylight the following day on bread and water, with no other snacks or meals. They were to spend this time until the end of the next day in total silence, even when enticed to speak. If there were three instances of failure to retain silence, they were either to repeat the initiation on another day or drop out of the organization. They were also to spend the day in assigned menial labor. Then, on the following evening, they would have their final induction ceremony. They were asked to accompany an OA representative back to their camping area to retrieve bedding, medications, a flashlight, and toilet gear necessary for spending the night in the wild. Again, this was to be done in silence. In preparation for difficult communication, each candidate was equipped with a pad and pencil. Hanno had no flashlight but was loaned one by a troop member.

With overnight gear assembled, the candidates were paired off and taken to assigned locations in the thicket of virgin woods. The partner assigned to Hanno was a high-school senior, Jack Finley, of Clear Creek. This was a village of about three hundred people near Bloomington. Finley had distinguished himself in elementary school as county champion in a spelling contest. In high school, he had become the state champion heavyweight wrestler on the Bloomington High School wrestling team. He was a huge, powerful, but gentle and handsome young person who had the charismatic quality to be known and respected by his peers throughout the county and state. Even those who did not know Jack talked of him during the week in camp. It was known that he had just won a competitive examination for appointment to the US Military Academy at West Point.

Hanno had not met Jack Finley and had known of him only since coming to camp. Jack now stood by him as a huge, muscular, athletic young man. Rather than an attitude of competition and threat, his warm, quiet demeanor conveyed one of liking and protectiveness toward others.

Hanno was to learn later that Jack graduated from West Point and finished a tour of duty in the US Army. Then he went to the University of Illinois to study engineering and was thereafter involved in the space program.

The candidates were escorted into a remote area of heavy forest. Hanno and Jack introduced themselves by smiling, nodding, and pointing to the things to get done to set up camp. With a storm on its way, both were mindful that time was at a minimum. The gathering thunderclouds shielded the stars and moon. One could hear the distant sound of thunder. It echoed through the wooded hills.

To Hanno's surprise, the gear that Jack had packed into his haversack included two shelter halves. They could be fitted together into a pup tent. After ridding the tent area of rocks, stubble, and saplings, they put down their sleeping bag and blankets within the tent. They finally wedged into the tent, got under their sleeping covers, and put out the flashlights. For the first time, they lay in silence without activity. Suddenly, the silence was broken by thunder blasts, which were getting louder and louder. Clearly, they were closer and closer. Shortly, Jack said, "Is everything all right with you?"

"Yes," Hanno responded, covering up his surprise that Jack had broken his silence.

All was quiet thereafter within the tent, but in the sky above, the curtains opened up to display the greatest electrical storm of recent years. First came that minute or two when all the birds and animals of the woods fell into deadly silence. Then came the loud crack of lightning striking about two hundred yards away with echoes reverberating through the woods and hills. Then came the sound of splitting wood as a huge branch were separated from the trunk of a tree. Then they could hear huge drops falling on the tent that Hanno at first thought were hailstones.

The galloping onset of more and more rain followed. It was heavy, unrelenting rain. Then more lightning flashed in all directions around them. They could count the seconds between the flash of light into the tent and the booming sound to follow. The shorter the time between lightning and sound, the fewer the yards the lightning strike was from the tent. They could hear more branches of trees split and fall to the forest floor. It was a time when in ordinary life one was expected to run for cover, get out of the storm, and not stand under trees. Do not get near the window. Do not sit near a heavy metal object, such as a pump or farm implement. Yet they were there, vulnerable and in the open. The downpour continued even harder as the lightning began to move farther away. The thunder occurred a longer time after the lightning, but still it rained. Hanno did not know whether either of them slept. The rain persisted heavily for over an hour. Within half an hour, it was clear that the rain was flowing as surface water on the ground beneath the tent. They both rose up to get gear onto the top of backpacks. As for their bedding getting wet, it was hopeless. They were being soaked.

The rain had not stopped. It had only slowed down, and Hanno, in his doze, thought he heard voices off in the distance. Then he heard Jack raise his head from an improvised pillow. He reached for his flashlight. Then, sure enough, there were lights from a miner's headlamp striking the roof of the tent as the rain kept splashing onto it.

They heard a voice say, "There they are! Hey! Over here! Come over here."

With this, Jack and Hanno began to crawl out of the pup tent.

"Hey! These guys have a pup tent. Where did you get that pup tent? No one said you were allowed to bring a pup tent!"

Hanno and Jack had already broken silence once, and now he was fearful that they had failed the initiation and would have to repeat it. Jack, however, only smiled with confidence and a sense of pride.

The OA members had brought dry ponchos for Hanno and Jack. They put them on. With a rare serious note, the rescuers asked about their welfare and asked them to gather up their belongings. The party helped Hanno and Jack carry their bedding and gear back to the dining hall. There, they were welcomed by a blazing fire and hot chocolate that had just been prepared.

The OA members continued to bring in candidates from the forest, all of them drenched. Jack and Hanno had already hung their soaked clothing and bedding over one of the many tables of the dining hall. Jack was lucky enough to have found a dry pair of Boy Scout shorts in his haversack but still had on a soaked white plain T-shirt. He sprawled over a rustic wicker armchair. His muscled neck was as wide as his face, and his broad shoulders and huge thighs were what one would expect of a heavyweight wrestler. A thin coating of hair could be seen across his forearms and legs, matching the sandy-red hair on his head. Without breaking his silence, Jack took no offense to the taunting by OA members but treated them with warm regard. Even without saying a word, he had an attitude of warm confidence and acceptance rather than arrogance or annoyance. He pointed to the Eagle badge pinned on his soaked Scout shirt that he had placed on the table to dry. On its motto scroll were the words "BE PREPARED." They laughed. Jack had won his point. While the rest of the group shivered, Jack, with his remarkable physique, revealed not a single goose bump.

The OA members enjoyed the frivolity of the occasion and the rare instance where they could dominate the conversation. In contrast, the Arrow candidates could only nod or jot something on a pad. The OA members brought in more towels for the wet candidates, and they raided the lost-and-found closet for clothing items to help get through the night.

Hanno felt himself the skinniest, the most shivering, the youngest, the least in rank, and out of his place. He was inarticulate in dealing with boys older than he was when they had confidence, pride, or sass. He had faded into the background, and he was happy for that. His mandate not to talk was a blessing. But once an Arrow member came by him to offer another cup of hot chocolate. He said, "You're that guy from over in Linton who has kept a troop alive for a year or so. Right?"

Hanno looked surprised and momentarily frozen. He could not have talked even if given permission. With an embarrassment he could not even explain to himself, he could not nod or shake his head. Hanno thought fleetingly of the grief and failure he had felt—and still did. He had never been one to brag or tell others that he had accomplished some feat, let along rescuing a troop. He also felt his reputation was misunderstood. It was not that he had rescued a troop but that three young boys in the troop had rescued him. Yet, if people wanted to feel he did that, he was not about to disabuse them of their distorted view and tell them they were wrong—like whether he deserved it or not. It is easier if people greet you with positive thoughts.

The OA member could tell that Hanno was troubled by his question. He did not know why. He simply said, "It's okay. You did a good job."

How did he know? Hanno wondered. The others seemed to know also. People seemed to treat him with a special regard.

At two thirty in the morning, once assured that all candidates were safe, the OA members continued good-naturedly to taunt (and secretly admire) Jack Finley.

"Where did you get a pup tent to take out with you?"

The next day's events seemed to confirm that all the OA members had this view of Hanno. Hanno was just beginning to know some of their names, and yet they all knew him. Why? How did this happen? One day, Hanno was to find out.

At about four thirty that morning, the OA members were beginning to reach the end of their socializing. The candidates were told to choose space—tables, floors, benches, or prearranged chairs—to find whatever sleep they could. They also appointed candidates to be in charge of the fire. In spite of all, when daylight came, the fire was out. All the candidates were still asleep.

Hanno reflected back on that evening. He was on a cusp of dealing with his moral view of life. If he were to follow the concrete and fundamental rules of the Order of the Arrow ceremony, the Scout oath, and the Scout laws, he knew a flagrant cheating had gone on that night. That Jack Finley should break his silence and speak up in the middle of the night shocked Hanno. It was a transgression. That he, Hanno, answered was another. That the OA chief and officers should interrupt their night in the forest and give the candidates hot chocolate and dry clothing was a further transgression. This, at first, bothered Hanno. He viewed their help as a sign of weakness and breaking the rules. But then, another part of Hanno was beginning to emerge. There was a higher order of interpretation. What they had done was exactly in the spirit of the highest values of the organization. The OA members, and Jack Finley himself, had all conducted themselves with brotherhood and a cheerful spirit in the face of adversity and efforts of rescue. It was a service to others that was greater than to themselves. They knew the candidates were in harm's way, so to give rescue and comfort was a personal duty. The written rituals and rules remained the same, but Hanno was changing. He was seeing a broader horizon. Hanno's transition was not an overnight one though. It took some time.

The OA candidates were apprehensive on the day of the initiation, but it was not all that bad. One could have taken a pass on the bread and water, in favor of real food, yet the idea of mastering this task of self-restraint had meaning. A Scoutmaster who had once been inducted into the OA compared the bread and water experience to the rowboat trip of the sailors when Henry Hudson discovered Manhattan Island. A detail went ashore to find a spring and get fresh water. Returning to the ship, one said, "That is a nice place to visit, but I wouldn't want to live there." The day's ordeal was indeed tolerable, but one would not want it as daily fare.

Later in the day Hanno became involved in chopping wood for the cook's stove in the dining room. That was demanding but somehow satisfying.

The most difficult task for most candidates was to keep from talking. Of all the candidates, Hanno had the least difficulty. Having been isolated for years on the homestead, he was accustomed to talking little. One boy, however, who grew up in a large family, put adhesive tape over his lips once he had spoken out by mistake twice.

Early on the day of initiation, Hanno, while working alone, realized that he had unfinished business. He had come to camp as a second-class Scout and had intended to get his swimming requirement met for his first-class badge. There had been so many rainy days during the week that swimming periods had often been cancelled. For one reason or another, he had not had a chance to get into the water. Although he could pass others on the swimming requirement in Linton, there was no one qualified to pass him. Now, unexpectedly, the Order of the Arrow proceedings were taking up Friday, and he would be leaving in the morning. Dick Johnson from Washington was the waterfront director, and Hanno could not get to him from his working post. However, the camp director was nearby. Hanno prepared a note for Johnson, explaining the situation. The camp director read the note and nodded. Hanno did not know what that meant and, of course, could not speak. The camp director left. He sent a young Scout to retrieve Dick Johnson, and soon, the two returned. Dick told Hanno that he had already started storing the waterfront equipment and that they should have the swim test now. Hanno put down his ax, wrote a note to his OA monitor, and began walking toward the waterfront.

"Don't you want to wear a bathing suit?"

Hanno looked surprised and embarrassed. In the Linton stripper holes, everyone swam in the nude.

"Run back to your tent and get your bathing suit. And a towel."

Hanno took off. He returned dressed only in a bathing suit. His towel was over his shoulder.

"Sorry I have to rush you. I have lots of things to put in storage, and I want to leave for home early in the morning."

Hanno nodded but, of course, did not speak. Dick Johnson had been in the OA group the night before. Dick was a handsome, well-built guy. Clearly, he was the most admired person on the camp staff. During the fireside dry-out, staff members were trying to persuade Dick to return to be the waterfront director one more year. He had just graduated from high school and had been on the football team. He had set his plans to go into the Navy a month after this summer camp was over. Like Leon Moody, he did not want to get drafted. Hanno had watched him and liked him. Hanno wanted him to return also. Dick sounded regretful about leaving, but his decision was fixed. He was going into the Navy.

When Johnson and Hanno got to the waterfront, Johnson got into the only canoe the camp had. Then he told Hanno to jump into the water. Hanno threw his towel down and began to take off his swimsuit.

"Keep your bathing suit on." Johnson smiled. "We assume everyone is male down here."

Hanno was mortified with embarrassment. In the stripper pits around Linton in summertime, where he swam almost daily, everyone swam in the nude. Hanno finally jumped into the water but without showing his male credentials.

Hanno was not unsure of himself. He had swum one hundred yards at Shakamak State Park once, and he was sure he could handle fifty. He did so with no difficulty.

The next morning, the end of camp had arrived, and parents were driving in to pick up their kids. Hanno's dad was working at the war plant in Terre Haute, and his mother got her brother Murl Oglesby to drive her down to Burns City to pick up Hanno. The one-armed policeman was glad to comply. Scattered out from around the dining hall were stacks of camping gear and mementos from camp and canteen. Boys were moving around saying good-bye to their newfound friends. The Scout executive was moving among the boys, shaking hands with them, wishing them well, and urging them to come back next year. Actually, this was the last year Camp Currie would ever be used.

Hanno saw his family car drive into the camp yard, and he started to pick up his stuff.

"Is that your machine that just drove in?"

Hanno looked up and saw Harold V. Boltz right in front of him. When Hanno affirmed, Boltz picked up Hanno's Flying Eagle patrol flag. He carried it horizontally.

"I want to meet your mother," said Mr. Boltz.

Hanno had a measure of shyness. He was not ever delighted when he had to introduce his parents to anyone. There was always a sense of shame and feeling they were out of place. Unfortunately he never lost that feeling.

Hanno's mother was standing outside the car, waiting to greet them. Murl stayed behind the driver's wheel and was already eager to get back to Linton. Hanno's father used to joke that Murl was afraid that they would take up the Linton sidewalks if he stayed away.

Hanno and Boltz went almost to the car, and his mother approached them.

"I have been wanting to meet you and to thank you for getting your son interested in the Boy Scouts. We hope he will enjoy it for many years to come."

Hanno's mother was always ready to accept a compliment. She wanted more compliments than she had ever received. They exchanged pleasantries—"Did you have a good drive down from Linton?" and all of that.

Finally, Boltz said, "Well, Hanno, thanks for bringing Troop 50 to camp. To organize it on your own wasn't easy. Congratulations on the Order of the Arrow. Keep the pot boiling."

"I will," Hanno said.

[24]

TRIP BACK HOME

Harold V. Boltz stood and waved as they left. It was the last time Hanno ever saw him. He was transferred to be Scout Executive in another state. He then died shortly thereafter of a heart attack.

In the car, an old prewar Studebaker, Mary Oglesby Buchwald sat in the front seat beside her brother. She was always anxious in cars. An unrecovered backseat driver was she. Hanno's father often said that she wanted to participate in the driving (although she herself could not drive) in order to watch out for the nails and glass on the road.

"What was that about? You were the only one he walked to the car with."

"I guess that's right."

"Why did he want to meet me?"

"I don't know."

"He said, 'Keep the pot boiling' to you. What did he mean by that?"

After a few seconds' pause, Hanno said, "I guess it's because Leon and Bob enlisted. So some of the guys along with me have been running the troop. I'm the oldest, so I get all the credit."

Pause.

"But what does that have to do with boiling the pot?" No answer. "Keep the pot boiling. He said that to *you!*"

Hanno became quiet. His mother began chatting with her brother Murl. Hanno was happy to be ignored. He fell deeply into his thoughts. It had been a big and different week in his life. He had much to think about. His mother, he felt, was out of touch. He could not blame her. It was still only a few months since Jay had been killed at Pearl Harbor. The grief was unending. He looked down at the second-class badge on his shirt pocket and remembered being rebuffed when he woke her to show it off the night it was awarded. He realized that the conversation that they had just had was another indication of her being oblivious of him and his life. With her intense grief, he knew he could not expect more from her. Her grief and concern over the surviving twin overpowered everything. With her crying for hours every day, Hanno no longer felt sympathy and compassion for her. Nor was he angry and frustrated with her. Things were just the way they were, and he did not count—not, at least, until the war was over and Ray was back home. For Hanno, there was only the meeting of basic needs.

Hanno began to think about the conflicting images that he portrayed. It was even clearer now that among those who came and went from the Boy Scout Council office in Bloomington, he was a hero. He had rescued and kept alive a troop in Linton. At Camp Currie, the OA members and the Bloomington Scouts all knew who Hanno was. With Mr. Boltz' generous farewell, it seemed that Boltz himself was a participant in the hero message. Yet someone who had contact with the office but also had broad contact with the Scouts themselves had been spreading the story of Troop 50 and how it survived. But Hanno knew not who.

Hanno suddenly realized that his own efforts were of great significance for Boltz. Boltz had put his heart and soul into working with Linton community leaders and chartering six new Boy Scout troops. Now, all of them had failed except Troop 50. Although a number of Troop 50 Scouts were working to keep it going, Boltz knew only of Hanno. It was Hanno who did the hitchhiking to Bloomington to get rank and advancement materials. As Boltz viewed it, Hanno finally realized, the efforts he made in Linton to create new troops would have been a profound failure had it not been for Hanno. Only Hanno, for a period, stood between Boltz and that complete failure. No wonder it was that Boltz and the Scout office had bestowed on Hanno this heroic halo. Hanno knew he did not deserve it. Boltz did not know the work of his fellow Scouts who had saved the troop. Meanwhile, Hanno did not believe the generous view bestowed upon him. Yet, he was determined to try to live up to the positive epitaph. Don't look a gift horse in the mouth.

The other labels, "model son" and "model Scout," he had to face. Hanno was heading back home. To be viewed as perfection and to be pointed to by parents to their sons was poison. It made him alienated from peers his own age. Being uncomfortable in making friends in his new environment was bad enough without having the hex of being seen as a "goody boy." Hanno knew he did not have the verbal skills to approach the issue directly. Simply to deny he was a Goody Two-shoes or wonderful model for a son would not have been convincing. So, the only answer Hanno could think of was to deal in a bit of mischief himself. What would it be? Throwing rocks and breaking the insulators of telephone poles on a country road? Slinging a rock through the window of a vacant house? Curse his parents? Hanno was caught in a dilemma. Having adopted the oath, laws, and other principles of Scouting as almost a fundamental religion, a very fine line was drawn between what would be rebellious behavior against the Goody Two-shoes image and a failure of devotion to some high spiritual commitment. Hanno would have to let time pass to deal with that question.

The third image was what Hanno considered the real Hanno. It was the image that had confronted him during the days when he was a profound failure in keeping decorum and successful operation of Troop 50. It had to do with his inability to fight for his own rights or speak up in his own defense. Hanno was left with the enduring feeling that he had no moral courage. He would not amount to anything in life. He could not stand before a group and give a talk. He had no natural power or dominance over others, and he never would have. It was the feeling that his personal intent of character was of no worth.

Once Hanno told his parents that he would like to see a psychiatrist, that there was something wrong with him mentally. They just laughed at him. Later, he realized that they did not have the money for such help, even if they had been sympathetic.

Hanno revisited and struggled with the images in his thoughts. The only one he had confidence in controlling (and negating) was the model son / model Scout image. To commit inappropriate or illegal activity for the purpose of being one of the guys would be no problem. One must only be mindful of the risk that it would backfire and create new problems. It was so very clear that others imposed the heroic image on him. It had two features; it was extremely attractive, and it was wrong. Hanno's resolution was clear: try to change reality by attempting to live up to it. As for the third image, it was the ghost that, on and off, could haunt him for the rest of his life.

Gradually Hanno realized he was hearing his mother's voice.

"Wake up! It is time to unload!"

Hanno, after his contemplations, had fallen asleep in the backseat. He had had a dream, and he was still left with the feeling of excitement and elation. He dreamed he was flying. Hanno would have this dream a half dozen or more times in his life, but this was the first. In the dream Hanno could move in the fluid air much as he could with underwater swimming. He found the sense of power in a flutter kick of his legs and feet. The movement was so powerful that Hanno would give a flutter of his ankles, stop, and glide a distance through the air around him. One rule within the dream was that Hanno had to believe he could fly. He had to have confidence. Should he be overcome with doubt, his body would automatically collapse and fall to the ground. This never happened, but Hanno was always mindful.

Hanno had three different levels of flying, each revealed by his visual experience. One level was about six to seven feet off the ground. On this level he could see things on the same level as if he were standing or walking. He was just high enough to avoid most of the obstacles. The next level was to fly and glide about three or four feet off the ground. This was an interesting way in that one had an entirely new visual experience. As he glided just above the ground, he could look closely at the detail of things one could not detect while standing, walking, or flying high. Another aspect of this level was the fun of weaving in and out among trees, bushes, or furniture. The skill of movement and dodging was satisfying. The third level of flying was up very high in the air, like a bird or an airplane. Hanno did not fly at this high level often because, should he lose confidence and fall, it would hurt more. It was like the canoeist who never capsizes when a mile from shore on a lake, but finds it better to be closer to shore—just in case.

[25]

WAR

I t seems that all people alive at the time remember where
they were and what happened to them on December 7,
1941. Hanno's mother had attended the First Baptist Church
that morning. With the time change, the Pearl Harbor
attack came around midday in Linton's time. Shortly after
noontime, Hanno was attending a matinee in the old Grand
Theatre. *A Yank in the RAF,* starring Tyrone Power and Betty
Grable, was playing. From the back of the theater came a
voice never heard there, before or since: "All newspaper
boys report to the newspaper office immediately."

It was Eskin Turner, editor of the *Linton Daily Citizen.*

On the way to the *Citizen* office, Hanno heard someone
on the street say that war had been declared (which was
not exactly correct). In the circulation room, the manager,
O. L. Barnes, said that the Japanese had attacked the US
Navy at Pearl Island. This statement was close enough

for Hanno to correct it to Pearl Harbor. He also noted that his brother was there. After linking his brother to this news event, Hanno was looked on with a bit of awe. The attention soon subsided.

The boys sat crowded on one long bench. They waited. Soon they were told that the printing press had broken down. Someone had already been called to fix it. It would be fixed soon, they said. Not so lucky. The boys sat and sat, and they became tired, restless, and hungry. Finally, Barnes sent his assistant John Richard Spice out to get sandwiches. Barnes kept repeating the orders. No one was to leave.

Sandwiches in those days were not the super ones we have today. Each boy ate his sandwich, with its two slices of white bread, and was still hungry. No more food was forthcoming.

Bulletins continued to come in by radio as the boys sat. Four battleships, including the USS *Arizona* and the USS *West Virginia*, and a number of smaller ships were reported sunk. Also came the report that all of the aircraft carriers were at sea and had missed the attack. In fact, almost the entire Pacific Fleet except the carriers had been destroyed. All had been damaged or destroyed except the USS *Tennessee*, which was moored side by side with the *West Virginia*, the latter protecting the other from incoming torpedoes. Even the *Tennessee* was temporarily disabled though. It was pinned between the shore and the disabled *West Virginia*.

Back in Linton, about eleven thirty at night, the press was finally repaired. The *Linton Daily Citizen* printed the only "extra" in its history. Hanno recalled that it was a newly prepared front page, but the remaining pages were the same as those printed the day before. Barnes, of course, wanted the boys to go out on the main streets downtown and sell the newspapers, yelling, "Extra! Extra! America at war!" just like in the movies. The boys tried this, but the streets, as expected on a Sunday night, were empty. Very few extras were sold. Instead, the newspapers were delivered to the regular route customers. The boys were still yelling, "Extra! Extra! America at war!" at each front door. For the few who came to the door, they were not impressed. They had long acquired the front-page information on the radio. The paper offered nothing new.

Hanno got home after midnight from delivering the newspapers, tired and hungry. His life changed greatly from that point. Hanno's parents were in a state of great fear about the fate of both of his brothers. They suspected that both boys had participated in the attack defense.

The amusing thing for the newsboys came on Monday morning. (As they chuckled, the fireboats in Hawaii were still working on the *West Virginia*. It was still ablaze.) Newspapers throughout the nation had front-page articles that Linton, Indiana, was the last city in America to learn of the Pearl Harbor attack. Someone had reported to the AP and UP news wires that the *Citizen* printing press had failed. Not correct in its conclusion, it nevertheless made a good story. No one took into consideration that Linton citizens owned radios.

* * *

Only after World War II could the juxtaposition of events in Hawaii and in Linton, Indiana, become clear. The following therefore represents information pieced together at a much later time.

Soon after Hanno's mother attended church Sunday morning (while Hanno stayed in bed), the crew of the *West Virginia* was experiencing the torpedo attack. A series of events led in short order to the ship being immobilized. Unlike on some other ships, the captain was on the bridge in command. However, shrapnel from the exploding USS *Arizona*, somewhat aft of the *West Virginia*, had struck him. He was carried away for medical attention but died shortly thereafter.

One of the officers believed that the assault was coming from airplanes and overhead bombing. (For some other ships, this was true.) So, all men on the top deck were ordered below to protect themselves from aerial assault.

Since the assault on the ship was judged to be nine torpedoes below the water level, the port (left) side of the ship was flooding with seawater and fuel from ruptured tanks.

At this point a major breach occurred in communication. The ship's intercom was disabled. Separate fires and water prevented any one officer from moving to all points on the ship to convey a verbal order.

Since the portside flooding was out of control and the ship was listing, two actions were necessary. One was on behalf of the men. The other was on behalf of the ship.

The order to abandon ship did not reach everybody. One or more officers would have to reach all areas of the ship to give the order vocally. Because of fires and direct torpedo damage in many areas, there was no way this could be done.

The order to counterflood the ship came from standard naval protocol. A ship can be more successfully salvaged and refloated if it is not capsized. This is especially true with ships in harbor at known shallow depth. This procedure requires opening the hatches in dry areas opposite the side of damage. These dry areas are then flooded to counter the list as a ship begins to turn over toward its damaged side. If a ship settles on the bottom on its damaged side, it becomes difficult or impossible to patch the damage. The extraordinary problem here was that the counterflooding decision had to be carried out with the abandon ship order not reaching the total crew.

This meant that some crewmembers were permanently blocked from escape. Others, who manned their assigned stations, may have delayed departure by their own judgment or sense of duty until it was too late to locate an escape route. Others who wanted to escape were met with the ambiguity of having been given no order to abandon. A review of this perfect storm series of events after the war found that no negligence could be assigned to any given officer for this tragic set of circumstances.

One well-documented example of this chaos during the morning was in a larger lower-deck compartment with several hundred crewmen up to their knees and then waists in a continually rising mixture of fuel oil and seawater but with only one escape hatch. This escape required ascending a ladder, one person at a time. Some dizzy and fainting crewmen were being lifted up the ladder first because of immediate risk of loss of consciousness. Others already on the ladder were dizzy or fainting. Those assisting below and above from outside the hatch were creating a natural traffic jam. The rate of successful escapes could not keep up with the rising water and the density of fumes causing the loss of consciousness.

Reaching fresh air and sunshine on the top deck did not ensure escape from danger. Fire on deck limited the exit routes from the ship. Some seamen jumped off the deck into water that was on fire with a heavy layer of fuel oil resting atop the surface. Finding and swimming to a dock ladder or entry onto the USS *Tennessee* was another option. One solution for escape was over a cable or hose line. At the time of attack and during prior hours, the *West Virginia* was refueling and the ship was 70 percent full at the time of the attack. Thus a hose line was available as a tether to the *Tennessee* and to the shore.

* * *

Around December 10, 1941, the Buchwalds received a telegram from Ray. He asked if they had any information about the fate of his twin brother. Amid the chaos and fear of invasion, Ray, in spite of being given time off to look for his twin brother, was unable to locate anyone who had information. Following the attack, all Hawaii was in turmoil, chaos, and hush. Even when allowed on what was left afloat of the *West Virginia*, he could get no information. Part of the top deck and the squirrel cage conning tower were above water as the ship rested on the bottom of the harbor.

Two more telegrams were to arrive later in the month with the same query.

In early 1942, Hanno's family got the telegram that resulted in one gold and one blue star on a pennant in the Buchwald front room window for the duration of the war. The telegram was a boilerplate form sent to hundreds of families of Pearl Harbor victims, with blanks provided for the name and address of the receiver and the name, rank, and relation of the victim to the receiver.

Telegram

MR. GENE BUCHWALD
R. R. 3
LINTON, INDIANA

THE NAVY DEPARTMENT DEEPLY REGRETS TO INFORM YOU THAT YOUR SON Jay Buchwald, Carpenter's Mate Third Class, U. S. Navy WAS LOST IN ACTION IN THE PERFORMANCE OF HIS DUTY AND IN THE SERVICE OF HIS COUNTRY X THE DEPARTMENT EXTENDS TO YOU ITS SINCEREST SYMPATHY IN YOUR GREAT LOSS X TO PREVENT POSSIBLE AID TO OUR ENEMIES PLEASE DO NOT DIVULGE THE NAME OF HIS SHIP OR STATION X IF REMAINS ARE RECOVERED THEY WILL BE INTERRED TEMPORALLY IN THE LOCALITY WHERE DEATH OCCURRED AND YOU WILL BE NOTIFIED ACCORDINGLY.

REAR ADMIRAL C. W. NIMITZ,
CHIEF OF THE BUREAU OF NAVIGATION

The telegram was not dated, owing partly to a clogged telegraph office. The sender, Rear Admiral Chester W. Nimitz, was later to be a full admiral and commander of the Pacific Fleet.

The phrases *lost in action* and *missing in action* (used in other official correspondence) became focal points in the thinking of Hanno's parents. Officially, these phrases meant that no body had been retrieved. With Hanno's parents, however, they represented the last but strong thread of hope. Even though the references were made to "death" and "burial," the telegram did not say Jay had been "killed in action." Although Hanno did not realize it at the time, his parents were hanging on to the idea that Jay was still alive.

Nevertheless, the Buchwalds got a telegram off to Ray, who, even then, had not learned the fate of his twin brother.

* * *

In late summer of 1942, after the USS *West Virginia* had been refloated, the family received a small package of "personal effects." It was Jay's Midland High School graduation ring and his Social Security card. The ring was badly tarnished from fuel and seawater, and it had a piece of skin stuck to the inside. Hanno took the skin off so his parents would not see it. his dad got home first, and Hanno showed him the package.

Gene left Hanno to shed his security guard uniform and prepare to pick up Mary. The two then drove to the Roosevelt Hotel where Hanno's mother was subbing for the maid and also doing heavy housecleaning. Hanno, in an unusual move, had taken the backseat. As Hanno's mother approached the car, she could see that his dad, in the driver's seat, was emotionally unhinged. She immediately assumed that he was drunk (not an uncommon occurrence during that period).

"Look at you!" she said, lashing out. "A fine state of affairs you are in! In the middle of the day!"

Hanno could see that he should intercede. He told her of the package they had received. However, sitting in back, Hanno did not know that his dad had been crying. Now his mother could see it all correctly. Gene handed the package to her and could not speak.

The complete emotional breakdown of his parents made him realize that neither of them had actually accepted the fact of Jay's death until that moment. They had not relinquished the hope that he would one day show up. The personal differences between them faded away, and on the way home, the two tried to comfort each other. It was a relationship that Hanno had never seen.

The period of apprehension and hope was over. Now came the period of true bereavement.

* * *

Next came the life insurance event. Hanno's folks had a Prudential life policy on the twins and Hanno for $1,000 each. That seemed to Hanno like a lot of money. Hanno's parents retrieved the policy, which Hanno examined on his own. He noted that certain conditions allowed the policy to be paid in double indemnity. Accidental death or death in a riot allowed double indemnity, but being killed in a war did not. Before Hanno's parents had time to file a claim, Oliver Marshall, Bill's dad, came to the house with a colleague and with a check for $1,000. Prompted by Hanno's information, his mother pointed out to them what Hanno had found and noted that war with Japan had not been declared until December 8, 1941 (and with Germany on December 11, 1941). Without a word, the insurance men left and in a few days returned with a

$2,000 check. Hanno remembered walking into town to deposit the check, feeling with fear that he was carrying all the money in the world.

*　*　*

In addition to the hundreds who drowned or escaped or were hit by missiles, a group of sixty-nine were found in one large lower deck compartment when the *West Virginia* was refloated. By reaching an air pocket they died of lack of oxygen rather than drowning—that is, as the water level rose in this large compartment, an air bubble was created at the ceiling, where the water could not rise. In effect, the air at the ceiling could not escape. The sixty-nine had climbed onto the plumbing near the ceiling. They escaped the water, but only a small amount of oxygen was available. So, when the ship was refloated, these sailors were found dead among the plumbing pipes.

*　*　*

Hanno found himself preoccupied with the fate of the three trapped men in the freshwater machine compartment on the USS *West Virginia*. Later on, when Hanno was a professor, he and one of his students tried to investigate. Reports made regarding the recovery of bodies during the refloating of the ship indicated that three seamen were found in the airtight chamber away from the seawater and fuel-oil mixture. However, the efforts by Hanno and his student to get the names and details of the three sailors met with refusal. After repeated phone calls and letters to the Navy Department, the Department of Defense, the National Archives, and other government agencies, no names or details were provided. While freedom-of-information guidelines made such information legally available, the resistance to cooperate was clear. Hanno knew that all next-of-kin were deceased, so that could not be the reason. Moreover, the agents admitted that the information was there—plus pictures. Eventually a vague reference was made to the view that such information might be detrimental to public morale and that the Navy, in particular, would have difficulty recruiting.

Hanno took great umbrage at this response. To him, these three men, living sixteen days in trapped quarters, had made an extraordinary sacrifice for their country and, given the recent policy, their names and uncommon sacrifice would be completely lost to history. For Hanno, somehow, it became a personal matter.

One day it occurred to Hanno why he could not let go of the plight of the three and move on. Early on, as a preschool child, he had been told by his brothers that they would butcher and scatter his body so that no one would ever remember that he existed. Hanno came to realize he held a strong identity with the three.

Then a breakthrough occurred. Hanno and his student learned of the annual reunions of the crewmen of the *West Virginia*. The crew had no prohibitions of government jurisdiction. The names and the deeds of the trapped men were well known. A play about them had been written and performed at the Edinburgh Festival. Siblings of the men had attended the reunions. Plans were discussed to change the date of death on the Navy records and on the tombstones.

When the ship was refloated, each sailor was lying on a bare storage shelf in his Navy blues. These are the warmer uniforms used in climates cooler than Hawaii. They had ample water from the freshwater-making machine. By good fortune some boxes of canned peaches had been liberated from the galley. Although nothing was left except empty peach cans on the floor, they had not died of starvation. Also on the floor was an abundance of used flashlight batteries.

The three seamen had made themselves heard during this period of entrapment. They used a wrench to tap on the plumbing and bulkhead. From the unique rhythms, people knew very well that someone was trapped. Fiske, a sailor on sentry duty at night, first detected and reported the rhythms. Learning of this, other sailors avoided the morbid nighttime sentry duty when the clanging could be heard above the other noises at the surface. Robert Fiske, who had been the bugler on the *West Virginia*, remained on the night duty. In time, the tapping became slower and less frequent. It finally stopped on December 22.

Rescue of these men was impossible. The attempt of a team of divers and welders to penetrate the hull of the USS *Arizona* had failed. An underwater explosion killed one of the divers in an attempt to drill a small air hole in the hull of the capsized USS *Oklahoma*. Immediately, the inside pressure caused the air bubble to escape out the hole, leaving the chamber completely filled with water. Making an escape hole big enough to allow a human body to escape or be extracted was impossible if the direction of water pressure outward exceeded the pressure of air inflow. So, no new attempt was made to rescue the *West Virginia* boys.

The three seamen trapped in compartment A-111 of the *West Virginia* had placed on the wall an eleven-by-fourteen-inch calendar on which the days between December 7 and 23 had been marked with an X. Questions were raised about how the trapped sailors could discern when a day had passed. This query was answered by the fact that an eight-day clock was on the wall in the compartment. Also, Hanno knew from research that natural body rhythms convey day-to-day time awareness.

When Hanno learned of this public recognition, a great burden was lifted. A sense of peace and justice prevailed. More would be done to ensure that these three human beings would not go unknown to history. It was as if something good had happened to Hanno himself.

The entrapped men of the *West Virginia* were Clifford Olds, age twenty, of Stanton City, North Dakota; Ronald Endicott, age eighteen, of Aberdeen, Washington; and Louis "Buddy" Costin, age twenty-one, of Henryville, Indiana.

A cousin of Clifford Olds learned of his fate while working in the Bremerton, Washington, shipyards, where the USS *West Virginia* was refurbished and upgraded for the later Pacific War. The cousin informed Duke Olds, Cliff's brother. Duke reported that his brother Cliff had almost always sent home to his poor family eighteen dollars per month from his twenty-one-dollar-a-month paycheck. Duke concluded that his parents did not need to know. He informed Cliff's sister, who attended some of the reunions of the *West Virginia* crewmen.

Ronald Endicott's parents' address became unknown in 1956, and it is assumed that no information about their son was available after this.

Buddy Costin's brother Harlan was the first family member to know of his fate. Harlan joined in October 1942 at seventeen and served on the USS *Tuscaloosa*. In 1944, he had a chance meeting with a friend who was serving on the rebuilt USS *West Virginia* and learned of the story from him. Harlan was determined never to tell his family. As in the case of Jay Buchwald, Buddy's parents got a "personal effects" package from the Navy when the *West Virginia* was refloated. It contained a lady's wristwatch, which obviously had been intended for his mother's 1941 Christmas. She had it repaired and wore it until her death in 1985 at ninety-two.

* * *

Over the years Hanno was able to learn of events that occurred on December 6, 1941, the day before the attack. He linked them to his own activities in Linton.

People were seeking good times on that evening in Hawaii. Jay had taken the shuttle boat (called the tender) to come ashore in hope that Ray would be available to go enjoy Honolulu. At about the same time, perhaps on the same tender, three other sailors from the *West Virginia* were also out to explore life ashore. These three men were Clifford Olds, Jack Miller, and John Szwerda. They made their way to the Monkey Bar, a well-known nightclub near the shuttle dock. Like almost all the enlisted crew, they were young, not long away from home, and just now learning what it was like to go into a tavern and order a drink. When a fellow sailor offered you a cigarette, you could not turn it down. It was part of growing up.

On this evening of December 6, one of these three sailors was Clifford Olds. A country boy from the Dakotas, his acquaintances were recent and he was pleased to have their company. He was also pleased to be there and to explore with them this new experience. After they were "set up" and "lit up," a cigarette girl / cocktail waitress came around with a camera to take their picture. After the picture was taken, they discussed it briefly and decided that it was a scam. They felt that the cost of a print of the picture was too much. They turned her down.

It was a good and memorable evening. Nevertheless, when they caught the tender back to their ship, Olds invited them to his special air-sealed quarters. He had in mind a bull session. On this night, however, the drink had been heavy and the hour was late. Shortly, everyone retired to his own quarters.

For Clifford Olds, this night was the last he was to see moonlight. It was the last he was to smell the flowering citrus of this tropical island.

Jack Miller, John Szwerda and Cliff Olds at the Monkey Bar, December 6, 1941.

Jack Miller and John Szwerda, the other two at the Monkey Bar, survived the attack. They got onto another vessel and went to sea. Jack, who had been a special friend of Cliff Olds, wondered if Cliff had made it. He kept remembering the photo. It was the last picture taken during peacetime for all of them. He did not know what had happened to the others, but he soon learned that Cliff was unaccounted for. After two weeks at sea Jack's ship came back into Pearl Harbor. As soon as he could get leave, he made a straight line for the Monkey Bar. He found the waitress who had taken the picture. He asked if he might buy it. She had indeed kept it, knowing that this was the last evening of peacetime for everyone. When she found the picture, she declined to charge him for it. She gave it free.

Now, on the wall of Hanno's study, in the Museum of the USS *West Virginia*, and in many other places is the famous picture of the three sailors in the Monkey Bar. They reached for the end of innocence, trying the new drink, accepting the cigarette from a buddy, trying out life. In this exploratory test, they were unsure of themselves, as the picture shows.

* * *

On the day of the attack Hanno was just over thirteen years old and in the eighth grade. As he later learned, on the evening of Saturday, December 6, 1941, before the attack, Jay took the tender that transports sailors on liberty to and from shore. Jay made his way off the boat to Fort Shafter to visit his brother Ray, who was in the military police battalion. Ray, unfortunately, was tied up in paperwork following some arrests made earlier in the day. He could not accept his brother's invitation to go out on the town. Jay left the MP station and caught the next shuttle back to the ship. On the ship, he ran into his friend Ernie Simmelink from western Kansas. The two had talked earlier of chess, and Jay had confessed he did not know the game. The Kansas buddy invited Jay to meet for an early breakfast and then to go to the carpenters' shop for a chess lesson.

They had almost completed setting the chess pieces upon the chessboard when a loud, jolting explosion knocked the pieces onto the floor. They looked at each other, and both had the same idea. They suspected a boiler on the ship had overheated and exploded. They got down on their hands and knees to pick up the chess pieces. Before they got them back into place, another explosion occurred. Immediately following was a call-to-quarters message on the intercom. They looked at each other again. Over and over they had been warned in the last few weeks that war was imminent and to be prepared. They realized that the time had come. Neither of them could fully comprehend what was happening.

As the ship was being flooded, Ernie ran onto the officer opening the hatches and got the abandon ship message. He fled the ship on the fuel line that tethered the ship. As Ernie reported, Jay did not make it.

* * *

The parents of the deceased men were given the choice of letting their sons remain in the Punch Bowl Military Cemetery or having them be shipped to another place for final burial. Jay's parents chose his return to Fairview Cemetery in Linton.

When the body arrived in Linton, the flag-draped casket was put on display at Welch and Cornett Funeral Home. Hanno became aware immediately that, compared to the traditional Linton funeral, there was very little for visitors to look at. So Hanno, with his parents' consent, got a large portrait of Jay in uniform and also the Order of the Purple Heart medal that had been awarded to all who were wounded or killed in action since the time of George Washington. These were placed on a table beside the casket. Hanno then asked one of his classmates, Frank Miller, to take a picture of the casket and display. Frank had just acquired his first studio camera.

After the funeral the casket was transported to Fairview Cemetery. The usual funeral tent had been set up in front of the casket and grave. The day was neither sunny nor rainy, so the tent served little purpose other than to block the breeze. A Navy noncommissioned officer had accompanied the casket to Linton. In the usual ceremony, the flag was removed from the casket and the naval escort and Hanno's cousin Martin folded it into a triangle. Amid the sobbing family, friends, and relatives, the naval escort, who took his job seriously and was just short of tears, took the folded flag and bent down on one knee in front of Hanno's mother. Hanno was sitting to the left of her on the front row. The escort said softly to her, so that Hanno could barely hear, "Mrs. Buchwald, the president of the United States, on behalf of a grateful nation, presents you this flag from your son's casket."

She nodded through her tears, and he placed the flag into her hands on her lap. The escort then arose and gave orders to the representatives of Linton's American Legion, who, dressed in Sunday church garb and their eternal Legionnaire overseas caps, conducted the three volleys of shot from four rifles. Then came the sounding of taps from a bugle just out of sight.

Hanno knew of the flag folding from summer camp. He knew the peaceful sound of taps. He thought of Ray, still on duty in the South Pacific, who would have wanted to be present. He thought of Okie Astrup, who, during the three years at the one-roomed Plum Branch School, had taught proudly of America, his country, and of the brave heroes who had given their lives for their country. At last, Hanno himself had tears falling down his cheeks. Then it was all over.

[26]

RAY'S WAR

Having viewed the war from Hanno's home front in Linton and from Jay's fate on the USS *West Virginia* during the Pearl Harbor attack, we now view the war from the perspective of Ray. Hanno spent hours listening and taking notes.

As the war broke out on December 7, 1941, Ray was a member of the 810th Military Police Company. Their police station was on the corner of Merchant and Bechtel Streets in Honolulu. The living quarters were in Fort Shafter about three and a half miles away. Before recounting Ray's experience, it is important to describe various background and cultural features that bore heavily upon His fate.

While Hanno and his brothers all shared an isolated existence on the homestead farm, Hanno's brothers, seven years older, would move directly from the narrow isolated homestead confines into the diverse culture of military service. This they did when they graduated from Midland High School in 1939. From a high-school class of only thirty, the twins left the jobless Depression to broaden their horizons.

Hanno went to a larger high school and was in a wider range of activities, including high-school drama, editing the high-school yearbook, making ice cream, waiting trade at the Rexall drugstore, and participating in the Boy Scouts. The Midland experience of Jay and Ray emphasized wood shop and art. This turned them inward toward their talents rather than expanding their social realm.

The twins encountered a culture shock entering the military, whereas Hanno remained cloistered in Linton. With the absence of the present information age and its exposure to diversity, it is now difficult to imagine how this isolation magnified differences when people of different backgrounds encountered each other. Stereotyping others was not just an unfavorable social habit but was a fixed first step in processing differences. To encounter a person with a different accent, a name spelled and pronounced differently from common English or European family names, or practicing a religion other than Protestant Christianity provided new categories to be processed before assimilating them as fellow human beings. Supplanted upon these prevailing stereotypes were the more recently fashioned ones of the voluntarily enlisted versus draftees and the West Pointers versus the officer candidate school (OCS) officers.

The differences in the lexicons of the country and city boys in service were immediately evident. The twins could not distinguish an egg cream, chocolate phosphate, subway entrance, corner peddler wagon, or the Brooklyn Dodgers. The city boys did not understand croppies, a doubletree hitch, smallmouths, four-tens, black-and-tans, or a fly reel. The boys from rural states tended to drift together, and the city boys did the same.

It is not surprising that the local Hawaiians had their own brand of stereotyping. Besides the conflicts that could arise from the Japanese, Chinese, Korean, and other East Asian cultures, Ray and Jay soon learned that students in Hawaiian high schools were taught to shun the American servicemen because they allegedly contained a high number of criminals and rapists who joined the service to run from the law.

Another important factor was that the Army and Army Air Corps practiced a tradition of transferring (dumping) overseas the various misfits, such as chronic liars, chronic fighters, alcoholics, gamblers, and incompetent officers. The prewar peacetime Army was to be greatly contrasted to the recent arrivals with the defensive buildup of the military forces. This difference bore heavily upon the series of experiences Ray encountered.

Before World War II, this dumping ground was Hawaii. Later, during Hanno's Air Force tenure, Korea (before the Korean War) was the well-recognized dumping ground. This meant that a new military recruit shipped to Hawaii did not experience the transient paradise of the tourist. Not only was there the clash of urban versus rural, East Asian versus Anglo and European, but there was also a rat's nest of personal problems existing among old-timer prewar officers and soldiers. The Navy was somewhat immune to this problem. Officers could not exert power from their own prejudicial and personal whims as easily.

Being sequestered on a ship allowed a more stable group structure. The use of testing to determine promotion eliminated politics and abusive power in the upper ranks.

By sheer fate, both Jay, in the Navy, and Ray, in the Army, wound up quickly in Hawaii. The buildup of military forces in Japan represented the greatest immediate menace to the United States. Pearl Harbor was the major fleet base away from the mainland.

As Ray and his infantry unit disembarked in Hawaii, they were heading for Schofield Barracks. A sergeant waiting on the dock approached Ray. In answer to two questions, Ray reported that he weighed 170 pounds and could type. With this information, Ray was immediately made an MP (military police) and was transferred to Fort Shafter within the Honolulu urban area.

The two Buchwald twins had chosen to be together on all possible occasions. Splitting into Navy and Army was not their will. Jay was the more assertive leader and planner. Ray was the more neighborly, talkative, and dependent follower. Ray did boxing for a while but turned to pistol marksmanship as a hobby. He very quickly made expert marksman and was winning competitive matches. Later on, when matched against the Norwegian national champion, Ray was the winner. Ray also extended his safety skills, passing the Red Cross requirements in swimming, life-saving, and water safety as an instructor. On regular duty, his typing was important in writing up the many reports. He had reached the rank of corporal in a few weeks. On the ship Jay qualified for carpenter's mate second class on December 1, 1941, just prior to the December 7 attack.

Jay visited Ray on the evening of December 6, 1941. Ray was busy with reports and could not go out with him. As it turned out, Ray had to work all night long, and Jay returned to his ship. Early the next morning, Jay and his Kansas friend Ernie Simmelink setting up a chessboard and Hanno was watching a matinee in Linton. Ray was trying to get some sleep. The first explosion from Pearl Harbor aroused him temporarily. He looked outside and was surprised to see fighter planes in the air on a Sunday morning. Going back to bed, he then heard more explosions. A small Motorola radio, owned by someone in the barracks, yielded the announcement that "Hawaii is being assaulted by enemies." This was Ray's first and only announcement of the Japanese attack. There were no official announcements, no orders in response, and no prior protocol to guide the action.

Before Ray went to bed, he had laid out his uniform with leather belts for a scheduled two o'clock parade. However, with the radio news, Ray donned his web belt that accommodated ammunition clips and a pistol holster. For the rest of the day, the orders were contradictory if not bizarre. At eight in the morning came the assembly order for roll call. The platoon leader immediately ordered Ray to return to the barracks and put on his leather belts. He did so and, upon return, was ordered to go back and shine the leather. The platoon leader oriented himself to preparing for the two o'clock parade, even though he was aware of the Japanese attack. As Ray attended to his leather belt, he noticed that others were ignoring the platoon leader and putting on the web belts. Ray did the same.

After roll call Ray immediately went to the armory to get his pistol and ammunition. There was a big line.

Ordinarily each MP was given his pistol and three rounds of ammunition. Now everyone wanted more. The supply sergeant, Marcoski, felt he had no clearance to give more than three rounds without the MP signing papers for each additional three bullets. Ray wound up signing his name seven times to get his pistol and ammunition.

Ray knew he was on the machine gun detail, so he got out the three guns assigned to the company. Since these machine guns were water-cooled, each having a three-gallon tank, Ray began filling the cooling tanks with water. He was interrupted by another corporal who said he was in charge of the machine guns. When Ray asked this unfamiliar corporal for his identity, he said he was Zimowich, the house orderly (dog robber) for Lieutenant Colonel Steer. Steer had sent his orderly ahead of his own arrival. The corporal ordered Ray to get a piece of twine in order to align the machine guns properly. Ray went to get the twine. When he returned, the machine guns were gone. Yet someone else apparently was in charge.

Sergeant Winters was on hand. Although a state of combat was under way, with ground and air exchanging gunfire, neither Sergeant Winters nor any superior had actually given an order.

Ray had had a previous encounter with the sergeant. A few months earlier, Sergeant Winters approached Ray and told him that he had rescued his twin brother Jay from "big trouble." The sergeant told Ray that Jay had been in a bar pitching dice with some Marines and was being accused of cheating. He was much in danger of a fight or a shore patrol officer arresting him. Winters said he intervened and got Jay out of the situation. If not for Winters, according to his own report, Jay would have gone to a lockup. Ray was astonished to hear this, until he got a postcard from his brother. He was with his ship in Bremerton, Washington, for upkeep repairs. Since Jay was at sea when the alleged event occurred, Ray realized he had been taken for a gullible country boob, to which Winters often made reference. Winters was part of the old prewar Army that was prone to making up their own rules.

Once the shooting began, Winters stood over and watched the firing of an antiaircraft battery. Ray approached and pointed out to Winters that the battery was using blank ammunition reserved for simulated demonstrations.

"How can you tell?" asked Winters.

"The puff of smoke is not dark as with real ammunition."

"You are a lying son of a bitch." Winters then ordered Ray to leave, and he continued to stand and watch the antiaircraft battery.

The soldier assigned to duty as guard at the front gate of Fort Shafter came running down a barracks street. Excitedly, he yelled that a plane had strafed and killed two pedestrians in front of Tripler Hospital. It was clear that the guard at the gate did not know that there was a war on. There was no telephone or other communication at the Fort Shafter guard box. Thus Ray marked another situation in need of correction. The guard returned to the guardhouse but with no special order following his report.

A truck was readied to transport Ray and others from Fort Shafter to the police station at Merchant and Bechtel. On the way, along King Street, a Japanese fighter plane fixed its aim on the truck but then suddenly veered away.

Ray and others assumed that the plane must have been out of ammunition.

About this time Ray's vision of the world made a dramatic shift. He realized from various reports that the main target of the attack was at Pearl Harbor where his brother was. Ray was stunned and began immediately to show the effects of traumatic shock. His memory became disconnected so that he could not piece together the sequence of events he was experiencing. This is the common reaction to combat, rape, severe auto accidents, natural disasters, or any other event that has traumatic shock.

Although he started out in a truck to the police station, he wound up in a truck going to Hickam Field housing. At Hickam he saw Japanese planes diving steeply, unloading their bombs on parked planes, and often failing to pull out of the dive in time, thereupon crashing into the hangars. It did not appear that they were crashing on purpose.

Ray was once on a road following a man in a modern World War II helmet. (The MPs at that time had World War I helmets.) A bomb landed nearby, and the man was killed by shrapnel penetrating both the helmet and skull. This was the first casualty of the war that Ray was to witness. The vehicle traffic at Hickam was maddening, with cars going in all directions.

By two in the afternoon Ray was back in the police station. A call came in that a "gook" (pejorative word for East Asian) was standing naked in the water offshore at Bellows Field. Colonel Steer had become the OD (officer of the day). He pointed to Ray. "Go find a driver and pick him up if he is still there."

Ray found Pfc. Wheeler available. Overwhelmed by the events of the day, Ray got into the back of the truck. Arriving on the scene, Ray found a Lt. Paul Plybon and Cpl. David Akui observing the man in the water but taking no action. Ray assumed that the naked person in the water was either drunk or mentally ill. Ray went to the shoreline and motioned the man to come ashore. He obeyed. When spoken to, the man responded only in Japanese. The truck had turned around in the road during Ray's apprehension. Ray and the arrestee boarded the truck. Ray sat down beside the man. Immediately realizing that his pistol holster was adjacent to the man, Ray moved to an opposite rather than adjacent position. Ray noticed a faint smell of perfume from the man but did not link it to Japanese ceremonial procedures.

Getting to the police station, Ray found Captain Benson on duty as OD. Benson decided to transfer the man to Fort Shafter, where there was more space and where language translation was available.

As it turned out, the man was a Japanese pilot of a two-man submarine. The steering mechanism broke, and the pilot was unable to enter the mouth of the harbor at the appropriate time. The sub ran aground off the Bellows Field Beach, and the pilot's partner had drowned. The man reported his name to be Kazuo Sakamaki. When asked who would win the war, he replied, "The Rising Sun." (Later, this POW was reported to have become the manager of Toyota sales in South America after the war.)

Next came another apparent mix-up wherein the MP company's gear was transferred from Fort Shafter to the immigration station near Pier 1. Ray lost all his leather equipment. His campaign hat was assigned to another corporal, but his uniforms and footlocker were transferred to the immigration station in good order. The apparent purpose of the move was to build slit trenches for machine gun placements. The entire Hawaiian community, civilian and military, was expecting invasion at any moment. The alarm and paranoia over Japanese residents was much greater than that on the mainland. A curfew was strictly enforced.

According to military custom, the privates and privates first class did all the digging, and Ray, as a corporal, supervised.

One day after the completion of duty he got the telegram from his parents back in Indiana that his twin brother, Jay, was officially missing in action. Ray had no misgivings, as his parents did, about the message. To him, it meant that his brother had died on the USS *West Virginia*. It is commonly argued that the loss of one's identical twin is greater than any other loss. Ray had the feeling that part of his body inhabited that of his brother and vice versa. He had not lost his arms or his legs, but from then on, he would never feel complete. Ray was a long way from home, and he had to go it on his own. Immediately, Ray lapsed into a state of depression as part of his bereavement. He could not eat. He could not sleep. He had a feeling of alienation from other people—no more neighborly talking "over the barnyard fence" with people. Finally there was the black mood. The best way to describe it was that, as he opened his eyes each morning, he knew he felt miserable and that miserable things would happen. If something good did happen, there was no sense of pleasure. It was not surprising that people who knew him earlier viewed him as a different person.

Then a series of events began in Ray's life that was impossible to comprehend. Sgt. Winters came to him with a shovel and a stick eleven inches long and told him personally to start digging each trench eleven inches deeper. When he asked about the protocol and said that corporals did not dig, Winters ripped the two stripes off his shirt and told him he was now a private.

The sergeant said, "I want you to get down into each slit trench and not raise your head up until each one is finished. If you do, I will hit you over the head with something. If you decide you do not want to dig anymore, I want you to go out this main gate and I do not want to see you again."

Ray felt he had nowhere to go. While his muddled state of thinking left him with no basis to retaliate, he began digging. He dug day after day until three weeks passed. Such an incident would ordinarily be subject to redress of grievances, but such redresses were not typical with the prewar peacetime soldiers in Hawaii.

Then Captain Benson visited him.

"Get up here. I have some questions."

Ray was happy to comply. "Yes, sir."

"What ship did you come to the islands on?"

"The SS *Republic*" was his prompt response.

"When did you arrive on the island of Oahu?"

"July 9, 1940."

"What is your serial number?"

"C990724."

"What is your pistol number?"

Ray gave the correct and prompt answer.

"Give me your shovel."

Ray did as told.

"I do not want you digging anymore until I hand you back this shovel myself. Do you understand?"

"Yes, sir."

Ray was happy to leave. He left the measuring stick in the trench. Neither the punishment nor the query by Captain Benson made any sense to him. He was too morally devastated to do anything about it. It was not until the end of the war that he got an explanation about why these events took place. He was too depressed to realize that a rift was forming among the officers and that the rift for some reason was centered on him.

The old peacetime Army with its prejudice, corruption, and arbitrary use of power for the sheer enjoyment of power was different from the new Army, which had elements of leadership, mission, and rules.

Time passed. Others advanced in rank. Others were recommended for OCS. Ray remained a private. One day, he returned from extended duty after Colonel Steer had made an inspection and gave a talk. When Ray entered the barracks, he was approached by three who were moderate acquaintances. It was Sidwell, Jones, and, later to walk up, Hullinger.

"Do you think you will ever get any rank in this outfit?"

"I hope so."

"Don't count on it. This morning Steer conducted inspection and gave a speech. In the speech he said that the only ones who do well in the company are the Catholic ones, especially the Polish. He said that if he had it his way, the entire company would have this makeup. Any chance he had to transfer a Catholic, especially Polish Catholic, into the company, he would do so."

Ray's response to them was somewhat passive and suppressed. He knew that such talk occurred, that he was looked down on as a country boob, yet he had the faith that people would be fair and honest in the long run. As time passed, however, it was evident that more Catholics were recruited in, more Catholics were getting promotions, those who were not Catholic were transferring out of the unit, and rank was being awarded almost primarily to Catholics. It was also notable that many Protestant soldiers began attending Catholic services.

A number of Ray's comrades had gone into OCS and had become commissioned officers. One day, Ray asked about being put up for OCS training and Benson wanted time to check on it. Benson returned and said that the current rules were that a person had to be of sergeant rank before being put up. There were officers, like Captain Benson, who were positive toward Ray or at least not negative. Ray did not speak up to argue his own case. He knew well that he was chosen by many of the others as a scapegoat and a loner. So it was with some courage that someone should go to bat for Ray. After all, he was still chronically depressed and still inefficient in his work.

Since Ray was pulling regular street patrol only as a private, he had the opportunity to learn more of the community. He learned that deserters from the military existed in close proximity. A huge rubber pile had been apprehended from the Japanese and was near the dock, ready to ship to the mainland for the war effort. As Ray did patrol, he could see two persons in the pile behind the barbed wire. They were watching him. He was walking, armed with only a pistol, so he waited until he was with a truck and an armed driver to approach them. He then stopped and asked for their passes. They, of course, had none. These were his first two deserter arrests.

After this, a local resident, Nancy Matsumoto, briefed him about how to spot a deserter. She said that they usually had dirty collars and cuffs, whereas other military were usually clean and neat. On the corner of Tin Pan Alley and Baiayasie, she pointed out one suspect on the street. Ray approached him, found him without pass, and arrested him.

It was easy to survive in Honolulu as a deserter. If in uniform, one could walk into any military mess hall or cafeteria and get food. After Nancy helped him get four additional deserters, he gave her his telephone contact number and then gave it to other East Asian girls working in shops along the main streets. In this way they could notify him of a suspected deserter.

As time passed, the 810th MP Company changed its commanding officer. For a period, Captain John Cutter was in charge. He was well known for walking on his hands. He was once measured to have completed three hundred yards. He also enjoyed playing follow-the-leader with his men. Once Ray was especially amused when Cutter led a three-hundred-pound man into a muddy water pit. In response, Captain Cutter ordered Ray to go through it three times in his parade dress. Ray had no recourse but to comply. Cutter then promised Ray a corporal rank if he would walk on his hands. Ray failed and was never promoted while Cutter was in command.

Next came another commanding officer named Captain Slob. Slob changed his name to Slobe when his children entered school. One day after Ray had been directing traffic in front of Fort Armstrong, he was called into Captain Slobe's office. Slobe told Ray that Lieutenant Evars had reported that the good-looking MP on guard duty at the gate flirted with his wife. Ray denied the charge but, upon further discussion, remembered previously established company protocol. If an MP salutes an officer's car but then recognizes that only the wife is in the car, he should change his salute to a tipping of the hat. Ray explained to Slobe that this was what he did. Ray failed to point out that he also gave the lady a nice smile. Slobe ordered Ray to go to the parking lot, identify Evars's car and tag number, and in the future to motion the car through without saluting or tipping his hat.

Captain Slobe assumed a fair (rather than scapegoat) treatment of Ray. In fact, he called Ray in and told him that he had a perfect record. He informed Ray that the 810th was splitting up into different locations. He said that Ray had a choice of either transferring to Kaneohe where a new radar station was being built or else transferring with a cadre to the United States mainland, where he could likely be sent immediately to combat in North Africa. He gave Ray two weeks off to make a decision. If he stayed, Slobe assured him that he would be in line for promotion as well as being recommended for OCS officer. The new job in Kaneohe on the other side of the island was to be head of buildings and grounds and head of security for the new radar station under construction. He would be made a corporal in charge of a working crew of privates to develop the grounds. Ray took the offer.

Life went well in this new position, and Ray could exercise his carpenter skills.

The unfortunate problem with the agreement was that Slobe was immediately transferred to the office of provost marshal. Decisions on Ray's rank went back to the core officer unit at Fort Shafter.

Another problem with this new environment was that no mess hall existed on this new compound. Ray and his men had to walk a mile to a cafeteria in a military hospital for each meal.

Ray reported later to his younger brother, Hanno, that a chill came over him when he found out that Lieutenant Evars was replacing Captain Slobe. Of particular significance was Ray's reason why. It was not because of Ray's promotion in rank or Evars's being a jealous husband, or oversight of duties. Instead, it was because Evars had grown up on the island and had absolutely no experience or understanding of the agrarian culture from which Ray had come. As Ray put it, "Evars could not carry on a conversation about a Greyhound bus, a wheat field, a forest, a cornfield, or anything in common except the island of Oahu and Honolulu. Evars had never been off the island of Oahu since age three. Moreover, Evars always wanted to kiss up to Lt. Col. Steer." Ray already knew that Evars would get along with the old system of giving the city guys all the credit and rank.

Clearly Ray was judging Evars on the basis of cultural grounds rather than military procedure. Evars was apparently doing the same.

An announcement came in to Kaneohe that the 810th MP Company was to have a New Year's Eve dance to celebrate the passing of 1943 into 1944. Ray did not know how to dance. He was not a big drinker. So he quietly decided, early on, that he was not going to go.

Ray's job at Kaneohe took him to different places each day. Since the clerk assigned to him was incompetent, he had to spend one day each week with the typewriters at the police station at Merchant and Bethel Streets to get caught up on all the reports.

As it turned out, Ray found himself working in the (empty) police station while the company was having its dance at the Immigration Station on New Year's Eve.

At nine thirty at night a car drove in and the driver reported he had seen an accident occur on a hairpin turn on the way down from the Pali. Ray had a jeep available. All other qualified personnel were at the dance. So Ray decided on his own to drive the jeep up the mountain to investigate the accident.

He arrived at a turn in the road on the mountainside where a truck was upside down and a black soldier was lying dead beside it. Ray, surveying the scene, realized that the truck actually had fallen sixty-five feet from the level above the hairpin turn. In spite of universal blackout orders, Ray managed to get one of the dog tags from the dead soldier and the number painted on the truck.

Ray then drove to the top of the Pali, where he could get good communication to a police radio. He reached Honolulu station KHAC and reported the accident. After standing by, KHAC came back to report that five soldiers had been on the truck when it left Honolulu. Ray asked to have an ambulance and a wrecker sent. Then he returned to the accident scene.

If there were four additional men in the truck, they had to be in a gorge in between the high and the low road. It began to rain. Lights being forbidden made the task difficult. Ray began to search the gorge and found one body. With great difficulty he dragged the body up to the curb of the road. He returned to the gorge and immediately found the other three. Two were dead, and the one still alive had a crushed skull.

This task of getting heavy soldiers out of the gorge by himself in the rain and in the dark was as difficult as anything he had ever encountered. After getting the bodies to the road, he went back to investigate the area. He discovered that a great deal of mail had been strewn from the truck into the gorge. He picked up what he could find.

By the time the ambulance and wrecker had cleared up the scene, it was seven o'clock and daylight. Ray then called the provost marshal's office to report the accident. Captain Slobe happened to be on duty as OD. He said the accident had been reported and that Ray should write it up while it was still fresh in mind. He requested that the report be separate for the truck and for the personnel. It turned out to be a most complex report because it involved two separate days, two separate months, and two separate years.

After he submitted the report Slobe called back to acknowledge and compliment Ray on it.

Back at the Kaneohe station, new problems were arising. A new officer, Lt. Marty, just out of OCS, was now in charge. He was new to Hawaii and felt that a greater wall of security should be built between the compound and the community. Ray, highly familiar by then with the islands' culture and people, had fostered the opposite idea. Marty wanted a fence built around the compound. Native Hawaiian civilians had been hired to run the radio communications. Marty wanted personal messages forbidden. Ray had allowed a message to be sent to a local old couple that the birth of the grandchild on Maui had been successful. Marty objected to this. Marty wanted

Ray to get all the troops together from their various work details and march to and from the hospital cafeteria for meals (six miles per day).

When Marty arrived, Ray had suggested the lieutenant, as with his own troops, go get a thirty-five-cent haircut by a sixty-year-old Japanese lady. Appreciative to Ray for all the business, she happily told Marty in her broken Japanese, "Ray my boyfriend." Marty later reported to company headquarters that Ray was shacking up with the old lady.

One day Marty lost his temper with Ray's work group. Many of the homes of the local people had racks of drying squid behind the house. As a gratuity for sending a radio message, one local family sent over some dried squid and Marty came upon the soldiers eating it. In a rage he forbade them to eat it and lectured on how smelly, rotten, and unhealthy this food was. Fortunately, Ray had not yet arrived to take his share. The men began to roll their eyes each time Marty's name was mentioned.

Unfortunately, all the negative impressions and reports of Lt. Marty were passed on to the new commander First Lieutenant Evars.

Lt. Marty was soon replaced by Lt. Sexton. Ray found on their first meeting that Lt. Sexton was intensely interested in Ray's knowledge of arrest slips. He was astonished and unbelieving when Ray said that he had completed over three hundred arrest slips. To demonstrate to Lt. Sexton how he had remembered various arrest codes and codes for articles of war violations, Ray showed him a little notebook he had prepared. It had not only code numbers but also different telephone numbers necessary when processing an arrest. Sexton asked to take the book to the Immigration Station, the new headquarters of the 810th MP Company.

When Sexton returned, he asked Ray to report to the new commander, Lt. Evars, at eight thirty in the morning. Ray knew the meeting would be important, and he hoped that Sexton's presentation of his book would result in a promotion. So he dressed well for the meeting. He reserved a jeep with Pfc. Mimzzura as the driver. As Ray rode over the Pali in reaching the Immigration Station, he reviewed his achievements. He had made fourteen of the twenty-one arrests of deserters by the company. He had earned all his swimming, lifesaving, and water safety instruction certificates. He held the company's record as expert marksman with the .45 pistol.

Remarkably, the most spectacular of Ray's feats did not ever occur to him. He was the first American in World War II to have captured a prisoner of war. At the time Ray had been in a cloud of disconnected thought about the fate of his twin brother. It seemed that his actions on that day had been carried out by someone else.

From the first contact with Evars in the hallway, the interview did not go well. Evars had been promoted to captain, and Ray acknowledged he had been unaware of it. Evars told him to go to his office but refused to tell Ray where his new office was. After finding the office he waited for Evars. When Evars entered, he stood facing the wall and read to Ray a set of orders that Ray had given his own work detail should they be involved in combat. Ray explained that he was already familiar with these orders. Evars, in rage, turned and ripped off Ray's corporal chevrons from his shirt.

"You have now been a private for over two weeks. Pfc. Mimzzura, your driver now outranks you, so you are to drive him back to your barracks. As soon as you get back, pack your belongings immediately. A truck will be there in an hour to get you."

Ray drove his driver back to Kaneohe, but first, he stopped at Fort Shafter to report the incident to the inspector general. The inspector general said he could have acted before the incident and before Evars prepared the order, but he could do nothing now.

When Ray arrived at Kaneohe, he explained to his men that he had been busted to private and that they must proceed to duty without any orders from him. The Sgt. Gilliland and Loomis expressed dismay at what had taken place. Loomis had spent the evening of December 6, 1941, on duty with Ray.

Soon a truck came by with a driver and escort to take Ray to a staging point. There he was assigned a bunk, issued a rifle, and told not to unpack. They were immediately to be shipped out to an unnamed invasion site. All who were in the staging tent were taken to a Pearl Harbor dock where troops were boarding a transport ship. As each last name was called out, the soldier gave his first name and serial number. The list was long, so Ray sat on a curb and cleaned the Cosmoline off his rifle. Soldier after soldier had his name called and disappeared up the gangplank.

A last name was called, the gangplank was raised, and the ship shoved off. Ray continued to sit there, now alone.

Finally Ray got up and went to the main gate, but the marine on guard duty would not let him out. Ray presumed that they had dropped him off at the wrong dock.

Ray remembered that he knew a sailor assigned at a radar station inside the Pearl Harbor perimeter. The sailor had married one of Ray's high-school classmates, and they now had a baby.

Ray visited him and explained his circumstance. They had breakfast together. The sailor had a canopied truck. They decided to hide Ray inside the canopy and proceed through the gate back to the staging area tent. The plan worked with no difficulty. When he got back, there was no one to report to at the staging area. Ray found the mess hall about a half mile away. On the way he saw a first lieutenant and explained his situation. This lieutenant told him to wait at the staging area while he made a couple of phone calls. Eventually he returned and told Ray to wait in the staging tent. A truck came and took Ray again to Pearl Harbor. This time he immediately boarded a transport ship. However, it was empty except for the crew. They told Ray where to sleep and where the mess hall was. They ordered him to stay below deck and not be seen.

After Ray went to sleep, he heard the ship move. Soon, it stopped and the ship began to load up with Japanese prisoners of war. The prisoners had been delivered from various destroyers. The trip to transfer the prisoners was short. Before daylight they were being offloaded into trucks. Ray was told to get onto one of the trucks with them. They were taken to a POW camp, and Ray was told where to bunk with four other soldiers.

With all that had happened, Ray was in a state of depression and spoke to no one. He knew not whether he was still on the island of Oahu. Meanwhile, he helped soldiers set up barbed-wire fences and covered them with burlap. He also helped with guard duty with the prisoners but continued not to speak unless spoken to. Finally, after two weeks, a call came for him.

"The Protestant chaplain wants to see you at Fort Shafter."

"How do I get there?"

"A truck will take you."

"Then I must still be on Oahu."

That afternoon a truck came to the POW camp and drove Ray to Fort Shafter. Ray knew the location well and directed the driver once inside the compound. A chaplain answered the door.

"What can I do for you?"

"I want to see the Protestant chaplain."

"Why do you want to see him?"

"I don't know. He sent for me. Are you the Protestant chaplain?"

"Why do you want to see him?"

"I don't know. I was sent. Are you the Protestant chaplain?"

"You don't know why you are here?"

The conversation continued without the chaplain giving his identity, so Ray abruptly decided to leave. Before leaving the base, Ray visited the personnel sergeant to see if he had a record of his recent activities. The only information he acquired while there was that the POW camp where he was assigned was Honowiliuileio. Ray also found that he was on record as having special assignment to the 811th MP Company but attached to the 624th MP Company. However, his pay was still coming from the 810th MP Company. This meant that he had not been transferred.

Two more calls came in to the POW camp for Ray. Neither of them led to any outcome. One was to have his bags packed and ready to leave. Another said he was to escort two prisoners of war to the United States and then be reassigned there. Nothing came of these messages.

Finally Ray was taken to the immigration station, still the base for the 810th MP Company. Ray continued to speak to no one unless spoken to. The first sergeant asked, "Who are you looking for?"

"I want to see Evars."

"He's gone for the weekend, and he doesn't want any trouble out of you."

This comment was the first indication that there could be a transgression against Ray or some other reason to cause trouble.

That night at the Immigration Station the corporal of the guard woke Ray up and asked him if he would stand guard at the gate near the civilian house. Ray agreed and served the 4:00 a.m. to 8:00 a.m. watch. At 7:30 a.m., Lt. Marty entered and Ray, who kept the rifle issued to him for the invasion, gave him a formal rifle salute. Marty stopped and told Ray he was too dumb to know how to salute. Lt. Marty had Ray lean the rifle against a fence and made the usual hand salute. Ray, without protest, did as he was told.

Evars did not show up but the tech sergeant said that they wanted him to work in the Criminal Investigation Department (CID).

Ray was openly bitter. "Well," he said, "everyone else has had a crack at me, so you may have yours now."

"Go to supply and get a web belt and pistol."

Ray went to Supply Sergeant Benny Marcoski, the same one who on December 7, had required a signed paper for each three rounds of ammunition. That day, he issued the web belt but refused to give Ray a pistol—on the basis that he was only a private.

"Do you know how I made expert on the pistol and how many years I have used it?"

"It makes no difference."

As Ray left, the supply sergeant replied, "You are like a chunk of snot that hangs around that no one wants."

Ray turned away and went out the door. When he reported to CID, he was told that they had enough parts to assemble a .45 pistol. Ray knew very well how to do this. So, the matter was solved.

In the CID, Ray found he was consistently treated well and was appreciated for his efforts. It was so much in contrast with the past that it left him confused and afraid of a trap. Even so, they prepared an ID card with his picture and laminated it. This card had unusual status for an enlisted man.

The most unusual thing that happened, as he related to Hanno after the war, was that Ray was sent to Bellows Field to participate day after day in a series of courts-martial. The incredulous thing was that all the courts-martial were ones where he had been the arresting officer or had participated in some way. Negligent filing was not a tenable explanation of why these courts-martial should be delayed. Some malicious steps, it would seem, were taken to delay or obscure the performance record Ray had accumulated.

Some events continued to occur that were incredulous and others Ray continued not to understand. He was assigned for his own use a new Plymouth car with three two-way radios for military and civilian communication. The CID wanted him merged into the community, so they assigned him living quarters with a local Smith family, a member of which was on the Honolulu Police Force. Specific orders were given to stay away from the Immigration Station. The reason was that evidence was being gathered to file charges against Evars for mismanaging funds to pay his tailor for uniforms previously made. Knowing the controversy that existed between Evars and Ray Buchwald, they wanted to avoid any complexities.

Ray's job in the CID was one that kept him in touch with much that was going on. Captain Losco was the head of the CID. Ray's office was just inside the front door, and he served as a receptionist and triage agent. As people walked in, Ray would greet them and direct them to the person most able to solve their problems. Most of the investigations assigned to him involved telephone calls only.

Captain Losco had a regular routine of entering at eight o'clock each morning. He would greet Ray and others and pass to his office. Once Ray was oriented to his job, Captain Losco would not only greet him but also ask how Eleanor was doing. Ray took it as some kind of joke he did not understand.

After two weeks with the same query, Ray confessed his failure to comprehend. It was the morning that Losco came in with major's insignia on his shoulders. Ray congratulated him and conveyed the mystery he felt.

Losco said, "If that is so, then I need to have a conversation with you. Drop into my office in a half hour."

When Ray arrived, Losco said, "Get yourself a coffee and have a seat."

Ray did so.

"Well, what I am about to tell you may come as a big surprise and also make you angry."

Ray remained quiet and attentive.

"I suppose you remember where you were last New Year's Eve?"

"I could hardly forget it. I was up on the Pali hauling bodies of dead black soldiers up out of a gorge. It was 6:00 a.m. when I finished the lifting. Clearing the area took another hour. Then the reports involved two different days, two different months, and two different years, separately for persons and vehicle! Major Slobe wanted the reports right away."

"Well, it may be that your having difficult duty all night was the luckiest thing to happen to you." Major Losco paused and took a sip of coffee. "Where should I start?"

"Evars's wife got drunk and left the New Year's Eve dance with some soldier. She did not show up until the next day. Someone, I wish knew who, put the finger on you as the one who left the dance with her. After the dance, Captain Evars went to Colonel Steer in a rage. He told him that you took his wife and got her drunk and spent the night with her. Her name, by the way, is Eleanor."

Lasco paused and took another drink of coffee and then a deep breath.

"Steer said, 'Bust the son of a bitch and get rid of him. Ship him off to combat. Anything.' Well, you got busted.

291

But shipping out? That was another matter. You have been falsely accused," continued Losco. "But look for a moment at the position Evars was in. He goes to the dance with Eleanor. They have a problem with each other. She goes missing. Someone tells him you are the culprit. They say that you left the dance with her and spent the night with her and slept with her. He believes it.

"Evars is smart enough to know he cannot take action against you that would expose his own problems with his wife. So he goes to Steer to initiate the order. Evars then calls you in to act on Steer's order. All is fine now with Evars until he gets the word that you were not even near the dance. He learns that you were up all night handling the Pali accident. Now he is in a bind.

"Meanwhile," Losco continued, "there were other officers who realized that things had gone too far. While we don't have evidence to bring a fellow officer to court-martial, we do know the orders issued for you. And that you have been mistreated. So we hurried up and called the shipping officer at Pearl Harbor and told him they had the wrong man. So it was not a mistake that your name was not called."

"You mean that someone took my name off? Someone took my name off the list?"

"That is correct. The problem was, we still did not know what happened. If you had actually gotten on the ship? Gone with the invasion force to Saipan? Finally, you turn up at this damned prisoner of war camp.

"With this, we went to Colonel Steer and asked him to reinstate your corporal rank. He refused. He said he had never done that and was not going to start. The real reason was that reinstating you would have opened up publicly a transgression in officer judgment and conduct, both for himself and for Evars. For them it was better to do nothing."

Ray was speechless.

Losco continued, "Now Lt. Sexton gets into the act. Sexton had been given the picture from both Evars and Steer that you had never made a single arrest in your career and would know nothing about how to fill out an arrest slip. They marked you useless as a soldier and as an MP. Yet, Sexton, in quizzing you out at Kaneohe, appeared to be talking to a different person from what they described. Not only did you teach him the codes for arrest information, not only did you claim the record for most deserter arrests, but you kept a little book with the useful code numbers and telephone numbers to process an arrest. Sexton could see that this was not a trivial difference that could be corrected with your book. There was some long-term vendetta that is being held against you. Those records of your arrests and also the performance ratings in your personnel file were being swept under the rug. Sexton also got word that Captain Benson intervened in your behalf early on by taking your shovel. Sexton decided to try to find what had happened to the records of your arrests in the 810th company files.

"Sexton also said that Lt. Marty did not do you any good. He had a list of complaints about your work performance and fraternizing. Their claim that you had not made one single arrest, however, was the clincher. When it was found that someone had jimmied the active files on arrestees up for court-martial, this was the final straw. That led us to getting you into the CID and physically separating you from the 810th MP leadership as much as possible."

At this point Ray had long finished his coffee. Not being a coffee drinker, he could not take another. Although Losco had predicted that Ray would be angry, he was not. He was quiet and depressed. Most of all he had been left with the feeling that he had been treated fairly and honestly by Major Lasco.

After Ray cleared his head from all the new information, he decided to contact each of his superior officers who had supported him. He asked each one for a letter of reference. His thoughts were to restore his identity and dignity. No retaliation, restoration of rank, or other issues drew his attention.

Following the long conversation in Major Losco's office, Ray's duty in the CID returned to normal. Advancement in rank was coming to the many draftees in the 810th MP Company stationed in the Immigration Station, but Ray continued to be a "hot potato" and no confirmation for advancement in the company headquarters was approved.

It was 1944, and with the war winding down, military servicemen were being sent to the mainland and discharged on the point system. Ray had spent four years, seven months, in the Army without furlough. Therefore, he had twice the required number of points for discharge. Major Lasco told Ray that if he stayed on with the CID, he would get his rank back. Ray told him that he had received a similar offer earlier on from Major Slobe when he accepted the Kaneohe job, but Slobe was immediately transferred away from command. Ray decided not to let the same mistake happen twice. He decided to go home, even though stripped of all rank.

* * *

The next significant event both for Ray and for Hanno was Ray's first visit home for three days before finishing his separation from service. Hanno came home from high school and found Ray and both his parents just inside the front door. It was a meeting that yielded silence as each brother scanned the other's features. Hanno cast his eye down upon a slightly slumped and underweight Ray. The visual image was more memorable than what was said. When they had last been together before the war, Hanno came barely up to Ray's shoulders. Ray now looked like a broken man, and Hanno's response was a feeling of sadness as much as excitement.

In the days to follow Hanno was surprised and impressed that Ray invited him to go almost everywhere with him, both for business and pleasure. In times past, Hanno would have been the first one to avoid.

After the short visit, Ray was off to Florida to complete his tour of duty and then go to Camp Atterbury in Indiana to receive his back pay and discharge. In Camp Atterbury, a delay occurred because records indicated he had received all of his back pay. The woman handling the separation had to request all of Ray's personnel records. Needing additional time to untangle the payroll problem, the agent asked Ray why he was in the Army almost five years and came out without any advancement in rank. he gave an explanation as best he could. Then when Ray's personnel records arrived, both of them were in for a surprise. A major portion had been blacked out with permanent India ink. No record was present of any promotions or reductions in rank. Instead, there was the single word "inefficient." The agent explained that this kind of deletion without signing and dating was illegal.

Thus came to an end the tenure of a common soldier. He lost his beloved twin brother in the war, and people will argue whether he also lost himself. Did he leave the Army as a hero or as a profound failure?

* * *

Bad events leave emotional scars, and for Ray, there was no exception. After having been a scapegoat and mistreated in his years in the Army, Ray developed an emotional disorder in situations where he was vulnerable to being turned down in a request. One day in Florida Ray, looking ahead to future employment, went into an upscale hotel, and asked, "What can I do to join this outfit?" With his suddenly whispered inappropriate comments, he was taken to a psychologist for examination. On another occasion, when Hanno visited him and needed to cash a check before flying home, Ray took him to the bank where he was very successfully employed to track down borrowers who had skipped town with unpaid car loans. Ray, in asking for permission for his brother to cash a check, made a verbal appeal so insecure and inappropriate that it drew attention from the bank employees. Ray was so disabled it was painful. Only in these specific stress situations did he show disabling stress symptoms.

Not always in this world do wrongs get to right themselves. When Ray lost his identical twin through death, he lost a significant part of himself. In some ways Ray tried to relive the life that his brother Jay had been denied. After a short time as a civilian he joined the Navy. He knew military life well, knew now how to stay out of trouble, and studied hard on the promotion exams. His officers were more rational and in no case did he have an unpleasant encounter. He moved up quickly in the ranks and retired as a chief warrant officer, the highest rank one could achieve with Navy enlistment.

While in the Navy Jay served on the USS *Worcester*, a light cruiser. Jay engaged in combat and was awarded various campaign ribbons as his ship and others shelled supply caravans along the western coastal highways in the Korean campaign.

Another way to reinstate a lost one is in naming a child. Ray named his son Jay after his twin brother. As a teenager, the boy drowned. The intensity and length of Ray's grief made clear that his pent-up grief from losing his twin brother had never been fully expressed.

Earlier, when Ray rejoined the service by entering the Navy, Hanno was entering college. Ray, as a civilian, had bought a fine new dark-blue suit and a new Chevrolet coupe. Going to sea, he generously left these items for Hanno. The items became crucial for Hanno getting jobs that would otherwise have been impossible. Ray's good will represented a contribution to Hanno's college support that was greater than any other single supporter.

Hanno, realizing Ray's storytelling skills, encouraged him to write a book about the stories handed down by their grandfather Oglesby. When the twins were young (and Hanno too young to listen and remember), their grandfather told of his own father who was sold into bondage at age ten in 1821. After living in a barn and eating with pigs, he ran away and made his way through many states to settle in Greene County, Linton, Indiana. As Hanno made this suggestion to Ray, he was the only one left alive who knew these stories. The resulting book

The Bound Boy was finished just as Ray succumbed into Alzheimer's disease.

With a supportive wife and family in his final years, Ray was dead at age seventy-five. He had a full military funeral with a flag on casket, gun salute, taps, and a bagpipe farewell of "Amazing Grace."

[27]

HIGH SCHOOL

Hanno entered high school with at least the same amount of uneasiness as other country kids. From fourth grade, when he entered Midland consolidated school, he knew he was more comfortable on the playground with kids two grades lower. He was skinny but average in height. He lacked the verbal facility to outpersuade, outcuss, outthreaten, or outshame others on the playground. His only redeeming playground skill was running. Whenever there was a race, Hanno was always first.

At the bottom of his skill ladder were baseball, football, and basketball. Never on the homestead did he ever own a ball, so his lack of experience foreshadowed his lack of skill. His parents saw him as frail. A baseball might hurt him, they felt. Also, there were the nosebleeds.

Moving on from Midland to Black Creek School for the sixth, seventh, and eighth grades, his role on the playground was even more fixed. If choosing up sides for baseball, he was either the last to be chosen and assigned to right field or else he did not play at all. If football, he was the linesman in charge of the ten-yard marker.

In informal activity of throwing and catching, the other boys always excluded him. So Hanno either quit, or it was a game of keep-away. Usually, Hanno would walk away, but on one occasion, he decided he was going to make a big lunge in front of the school's first baseman to intercept the ball. The first baseman lunged as well. The two collided, and a front big tooth of the other boy broke off and lodged in Hanno's forehead. This was a tragedy for the other boy, in that he spent years with dental work and bridges. For Hanno it was only a matter of removing the boy's tooth and cleaning and bandaging the puncture wound. After a month the wound failed to heal, and then Hanno found another larger piece of the tooth more deeply lodged.

The playground ethics following the accident cast blame on neither boy. There was no animosity between the two. The teacher did not punish them. However, the playground dominance did not change. Hanno continued to be excluded from the informal sessions of catch.

Once Hanno had a large rubber ball that he was bouncing off the side of the school building. With a hard but uncoordinated throw, he hit his eighth-grade teacher in the side of the head. Hanno may have been punished had it not been that the teacher before recess had complimented him for being the only one to complete his homework. He also knew of Hanno's poor coordination.

A bizarre outcome resulted from Hanno's exclusion from the boys' ball games and the fact that Hanno and one other boy were ticklish. The teacher, the girls learned, liked to do the tickling. They knew that Hanno was the fastest in the school. Some girls matured fast. Their crush on boys was not reciprocated. Some girls had a crush on Hanno. So, for each recess and noontime, day after day and week after week, they would chase Hanno and try to capture him. About once every three weeks, they would successfully trap him. At this point the smelly, sweaty girls would drag smelly, sweaty Hanno into the schoolhouse to be tickled by a smelly, sweaty three-hundred-pound teacher. Hanno at first resisted giggling or laughing. Finally he would lose all control. His limbs would go limp, and he laughed uncontrollably. On other days, the other boy, Billy, met the same fate.

Meanwhile, during class, Hanno excelled. He was either the best or one of the best in schoolwork.

The city kids were different. They had a sense of presence and ownership of any situation. The trash talk was sharper. Their interests were broader. Their vocabulary was advanced. With more access to radios, jukeboxes, pianos, and phonographs, it seemed they knew all of the modern hit songs and who the performers were. They always had nickels to put into the jukeboxes or even to buy a record. The country boys might well know Lulu Belle and Scottie, Uncle Ezra, or Red Foley on the Chicago WLS National Barn Dance, but the city kids would know who Spike Jones, Glen Miller, and Benny Goodman were.

City boys had the gift of gab—a glibness that country boys could not muster. If told it was going to rain tomorrow, a city kid would never say, "I reckon as how it might." The city boys would chase after the good-looking girls. The country boys stood by or chased a safe girlfriend (not pursued by the others).

Hanno was not daunted by the city-country differences. He was learning the city language and ways. He acquired them from his Boy Scout troop, from city friends, and, finally, from a girlfriend who was from the city.

Another insecurity entailed Hanno's physical appearance. Early in adolescence he obsessed about his thin wrists, his blackheads, and his big nose. Whenever he was kidded about these things, it hurt. He learned that to ignore remarks helped make them decrease. So long as others came to ignore the imperfections, Hanno was willing to do the same. The exception was his big nose. As noted earlier, Hanno leaned he had a remote uncle of the 1600s, Oliver Cromwell, whose big nose gave him the nickname "Nose Almighty." From this fact Hanno felt he had a legacy to uphold. An exception occurred when Hanno was holding a baby. If the baby grabbed his nose and held on for security, Hanno, even as an adult, could not tolerate it.

Just as Hanno battled with his physical insecurities, he also battled with the reputation he had gained among the parents of Boy Scouts as the perfect model boy. As already mentioned, Hanno felt compelled to misbehave occasionally just to prove that he was a regular kid.

In Hanno's sophomore year he decided to join an underground newspaper in protest of his English teacher. When viewed after the fact he could see that the teacher, Miss Gladys Terhune, was an outstanding teacher and taught the course well; however, the required English classes were not the cup of tea for most high-school boys at that time. So, a newspaper was printed with Hanno as assistant editor. The paper was called *Tertorchaca*, meaning Terhune Torture Chamber Club Associates.

A feature article on the first page was a paraphrase of Portia's speech from Shakespeare's *Merchant of Venice*: "The quality of mercy is not strained. It is dehydrated."

With only one issue, the editor and the business manager were summoned to the superintendent's office and expelled for a week.

The superintendent interrogated them about who the assistant editor and other newspaper staff were, but out of their own personal ethics, they refused to divulge the information. To apply pressure on them, he told them that if they did not cooperate, their punishment would be worse. They held their ground. Had they informed on Hanno, his future path in high school might not have been so bright.

There is another (throwaway) story about Miss Terhune that may as well be told. One of Hanno's high school classmates (and a buttercupping companion) had Miss Terhune as a teacher in the fourth grade. His understanding was that her name was "Mister Hune." He could not understand why all the other women teachers were called Miss and Mrs. But she was called Mister. He was afraid to ask. Notably, his first name was Shirley.

Also, in Hanno's sophomore year, there was a fundraising movie. Hanno got up the courage to ask Becky Ann to go to the movie. She was an attractive girl and intelligent. He had known her in Baptist Church activities. Along with Hanno's attraction to her, she instilled the least fear.

Hanno's unclear communication made it necessary for Becky Ann to return to Hanno to confirm that he was actually going to accompany her to the movie. It was indeed a pleasant first date. It began two years of going steady in a comfortable, loving relationship but did not improve Hanno's social communication.

Most of their dates were last-minute invitations to movies after the Sunday evening church youth meetings. Becky Ann did not know until the last minute that she was being invited. This situation led Becky Ann to accept a blind date with another group one Sunday evening. They picked her up at the church. Hanno was expecting to take her to the movie and, as usual, took it for granted. This was a heartbreaking experience for Hanno, and it eventually led to their relationship breaking up. It was a major learning experience for him. He learned not to take girls for granted with last-minute invitations.

In Hanno's junior year, an unexpected but major event occurred. He was invited to play the leading role in the spring play. Hanno was not a member of the dramatics (Scitamard) club, but faculty sponsors decided that he was the right one for this role. This casting meant that Hanno and the other cast of *And Came the Spring* had to return to school each evening to rehearse.

One evening during a period when Hanno was off stage, he and other students were waiting out in the hallway by the clock and trophy case. Someone mentioned how nice it would be if the morning buzzer call to classes did not ring. Classes would be delayed. All agreed. Someone then found the clock door unlocked and the fuse box easy to open. Then came the discussion of who would like to stop the morning buzzer. All hesitated except Hanno. He saw that simply removing the two fuses and placing them at the bottom of the box would stop the class buzzer system until someone replaced them. He did so.

The prank backfired. The next morning, instead of replacing the fuses, someone called a clock repairman. He dismantled the clock and then was unable to reassemble it. The result was that the school had no buzzer system for the rest of the year. No one spoke.

Hanno's prank and the decision of his fellow actors to protect him led to uncommon guilt. Although he did not want the good-boy image, he also did not want the result of his actions to be detrimental for others. During the months to follow, Hanno selected many assignments for himself as reparation for his wrongdoing.

The faculty sponsor and director maintained her cool one evening in rehearsal when Hanno slipped up on the line, "I do not see why three grown children should sit through supper arguing." When Hanno used the word *shit* instead of *sit*, she joined the laughter and then gave him a substitute sentence. On play night, however, Hanno was determined to return to the original line, and he did it correctly.

The student cast bonded as the performance day came near. Not having had sisters, he was amazed at how composed and efficient the cast members were when girls and boys had to change clothing together backstage in close quarters.

Hanno wondered if he would freeze up and be unable to give his very first line. When the time came, he could think only of his obligation to fellow cast members and gave the line without a wavering voice.

After the play, as his makeup was being removed, Hanno was startled by the superlative comments, like "Hanno should be in Hollywood." Hanno could now see many places in the play where he felt he had done poorly. He did not fully accept the applause and enjoy it. Instead, there was an edge of anxiety because people were expecting more and more of him until one day they would discover his personal inadequacies.

During the four years of high school, Hanno's interaction with his parents was minimal. As mentioned earlier, both parents were in a stage of prolonged grief and did not participate in the Boy Scout movement, school PTA membership, or other parental activities. When Hanno had good grades or advancement in the Boy Scouts, he received fleeting approval but little or no attention except for proper food and lodging. With food it was often the same thing daily. Hanno understood this as an indirect effect of the war.

Hanno did not want to withdraw into the isolated country society from which he had come. He was ambitious, sometimes to his benefit and sometimes not. He held the best grades in science courses, but two girls, one his own girlfriend, surpassed him in overall grade average. He was also capable of being lazy. He was happy to copy his girlfriend's homework when he had not completed his own. She did not mind, but she was annoyed when Hanno then made a better grade when a test was given on the homework.

In general Hanno would press himself to excel. Once Hanno's father had bought him the youth novel, *Dick Prescott's Second Year at West Point*. The book inspired Hanno toward seeking an appointment to West Point.

The book dealt greatly with sports and friendships. It also presented the rich history of the institution.

This was not the first time Hanno had attached himself to goals without having a firsthand experience. Early on, after mowing a lawn at Markle's Service Station across from the park, Hanno was getting a Coke in the station, and a truck driver advised Hanno to get as much math as he could in school. He said you would always use it and never regret it. From that time on, Hanno made straight A's in his math courses in high school and college. He did not regret the advice of this unknown truck driver.

Later on in high school Hanno was sitting in the backseat of the family car. Two relatives had come from Terre Haute to go hunting. Somehow, the word *psychology* came up in the conversation. One of the relatives said that psychology was a "very deep" subject and required great intelligence to study. The word *deep* caught Hanno's attention, and he decided he wanted to show that he could master anything deep. So, he decided that psychology would be his subject of study. He did not know fully what psychology was. He had never seen a psychologist, even one crossing the street. Yet, Hanno was choosing his life's profession from a personal drive for achievement. As with his choice of mathematics, it went well.

Late in the third year of school Hanno underwent a major emotional breakdown. It affected him for decades and, to some extent, for the rest of his life. One day in English class, shortly after he performed in the play, he was to give a five-minute speech on the Elizabethan theater. He found himself locked into silence, unable to open his mouth. The experience was so profound and so traumatic that the perfect storm that led to it should be recounted.

In a sprint toward extraordinary achievement Hanno had committed himself to the point where there was no free time. The ordinary course load in his high school was four courses daily. This allowed for a study hall and a library period to fill out the six-period day. Hanno, against teacher advice, was signed up for six courses. This meant that all his homework had to be done outside the school hours. Hanno was managing the full course load well. It was the first time in his life that he was making straight A's on all of his subjects. When there was no time to play around, Hanno could discipline himself in his time use.

The second factor was his commitment to working twelve hours per week at the Rexall drugstore. When school began in the fall, Hanno dropped from twenty to twelve hours per week. This involved mopping the white marble tile floor each morning before he opened the store, making Borden's ice cream, and extracting it into quart cartons and large soda fountain containers. He also worked at the soda fountain, making ice cream sundaes, banana splits, ice-cream sodas, milk shakes, and malted milks. Lemon Cokes and cherry Cokes were especially popular. He had to keep the Coke syrup and all the special flavor dispensers filled.

At the beginning of the summer Hanno got offers from both the Rexall drugstore and the Boy Scout canteen manager jobs. With his eager ambition he wanted both very much. He found a private spot and cried when he had to make the decision. He was humiliated at his own behavior. Boys at this age in Linton did not cry, especially when choosing between two positive job opportunities.

He accepted the Rexall drugstore job because the work (and money) would extend on into the school year.

As good fortune would have it, his visibility did not diminish in the Boy Scouts over the year, and a much bigger job was in store for him the following summer.

As a kind of rebellion against his parents, Hanno had not told them that he had applied for and was offered the Rexall drugstore job. Had his mother known about it, she would have been full of advice on which pocket to keep his handkerchief in and how to part his hair. So, on the evening before he was to open the store and mop the floor for the first time, he asked her how one used the commercial mop bucket with a wringer operated by a foot pedal. She was floored. He then advised her of his duties the next morning and the job he had accepted.

With his evening work at the Rexall, it was apparent that there was no time for Hanno to walk the mile home to Black Creek Road for supper and still get back to work at six in the evening. Hanno's mother made arrangements for him to go directly from school to her brother Murl's friend Trella to have evening board and to do a little homework before going to the Rexall.

Making Borden's ice cream in the back of the drugstore was not difficult. First, you turned on the freezing unit. Then you poured in the disinfectant water, turned on the beater, and then emptied the water out the bottom. By this time the machine was cold and ready to freeze. You then poured in the ice-cream mix and the base in the top and turned on the beater again. When the beater motor began to labor, you knew the ice cream was done. You turned off the freezing unit and let the ice cream fluff itself to almost double in volume with air. Then it was extracted and put into the containers. Without adding air to the finished ice cream, it would have been a solid brick, penetrable only with an ice pick rather than a spoon.

One day the freezing unit failed. Hoping it would eventually kick in, Hanno poured in and extracted the disinfectant water. Then he stuck his fingers inside the extraction door to see if the freezer cylinder was beginning to cool. Unfortunately, the beater inside, when turned off, slowed down like an electric fan. One cannot tell when it has stopped. This time it had not, and the beater knocked the top joint of Hanno's middle left finger loose and bleeding. Bill Sahm, the manager, helped wrap the bleeding hand in a soda fountain towel and walked down the street with Hanno in search of a doctor. Although elderly, the doctor was experienced. He had lost three fingers from radiation when he purchased X-ray equipment as a young doctor. He completed the amputation of Hanno's finger, sewed up the end, and bandaged it. To reduce the extreme throbbing, Hanno had to keep his hand elevated well above his heart. He quickly learned to sleep with his arm elevated and resting on his elbow. Should he lower it (or should it fall while he slept) the pain would wake him up.

With the loss of energy from lost blood, Hanno did not have the strength to walk the mile out of town to Black Creek Road, so he was cared for overnight by Elva and Martin.

Hanno had earlier made arrangements for a movie date that night with Becky Ann. Since Hanno was bedridden, Elva called Becky Ann and she came to their house to visit Hanno. After she left, Hanno did a little homework and then tried to sleep.

The next morning Hanno awkwardly ate breakfast with a single hand. His left hand was in a sling and atop his right shoulder. The throbbing had barely lessened. He was driven home. Before he crawled into his own bed, he grabbed a book from his bookshelf. It was the catalog for the United States Military Academy at West Point. In a moment, he happily announced to his parents that his accident did not disqualify him for West Point. Only if his trigger finger had been amputated would he have been disqualified. Hanno's parents were surprised at the extent of his interest in West Point.

Flat on his back with one hand pointing to the ceiling, Hanno still found time to concentrate on his homework. His "straight A" record in his six subjects was not disrupted.

Hanno's next commitment was his Boy Scout troop. During the summer following his junior year in high school, Hanno was given the top job, waterfront director, at the summer camp. He retained that position until the summer following his college junior year. During that summer he went to ROTC camp. Also during the final Scout summer he was waterfront director for the Girl Scouts' two-week camp.

More relevant to the pressures during his high-school junior year, Hanno's troop had participated in a statewide first-aid contest held in Alumni Hall at Indiana University. To their surprise they scored among the top ten troops in the state. This year they decided to go at it seriously and try to win the state championship. This led to Hanno composing a number of complex first-aid problems beyond the practice problems provided by the Boy Scout Council. The only typewriter available to the troop was the one in Dr. Ben Raney's office. The father of Scout Ben

Raney Jr. had long been gone to war and his medical office was closed. Ben Jr. liberated the key to the building from his grandmother, and Ben and Hanno had an ideal quiet setting to prepare these practice first-aid exercises. One day Ben had to go out on an errand and left Hanno working alone. After an hour, Ben returned.

"Guess what!" said Ben.

"What?"

"President Roosevelt is dead."

Hanno paused from his typing and said, "I don't get it. What's the catch?"

"President Roosevelt is dead."

"Yes, but what is the punch line?"

"No punch line. It is really true."

"You mean President Roosevelt is dead?"

"He just died, and Truman is going to be the new president."

Hanno stopped typing. It did not seem possible. Roosevelt had been president into his fourth term. Hanno could remember going to the polls with his father when Roosevelt was running against Hoover. For Ben, there had been no other president in his lifetime.

The other major time commitment for Hanno was his girlfriend Becky Ann and what they shared in the church. Hanno attended the Sunday morning church services and sermon. Recently, his cousin Martin, a deacon in the church, had been having Hanno participate in the collection ceremony. Hanno remembered one day some young boy dropped a marble in the back row of the sloping auditorium. The marble began to roll. As the marble proceeded, it managed to miss all the shoes and purses, roll to the front of the auditorium, bounce off the altar, and stop. Suddenly the minister burst into loud laughter.

On Sunday evenings the Baptist Youth Fellowship met, and once in about every two months, it was Hanno's turn to prepare the program for that evening. Then, almost always, Hanno and Becky Ann left that meeting to have a movie date at the Ciné theater, only a block away.

With these time commitments came the incident one morning in English class. Hanno had to give a five-minute talk on the Elizabethan theater. He had been agonizing over it and was unable to sleep. When he arose to give the talk, he became completely mute. He could not talk or answer any questions. He knew the word *stage fright*, but this seemed much worse. His thoughts were completely blocked off so that he not only could not remember the words, but also he could not even remember why he was there. For Hanno it was no small event. It was as if the world had come to an end. He was certain that he would not ever be able to stand in front of a group and give a speech. He would have this disability for the rest of his life. For whatever aspiration he might have for making something of himself or doing something for the world, it all came to nothing and he would return to the countryside in obscurity.

As might be expected, Hanno's collapse in English class drew a good deal of attention. The mystery was why he could perform so well in the spring play a month earlier, lead Boy Scout activities, and preside in BYF meetings, yet was unable to talk five minutes in front of the English class.

Hanno's teachers were silent in the matter but were sympathetic and supportive. His girlfriend was likewise.

Some of Hanno's buddies and some of the students in the English class were suspicious. They knew that Hanno had just finished the big play. They knew that he had the leading grades in class. They concluded that he was capable of about anything and that he was probably pulling a prank.

For years Hanno would not describe it. No words came that seemed right. Finally, much later, he felt it necessary to try to explain it to himself. As best Hanno could describe it, there was a huge difference between the play and the classroom talk. The play was not Hanno's words. The words came from the playwright. They were not Hanno's creations. From the words he uttered in the play, Hanno himself could not be scrutinized. The words of the classroom talk, however, were all of Hanno's doing. If the classroom, other students, the teacher, and the world were exposed to Hanno's genuine creations, they would find no merit, not even mediocrity. They would find only a complete void. What people ordinarily saw in Hanno was a big facade. To give the talk, even to start it, would be revealing a nothingness that left no redeeming feature of Hanno to be of merit. In the end, all was panic. Neither the words nor the reason for being was left.

This "blanking out," the blocking of attention, persisted for the rest of Hanno's life. For a few years he did not know how to deal with it. He would escape every instance where he had to stand before a group of people and talk. In college, if he found he had to give a book report or other talk, he would drop the course, no matter how much he was interested in its content.

The one exception to this escape strategy came when Hanno was required to give a half hour lecture in ROTC class. To withdraw from the class meant to have to withdraw from ROTC. To withdraw from ROTC would mean he would lose the stipend that helped support him in school. He could not escape. Following the instructor's suggestion, all cadets began their talks with a joke—"to loosen themselves and the audience." Hanno began his talk by making reference to a quandary: "What has the greater sex appeal? A banana or a doughnut?" Hanno's comment caught the cadet audience so that they laughed and laughed. The laughter was so prolonged that he could not continue. While others might have seen this as a success, Hanno became unhinged. Just as after the high-school play, Hanno felt that people would now expect more than he was capable of providing. To the surprise of the cadets and the instructor, his voice trembled and quavered for the rest of the half hour.

Finally, Hanno began to adapt to the disability. He discovered that all he had to do was to do nothing. If he were quiet for a few seconds, his attention would return. Seldom did the general audience discover these episodes of attention loss. Only keen observers, who already knew Hanno, and his problem, could detect them. The pauses and silence to regain himself did not penetrate the audience's attention. They did not detect the panic and loss of sense of direction. Later, his failure in eyesight when reading a paper created a greater problem than the panic about speaking.

Decades later Hanno reflected upon the attention blocking (blanking out). What would have been the outcome if at the beginning Hanno had merely admitted he had bitten off more than he could chew? He will never know.

As Hanno's senior year began, the administration was determined to abolish the tradition in which the senior boys paddled the incoming freshman boys. When Hanno was a freshman, he paid his dues with many wooden paddles reaching his backside. For Hanno and his fellow seniors, this was a difficult tradition to give up. Consequently, he continued the practice as usual. In fact, many boys, unsure of whether they would comply or resist, saw Hanno with his good grades and model boy reputation and wooden paddle, as an example to follow. Summarily, all boys who paddled—fifteen in all—were called to the superintendent's office and expelled from school for three days.

Hanno envisioned the expulsion as an extension of summer vacation, but his mother had other ideas. Hanno was pressed into picking apples for three days, eight hours a day, in a neighbor's orchard. Hanno's mother collected the salary, and Hanno collected a large dose of poison ivy rash from the vines under the apple trees. He had to deal with it for a week after returning to school. Even in the evenings, after picking apples all day, Hanno's mother kept his nose to the grindstone.

Hanno's final year in high school took on a focus with his being appointed editor of the yearbook, *The Revue 1946*. That was a high honor for Hanno. He was not only very ambitious but also skilled in many of the things that the job required. The faculty advisor for the yearbook was Estelle Phillips, an older member of the faculty. Ms. Phillips had taught Hanno plane and solid geometry and then trigonometry. Although he did well, Hanno was given no impression that he was favored more than anyone else in the class. Then Ms. Phillips became the principal of the high school, second only to the superintendent.

Her invitation to Hanno came as a surprise, just as the leading role in the spring play had come as a surprise. Given the very public emotional breakdown he had had late in his junior year, Hanno always wondered if the appointment might in some way be intended to rehabilitate him, but nothing was ever said of this. Hanno had many new ideas of how the yearbook should be improved, and with eagerness and excitement, he often made decisions and reviewed them with Ms. Phillips after the fact. She consistently gave Hanno free rein and never rejected or modified any of his decisions. One could only describe her role as encouraging and enabling.

While Hanno's performance measured well in terms of the product completed, it was far less than perfect in dealing with his fellow yearbook staff. Various students with delegated duties in the written and graphic aspects of the book had their own ideas. When Hanno felt these ideas came up short of his own, he would not easily resolve the differences. In his eagerness and drive, he sometimes went too far in imposing his ideas onto others. Hanno learned awkwardly when to yield or withdraw his authority. He had to allow someone else's creativity to be expressed.

Perhaps Hanno's major transgression was that he failed to include the coeditor in many of his decisions. Ideally, he would have discussed all plans with her before taking action. Instead, without dispute, Hanno saw immediately what was to be done and wanted to do it all himself. Although this did not create any open conflict, it might have. With Hanno's history of isolation, he was shy in approaching the coeditor, shy because she was attractive. He was eager to work alone and therefore did not allow her potential to be fully expressed in the product.

One evening Hanno had an extended meeting with Ms. Phillips about some technical details in preparing copper plates for printing photographs. During the meeting Ms. Phillips mentioned that she would like to catch the last showing of a Technicolor movie at the Ciné. It was "A Song to Remember," about Frederic Chopin and George Sand. Cornel Wilde and Merle Oberon were the leading actors. As Hanno and Ms. Phillips finished their work, Hanno gave thought to the discomfort women in their fifties or sixties would have in attending a movie at night alone. It was also unusual for a high-school boy to accompany a teacher to a movie. Hanno decided to ask Ms. Philips to accompany him to the movie. After the movie, he walked her home. After the fact Hanno realized that in their quiet relationship, he had a bond that did not occur with any of the other high-school teachers.

The war was winding down, and V-E and V-J days were prominent events of celebration. Rationing was over, and a new optimism and budget loosening seemed to be available both in the high school and in the offices of the *Linton Daily Citizen*. The yearbook was printed on the *Citizen* press.

Hanno produced the first hardcover yearbook since before the war. The artwork by Frank Miller helped communicate the dedication and separate the respective sections of the book. For example, a drawing was made for each section of the book and these same drawings were shown white-on-red on the inside hard covers. Hanno wanted a running script of split sentences going throughout the book to replace traditional titles at the top of each page. When Hanno asked the *Citizen* press staff for a script font, they gave him a catalog and let him choose the style of script in all font sizes necessary. Also, as the various chores of copy and pictures converged upon the final deadline, he was amazed that Eskin Turner, the editor, would loan Hanno his new DeSoto to transport material from the high school to the printing office. Hanno had been licensed to drive only a year. Finally, as the last items were being proofed, the *Citizen* staff was in a high mood with the yearbook staff. They provided Hanno with a desk and chair to do proofreading and editing of copy on site. Once a page was done, the head printer in black apron and translucent billed cap would in jest whisk the copy and run into the other room to the press. The relationship between the *Citizen* office and the *Revue 1946* staff could not have been better.

On graduation day Hanno received the Bausch-Lomb Science Award for the best science grades of the graduating class. He was greatly relieved when he learned that he did not have to give a talk of acceptance. Hanno received a forty-two-dollar merit scholarship for his first year at Indiana University. Having focused upon West Point, he had no realistic idea what total college expense would entail, with tuition, textbooks, supplies, room, board, and clothing. He assumed that he would be working his way through.

[28]

DAD: THE LATER YEARS

During these final years that Hanno spent in Linton his father's alcohol addiction proceeded to cause his downfall. One day, after a typical dispute between his parents, his mother came to him.

"You are a grown person now and strong enough to control your father. He is leaving. Who knows when he will come back? It is time for you to take responsibility to keep him home."

With this very direct confrontation, Hanno arose and went to his father. He asked him to stay home.

"I'm going."

"No, you're not."

"I'm going."

Gene began to leave the basement kitchen they were in. Hanno grabbed him by the shoulder.

"Let go of me."

Hanno held him. Gene didn't think he would persist. But he did. They struggled and went to the floor. Hanno was on top of his father and had him held down helplessly. He was surprised at how frail his father had become. Gene quit struggling and looked off in the distance. He would not look at Hanno. Hanno tried to give him a lecture. It was hollow. Gene's eyes indicated that he was not there; he was not in audience. Hanno sensed that he was waiting. Neither wanted to accept that they were in this fight with each other. Hanno knew that no matter how long he held his dad down, he was going to go as soon as he was loose. There was no other recourse. He had to go. The only path to dignity was to go. There was no freedom, dignity, or pleasure where he was. Dignity was the last to go, and with Hanno on top of him, it was going also. Hanno, if not having lost esteem, was in another world where he was not holding his father to the floor. Hanno let him up. They did not look at each other or speak. Gene went out the door and down the lane to Black Creek Road. He was gone.

When they met again, they were their same cordial selves to each other. Both had cast away what had occurred.

On another occasion during this period, Hanno's uncle Murl came to the house. He asked Hanno to come to the car. Hanno got into Uncle Murl's car. Murl said, "Your dad has just been thrown in jail. He was still drunk early this morning. He drove into and damaged a parked car and was thrown in jail. What they usually do is keep them overnight and let them go."

"Is there any way you can keep it out of the newspapers?" Hanno asked. "Can you tell the chief of police, the justice of the peace, or the judge not to report it?"

Hanno recognized that the owner of the damaged car was his own sixth-grade schoolteacher, who had tickled him so much. Hanno spoke nothing of it.

"I'll try. I will see what I can do," said Murl.

Years later, Hanno reflected on the fact that Murl, in the role of policeman, contacted Hanno rather than his own sister, Hanno's mother.

Soon after Murl left, Frank Miller came by and picked Hanno up to go to Shakamak. They had packed their lunches and had planned to stay the day. Frank liked to jump off the thirty-two-foot platform into the lake. Hanno sat on the pier in the sun.

"What's wrong with you, Hanno? You are so quiet. Is something wrong?"

"I'm fine."

By the time they left to go home, Hanno had not changed.

When Jay and Ray were high-school students, they spent the entire winter trapping ground animals, stretching and drying their hides, and selling them to Sears Roebuck. They expected to make a pile of money to buy fishing equipment and another gun. Instead, they got a check for only nineteen dollars. They were very disappointed. Then, as life fortune would have it, their father Gene stole the money and gambled and drank it away in a day. The twins never forgave him.

Hanno could understand why the twins felt the way they did. He could not blame his dad or them. To them Dad was all evil. To Mary he was all evil. Hanno could not bring himself to this conclusion.

A year passed and Hanno also became the victim of Gene's misdeeds. Gene sold Hanno's bicycle and used the money for gambling and drinking. It was the bike Hanno's brothers had bought him when in military service before the war. The bicycle was no longer in daily use, such as for a paper route, yet Hanno had need of it. He bore no ill will toward his father. Instead, Hanno felt his dad was a tragic victim of circumstance. He felt sorry for his dad.

Looking back years later it became clear that these two events signified that Gene was moving into a more serious state of personal deterioration, and these were the first major indications. On no previous occasion had he ever acted in a way that transgressed against his own children. In the final year of his life, he would even transgress against the needs of people in his immediate company if it allowed him an escape to get alcohol.

Hanno's view of his father was not simple. Foremost in his thoughts was the affection he had always received from his father. Hanno and his father always knew that they were on each other's side. Sometimes Hanno felt strongly that his mother's relentless tearing down of Gene's esteem was the sole cause of his alcoholism and uncontrollable behavior. On other occasions Hanno saw his two parents as locked in a spiral, each one acting negatively to the other's behavior and responding in a way that drew greater retaliation from the other one. Sometimes he viewed both parents as bringing problems into the situation that were there long before they met each other.

The later years of Gene Buchwald were ones of an uneven downhill trajectory. This same period was one in which Hanno was taking serious stock of major issues in his life. To track Hanno's story, the story of his father is continued to the end of his life.

Seldom was a time when Hanno's father could be described as happy. One of these times was when his stomach problems got so bad that doctors concluded he needed an operation. It was early December. Gene took a Greyhound bus to Indianapolis and checked in at the VA Hospital. Mary stayed home with her housecleaning job in the hotel and with Hanno in school. It was a time when the procedures of surgery had not progressed, and everyone was mindful that this might be the last they would see of Gene. Gene felt the same, even more so. During the surgery prep and recovery, the hospital staff became his support group. He had a respite from the fireside quarreling at home.

The ulcerated portion of Gene's stomach was removed. Besides a phone call to say that he had survived the operation, the family, unexpectedly, began getting postcards from Gene. Then came complete letters. His mood became increasingly positive.

When Gene came home, he was in a state of mild euphoria, such that Hanno had never seen. Happy to have faced death and survived, he talked often of the support of the VA hospital staff who took care of him. He claimed he had the Christmas spirit for the first time in decades. In the hospital he had bought Christmas presents for each member of the family. Usually Mary did the Christmas shopping and dispatched gifts under their joint names. This euphoria lasted a few days. Then old habits and renewed quarreling resumed, and Gene's attractions to alcohol, gambling, and escape from the house were back to where they were before.

After the security guard position in Terre Haute, Gene became a security guard at Crane Naval Ammunition Depot.

During brief visits to his father's workplace and when sharing a train ride back to Linton, Hanno discovered that his dad had been selected by a sizable group of young men for taunting and ridicule. They referred to him as a Smokey Bear because of his campaign hat that all guards wore these hats. They jeered that guards did nothing to earn their pay and were useless.

Unfortunately this taunting occurred also in the Linton bars to which Gene escaped for solace. Since Gene was a runt, becoming elderly, he was an easy target to bolster their egos.

During a period when Hanno was home from academic chores and Ray was home from service, Gene became so angry with his persecutors that he wanted Hanno and Ray to join him in a barroom brawl to beat up on them. Gene brought it up to Hanno more than twice, and Hanno ignored it. Hanno was not a physical fighting person, and even if he had been, he would still have thought this a bad idea. Finally the matter could not be ignored. It was clear that Gene would view Hanno's aversions as a lack of personal support. He hoped that the outcome would not come to that, but he went to his father and said, "Okay, let's get this over with. Find out when this guy will be in the bar, and Ray and I will go there with you. We'll beat up on him if he wants to fight."

"Is Ray willing to do this with you?"

"He will if I ask him."

In less than a day Gene came back to Hanno.

"About fighting this guy in the bar, I have changed my mind. Forget I ever suggested it."

Why Gene changed his mind is a matter of interest. Hanno may have confronted his dad with the realization that a public issue would be created by having an open brawl. He may have decided that he should handle his own affairs or give the appearance of doing so. Hanno's best guess was that the major thing that his father needed was a signal of personal love as a human being. Once he got that, the barroom issue faded from importance.

As the naval munitions activity continued to wind down and various jobs were closed, Gene became a janitor. The munitions workers at Crane viewed janitor's work as being in a class far below their own. So they continued to taunt Gene on the train rides to and from work. Hanno was surprised, almost displeased, that his father appeared to absorb these darts without response. Gene was getting a full-time paycheck, and it seemed he did not want to jeopardize it.

Hanno became aware that while most people of the world sized up and rated the work of doctors, lawyers, teachers, and others, few people distinguished between a good or poor janitor. Hanno was proud of his father and felt that he was an outstanding janitor. As time passed, health problems forced Gene's retirement.

Many conflicts arose with Hanno's mother whenever Hanno wished to give attention to his father or just enjoyed being with him. But, for Hanno, it was more than that. The quiet long talks with his dad gave him a strength he needed to deal with the growing stresses in his own life. The following story not only tracks the trajectory of his father's downfall but also reveals Hanno's stresses while becoming an adult. To follow his father's time line, Hanno flashes forward and then returns later to the events of World War II and high school.

The summer of 1950 had been highly eventful. In late spring, Hanno graduated from Indiana University with a degree in psychology and a commission of second lieutenant in the US Army Air Force. As well, he was accepted into graduate school at the Ohio State University in clinical psychology. He was engaged to be married later in the summer. His financial resources had been expended to get through college, and immediate entry into military service would provide a source of income. After weeks of poverty and waiting, the orders finally came for him to report to duty at Selfridge Air Force Base.

As history would have it, the U. S. Army Air Force was changing to the U. S. Air Force, and new blue uniforms were required. He could not wear the olive-and-pink uniforms that came with his commission. As an officer, he was required to purchase a new set of summer and winter "new blues." He took out a loan.

As a few years passed in Hanno's career, his personal problems came to overwhelm him; what looked like a successful career was complete unhappiness. Hanno had a separate need to get away and visit his father, if not also have time alone.

To get any money for survival, he knew his dream of graduate school and a PhD in clinical psychology would have to wait until the military payroll produced the needed fluid cash.

Within days following his entry onto active duty, the Korean War broke out. All discharges from the USAF were frozen. Again, history intervened. A crisis had occurred in the Veterans Administration (VA) hospital system in that, with aging World War II veterans, the VA neuropsychiatric wards were overflowing with admissions. Because of the priorities of war, the number of mental health professionals trained to meet the national need was far inadequate. Once Hanno's admission to graduate school in clinical psychology was identified, orders were cut immediately, in spite of the Korean War, to discharge Hanno from active duty provided that he enter clinical psychology training immediately. In quick succession, Hanno was discharged, his wedding took place in East Chicago, the went on a honeymoon to Indian Lake, they moved into an apartment, and he enrolled in graduate school in Columbus, Ohio. Hanno had become a veteran hitchhiker, which helped eliminate a travel bill when possible.

Settling into a program of graduate study, Hanno discovered that the program, highly competitive for admission, was immediately dismissing people for reasons that they were not cut out to be clinical psychologists. From September to Christmas break, six of the eighteen new admissions were asked to leave. Of the others, Hanno was under pressure for lack of tuition money to get through the first year. It was under these circumstances that he received a phone call from his mother. Hanno's father had just been rushed to the VA hospital in Indianapolis with another stomach bleeding incident. She made it clear that it was possibly life threatening.

With concerns about both school and money, Hanno nevertheless made arrangements with classmates to take notes in his absence, and he took a plane from Columbus to Indianapolis to see his dad. It was his first commercial plane ride. The plane was the "old DC-3" whose tail dropped down to the ground and sat on a strut during takeoff and landing. During the night Hanno reported to the flight attendant that sparks were coming out of the exhaust of the left engine. She reassured him that the sparks were normal. The engine was not on fire.

As Hanno became accustomed to the loud motors of the propeller engines, he was lulled into a panorama of landmarks of his recent existence. These landmark vignettes came to his thoughts as he set aside his preoccupation with lack of tuition money. The first milestone he wondered about was whether he had had an adequate preparation for clinical psychology in the strongly experimental psychology program at Indiana University. All that was behind him though. Now he was indeed in an advanced graduate program, and, mixed with this fact, his father may not be living when he arrived.

How did this all happen? Perhaps Hanno himself could not answer this question. And some landmarks were absent. One occurred the night he was awarded his second-class badge at a court of honor, and he immediately woke his mother to display it proudly. His tired and grief-stricken mother scolded him and went back to sleep.

Another milestone occurred when Hanno wrote a formal letter of application to the Boy Scout council office for a job on the summer camp staff as canteen manager. His parents read it quietly and handed it back with approval and no comment. Hanno suddenly realized that neither of his parents had ever applied for a job that required an application letter. (Hanno got the offer but went instead to the Rexall drugstore for the summer.)

The next landmark occurred when his parents (and all his relatives) endorsed his attending the U. S. Military Academy at West Point. His turning down the West Point appointment in favor of aspiring for a doctoral degree in psychology brought open criticism from relatives and friends alike. They did not see West Point as a type of college but instead solely as officer training. Having lived through the Great Depression, they were mindful of the value of a job guarantee, which they associated with the status of West Point. After that decision was affirmed, Hanno recalled the one and only comment made about his going to graduate school. His mother had said, "I can understand anyone wanting to have a college degree. But why would anyone want to have three?"

The loud, unrelenting propeller engines on the DC-3 also lulled Hanno into a subjective review of his own life. The summer and fall of 1950 had gone by so fast that he lacked time to put it in perspective.

This persistence led him into his love to daydream. He reflected back to early high school when his parents could not advise him on a job application letter. As he became more distant, they did not intervene in college decisions. As he flew, he came to realize that he was en route to visiting his father from a doctoral program. His parents had neither complimented nor questioned him when he took this step.

Hanno's daydreams were interrupted when the DC-3 made preparation to land.

Hanno found his father in the hospital in a weakened condition. He was surprised and bolstered to see Hanno. He had not yet had surgery. His dad had about a week's growth of beard, and no orderlies had been available to clean him up. Hanno shaved his father's face with his new Remington electric razor. Gene had never had the experience of an electric razor, and both of them were interested in this device introduced only in recent years.

Hanno returned immediately to Ohio State, and he reported to his mother on his father's condition. His mother was furious. How could Hanno visit his father without bringing her? Considerable time was spent explaining how it would have been impossible to spend an extra day or two away from classes to get to Linton (which had no air service) and to get to Indianapolis and then get her back home and get back to Columbus. She was not consoled by these explanations.

Hanno's mother's rage was even greater in later years when Hanno's father was permanently hospitalized in the VA hospital in Marion, Indiana. Hanno was a college professor in Nashville, Tennessee. He had not seen his father in many months, and he wanted to have some uninterrupted time with him, father to son. It was summer, and Hanno drove there with his three children. They greatly enjoyed the trip alone with their father. On the road, Hanno entered into play with them. He found a motel with a swimming pool. He checked his father out of the hospital, and they sat in the motel room to talk. Hanno had lunch brought into the room and for his children at the pool. Memory could not overlook that escargot was on the menu.

The conversations were relaxed and broad in content. They reflected upon Hanno's present professional life and upon Gene's early life. Gene said he felt as if he had fallen off the wagon (with his permanent hospitalization). The rest of the world was moving on without him. It was a highly memorable visit for all of them.

When Hanno told his mother about the visit, she was outraged. It was unforgivable to her that Hanno did not come and get her first and then go on together to Marion VA. In fact, this was exactly what Hanno wanted to avoid. He knew that she saw it as her duty to frame and control the conversation. She was committed to placing negative comments and blame on her husband and to ensuring that neither Hanno nor anyone else should see family matters as anything but the way she saw them. Whenever his mother was present, none of her children denied her that opportunity. Any rejection of her negative labels and blaming of her husband she would have received as a rejection of her.

Hanno defended himself and his decision by explaining that a trip to Linton would have cost him one day, if not two days, away from school. trip as one where a trip to Linton would have cost him one day, if not two days, away from school. With Mary's poor understanding of the map, this explanation had no merit to her. So Hanno was never fully forgiven. The issue was not that Hanno never visited her in Linton. Hanno's visits to see her in Linton occurred far more often than his visits to see his father. The issue was that no visit by Hanno with his father should occur without her supervision.

This dispute led Hanno to the decision that he simply would not inform his mother of future visits to his father. Because of Hanno's devotion to a busy academic and research career, these visits to his father were sparse: no more than once or twice a year. Hanno felt guilty for neglecting his father. He visited his mother and people in Linton far more often.

The next time Hanno visited his father he did not tell his mother. Again, it was, as always, an enjoyable and fulfilling visit between father and son.

On the way home on the new interstate highway, he witnessed a near accident. A man was teaching his wife how to drive. On the four-lane highway she had driven in a circle and then stopped, blocking two lanes. Ms. Phillips began going in reverse at high speed, making circles across both the southbound lanes. Hanno stopped in time to avoid mishap. The husband jumped out of the car and headed to Hanno's car apparently to apologize. He then thought better of leaving his wife alone, so he returned to his car and they soon drove on.

Then it began to snow. It was not just an ordinary snow. Rather than sliding in the new snow, the problem very quickly became one of Hanno knowing if he was in his lane or even on the road. Hanno stopped under an overpass to get his bearings. Traffic on the road had ceased completely. He reached the obvious conclusion that the road was impassable and that he was not safe. He drove forward slowly with fog lights on at midday. He came upon a set of tourist cabins. (Tourist cabins were soon to be replaced by strip motels for lodging.) As he pulled off the road, there was no way to tell whether he was on a driveway, a lawn, or a flowerbed. He immediately mired down in a drift, but he was safe. He was the only guest at the tourist cabins where he took refuge while hundreds were stranded elsewhere.

The innkeeper turned the heat on in one of the ten tourist cabins. Hanno was alone without phone, radio, or television for the rest of this day and night.

Hanno had a briefcase full of academic work and some simple snacks. And he had a bottle of Vat 69. He spent hours taking stock of his life and why he was so unhappy. During that night, he made two major decisions. He belonged to ten national and international committees, and he decided to resign from all but one as soon as he arrived home.

Also, in recent years, he had been using telescopic lenses as optical aids to get his professional work done. Hanno had been fearful that the public display of these aids would spread the word that he was handicapped. If so, his professional career opportunities would thereby be constrained. He had used these glasses only at home or when his office door was shut and locked. During this snowbound evening Hanno decided not only to use these optical aids publicly but also literally to place his impaired eyesight up front as an excuse for getting out of committee and other assignments. A great burden was lifted. Hanno went home a happier person. His mother never knew of the trip.

Gene Buchwald's permanent residence in Marion VA Hospital was due to transient ischemic attacks (TIAs) and multiple ministrokes at different sites in his brain. These ministrokes continued even after his entry into permanent residence.

On one occasion, when bed space problems arose on the neurological wing of the hospital, Gene was assigned a bed on the psychiatric wing. While Gene was sympathetic to fellow patients with paralyses and tremors, he did not take kindly to patients who heard and answered voices, who saw visions, who talked in meaningless sentences, who laughed or cried with no reason, or who were convinced they were Christ or that the FBI was after them. "There was no one to have a decent conversation with," he said.

One day when Gene could not be moved back to the neurological or general medical wing, he went AWOL. In three days he appeared at his home in Linton. On the afternoon of his arrival home, the VA hospital informed Mary Buchwald that he was missing. Gene had no money, only the hospital clothes he wore on the ward. He would not discuss with anyone how he managed to hitchhike two hundred miles across the state of Indiana by himself. The freedom of being home in his own bed was superior to being locked up with schizophrenic patients.

That Gene had the ingenuity to go AWOL and find his way hitchhiking across the state was all the more remarkable because, when traveling in the company of family or friends, he became so socially dysfunctional that someone had to look after him during a stop for gasoline or rest. Gene would try to steal away from the car to find where he could get a drink. The entire travel party would be held up in their schedule in order to look for him. Otherwise, he would be left in a strange city alone to fend for himself. Even on Sundays when bars were closed in many states, Gene was uncanny in finding a drink at a back-alley door.

Once, during Gene's last year of life, Hanno and his wife brought Gene and Mary to Nashville to visit in their partially completed home. It was not an entirely happy visit. Hanno and his wife did not anticipate that the noise and boisterous behavior of their children would be so discomforting. Advanced age had made both Mary and Gene unable to tolerate it.

In great part the visit reconfirmed to Hanno that he had grown into a world foreign to his parents. When a visiting student addressed Hanno as "Dr. Buchwald," his mother was dumbfounded. They had both grown feebler with age. On one weekend Hanno was in the backyard of the wooded acre lot splitting up fallen trees with a chain saw. Gene came out to help. With one difficult log, Gene began to put his hand on the top of the moving chain saw teeth to press down and get the saw through the log. He did not recognize that the chain on the saw was rotating across the top. Hanno grabbed his father's hand just in time.

The basement of the home had not been finished. There was need for a stairway railing, at least temporarily, so that someone would not fall while carrying laundry to the basement. When Hanno went to work, Gene decided to attach a temporary railing himself. He got a two-by-two piece of wood at the right length and nailed it onto the wall studs in the stairway. When Hanno came home, he could see that the railing was properly waist high at the top of the stairs but shoe-top high at the bottom of the stairs. Clearly, Hanno concluded, his dad had developed a perceptual disability he did not have before. His father could not detect what he had done wrong.

Looking in the clothes closet one day, Gene was amazed that Hanno owned three suits.

"I have never had more than one suit at any time in my life," Gene said.

"But these are my work clothes. I go to work in them every day. You have more than one set of work clothes, don't you?"

Hanno's father remained quiet.

Another awakening came when Hanno fixed his father a dry martini before dinner. A martini cocktail before dinner had become a custom for Hanno and his wife. His father acknowledged that he had never had a martini before, in spite of his alcoholism. As the two sat and talked before dinner, Hanno's dad kept eyeing the martini but without touching it. There seemed something sinister about it. Finally they were called to dinner. As they arose, Hanno's dad grabbed the martini and belted it down all in one continuous swig. In Hanno's new world, a cocktail of hard liquor was something to be sipped as one enjoyed conversation during a pleasant hour of the day. In his father's world, however, such drinks required showing one's masculinity by slugging them.

Once while Hanno and his dad were driving, his dad apologized to Hanno for having been a failure in his life and as a father. Hanno, partly because of the traffic and partly because of his resistance to pursue the comment, passed it off without response. Here rests an incident—a transgression of omission—that Hanno regretted for the rest of his life. To Hanno, Gene had been a good giving and loving father. He was all that Hanno ever wanted from a father. There were times when Hanno was so down and out that he knew that he would get support from no one else on earth. His father was always there, regardless of whether he thought Hanno was in the right or in the wrong. Hanno let his father die without ever telling him how he felt about him.

Hanno was reminded of the brief visit to Uncle Hanno in 1961 in Seattle. He met his uncle for the first and last time. Uncle Hanno would not talk about himself but continued to query Hanno about his achievements. Again, there was a bottle of Vat 69. When they parted, Uncle Hanno said to his nephew, "If I had known that I was going to have someone like you named after me, I would never have changed my name to Roy Lee."

These were precious words from Uncle Hanno to keep for a lifetime. Uncle Hanno was dead within six weeks with cirrhosis of the liver. Hanno lives with the fact that he never accorded his own father with such kind words.

Gene Buchwald's death did not surprise anyone. He had again run away from the Marion VA hospital. He had hitchhiked home one last time. He died of a stroke while lying on his day cot, the same one on which Granddad David Oglesby had died.

Hanno and his family drove up from Nashville, and Ray flew in from Portland, Oregon, for the funeral. In the casket Hanno's father provided an image he had never possessed in life. His jaw formed itself in a sturdy, confident manner. He had on a fine suit. One could not discern his short stature. At eighty, his hair was still dark. As Gene Buchwald would have said of himself, he looked like "a Philadelphia lawyer."

As per custom, the members of the immediate family were seated in the front row of the funeral home chapel. As Hanno sat there in silence, he was convinced that he was the only one in the room who knew his father. He knew that everyone else in the room had viewed him disparagingly. Whether true or not, Hanno viewed himself as the only one who really cared.

Hanno picked up the program of the funeral service. The organ began to play, and the service was under way. Hanno noticed immediately the songs that had been selected for the service. During his father's life, he had repeated that the one song he wanted played for his funeral was "In the Garden." The song was not listed in the program. His mother, with her aging, had forgotten his wish. The minister was about to rise. Hanno knew the organist—a Breck girl that he had been in school with. Hanno arose from his seat with no one knowing why. He went to the organist and asked her if she could include "In the Garden" among her pieces. She nodded immediately without missing a beat. Hanno returned to his seat. In a few minutes came "In the Garden." When it began, Hanno cried for the first time. There had been only seconds to act. If he had not acted, the chance to complete his father's wish would have been gone forever.

In the years that followed, Hanno had many disturbing dreams about his father. The dreams always followed the same theme. He had killed his father and had buried his body to hide the murder. In one way or another, through an animal digging or a creek flooding, the body was arising to the surface where someone was going to discover it and realize what Hanno had done. Hanno was in mortal fear of being found guilty for the killing of his father.

People interpret dreams in different ways. One way was that Hanno had a repressed anger toward his father and that anger was never allowed to the surface. Another way, as Hanno preferred, was that, during his father's final years, when he needed Hanno, Hanno was too heavily scheduled in an academic and research career to see him. Hanno knew that his father needed him, and he

339

did not respond. Hanno, as an act of omission rather than commission, had killed his father.

Yet Hanno still could hear his father's salutation. For his father's own amusement, he would often address children by a name that was unfamiliar in order to note their reactions. Hanno could still hear his father say to him, "How are you doing, Bill?"

[29]

MOM: THE LATER YEARS

Although Hanno had left Linton, had struggled through nine years of college and graduate school, and was on the career ladder moving to his fourth university faculty position, there was one remaining bond that brought him back to Linton—not as a visitor or tourist, but as one of them. This bond was the funeral of his mother.

As Hanno's mother took on the shawl of widowhood, an emancipation and joy of living began to engulf her. It was a view of the world she had never experienced earlier in life. She was shed of the responsibilities of being a daughter, a wife, and a mother. A national organization, Mothers of World War II, sprang up. Like the American Legion after World War I, each chapter or post was named after the first local person who had been killed in the line of duty. Thus the Linton chapter was named the Jay

Buchwald Chapter of the Mothers of World War II. Mary was made the first president of the chapter. In many ways, the duties of president brought her out of her reclusive grief. She shared her loss with others and gave support in return. She had a responsibility one day to make the organization run.

A flagpole and stand was secured, and Mary donated the flag that had been atop Jay's casket when his body was returned. With this honorific position, Mary was called upon for various public appearances. One was a photo opportunity with the mayor of Linton, as the two cut the ribbon at the opening ceremony of the new JC Penney's store. A country girl was getting her picture in the newspapers.

With the loss of a son in the war, Mary's emotions changed somewhat from grief to enjoying her status. During church services it was customary for a widow or person otherwise struck by tragedy to remain seated during the singing of hymns, while the congregation stood up as outright Baptists. Mary remained seated. Especially notable was this choice since her Aunt Lizzie, who was always sitting beside her, stood up—albeit Aunt Lizzie was about twenty-five years her elder. Mary's donation to the church consisted in the many chores and deeds while helping with the Sunday school. Twenty years later, church elders spoke of her good deeds as if they had occurred last week.

Mary lived in a house, now her own, in the near northwest side of Linton. To go shopping or to church or to a funeral, she would walk. She was not lonely. Next door was a young woman caring for her aged father. He was lonely during the day, as his daughter had gone to work.

He soon began to spend each day in Mary's house. Soon she was sharing lunch with him. Although they were fond of each other, Mary respectfully called him Mr. Leslie. Mr. Leslie it was, as long as they lived. He was a handyman and helped Mary with chores and minor repair work.

A split in attitude arose regarding the propriety of their relationship. Hanno, his brother Ray, and the neighbors around the block accepted them naturally as a couple who happily lived their daytime lives together and then at suppertime he would return next door to his daughter's house to assume his role with her and her two children. Hanno and his brother, living far away, were happy that their mother had company and help in an emergency. Some of the uppity relatives did not feel this way. They felt a loss of face by the family for fear the old couple might be seen as conducting an affair. For example, one day someone walking by saw four feet protruding from the shrubbery up against the house. Coming closer, they discovered Mary and Mr. Leslie were lying side by side engaged in conversation. A downspout from the roof guttering was clogged, and they were trying to understand and repair it. Some people were appalled that an old widow and widower should be "carrying on." Others were pleased by their happiness as they worked together.

Another significant aspect of their relationship was that Mr. Leslie did not know how to read or write. When his daughter found her children complaining about him using their coloring books, she bought him a coloring book and a box of crayons of his own. Very shortly, he moved his coloring book and crayons next door to Mary's house. When there were no chores to be done and no dishes to wash and dry, they would sit in the dining room as Mary read the newspaper (and sometimes read to him), and He would color in his books (now more than one). Along with their compatibility, Mary did not have to assist her dominance to a male figure. He knew Mary was failing in memory and would assist her in that regard; however, he would not intervene to make decisions. Mr. Leslie did not have the initiative to become the dominant member of the duo.

When Hanno brought his family to visit, Mr. Leslie was the center of attention for the children. They were in the coloring book stage, and they would often read to him the dialogue of the cartoon characters they were coloring. Back home, they would talk more of Mr. Leslie than of their grandmother.

Mary had a fear of entering a nursing home and losing her much-valued sense of control. She would write Hanno and Ray a postcard every week to assure them that she was doing fine and that Elva was handling her finances. She would mail packs of postcards for them to answer. With his busy life and his work slowed by limited vision, Hanno seldom wrote. However, Mary would sometimes forget and write two postcards in the same day, always relating the same message.

Hanno always chose Thanksgiving among the times to visit Linton. A dessert highlight of Thanksgiving was strawberry shortcake from strawberries frozen fresh during the summer.

One year Hanno's son Joe Dean was the first at the table to get to his strawberry shortcake with its generous topping of whipped cream. With his first spoonful came his response, "This tastes like *soap*."

Joe Dean's mother was quick to reply. "Young man! Your grandmother made that for you. You *eat* that, and don't let me hear another word from you until you have finished."

In a few minutes the eldest child, Donna Lisa, got to the dessert. "This is not whipped cream. It is shaving cream."

Donna Lisa, eager to do things in the kitchen, had more authority than her brother, who was four years younger. Immediately, her mother and grandmother went to the kitchen to investigate. Lita Lorraine, two years younger than Donna, decided to wait for a verdict.

In a few minutes the two women came out of the kitchen with the answer. Hanno's mother, a few days earlier, had broken her bottle of vanilla extract. A survivor of the Depression, she poured what vanilla she could into an empty bottle that had contained Breck shampoo. She had thought it was empty. Grandma had failed to wash out a small amount in the bottom. The strong bitter taste of the shampoo prevailed.

They all then made do with a serving of the bun cake and strawberries without the topping. As the new dish was brought forth, all eyes were set upon preschooler Lincoln Harrison for the first time. Lincoln, who was too young to have listened to the conversation, had eaten all of his shampoo-flavored strawberry shortcake and was happy for having done so.

Mary begged Hanno and his family to return for Thanksgiving the next year without the dessert á la Breck. Unfortunately, that was the last Thanksgiving she was ever capable of preparing.

During the year to follow, Mary had her last enjoyment of control and independence taken away. Yet she knew she was ready. Other signs of memory loss were more and more apparent. Various relatives were critical of Hanno and Ray for not putting their mother in nursing care. With her begging to stay free, Hanno and Ray were of a mind to let her do so until she chose to go. It was a gut reaction. They had no idea if they were doing the right thing.

If Mary had any consolation about going into a nursing home, it was that the venue would be Rest Haven. Rest Haven had been founded by the female minister of Glenburn Mission, Miss Yoder. Although she did not know the Buchwald family, she was the first one to come to their home when the news came that Jay Buchwald had been lost at Pearl Harbor. She was already developing ideas about Rest Haven. Its great success and service to the community made Miss Yoder a part of Linton history.

Those who were negative about the relationship of Mary to Mr. Leslie and even those who were not anticipated there would be a problem with him. He would no longer be able to spend the day next door with Mary. Sure enough, Mr. Leslie promised Mary he would come to the nursing home each morning and spend the day with her. This led some well-intended persons to go to Rest Haven in advance and request, for the best interest of all parties concerned, that Mr. Leslie not be allowed to visit Mary. Accordingly, on the first day Mary was admitted, Mr. Leslie came and he was turned away. For the next three days, he sat on a bench outside the nursing home, hoping to get a glimpse of her. After the third day, he was chased away. Six weeks later, Mr. Leslie passed away. Beyond doubt, he took his place at the end of a line of people in the world who had died with a broken heart.

Mary knew of none of this. Soon after she was admitted, she dressed up and fetched her purse from the drawer. She asked to be let out the front door so that she could go downtown and buy her week's groceries. She was politely reminded that all the meals were served to her and she need not go. Like her father thirty years before her, such explanations did not suffice for Mary. Although she had lost her memory, she had not lost her stubbornness and need for control. She insisted upon leaving, and they held her back. Mary fought back. In the altercation that followed, she swung her purse and hit one nurse on the side of the head, knocking her to the floor. The scuffle ended with Mary being strapped into a geriatric chair and immobilized. Still not cooperating, she was administered psychotropic medication. This tranquilized her for extended periods.

One day a drug salesman came into Rest Haven and stopped at the front desk to make his usual hellos.

"By the way," he asked, "are any of your residents missing?"

"Oh, no. I believe they are all here. Why do you ask?"

"Well, as I was driving here, about two or three blocks down the street, there was this old lady on the sidewalk, hunched over, with a jerry chair strapped to her back."

A nurse went to the lounge area and found that the geriatric chair used by Mary was missing. The nurse became disquieted.

Mary was retrieved, along with the chair. She ate a fine lunch after her adventure. As time went on, she attempted fewer escapes and became more accommodated. One wonders if Mary had remembered her late husband running away from the VA Hospital and hitchhiking across Indiana to reach Linton. One is left to wonder how Mary got the heavy chair aloft and on her back. One wonders how she made it out the locked door. The mystery will never be solved.

A year later, Hanno came to Linton to visit his mother in Rest Haven. He did not realize it, but it was to be the last visit. It was a time in life when Hanno was pressed for time away from his busy career. Each evening after getting the kids to bed, he would return to his office and lab, work with his graduate students for two or three hours, and then go home to retire. It was a time when his research took him to Europe to oversee different projects. It was also a time when money was always short. He was always mindful that he needed a secure job; he had no savings account or rich relative to provide a safety net. Moving on from the chalk rings of Plum Branch School, Hanno kept to the grindstone.

Hanno's visit was indeed an uplifting one. Staff members brought Mary to the front desk and warmly greeted Hanno. They had Mary dressed in suitable attire for the two to take a walk to the end of the block and then return to a private visiting room. Mary was in good spirits. Out on the sidewalk, she began her query.

"May I ask who you are?"

"I am your son Hanno. Do you remember Hanno?"

"I don't reckon that I do. You say I had a son named Hanno?"

"Yes."

She looked at Hanno closely. "I don't remember any son Hanno."

"Do you remember I have a wife and family?"

Hanno named off his wife and children slowly, and Mary shook her head to each one.

"I never heard of any of those people. But I am glad you have come to visit me!"

"Do you remember having given birth to twins? You also had a couple of twin boys."

"Yes." Pause. "I do sort of remember I had twins. The twins. But somehow I do not remember their names."

Hanno recited their names, but they did not ring a bell for her.

"You're dressed in a suit and tie. Do you live here in Linton?"

"No."

"I thought not."

"I live in Rochester, New York."

"New York!"

"Yes."

"I've got visitors from New York! Wait till I tell the nurses and the girls in the kitchen! They'll think I'm somebody. I have a visitor from New York!"

Except for a short period in Anderson, Indiana, during World War I, Mary had never been away from the Linton area. To have a visitor from a great state like New York was something indeed for this farm girl.

Mary giggled at the thought of telling the staff of her important visitor, and Hanno had a warm feeling come over him as he was reminded of his preschool days with his beloved grandfather.

Hanno and his mother returned to the private visiting room.

"Don't let me forget. In a few minutes, I must go to the kitchen and start cooking dinner for you. I must also get the spare bedroom ready for you. You are going to spend the night, aren't you?"

Hanno smiled. He already knew from the wonderful days with his grandfather that he would hit a wall of resistance if he tried to reorient his mother to real time and space. So, he merely said, "I won't be able to stay that long. Let's talk. I have something to show you."

Mary sat down. Hanno reached into his briefcase and pulled out an old picture, tattered on the edge and mounted on cardboard.

"This is a picture of the Plum Branch School children when you were in the first grade. It was 1899."

"Yes. Yes, I know. Where did you get it?"

Mary did not wait for an answer. She started naming off the first- and second-graders, all in the front row. With each one she made an annotative comment. This one married (so and so) and had three children. This one took over his father's farm. This one's house burned down. Here I am here. The barn burned down for this one, and they used the insurance to buy a car. This one died of consumption when she was in the sixth grade. Here in the next row above is my sister Zelma." Mary had perfect memory for all those in the front row, and she showed her happiness to see the pictures of her schoolmates again.

Taking the picture back after looking at her classmates, Hanno said, "You have a very good memory of the old days."

"Sometimes my memory is not good. You know, a lot of people in here have bad memories. The other day, I went into the lounge and Ms. Hamilton was sitting there by herself with one arm raised in the air.

"'Ms. Hamilton,' I said. 'Why are you sitting with your arm in the air?'

"She looked up at the arm and said, 'Well, I reckon I don't know. What do you think?'" Mary giggled, and Hanno laughed.

Mary's limited vision caught the reflection from Hanno's recently shined shoes. With curiosity, she leaned over toward Hanno and reached out to explore the reflection.

"Don't get your fingers dirty," said Hanno.

For an instant, she pulled her hand back. "Oh!" she said. "I thought you were going to say, 'Don't get my shoes dirty!'"

Hanno was surprised at her response. He laughed, and Mary giggled at her own comment. It was the giggle of a carefree schoolgirl. Mary was revealing a part of herself that Hanno had never known. She had become unchained from the duties, pains, and sorrows of the real world. She was in a world of her own. She was a girl Hanno would have liked had they grown up together. It was not the mother telling him to exchange his dirty handkerchief for a clean one. It was not the mother who kept telling him to comb his hair.

Hanno then got a pad of paper out from his briefcase and told Mary he would like to take some notes on family relatives, the aunts and uncles, nieces and nephews, he was never clear about. Although there were a few blank spots where Mary could not remember, she was enjoying the discussion and had a sense of wit as she spoke of certain relatives.

As Hanno and his mother talked, Hanno's thoughts went back to times when he was so annoyed that he could not respond civilly to her. Once when Hanno was home from college, he had some appointment to keep. His mother, as usual, had her unending advice about how to act and how to be courteous. Hanno was so fed up with the advice that he carefully opened the front screen door and closed it behind him. As he walked down the sidewalk, almost a block away, he could still hear his mother from the screened open windows, talking from the kitchen and telling him which pocket to put his handkerchief in and to have some extra change in his pocket if possible. Almost out of hearing distance, he could still hear her talking.

Then there was the earlier time he came to visit from his home in Nashville and his mother brought out leftovers to give him a late snack. He sat at the kitchen table trying to have a conversation with his father. Even though his plate was full and he would likely be unable to clean it up, his mother kept offering him dishes of various kinds. A verbal "No, thanks," did no good. She would hold them in front of him and point to a small empty spot on his plate. If he handed the dish back to her, she would hand it back to him in two or three minutes. So, he then decided not to refuse but to take the dish and set it in the middle of the table. In a couple of minutes, she would pick it up and offer it to him and interrupt his conversation with his father. He learned then that he had to take the dish and set it down on the far side of the table away from her. She soon felt he needed the dish and reached across the table to give it to him. In desperation, Hanno began kindly to take each dish in turn and put it on the floor on the far side of his mother's chair. This annoyed her, as he well knew, and was unkindly intended. His father was surprised and amused.

Now, in the nursing home, Mary was released from reality and from placing demands and obligations either upon Hanno or upon herself. They were simply having a good time talking about things of common interest. As he drove home from the visit he marveled at how her Alzheimer's disease had uncovered a witty, joyful part of her that he had never known.

Hanno's next visit to Linton was to his mother's funeral. Over many decades, his mother knew what a Linton funeral was all about. Well in advance of her Alzheimer's, she therefore planned her funeral in great detail. She knew all the funeral directors at Welch and Cornett, so she had several meetings with them. She selected the casket and vault she wanted. She selected and bought the pink dress in which she wanted to be buried. She had a photograph taken to show the hairdo that she wanted. She selected the minister, organist, and singers. She prepared a stipend for each. She chose the hymns to be sung and wrote as much of the obituary as possible.

People came from all directions onto the porch and into the front doors of the funeral home. How they acted upon entering told more of the meaning of the word *Linton* and of the people in it than could ever be set down in the words of a book. There was the social gathering to give and take back a spirit of goodwill. If that required words of comfort to someone who needed it, as was most often the case with young death, then that was there to give and receive. More often, it was the chance to get together and touch upon the moments of the past, good and bad, they had had together. It may have been with people they had seen two days ago or at the last funeral or decades back. Life was seamlessly woven with death. The sum total of these actions was the sum total of what Linton was all about.

Perhaps the most important thing that Hanno saw was a level playing field. Large numbers came in from the Roosevelt toilet set. Some came in from the corncob circuit, and most from the indoor plumbing brigade from the city. Yet others came from the doubly used Sears catalog society. Once there, the class distinctions among them were absent. The high city official chatted with the corncob affiliate about his family and the crops.

Leon Moody was one of the first to arrive on visitation night. No one, including Leon, came just to sign the register, view the corpse, glance at his watch, and leave. Thirty-two years earlier, Leon had been Scoutmaster. He had left Hanno behind to go to what was a devastating war, still having its stressful effects on him. Hanno and Leon spent most of the visitation time together, as others joined them for fifteen minutes or half an hour and then moved on.

There were no words about Hanno's achievements either in the Scout movement or in his career or research. Nor did they talk about how the war had scarred Leon. Leon was there because he was from Linton. Hanno was from Linton, and that was what people from Linton did. The evening was like a Boy Scout Jamboree, a high-school reunion, and a family reunion, plus more, all rolled into one.

Karl Keller came by. He had been a very close friend when Hanno was at Midland School during the fourth and fifth grades. He had to identify himself. The two had not met together or talked in thirty-two years. He had been a red-haired boy with a sturdy athletic build. Now as for hair, there was less red and less of it. They asked each other about common acquaintances and talked of experiences they had had together. A lady came up who had dropped out of high school with a nervous breakdown. She knew all about Hanno, but Hanno, without revealing it, could remember nothing of her. There was the Charles Buchwald family who drove down from Terre Haute. Hanno remembered very well their quail hunting and their card playing. There were the local Oglesby relatives, some of whom Hanno remembered. Some relatives remembered that Mary had been in charge of the Richard Oglesby family reunion for a couple of years.

None of them came to mourn the loss of the deceased. Their mere presence said all that needed to be said. It was loud and raucous at times when family stories were told. Hanno's wife, growing up in the suburbs of Chicago and expecting an uncomfortable somber evening, watched in silent awe and disbelief.

"Hanno, you don't know me, but I was the mechanic that helped your dad loosen those lugs on your Studebaker that night you had a flat tire and turned them the wrong way."

"Hanno, you don't know me, but your mother was a life saver for us for years as she cleaned the house and took care of the baby. My wife and I had long hours in the accounting office. Your dad would come in voluntarily to watch and play with David. Your dad was an expert in watching David's face and telling exactly when he was filling his diaper with poop." David was now preparing to enter college.

"Remember—you and I got expelled from high school together for paddling freshman boys. That was the last year for that tradition."

"Have you ever seen or heard anything from Bobby Hall? He left town in the fourth grade."

Hanno would occasionally glance across the room at his brother Ray. He was also the center of a throng that included high school classmates from Midland and Jasonville. Besides his first-grade teacher, Mr. Fiscus, there were many hunting and fishing friends. Many of the farm neighbors near the Oglesby homestead, reminded again of Ray's neighborliness, had drawn up chairs into his circle. As if according to protocol, there was no talk of his lost brother or lost mother. None of them knew of or had interest in the abusive treatment he had encountered in the war.

On the next day the Oglesby, Buchwald, and Malone families followed the tradition of bringing loads of casseroles, cakes, and pies to an open-house family dinner at the home of Elva and Martin. Again, the spirits were high with favorite family stories. They asked Lincoln to play a few tunes on the banjo. The funeral, which followed thereafter, was clearly scripted according to Mary's directions. Less opportunity was given for communication, except for one Baptist church member who sought out Hanno and Ray to praise Mary once again for all the work she had done for the Baptist Sunday school program. His words made it sound as if she had done these deeds the previous week, but, in fact, she had been unable to attend church for twenty years.

After the funeral service, the procession of cars was arranged to go to Fairview Cemetery. Hanno's main memory from the cemetery was of his son Lincoln performing his pallbearer tasks. Lincoln, Martin, and four others of the Buchwald family carried the casket from the funeral home to the hearse and from the hearse to be placed carefully on the elevator straps to be slowly lowered into the grave.

After the ceremony at the cemetery, the congregation said their final good-byes and dispersed. After a brief supper, Ray wanted to spend some time with Hanno. He suggested that they pay a visit to Okie Astrup. Not only had Okie been Hanno's first-grade teacher in the one-room Plum Branch schoolhouse, but also Ray had him for the eighth grade. He had also worked with Okie as a farmhand for three summers. Ray had been present on a February day when some local young men devised an impromptu hockey game on the frozen Plum Branch Creek. Okie broke his collarbone.

Hanno, Lincoln, and Ray drove to the Astrup house and knocked as darkness was falling. Okie and his wife were at home and most pleased and honored that they should be the ones chosen to visit after the funeral.

Very soon after settling down in the front room, Ray introduced the topic of music. Knowing that Okie and his father had natural musical talent, he told Okie that Lincoln played the banjo and guitar. Okie eagerly said, "Well, let's hear something!"

So, eagerly, Lincoln went to the car trunk and brought in his banjo case. He tuned up his instrument by ear and then, to warm up his fingers, did a couple of lines of Earl Scruggs's three-finger bluegrass picking of "Foggy Mountain Breakdown."

"Oh, I see. You've had lessons!" he exclaimed in an air of both disappointment. A pleasure.

At first Hanno was disappointed. Clearly, Okie held a preference for pure folk music, home written and home taught. Formal music lessons and commercially written music were somewhat like cheating to him. Hanno quickly had to reorient himself. A full measure of status and dignity was extant among those with songs self-taught and lyrics self-written.

Lincoln was fully aware of the distinction that Okie was making. One difference was in the banjo picking. The Kentucky Blue Grass tradition of Flatt and Scruggs involved a three-finger picking style that had become so popular and commercial that it was no longer considered by the purists to be genuine folk music. "Foggy Mountain Breakdown" and "Orange Blossom Special" would be examples from this more popular style. For the true homespun folk music arising from the front porches of Appalachia, one turned to a picking and fretting style called "frailing" and "clawhammer." Examples would be "Barb'ry Allen," "Come Along and Be My Salty Dog," and "I Found Her Little Footprints in the Snow."

This mixture of folk music and stories of Plum Branch School during the early 1930s led to a rich and fulfilling evening. The two Plum Branch graduates paid their homage to a one-room Hoosier schoolmaster of years past.

[30]

LEAVING

High school was over, and the final day approached to go to Bloomington. Hanno had arranged to room at the home of a Scout acquaintance across town from the university. He had also arranged to work as a waiter and dishwasher in the kitchen of Lincoln House, a small girls' dormitory. Hanno's dad was working at a defense plant in Terre Haute, so Harry Welch volunteered to drive Hanno and his mother to Bloomington. Hanno's postal address would no longer be in Linton. This small fact was flooded with both memory and anticipation.

Time passed and a news item referred to Hanno as a "former Linton man." "Former" seemed wrong. He would always be a Linton person.

On the day before he left, Hanno realized that he needed an alarm clock. He had to get to the dormitory to work morning breakfast. With no money in the house, this was a crisis. Later in the day, his mother somehow came up with the money. She never told him how. Hanno left town with a six-dollar black-face Baby Ben clock with an illuminated dial.

During Hanno's freshman year at Indiana University, he took a bus from Bloomington to Vincennes to take the competitive examination for West Point. In a few weeks he was told he had won the appointment. By this time Hanno was in a rooming house near campus along with many veterans on the GI Bill. They were tired of war, hated their tenure in the military service, and felt a chunk of time had been torn from their lives. When they heard that young, innocent Hanno had won the West Point appointment, they had a private meeting without him. They firmly felt Hanno's life would be wasted in a "peacetime" military career. They agreed to persuade him in any way possible to turn down the appointment. This included loaning him their cars to go on dates, double-dating with him, setting him up with blind dates, and being true companions and buddies. Hanno listened to their arguments and their military experiences. He indeed turned down the appointment but instead entered the ROTC program at the university. Upon graduation, he acquired a second lieutenant's commission in the U. S. Air Force. The veterans who assumed West Point would take Hanno into a peacetime military were in error. Of the West Point class that Hanno would have graduated in, eleven lost their lives on the front lines in Korea.

*   *   *

And so that is the way Hanno left Linton. He came back, of course, but never to call it home. He loved to come back. He could come back every week—every day—because he was a dreamer. Linton does not exist. Hanno made it up. And for that matter, he made up Indiana too. And, yes, Hanno made up himself. How else can one tell the truth?